For Two Young People

Dreams are what we would like to happen.
Reality is what actually happens.
To attain the perfect balance may be impossible;
But we try.
It's called life.

ACKNOWLEDGEMENTS

Chris and Ron for their help with the finer points of the computer. Margaret, for her help with the text, especially the grammar. Fay for her honest opinion. Alan Jonathan and the ladies at Hartlepool library for without their help I would still be researching.

MICHAEL HAGON

A native of Hartlepool, Michael Hagon spent his childhood in Belle Vue, attending St Cuthberts Secondary Modern School before joining the Royal Navy in 1963. In 1973 he decided on a career in the then West Hartlepool Fire Brigade prior to its amalgamation with Cleveland County. He retired after twenty-five years' service as a firefighter and is currently employed by Asda/Walmart as a part-time handyman.

The Legend

Towards the end of the eighteenth and during the beginning of the nineteenth century the war against France resulted in widespread fear of an invasion of English shores.

Such was public concern that fear quickly turned to paranoia, all outsiders regarded as infiltrators and spies. It was during this period that a shipwreck ocurred off the coast of Hartlepool, the only survivor a monkey, dressed in the uniform of a French sailor.

Captured and questioned by local fisherman, its inability to speak was taken as an admission of guilt, and therefore only one sentence was possible.

A gibbet was hastily erected on the beach upon which the animal was duly despatched.

From that day forth the inhabitants of Hartlepool were known as the 'monkey hangers'.

THE TAKING OF A MONKEY HANGER

A Novel By Michael Hagon

'Birth. I know nothing but that
Which I am told.
My father's plans, not mine.
In time I learn not to join
The fold.
Better to chalk my own line.'

Michael Hagon 2005

PROLOGUE
Florida Straits, 1963

The red lighting gave the whole room a surreal appearance as if viewed through tinted glasses. It was not, however, switched on to pander to the more artistic among them, the intention far more practical. The men who moved between light and darkness needed to adjust quickly and working 'in the red' enabled them to achieve just that, without too much inconvenience to their quality of vision. The Operations Room on board the British warship was its heart as well as its brain, continually pumping information to various locations, supplied by a barrage of highly sophisticated machines positioned on the room's periphery. The responsibility for operating the equipment lay with four sailors, each trained for his particular area of expertise - surveillance radar, weapon tracking radar, sonar and radio navigation aids, each position manned twenty-four hours on a watch basis. Watching over them and at that moment in complete command of the ship and its two hundred and fifty officers and ratings stood a Sub Lieutenant, their safety and that of the ship in his hands. It was two hours into the middle watch, that period between midnight and 4am loathed by watchkeeping sailors the world over.

HMS Whirlwind had been deployed to the West Indies station some five months previously together with her sister Type 15 frigate HMS Rapid, both ships to undertake hurricane guard ship duties together with an American coastguard cutter. Their brief, to identify, locate and track any unusual weather phenomena in their designated area and relay the information to the appropriate weather agencies, thereby providing as much warning as possible of impending disruption.

The officer recalled the mock exercise they had carried out during workup in Portland, the ship simulating a call to an island devastated by a hurricane and requiring urgent assistance. So far it had been their only experience of that type of disaster but it had prepared them well for what could happen and he understood fully that particular duty. Why they were patrolling the Straits however was another matter. After spells in the Atlantic and Caribbean Sea, the Captain had informed the ship's company that their new area of operations would be the ninety mile stretch of water between Key West and the coast of Cuba, the ship's present position. During his last visit to the wardroom for a mess dinner, the ship's two midshipmen, the courage of several pink gins coming to the fore, had endeavoured to prise from the 'old man' the reason for this new task. Smiling to himself he recalled the Captain's riposte, given in the 'old man's' native Yorkshire slang:

'If everybody knew everything, then nobody would know nowt, but because I know what you don't, it gives you summit to think about.'

There were probably only two other people on the ship who knew the full implications of their orders, the First Lieutenant and the Royal Marine Officer, both trained like the 'old man' in the 'need to know, loose lips sink ships' tradition, he thought.

'Sir.' The monotonous 'pinging' sound of the sonar broken by the voice of the radar operator.

'I'm picking up a faint target every third or fourth sweep, range three miles, bearing two three one, and steady.'

Five feet away the sonar operator anticipated his question.

'Nothing on sonar, sir.'

Two pairs of eyes now searched the radar display, looking for the tell-tale glow that would indicate a possible target, the coast of Cuba clearly defined on the screen. It was conceivable that what they were looking for wasn't there at all, a false echo, maybe. It was a common occurrence, capable of fooling the most adept operator.

'There it is, sir.'

They saw it simultaneously.

'Any ideas?'

The rating was the expert and therefore his professionalism always demanded a high degree of respect.

'It's too small to be a gunboat, that's definite, possibly a very small fishing boat with a good masthead reflector, but because it's intermittent I can't be certain.'

The procedure now had been hammered home night after night at Dartmouth until it became second nature to him, plot and track the presumed target until a positive identification was established, only then would he inform the bridge.

'It's on the screen as a steady target, Sir, range two miles.'

The Officer of the Watch had left him temporarily in control of the ship whilst he had taken his customary turn around the deck. These new developments now required him to return control to the bridge, who would in turn inform the Captain.

Commander Harvey Dentford lay on his bunk, hands clasped behind a head of black hair that many a man half his age would have been proud of. He slept very little at sea, content to snatch two hours at a time, usually during the middle and afternoon watches, catching up on any 'shut-eye' when the ship was alongside the wall. He had been awake for some time, thinking mainly of Yorkshire and family, occasionally of the ship's efficiency - although that was principally the First Lieutenant's responsibility - but at that moment it was his orders from the Admiralty occupying his mind.

The first part had been relatively straightforward. Although the great British Empire had all but collapsed, thanks to gentlemen privateers such as Hawkins and Drake and to a lesser extent Mansfield and the notorious Henry Morgan, Britain still possessed quite a large number of island dependencies. It was because of these colonies that he now found himself and his ship in a protective role, and whilst they were also expected to 'show the flag', chasing hurricanes was the priority. It was his second set of orders that gave him most concern, causing him to discuss them with his two senior officers. Shortly after leaving the Azores, his First Lieutenant or 'Number One' as he was popularly known, together with the Captain of the Royal Marine detachment, had joined him in his cabin late one night, an event which sent several rumours scurrying to the lower deck.

'Most of what I am about to tell you is common knowledge gentlemen, but for the sake of continuity I ask you to bear with me, so let me begin with the events of 17 April 1961, the abortive Bay of Pigs invasion. On that particular date 1500 members of the 2506 Brigade, a collection of anti-Castro Cubans living in Miami and supported by the American CIA, landed at Playa Giron in Matanzas Province with the intention of overthrowing the Castro regime. Although obviously never admitted, the plan was formulated by the combined efforts of the CIA and the US Joint Chiefs of Staff which, bearing in mind the force's defeat after two days, caused the Americans considerable embarrassment, compounded by the capture of 1100 activists. Then only last year, two more episodes caused them more loss of face. The most serious of the two was the six days of tension brought about by the flotilla of Soviet ships, transporting a cargo of nuclear weapons to the island and only resolved by an American agreement to dismantle all their warheads sited in Turkey. Finally, the Cubans agreed to return the 1100 activists in exchange for $50 million worth of medical provisions, a virtual confession by the States that they were behind the Bay of Pigs fiasco. So gentlemen, in the space of two years, the Americans have taken quite a battering, to say the least, and now they have introduced plan B, a plan which our Government isn't particularly happy about, although to say so publicly would have serious ramifications for both sides.'

Captain Robert Morrow was familiar with all that had been said so far, not only was he in charge of the fifteen marines on board, he also doubled as the ship's Intelligence Officer, and as a prerequisite for assuming that role, had studied both Cuban history and the Spanish language. He was, however, more interested in what his superior had not said. Far from being a dyed-in-the-wool cynic, he was not naïve enough to believe that Admiralty orders didn't sometimes contain hidden agendas.

'How much of a smokescreen is the hurricane guard ship duty, sir?'

'It isn't Bob, but it is secondary and in a moment I'll tell you why.' He paused to fill and then light a pipe that had seen better days. 'There are still hundreds, if not thousands of Cubans who are extremely unhappy with Fidel and his regime. Some, because they have no choice, are still on the island. Others 'en exillo' are living in makeshift camps in Miami. Whilst it would appear to the outside world that the Americans have decided to let sleeping dogs lie - at least for a while - they are, in fact, encouraging small groups of these activists to carry out hit-and-run raids along the coast of Cuba. There is a problem however. They couldn't be seen to arm them in the States and then plead ignorance when something went wrong. The answer lay on the small, uninhabited islands or cays of which there is an abundance in the Caribbean. The CIA then proceeded to stock these cays with weapons and explosives, creating staging posts, the inflatable boats to get there provided quite openly and explained as encouraging the exiles to fish for a living.'

He paused deliberately, wondering who would ask the inevitable question.

'But how is this cloak-and-dagger business any of our affair?' His Number One.

'Because many of these islands that are being used belong to us, and although they are only inhabited by mosquitoes, they are our mosquitoes.'

It was the first display of humour during the meeting and all three men greeted it with subdued laughter.

'I know what you are thinking. Why don't we just tell the Yanks to clear off? That I can't answer. The politics of the matter lie elsewhere and rightly so. Our orders, gentlemen, are to keep an eye on our property, taking any action appropriate at the time.'

He smiled, a mischievous parting of the lips showing tobacco-stained teeth.

'Now let me tell you my interpretation of appropriate action.'

★ ★ ★

He was already dressed when the call came, anticipating it, having heard the tannoy requesting the Officer of the Watch to the bridge. His initial orders, given over the telephone, would be implemented by the time he left his cabin. Meanwhile, he waited until the sound of pounding feet abated. No point in getting in the way of eager, young sailors. The corridors, bathed in the soft red lighting, were empty as he made his way to the bridge and his command position, a raised wooden chair which, judging by its appearance, had fared as well as his pipe, someone had once quipped.

'What's the state of play Number One?' His eyes already absorbing the twinkling lights of Cuba through the bridge windows.

'Ops report a small boat off our starboard bow, range one mile, no lights and not making way, Sir.'

'What's our position?'

'Six miles north-west of a place called Mantua.'

The Royal Marine Officer had moved closer to the chair anticipating that the next order would be directed at him. It was.

'Put your lads in the water, Bob, go and see what we have. If it smells American leave it.'

He lit his pipe. Apart from anything else, it gave him time to think, casting his mind back to the last occasion they had investigated a foreign body, or to be more precise bodies - dead ones. Under similar circumstances they had discovered a drifting raft carrying two men and a woman - shot to pieces, he presumed by gunfire from one of the patrolling Cuban gunboats. The episode had upset quite a few of the crew. The upside was that it had reminded them that this was no 'banyan'.

The two fast inflatable's containing Morrow and his marines sped into view. He had taken a liking to him, even if he was a bootneck.

It was like driving a car at 50 mph over sleeping policemen, Morrow thought. Still, they were designed for speed and manoeuvrability, not comfort and, due to both characteristics, within ten minutes he had the boats adopt their approach positions. The man was now clearly visible, the beam of the powerful searchlights causing him to shield his eyes with one hand while he waved with the other. Morrow's voice, amplified by a loudhailer, carried clearly across the short stretch of water.

'¿Habla usted inglés?'

'Yes, I speak English.' The answer barely discernible, yet they were now quite close.

'Are you alone?'

The man replied that he was, adding that he required assistance, the words hardly out of his mouth as both inflatables made him the meat in the sandwich. It was hard to decide who was in the worse condition, thought Morrow, the man or the pathetic craft he was sitting in. One near to collapse, the other to sinking. Two marines manhandled him into the second of the inflatables, one of them providing him with a canteen of water, which he gratefully accepted, then watching as his boat was scuttled. Not a word was spoken on the way back to the warship, that would come later. A report on the incident and the man himself would be transferred to the

American cutter. A life saved, but Morrow knew that they were only delaying the inevitable.

* * *

'And the Lord said, 'Let there be light,' and behold there was light, and you could see for fucking miles.'

It was said to nobody in particular, it just happened to be the young sailor's favourite quote - irreverent, he knew, but surely God had a sense of humour. Apparently, so had someone else in the vicinity, a quiet chuckle causing him to turn and locate the source. The man was standing next to the guardrail - tall, tanned and dressed in a white shirt and officer's trousers, watched over by a marine.

'Morning.'

The young matelot returned the greeting, but continued his repair of the upperdeck light fitting.

'You are an electrician, yes?'

'And you must be the bloke swanning about in the ropey old boat we picked up during the night?'

'Ropey? I don't understand.'

Obviously not a popular word in the Spanish vocabulary, 'ropey,' he thought.

'Not very good.'

'No, once again I have been fortunate.'

'Do it as a hobby then, do you?'

The man smiled at his sarcastic remark, but he could see that it was more of a polite gesture than an appreciation of naval humour.

'I had been searching for my son, again.'

The seventeen-year-old rating suddenly felt very guilty, flippancy was not what this man needed just now.

'I'm sorry, but that's not usually the reason people give when we find them in your position. How old is he?'

'He was sixteen when the Cuban military captured him two years ago, following the disaster at the Bay of Pigs. I have not heard from him since then. So, I will continue until my Guardio Destino decides otherwise.'

For no apparent reason the word 'rum' suddenly entered the sailor's head. At present, he was too young to receive the daily quota issued to the more senior members of the messdeck. Not even allowed at the mess table until they were finished, unless invited. Favours, such as pressing uniforms, cleaning shoes and standing someone's duty watch were methods of receiving that invitation. The same applied if you had a story to tell, maybe the stranger's story. He sat down on a wooden grating some six feet away under the watchful eye of the marine.

'What is this Guardio Destino?'

It was still quite early and yet the heat was already overpowering, even causing the Cuban to remove his shirt, revealing a tattoo depicting a simple cross above his heart.

'In English it means Guardian of Destiny. It is the force that decides how we live. It is the power that makes our lives easy or hard, and eventually when and how we die. You live in a society that allows you a comfortable lifestyle, while on the African Continent a boy your age must walk miles for a drink of water. An accident of birth perhaps? I think not. I believe that the soul is returned to a different shell, to be tested continually until it is worthy to take its place among those who influence the scheme of things. You will see the cross above my heart. Let me tell you of its origin.

I too was captured at Playa Giron and sentenced to die at the hands of a firing squad. As a twisted attempt at humour, the guards would mark those about to die, saying, 'the cross marks the spot'. Three days before the sentence was to be carried out, a hurricane passed over the island causing devastation and confusion at the prison and allowing most to escape. I eventually made my way to Miami where I was encouraged to return to Cuba as part of a small armed force. I did so, but not to fight. It was an opportunity to enquire about my son Raul, but without success. Again, I had to leave the island in some haste and in order to do so, stole a small boat in which I survived for four days. On the third night, as I lay exhausted, I saw my father's face and then I crawled over the side and into the water. It was this strange occurrence that saved my life. Shortly after, my small boat was the target of machine gun fire from a gunboat.

'Many things have happened to me, strange things that I cannot explain. It is as if I was being guided, sometimes advised, maybe even controlled, but certainly saved. Now I think you have heard enough, yes?'

He didn't know whether he had or not. His life so far had been steeped in Roman Catholic dogma, never allowed an original thought, the catechism his only set of rules, and now he had met a stranger who had given him the opportunity to question those rules.

'I must go, I have the forenoon watch,' he replied, reluctantly. 'But I wish you luck in the search for your son.'

The stranger shook his hand.

'You have your duty and I have mine. Yours is to your ship, mine to my family, but if I do find my son, luck will not have played a part, believe me.'

For some unexplained reason the sailor did, and at midday he kept clear of the messdeck. The man and his story were worth more than rum.

Neither did he see the coastguard cutter that came to pick him up and take him to America so that the circle could continue, until the Guardian of Destiny deemed otherwise.

★ ★ ★

ATLANTIC OCEAN. JANUARY 1963.

It was the second hurricane of the season and so they named it Bertha. The first had been Alice. The fact that they were named after the female species was no accident. They had so much in common - changing direction several times a day, unpredictable and illogical. Bertha was no exception - a real handful, gathering speed and strength one hundred miles east of the island of Barbuda, she had suddenly turned south, on course for Guadeloupe. They had followed at a discreet distance, but she had been leading them on, like a wounded animal she had turned on them, bearing her teeth, venting all her wrath on the helpless frigate. They had tried to steer clear of her but she had been too quick and eventually enveloped them in a seething, wild frenzy of wind and water.

He lay lashed in his hammock, the usual routine for off duty men until they had hopefully passed through or round her, staring at the deckhead where a small card looked down at him.

O Lord, thine Ocean is so big
And my ship so small…

As the ship snaked and tossed, rivets popping, the dark water covering the portholes, he thought of the idiot who had written Rule Britannia. If he thought Britain ruled the waves why was he a musician and not a sailor? Then the lull, the centre, a brief respite for both ship and crew, then out the other side, a gentle roll at first building to the inevitable roller-coaster ride. For no apparent reason a picture of the ship's crest entered his head, a strange head with wind coming from its mouth, the motto underneath, 'Tot Itinera Tot Venti'. Translated, it meant, 'every voyage has its gales' - a slight understatement.

★ ★ ★

Bertha claimed her man some time during the morning watch. The bridge lookout had spotted someone through the spray, heading for the upperdeck vegetable locker, but at the watch changeover he was unaccounted for. The leading hand of the mess had called them all together later that morning, an old three badgeman steeped in rum and tradition, the Navy his life.

'It's sad about the young lad,' he began, 'but he either didn't know or forgot the tenets.'

They all looked at him as if he had asked them each for a ten bob note; nobody had mentioned these tenets at HMS Ganges.

'Live by those and you won't go far wrong. It might be the wrong time but I'm saying it anyway. What he did was not good sense.'

'What's these tenets then?' someone asked, speaking for everyone.

'It will cost ye.'

They were talking rum, the most valuable commodity on board any naval ship, a tradition not yet afforded to young sailors like him.

'Gulpers,' the same voice.

The drinks came in three measures depending upon the importance of the favour or information: 'sippers' which meant just that, 'gulpers' a good mouthful, or 'see it off' which could mean a whole 'tot' and for which you virtually had to lend someone your wife for the night. The badgeman agreed on 'gulpers'.

'The eight tenets are beliefs, principles and standards, handed down over the years by the earliest seagoing men, Phoenicians, Romans, Vikings, men who sailed with Drake and Nelson, men who followed the code of the sea. They possessed courage, tenacity, honour and honesty, they were loyal and had good sense, and when things got rough, they relied on humour and whatever they believed in as a god to see them through. It was hardly good sense to go on the upperdeck in a hurricane even attached to a line, which he wasn't. So take heed.'

Take heed the young sailor did. And for the second time that tour of duty he had heard something which he would remember. The tenets would be his.

* * *

FLORIDA STRAITS. JANUARY 1963

It was to be their last patrol before heading home and most of the thoughts of the ship's company were concentrated on family and friends. He was no exception; images of his native Hartlepool becoming stronger as the days went by. Only a small town on the north-east coast of England, but because of its long history, mainly associated with the sea and ships, it was a natural breeding ground for sailors. He had maintained the family tradition following in the footsteps of his father, grandfather, uncles and even aunts - a long line of seagoing men and women who he had never tired of listening to.

'Special sea dutymen close up. Marines muster starboard side of boat deck...'

He slid over the side of his hammock, already dressed in working rig, and made his way to the bridge, his part of ship, the routine now a regular occurrence as more and more Cubans joined the 'let's get rid of Fidel' campaign. Fifteen minutes later the marines returned, a small, black inflatable boat in tow.

'Duty electrician to the deck.'

He reported to the seaman Petty Officer who was supervising bringing the inflatables back on board and was told that the searchlight used in the operation was defective. Not unusual, he thought as he replaced the plug in its socket. He positioned the light so that it shone down into the recovered craft, illuminating the two bodies that lay still and covered in blood, the sudden urge to be sick adding to his increasing sense of sadness. He recognized the older man instantly, the cross clearly visible over his heart. The other, his own age and although unfamiliar he knew who he was. As he climbed back to his station he recalled the Cuban's words. Perhaps he had passed the test set for him by his 'Guardio Destino', even now sitting with those who control the scheme of things. One thing he knew for certain, his outlook on life would alter radically. No longer would he be tied to an ancient doctrine, a dogma that survived on interpretation and fear. He had, during that voyage, formed his own set of ideals.

CHAPTER ONE
Curaçao, Netherlands Antilles, May 1994

The table was large and oval, expensive like everything in the room, exemplifying the opulence of the Curaçao Plaza Hotel and Casino, a fact much appreciated by the various Government representatives gathered within its walls. For the majority of the year it was home to the Netherlands' more affluent members of society, the casino playing host to many of the richest people in the world or, as one of the croupiers had been heard to say, 'the Dutch with much.'

That particular day, however, it was a different sort of clientele occupying the ten chairs around the table. They were men who had decisions to make. They had arrived on the island the previous day. For some it had been long and tiring, for others - the delegate from Venezuela for instance - a short hop. But without exception, they had all taken a risk to attend. The conference had been convened under the auspices of ALADI, the Latin American Integration Association, formed in 1990 to create a common market in South America. The meeting, however, had more to do with termination than with integration, which was why an American and a Dutchman had been invited.

Since the early eighties, Colombia had been waging a lone war against the many drug cartels that still existed within its borders, but with limited success - filling its prisons with suppliers and users, but hardly scratching the surface so far as the major players were concerned. Such was the contribution of cocaine to the economic wealth of the country, successive administrations had all but turned a blind eye. People in work reflected well on the country, irrespective of the legality of their labours. A serious attempt at making inroads had been made in 1984, following the assassination of the Minister of Justice and again five years later when a leading presidential candidate had been killed. But a concerted campaign by the traffickers, including bombings - during which hundreds of innocent civilians died - had brought the attempt to an end. In 1993 the Government forces achieved a major success when, while trying to avoid arrest, a leading drug baron was killed. Pablo Escobar Gaviria was the head of the largest of the Medellin Cartels until his arrest in 1991. The following year, he managed to escape and evade the police for a further year before being shot. It should have signalled the end for the traffickers, but unfortunately it was not to be, and in the last twelve months there had been a significant resurgence in drug activity to such an extent that non-Latin countries were increasingly feeling the effects.

Renaldo Hernandez reflected on his country's turbulent recent past as he waited to be introduced to the waiting delegates. A formality as, apart from the Dutch and American members, he had met the remainder on several occasions, sometimes not enjoying the experience one bit. This conference too would be especially difficult for him. The fact that Colombia had called for outside assistance would not go down well with his fellow South Americans - a fact that his Chief Minister had brought to his attention three days before.

'Do not take things personally,' he had begun. 'To stop the drug trade completely is not only impossible, it is for some countries political suicide. You must remember, Renaldo, that in large areas of our continent the people are only capable of working in the drug industry, and unemployment means the difference between votes and apathy. The secret of diplomacy can be summed up in one word, face. Never show your real one and most important of all, try not to lose it.'

It was easy for him to say. Whilst most of those in the room were hardly in the same league as Colombia, they had the same voting rights, and a veto from the likes of Bolivia would almost certainly make any agreement untenable.

'Please gentlemen can I have your attention?'

All eyes focused on the Dutchman who was to chair the meeting.

'Can I introduce Seňor Hernandez who will briefly explain the aim of this conference and the purpose of the proposals on your agenda.'

Renaldo rose to his feet, both hands resting on the highly-polished table, his spectacles automatically falling to the end of his nose.

'The aim, gentlemen, is quite simple and that is for us all to agree that the trafficking of drugs is something that we will no longer tolerate. The proposals to help us achieve that end, whilst in some quarters may seem unpalatable, are I assure you, necessary. For the last thirty years the continent of South America has yielded more and more of its natural resources. Argentina with its large reserves of oil and gas, Bolivia tin, Brazil diamonds, and my own country with its large deposits of emeralds and increasing reserves of oil. They are commodities which are quite capable of sustaining our economies legitimately, as opposed to a product of which none of us should be proud. Since 1989 my government has intensified its efforts to prevent the growth of that product. Unfortunately, we have succeeded only in treading water. But gentlemen, with your assistance and that of the United States and Europe, we intend to apply more pressure on the cartels, by becoming more selective. We will in future concentrate all our resources on one major cartel at a time, instead of spreading our forces too thinly, as we have tended to do in the past. The government of Colombia will provide the force of arms. Where we need your assistance is in limiting the amount of coca leaf that is produced, or that passes through your country.'

He paused while empty cups were refilled with coffee.

At the far end of the table Ricardo Punta leaned lazily back in his chair, already bored with the whole proceedings, and wishing that he had been allowed to stay in Bolivia. He too had been well briefed by his Minister, the phrase 'do not make any promises that you know may be difficult for us to keep' never far from his thoughts. And if he needed reminding, there was the American sitting opposite. Half a lifetime spent in politics, his memory as dependable as ever, he recalled how the United States had, over a period of years, so readily given and taken away aid packages depending upon how much influence they could wield in his country's affairs. The 1967 uprising led by Che Guevara had allowed them a foot in the door, helping his country put down the insurrection. But things had not gone according to America's plans, mainly due to countless coups and subsequent changes in leadership. It was mainly due to the coup led by General Luis Garcia that the honeymoon had finally come to an end. Corruption and drug trafficking allegations were mainly responsible for the cancellation of US aid, and although restored three years later, relations between the two countries had never been quite the same. He must now, however, tread warily and not let his antipathy jeopardize the special relationship - unofficial as it was - that his country had with Colombia.

That relationship depended on two factors, Bolivia's continuing reputation as the largest producer of the coca leaf, and Colombian expertise at converting it into the finished cocaine and distribution, through its many contacts, worldwide. He suddenly felt the urge to ask a question.

'Would I be correct in thinking that your proposal involves the complete destruction of the coca crop, Señor Hernandez?'

Renaldo knew that it would be only a matter of time before Punta would try to influence the meeting.

'I would prefer to call it a replacement program, and I have no illusions about the difficulty of the task should we agree to carry it out, as I am sure you are aware.'

'Only too aware, but like my Government, I fear that in solving one problem we create another. How do we compensate the growers for the loss of their livelihood?'

There was a murmur of agreement around the table. Not all the countries represented would have the problem, the plan involving some more than others, the potential main stumbling blocks being Bolivia, Peru and, to a slightly lesser degree, Brazil, who would be asked to monitor the Amazonian waterways and jungle trails.

'It is hoped that all our Governments will seek to negotiate an agreement, culminating in payments being made or suitable land being made available to them, Señor Punta.'

'And the Americans, they will help us, again, and at what cost?'

The cynically expressed question had caught Byron T Hollingsworth a little by surprise, and although he had expected to be brought into the discussion at some point, he hadn't anticipated the suddenness of it.

'Before I begin to answer the last question gentlemen, let me say that it is in the interests of the US and Europe that we reach some measure of agreement today. Let me also add that I am here at the invitation of the Government of Colombia, to do nothing more than help. The US Treasury Department in partnership with the Inter-American Development Bank has already made available a substantial sum for this project. In addition, they have promised to finance any other resources that we deem necessary. As you well know, millions of American dollars are spent each year on operations to halt the influx of drugs into my country, either through Mexico or directly to the ports on the East Coast. We have for some time thought that the money could be utilized much more efficiently by prevention at source, as outlined by Señor Hernandez.'

He was about to continue when Punta interrupted him.

'Is it true, Mr. Hollingsworth, that part of the plan would be to educate the peasants to grow alternative crops?'

'That is a possible solution.'

'And you will also provide the soil?'

'Soil?'

'Yes, soil, because, you see, in much of my country the poor soil is only suitable for growing one crop, and it is not strawberries.'

Carefully concealed smiles and grins by some, outright laughter by Punta's supporters forced Hollingsworth onto the back foot for a moment, but only for a moment. He leaned forward, arms on the table and looked straight at the Bolivian.

'Let me clarify my position once again gentlemen, my only intention here today is to assist you in the elimination of the drug cocaine, by whatever means necessary. My country does not have all the answers, and indeed, as you have just proved, we are not aware of all the problems. I will say this to you, if the solution is soil, Señor Punta, I would willingly transport the whole of the American mid-west sack by sack, bucket by bucket to your country. Furthermore, if it's strawberries that you want, I would plant every last one and even milk the cow to make the fucking cream. Now if you don't mind. let's cut the crap and the one-upmanship and hear something constructive.'

A product of the diplomatic school Byron was not, but he felt it had needed saying, and he suspected that his outburst had gained one or two friends, in addition to the wink from Hernandez. Punta he knew would never change, and yet he felt no animosity towards the man, to a certain extent even understood him. Like quite a few Latin officials they had attained their power on the backs of the people America was now attempting to close down. Resentment was inevitable.

The small outburst had its effect and for the next hour the meeting continued with an increasing number of delegates contributing, as opposed to relying on Punta to be their spokesperson, which Byron had suspected all along, was the original plan. He had resisted the assignment from the very beginning, preferring to remain a doer rather than a talker, not comfortable in the company of politicians of any country or persuasion. It was obvious now that it was an appointment of appeasement, forced on him due to the increasing internal furore that was threatening the US administration. The decoy duck on a lake full of piranha, was the analogy that came to mind, he thought.

For twenty-five years he had been a respected agent of the Drug Enforcement Administration, enjoying the freedom of fieldwork until a near fatal experience had led to a desk job. A phone call from the Head of the Washington Field Division with an invitation to meet the Director had interrupted his sedentary way of life. The meeting had been amicable at first, but as his resistance increased, so did the impatience of his superior. At the meeting's conclusion he was convinced that he had been told more than he should have been, in order to secure his cooperation.

'In recent years Byron, our relations with OPEC have deteriorated to such a level that we have for some time been increasing our import of Colombian oil. Unfortunately, they are experiencing real problems in meeting our requirements, their production targets are nowhere near what they expected, and so for some time we have been providing assistance in the shape of geologists, construction engineers and production operatives. The fact that we are getting the oil cheaper than we were, and thereby saving the country millions of dollars, has failed to register with some who only see us trading with a country responsible for flooding the States with 'crack' cocaine. The present administration is under increasing pressure from the anti-drug lobby to terminate any trading between the South Americans and ourselves.

Terms such as 'hypocritical', 'two-faced' and even 'supporting the trade' are coming from the Senate floor.'

'But this conference, sir, it's a bit out of our jurisdiction, surely. I would have thought the State Department would have been involved,' he interrupted.

'You spent a lot of time out there in one guise or another. You also speak their language and understand their ways. Besides, all you'll be doing is reporting back with the results of the meeting. State will do any signing that has to be done. There is also a reason of my own that makes me think that we should be involved as a department, and I warn you, that if any part of this conversation is repeated outside of this room, I know who to sack without a pension.'

Byron had suddenly become more than a little interested.

'As you know as well as anybody, this Agency, for as long as I can remember, has fought an uphill battle, not helped I may add, by the sheer size of the country. Logistically it is a nightmare to police effectively, even the setting up of our own State Offices from the Canadian border down to the tip of Florida and from coast to coast, has done very little to alleviate the drug smuggling problem. Miami is quickly becoming the Medellin of America, made easy by the apparent 'open door' policy that we seem to have adopted, because I have to say that sectors of the immigrant population have contributed more than a little to our predicament. In addition to the South American, West Indian and Chinese communities, we shot ourselves in the foot again in 1980 by allowing the Mariel Boat Lift - a God-given opportunity for Fidel to empty his prisons of undesirables and offload them onto us.'

Byron remembered the event well. It was as if Castro had said to them, 'If you are all so concerned about human rights, then allow them to enter your country,' and they had fallen for it, curing a large headache for the Cuban leader.

'Anyway I digress. The bottom line Byron, is that the administration has demonstrated by accepting the invitation to attend this conference, a desire to fund ways and means of combating the cocaine problem. If they can do it abroad then they can damn well do it here, a fact of which I will be reminding them when I submit my budget proposals. If I can get the backing of the State Department, all the better and they may feel that by us doing them this favour they are beholden.'

He leaned forward and Byron caught the faint but unmistakable smell of whisky, and only ten o'clock in the morning, he thought.

'I sometimes ask myself what happened to 'organized crime,' at least you knew where you stood with the Mafia. Instead of the chaos we have now, where it appears every man and his grandpa are involved in something or other.'

'Is there anything else I need to know?' It was acceptance.

'Good man, you'll get a proper briefing before you leave, but don't take any crap from any of them, I don't care how far up the beanstalk they are.'

* * *

They called a halt for lunch, a six-course affair, and a far cry from the tuna sandwiches that he usually ate at his desk, and being first to finish his coffee, he wandered back into the conference room. He was not a great lover of art, but he envied talented people and it was obvious that the paintings adorning the walls were by someone special. Their themes were varied and he was standing in front of a very fine-looking, naked woman, when he noticed that the Dutchman had joined him.

'You like art, Mr Hollingsworth?'

He replied without taking his eyes off the painting.

'I admire the expertise, but I can't say I understand most of it - apart from this one of course.'

They both laughed for the first time that day.

'It is a Rubens - a very famous sixteenth century Dutch artist, who was also a scholar and diplomat, unlike yourself I think.'

'You didn't need a sharp eye to notice that.'

They laughed again.

'And how sharp are your eyes?'

Unnoticed, Hernandez had joined them.

'You'll have to explain, I think I'm missing something,' replied Byron.

'Indeed you are, look at the left eye of the nude, what do you see?'

They both took a step forward, peering up at the face of the woman. It was not obvious, but the discrepancy was there, the centre of the eye was missing, and where it should have been was a small hole.

'I take it the hole is of some significance Seňor?'

'It would have been had we not found it, my Dutch friend.'

They both turned and faced him, the question written on their faces.

'Please sit down and I will explain.' He walked to the huge pair of doors and closed them before joining them at the table. 'One of the disadvantages of being an official in my country gentlemen is that I am continually under threat, not only from outsiders, but from people and organizations within Colombia. I have therefore found it prudent, if not absolutely necessary, to have trusted people accompany me on most occasions. This visit was no exception. They arrived here late last night and immediately swept the room for any hidden devices, and it was during this search that they observed something out of character. The spotlight above the painting was pointing at an unusual angle. On closer examination, my men found that a powerful halogen lamp had been inserted which, had it been switched on, would certainly, very quickly, have damaged the painting. It was then that they noticed the hole and decided to remove the Rubens, discovering a small electronic device secreted in the wall directly behind the damaged eye. On closer inspection it was found to be a complicated control device capable of remotely detonating explosives.'

The American was the first to react to the revelation, intrigued by the use of the light bulb.

'I am not an electronics expert by any means but the method employed was explained to me like this. The effect of the light on a photoelectric cell would have produced an electric current, enough to close a switch and activate the detonator, which in turn would then cause the explosion.'

It was the Dutchman who this time asked the inevitable question.

'And the explosives?'

'They were found in the upholstery part of Mr. Hollingsworth's chair.'

Nothing was said for a minute or so, Byron taking in the fact that he had been the flick of a switch away from a fragmented death, presumably along with the rest of the delegates.

'Do you know who was responsible?' he asked, recovering.

'I'm afraid not, we very rarely catch the people who carry out this type of thing. If they were from Colombia they are well practised in this form of assassination. The truth is that as the wealth of these cartels increases so does their power, and I'm afraid that anyone who attempts to threaten the effects of that power do so knowing the risk to their continuing survival. Since 1980, in my country alone, eleven members of the Supreme Court have been murdered, over one hundred and fifty judges, even the Police Chief of Cali, together with the editor of Bogotá's leading newspaper were not immune. Quite simply, the cartels' influence in Colombia is now so extensive that I sometimes wonder who is in control. The irony is that although most of us look on these scum as purveyors of misery, they receive more than a small measure of allegiance from the peasant population, who benefit from the proceeds of the trade by way of schools, sports stadia and even churches.'

Byron nodded, he had witnessed at first-hand the influence of the traffickers several years before, whilst working in Bolivia.

They were interrupted by the return of the remaining members, suspicious glances aimed in their direction. The meeting resumed. As far as Byron knew, only the three of them aware of how close they had all been to not resuming their seats.

* * *

It was six thirty in the evening, and the two men sat in the rear of the Mercedes as it sped towards the airport. The conference had ended an hour earlier, both men sceptical as to its contribution to solving the drug problem. Hernandez had put it in perspective, thought Byron.

'Make no mistake my friend, the task we have set ourselves is impossible to achieve without some degree of force, because it relies on changing the ideas and strengthening the will of millions of people. Let me simplify the situation. Many years ago when the coca leaf was discovered, the peasants would chew it raw. For a few moments they were magnificent Inca Emperors, instead of poor Quechua Indians. But, like any anaesthetic, it loses its effect and the pain and suffering return. Take a good look at the world my friend. Ordinary people, not unlike you and me, are growing and cultivating cannabis and cocaine in small back rooms, huts in their gardens, even the window boxes of their apartments. The shame of it is, because of their economic plight, they sell it on, capturing, snaring and destroying future generations, and if they can't grow it, they manufacture it - inventing synthetic chemical substances. It's a grim picture I paint, Mr. Hollingsworth, but if people like us don't attempt to halt its progress, this planet will become like a dark Cronenberg Movie.'

Byron shuddered at the thought, but the man was right.

'I agree, but at the moment we can't even trust ourselves.'

'What makes you think that?'

'When the Bolivian asked you who was first on the hit list you evaded the question.'

'Check the definition of trust, I think you will find it reads: a person in whom confidence or faith is placed. I am confident that he will do what he can. I have, however, no faith in his motives for doing it.'

'And me. Am I to know?'

Renaldo Hernandez smiled.

'If we meet again my friend you will know, if we do not, there was no need.'

It was the diplomatic answer that he expected.

CHAPTER TWO
Bangor, North Wales, 1994

The day that Simon Halkin had been dreading for some time had finally arrived - a cold, miserable day, not unlike the way he was feeling. It was his graduation day. As far as he was concerned, a day to endure rather than to enjoy. Lying on his bed, hands clasped across his chest he tried to force himself into a more congenial mood in readiness for the approaching ceremony.

Since his early schooldays he had shown a reluctance to be the centre of attention, preferring to blend into the background. Unfortunately now that he was twenty-two years of age it wasn't so easy. At six feet three inches, with a shock of black curly hair and green eyes, he knew that he was the envy of many of his much shorter friends. He, however, saw it as an obstacle to retaining his privacy, his 'own space' being very important to him. In a little under two hours time that space would be shared by four hundred other graduates. For approximately twenty seconds, as he received his degree in History, he would be the focus of everyone's attention, and it was twenty seconds too long. The photographs with doting parents would then follow. Evidence to be shown to other family members and friends that their offspring had done well. How he detested the whole charade.

He raised himself, resting on one arm, and switched on his small portable radio, already tuned to his favourite station. He loved music. His kind wasn't everyone's cup of tea, but he found a certain inspirational quality in Iron

Maiden and Black Sabbath. A huge poster of the former adorned his room, depicting a futuristic warrior. It was a prized possession, like his collection of picture discs produced by the same pop group. To a certain extent his taste in music revealed a lot about him - not one to go along with the crowd. He was nevertheless well liked, if on some occasions looked on as a little eccentric with regard to his views. Outspoken and forthright, yes, but never in a vindictive way, which made his circle of friends small, but loyal. He was jolted into action by the 9am news bulletin and, leaving the unmade bed behind, made his way down the long corridor to the communal bathroom already occupied by most of the students on his floor.

'Morning Simon,' the greeting coming from Giorgio, the young Italian who occupied the room next to his, and whose family owned acres of vineyards, or something of that sort, in Corsica.

'Is the Cosa Nostra making an appearance today?' Simon quipped.

The young Italian had over the last two years become accustomed to the sarcastic humour of his friend, even learning to give as good as he got.

'I think my Godfather is making an appearance,' he replied.

They both shared the joke. He had taken to the short, swarthy Italian and even more to his native food, which he had been introduced to on a number of occasions. They discussed the forthcoming day's proceedings while they showered and shaved, and then walked back to their respective rooms, still in conversation.

'So you will return home and learn the business of winemaking, will you?'

Giorgio nodded in agreement.

'That is the intention, although the thought of treading grapes for a while depresses me somewhat.'

'You can always try one at a time, just for a change,' joked Simon.

Back in his room he sat in his underwear, putting off getting into his suit until the last possible moment - a mode of dress he was unhappy about wearing, but on this particular occasion convention required it to be worn. He was in the middle of packing away a few bits and pieces ready for his return to Teeside, when he heard the heavy knock on his door.

* * *

The green Toyota saloon car did not appreciate the hills of Bangor and at that moment neither did its driver, George Halkin, who was wondering why his son hadn't chosen to attend a university situated on the flat lands of Norfolk. As he continued to wage his private battle with the gear lever, his wife Joan watched his exertions.

'Would you like me to drive us to the University, George?' she volunteered.

'No I'm all right, it's just all these damn hills.'

'Isn't there another road we can take?'

Sweating profusely in the morning sunshine he thought about answering, but then bit his lip. He would have liked to have told her that there was an easier way, but because it was Lent and a time of penance, he had decided on the difficult route, but he didn't. Women had always been a complete mystery to him, convinced that they had been created to test men, starting with Adam. He thought of her friend Barbara who the previous week had failed the driving test, her fifth attempt, which was hardly surprising if her driving ability had been on a par with her answers to the Highway Code. He had overheard the two discussing her latest failure.

'And when he asked me to name some common signs that I would see in the countryside and I told him, 'fresh eggs for sale' and 'pick your own strawberries', he just laughed Joan, and said 'I'm sorry, but you must spend more time reading the code'.'

Whoever had made the decision to site traffic lights at the top of a 25% hill had either a masochistic sense of humour, or detested motorists intensely, particularly the people of Bangor. Somewhere, he thought, there is a sad little man with a pair of binoculars watching these lights and wetting himself every time a vehicle climbs this hill. On green he turned left, following the Prifysgol Cymru sign that would eventually lead them to the University of North Wales, and their son's accommodation.

He was pleased that they had decided to drive across from Teeside the previous night when the A55 was much less congested. Journeys in the past had been horrendous affairs, taking as much as two hours or more to pass through Conwy. Simon had arranged for them to stay overnight at a local public house, which had been nice and clean, and a bonus was its location which gave them a magnificent view across the Menai Straits to Anglesey. The local people had been friendly enough, but lacking the genuine openness to which anyone from the North-East was accustomed - talking to them in English one minute but switching to their native Welsh for conversation between themselves.

They had been awake early that morning and eaten breakfast alone. Then dressed for the forthcoming occasion, they sat on the veranda and drank coffee.

'Joan why are you taking that umbrella? The sun is shining, there is no forecast for rain, its just something extra to carry about.'

'If I take it then it will keep fine,' she had replied, seriously.

He had come to the conclusion early on in marriage that logic came in two varieties - a reasoned thought or argument, as distinguished from irrationality, and then the female variety which had much in common with the Japanese kamikaze pilot who wore a crash helmet.

The car park was, even at that early hour, fully occupied, and so he was forced to leave the Toyota on one of the ubiquitous Bangor hills, and make the short walk to Simon's lodgings. His room was on the third floor and by the time they had climbed the stairs, although only in their late forties, both were breathing quite heavily. Ten minutes later through a maze of corridors they located C138, guided the last few metres by the sound of loud, heavy metal music, and knocked loudly on the door.

* * *

He hurriedly switched off his cassette player with one hand while opening the door with the other, and was immediately enveloped in his mother's arms.

'Have you been all right son?'

Eventually releasing him and allowing an answer.

'I'm fine,' he replied, shaking hands with his father.

'You're both looking well even if you don't sound it.'

He noticed his mother already searching for a refuse bag; his father comfortably seated in the room's only chair, tobacco tin in hand and about to roll a cigarette.

'And when was the last time you went to the launderette, Simon?'

George lit the cigarette and smiled in response to his son's raised eyebrows, he was a credit to both of them, even if he did say it himself. At one time they had talked about his following in his father's footsteps, but he had ideas of his own and rightly so. They had more in common than either would admit, which was not surprising, both being the first offspring of their particular families. He also suspected that they had inherited most of their ancestors' qualities, in addition to one or two less attractive characteristics, and there had been occasions in the past when he had recognized himself in the actions of his eldest son.

He had once taken a keen interest in the family history, managing to trace the bloodline as far back as Hakon, the half-brother of Eric Bloodaxe. Hakon, who had been raised in the English court by Athelstan, was brought back to Norway and installed as King by a powerful group of landowners, opposed to the strong and wilful Eric. Bloodaxe and his supporters were forced into exile by the King and sailed westwards. Hakon, during the years that followed, produced many alliances between Norse and Celt - formidable stock. There was no doubt that both he and Simon had carried on that which Harold Finehair and Ragnild, Hakon's parents, had begun centuries earlier. The Celtic love of music and the Norse obsession with exploration and adventure, two examples of how the bloodline had remained intact.

He watched as his wife attempted to tidy the bombsite that had been home to his son for three years, and then listened as she spotted his tin.

'Can't you buy some proper cigarettes just for today George? I shudder every time you get that old thing out in company.'

She was right. It was a bit of an eyesore, but the tin didn't only hold tobacco and papers, it contained memories of times past, places visited, crisis and joy. It had been his constant companion for over thirty years.

At eleven o'clock they left the room and made their way down the hill to the Grand Hall of the University, his elder son asking after his younger brother on the way.

'He's okay, sends his regards but it was impossible to get the day off.'

Nicholas Halkin had joined the Fire Service the previous year and was still in his probation period. A popular lad, mainly due to his laid-back attitude to almost everything. He was extremely fond of sleep, and George was convinced that although he was eighteen years of age, he had only been awake for ten of them.

The three of them parted in the entrance hall of the main university building - Simon to collect his cap and gown, Joan and himself to take their places in the magnificent hall, that was rapidly filling. At half past eleven precisely, to the strains of Bach's 'St Anne' played on the huge organ, the graduates slowly made their way down the central aisle and proceeded to occupy the front benches. After a short speech by the Chancellor, the ceremony proceeded much like a school prize-giving, a long period of boredom punctuated by one special moment, as Simon received his 2:1 in History.

The courtyard was crowded by the time they found it. Families occupied every bit of available space, the flash of cameras everywhere, which he expected to be the case. His wife had insisted on buying a glass paperweight and a video of the ceremony, the cost of which would easily have paid for a child's education at a private school.

'How about a drink?' suggested Simon. 'I've arranged to meet some friends before we go our separate ways.'

The lounge area was already quite busy and while Simon went to the bar, he found a free table. They had just sat down when their son returned, accompanied by a tall, thin girl he introduced as Deborah, who in turn presented her parents. James and Gloria owned a farm in Lincolnshire and Deborah was the second of their daughters to graduate, they were informed almost immediately, without asking.

'Do you work, George?'

He wasn't sure whether he was just feeling a bit sensitive that day or that he had taken an immediate dislike to Gloria, who was obviously under the impression that anyone north of the River Humber in full-time employment was the exception rather than the rule.

'I'm retired now, but I was a firefighter for quite a few years,' he replied, trying his best to sound cordial.

'That must have been interesting, I imagine you have a story or two worth telling.'

He agreed that he had, but thought they were not the types to appreciate any of them.

'Is there one that springs to mind?' asked James.

He hesitated, uncertain of his next move. How involved was Simon with this girl? Would it cause embarrassment to him? What the hell, he thought. They did ask.

'As a matter of fact,' he began, 'about two years ago I attended a large fire in a fruit warehouse. Once the fire had been extinguished, we entered the building hoping to discover the cause, only to find in the ash a one-hundred-year-old rat.'

He caught his wife's disapproving look as the battered 'baccy' tin was placed on the table and he began rolling a cigarette.

'Amazing, but how did you discover its age?' asked Gloria.

He delivered the punchline in a way in which Clark Gable in *Gone With The Wind* would have been proud.

'Because there was a date up its bum, my dear.'

He saw his son drop his head to hide a smile, saw his wife look away, and had his suspicions confirmed about the family from Lincolnshire by the absence of any reaction at all. The penny eventually dropped with James.

'Fruit warehouse and dates, very good,' he admitted, reluctantly.

The conversation from that moment on could take only one path, and it did. As steep as any hill in Bangor, it plummeted downwards, until they all decided that other things required their attention, and parted company.

* * *

Simon spent the remainder of the afternoon saying his farewells to friends and tutors while he and Joan took the opportunity for a nap. They had reserved a table at a restaurant just outside Beaumaris, on the Isle of Anglesey, for seven thirty that evening, and having collected Simon, made their way across the rebuilt Telford Suspension Bridge to the island. It had been an excellent meal, expensive by their standards, but it was a special occasion and so they had no regrets about the cost. Unlike an experience in London, which still haunted him. It had been their first and certainly last visit to a well-known chain of steakhouses, and upon receiving the bill, had asked the waiter how often they would be informed as to the performance of their shares. The waiter had no sense of humour.

It wasn't until the arrival of the coffee that he had the opportunity to enter into any meaningful conversation with his son.

'So what are your immediate plans,' he enquired.

Simon Halkin looked at both of his parents in turn, he knew what they wanted to hear, particularly his mother, unfortunately the reality was quite the opposite.

'Nothing concrete at the moment, although I intend returning home and staying for a week or two before visiting Europe - backpacking with a friend for a month or so. Following that, my future plans are dependent on my getting a job.'

Joan stared at her first-born. No longer a child, now a young man talking enthusiastically about his travel plans, exuding the fearlessness of youth.

She loved both of her sons equally, had always treated them so, and yet there was something. George was forever telling people when the situation was appropriate, 'Never come between a mother and her first-born, it's the worst kind of grief.' Maybe that was the difference.

'And I don't intend to wait until it's too late to visit the places I've always wanted to see,' her son was saying, as she returned to the present conversation.

'To be perfectly frank son, and your mother isn't going to thank me for saying it, I would encourage anyone your age to travel. It wasn't easy in my day. In fact the only way was to use the Ministry of Defence as a travel agent, and book a passage on the Grey Funnel line.'

Her husband was right. She was not happy about it, and her son was well aware of the fact.

'It's as important a part of my education as my university studies, mam, and anyway I'll probably have to move away to find work.'

It was probably the wrong time to mention that fact, but at least he had kept from her - for the meantime at least - that Europe was only a stepping stone across the pond, that eventually he would take a giant leap to the other side of the world.

★ ★ ★

IBARRA, ECUADOR, 1994

The town of Ibarra, the provincial capital of Imbabura, is on the other side of the world, and situated some 135 kilometres north of Quito, the capital of Ecuador. The attractive colonial town with a population of 80,000 consists mainly of blacks from the Chota valley and Otavalenos and is not renowned for anything remarkable. Its only claim to fame being the starting point for the train to the Pacific Coast. It was 6:15 in the morning and Maria Sandino and her two friends, Anita and Patti, were excited at the prospect of a weekend on the beach at San Lorenzo - a journey taking some five hours to complete. They had arrived early to buy their tickets, which were only available on the day of departure, and already their light cotton dresses were sticking to them, due to the hot and humid conditions.

As seven o'clock approached, crowds of men, women and children pressed forward towards the edge of the platform, all eager to get the best position possible on the train. The three young girls, carried along by the crowd, called to each other to stay in touch as they were bustled into a carriage. As their fellow travellers climbed and tumbled over the backs of seats, the three found themselves squatting on the platform between two carriages.

The journey, although long and uncomfortable, did have its attractions. The scenery was spectacular, not least in its diversity of colours - continually changing as the train dropped from 2,225 metres to their sea level destination.

At 22 years of age, Maria epitomized the South American woman. Not tall, at five feet and four inches she was slightly smaller than her two companions, but it was her eyes and long, jet-black hair, together with her natural light-brown skin colour that made her so attractive. Her attributes however were not only on the outside, a bubbly personality and warm smile adding substance to her more obvious assets, which had been recognized immediately by the manager of the Hotel Gran Casino, situated in Quito. The three friends had made the two-and-a-half-hour journey from their small town to the capital looking for work and, quite by accident, she had discovered a vacancy at the hotel for a receptionist. The job was not well paid but she enjoyed it, and it had allowed her to rent a small flat, in the capital, which she shared with her friends. She returned home every three months to visit her family and contribute to the household budget.

Apart from her mother and father, four other people and her dog shared the house - two brothers and a younger sister, and also her grandmother, who had been compelled to join them because of ill health. Her grandfather was a family mystery and she had never seen him. His name was rarely mentioned, although occasionally she had seen her grandmother holding a photograph of a man and herself, which she kept in her room. The only thing she really knew about him was that they had parted when her mother had been very small, and even she had no idea of his whereabouts.

'Shall we go up to the roof?' shouted Anita above the incessant noise.

Nodding in agreement, the three girls, clutching their woven bags, clambered, one at a time, up the vertical ladder and onto the roof of the train - a position from which they could view the numerous villagers who lined the track, all trying to sell their various wares, principally to tourists.

'I was going to tell you on the return journey,' began Maria, once they were settled, 'but I must tell you now, I am going to Europe in five weeks' time.'

Had one of them fallen from the roof of the train, the impact and expression on their faces could not have been greater, she thought.

'When did you decide?' asked an incredulous Patti.

'I have known for about two months, but before you ask any more questions I will tell you how it came about. I happened to become friendly with a couple of English people who came to stay at the hotel for a few days on their way to Peru. During a conversation with them, I mentioned that I would one day like to visit Europe, of which I had heard so much, and that as soon as I had saved enough money, I would go. She then told me that they had a young son who was in need of a nanny, and asked if I would be interested in filling the position. But I was not to give them an answer then, as they would ring the hotel upon their return to London. The telephone call came three weeks later, and they told me that, providing I could afford the air fare and obtained the necessary documentation, the position was mine.'

'It will cost much sucre, will it not?' interjected Anita.

At that point the train made one of its many stops to allow the local people to board and offer their produce. Patti was busy buying some fruit from a small boy and so she waited for her to return before continuing.

'I have saved some myself, and my grandmother, Hermania, said she will give me the rest.'

'And have they rung you again?' asked Patti.

'Oh yes, many times,' she lied. It had in fact been some time since she had heard from them, but the absence of any word had not stopped her booking her plane ticket and visiting the Consulate in Quito for the required paperwork.

The questions made her head spin.

'What about the people, the language, and the culture?'

But she had a reply for each of them, and, try as they would to dissuade her from going, she knew that they would not succeed. They eventually all lay exhausted, hands behind their heads, each with their own thoughts, listening to the click of the wheels on the track as the train continued its journey. This time she knew where she was going, if only the future was as certain.

She accepted the fact that she would miss her two friends and family, but she had ambitions and they would not be realized in Ibarra or even Quito. The prospects for her were extremely limited to shop work, waiting on tables and of course receptionist. Besides, she was capable of greater things. She smiled. There was also the possibility of meeting a boy. She thought about what the future held for her two companions. They would marry men, probably from the town. Men who did nothing domestically, preferring to sit and talk - hardly a recipe for a long and happy relationship. They would bear children and be destined to a life of servile drudgery from which there was no escape. But she had no illusions that the path she had chosen would be any easier at first. Her friends were right. She knew very little of the English language or the people. It would take time to come to terms with a new culture, and yet the thought excited her.

The train slowed once more, approaching a cluster of small wooden buildings, which were surrounded by a few metres of poor soil. A man leaned on a gate, his only purpose in life to grow a few vegetables with which to feed his family. He would never see the strange and wonderful things that the world had to offer. The scene reinforced her will.

CHAPTER THREE
Medellin, Colombia, 1994

The man who showed himself into the dining room was careful to remove his boots before he entered - leaving them on the porch and walking onto the expensive Persian carpet in his stockinged feet, as he had done for more years than he cared to remember.

'You have news, Alfred?'

'I have, Rodrigo,' replied the man without the boots.

'Well, what are you waiting for? Tell me the details.'

'The truck has been loaded with the merchandise and will leave tomorrow for Santa Marta, it will be loaded onto the ship which will sail on the evening tide.'

'And how will it be transported?'

'In bananas. We confiscated a legitimate load on its way from Ecuador two days ago and have substituted boxes of our own.'

There was an uncomfortable silence before the questioning began again.

'You will supervise the consignment personally - from a distance of course, yes?'

'As you wish,' replied the visitor.

'And what of the other matter?'

The man called Alfred silently walked towards a large oak table on which he placed an envelope.

'All the details are there, apart from an incident that happened earlier today. There has been a shooting.'

'Who and why?' The tone of the voice had changed, markedly.

'A Frenchman. We discovered later he was ex-Legion and so more resourceful than the others. He somehow managed to break loose and overpower our man, escaping with a weapon. But he was tracked to the town of La Ceja, and after a short exchange, he was killed.'

'Photographs?'

'Yes Rodrigo, we took enough before we buried him.'

'And the idiot who was the cause of this escape, what of him, Alfred?'

It was the question he had feared.

'He has been a good man in the past, one of our best.'

'But it would appear no longer is he one of the best. But I will let you decide. That is all. You may go.'

Curt and to the point as usual, he was dismissed, and returning to his boots found them clean and highly polished.

Rodrigo Cesar Betancur picked up the envelope and slit it open with a gold knife, the handle of which contained a single emerald - an acquisition from a fellow trafficker. Its use brought back memories of days when he had been able to use his real name and not, as now, an assumed one. But he also knew that it was a name to be feared throughout Colombia. He was now in his mid-sixties and felt it. Not a well man, but still retaining the streak of ruthlessness and business acumen, along with the same enthusiasm that had seen him reach the top of the ladder, so far as the cocaine trade was concerned.

He looked around the large room, at the fine trappings with which he had surrounded himself, but not without cost, he thought. The wheelchair, his constant companion, a reminder of the violent world in which he existed. He rarely left the estancia, situated on the outskirts of Medellin. For years it had been his home, his office, but also his prison, remaining within its confines, and only very occasionally taking to his helicopter to visit his empire. He now controlled that empire by computer, telephone and fax machine, still managing to keep his finger on the pulse - until recently that is. The envelope brought by his rare visitor, more evidence that his business was under serious threat. The wheel has come full circle, he reflected, as he read more of the contents of the envelope.

Times had been difficult in the late '70s, but then, during the boom years of the early '80s the Colombian cartels had controlled 80% of the world's cocaine market - plantations and laboratories appearing overnight, transport companies changing hands, protection becoming a way of life for many. It was not until 1983 that the Government forces had launched a serious campaign against the drug trade, eventually turning the conflict into a real war. It was also during this period that he had been shot, taking a bullet in his lower back, which smashed his spinal column. Lengthy surgery had removed part of the offending bullet, but the damage had been substantial and from that day he had been confined to the chair.

Two months later, the leader of the guerilla group to which he belonged, Carlos Pizzaro, had been assassinated, signalling the break up of Morimiento 19 de Abril or M19 as it was popularly known. Although still extremely ill, he had with the help of Alfred and several other loyal field commanders, managed to hold together enough of M19's cocaine interests to make it a viable proposition. Whilst many of the cartels had become involved in long and expensive terrorist activities against the Government of Conservative President, Belisario Betancur, his namesake, but nothing more, he and many others had accepted the offered amnesty, whilst still retaining the drug interest. He had kept a low profile, steadily expanding his area of operations at the expense of others and trading quite freely under the protection of the amnesty. Now, however, he had been drawn into conflict with the Colombian Government, who, with the assistance of the US Drug Enforcement Agency, had forced him into a corner from which he was finding it very hard to extricate himself.

★ ★ ★

Alfred Jaramillo no longer looked to see if his boots had been polished, unlike some that had visited this estancia, he thought. The tradition was, in fact, a code known to all those who were employed by his friend and boss, and it was an indication of one's future well-being. Over the years many had returned to collect their footwear, and finding it untouched, knew that their employment had been terminated. A clean pair of boots was not a prerequisite for meeting your maker.

From his position at the top of the steps leading to the main house, he could see the extent of the protection that his friend had found necessary to ensure his safety. Immediately below him the courtyard had been covered with razor-sharp stones that ringed the house, and a further reason why Rodrigo permitted only bootless visitors. The theory was simple, anyone attempting to escape from the house quickly, for whatever reason, would not have time to don their footwear, and progress across the stones without, was both painful and slow. The remainder of the security was by conventional equipment - CCTV in abundance and beyond the courtyard, the compound enclosed by barbed wire fencing. The whole area was dominated by the watchtower, from where the many huge searchlights were controlled.

As he strolled across to his waiting helicopter, he thought about the recent events that had brought him to the estancia, a report of these he had just delivered in an envelope to his boss. The situation in which they now found themselves had come as no surprise to him. It had been gathering momentum for some considerable time, at least seven years, and since the capture of Pablo Escobar Gaviria.

Gaviria had been one of their main competitors, until quite suddenly in 1991 he had surrendered to the Colombian authorities under a plea bargaining programme, which promised that he could not be extradited to stand trial in the USA. In 1992 he escaped and despite a multi-million dollar reward being offered for his recapture, he remained a free man until the following year, when he was shot dead. His death moved the focus of the authority's attention to them, and although they had a brief respite when the US Congress decided to deny aid to the country through de-certification - which meant in effect that Colombia was removed from the list of countries making progress against the drug traffickers - they had come under renewed scrutiny the following year. Since then their position had gone from bad to worse, losing valuable shipments worth millions of dollars and eventually forcing Rodrigo's hand.

The helicopter took off from the pad and circled the compound, the well-armed guards watching his progress, probably wondering if he had been the bearer of more bad news, which he had.

* * *

The envelope contained the particulars of seven people - three women and four men, and although of differing nationalities they had one thing in common, they were tourists and therefore prime targets for what he intended. Unwittingly they had become potential levers, a means of bargaining, their names unimportant, their country of origin the real source of value to him. Two Americans, and one of each from Japan, China, Belgium, India and at that moment the most valuable, one dead Frenchman, made up the list of hostages held at various locations, which were known only to Alfred. The days of large amounts of money finding their way into officials' bank accounts had long since disappeared, due to the intervention of outside agencies who had made it increasingly difficult to sustain. He still had valuable sources of information within the security forces, of course - people who gave him warning when there was about to be a raid on his estancia, allowing him enough time to take a short trip to Alfred's hacienda. It had also come to his attention that feverish negotiations had already commenced with the countries who had people missing, the obvious question being asked. What were the Colombian Government doing about it? He knew exactly what they were doing, but in a country equal in area to France, Spain and Portugal combined, the possibility of the police and military discovering the locations of the hostages was remote. In reality, they only had one option, to buy their release, and the price was to concentrate their efforts on activities other than cocaine production.

A knock on the heavy door, followed by the entrance of three men, interrupted his train of thought. Two of them were his and armed, the third, a stranger, showed visual signs of uneasiness.

'Who is this?' he asked, not happy with the intrusion.

'He applied for a job as a gardener at the hacienda of Alfred Jaramillo some weeks ago and he must be very good because we have discovered that until recently he was employed by the Ministry of Foreign Affairs in Bogotá, Señor Betancur.'

Over many years spent in the company of men of questionable character and ethics, he had become very adept at recognizing the genuine, or otherwise, nature of his fellow man. It had saved his life on many occasions, and he accepted nothing at face value. He had adopted the golden rule of his former leader Pizzaro, 'Where there is doubt there is danger. Where there is danger, death. Whose death depends upon your actions, but in our business there is never a place for doubt.'

He looked the man in the eyes.

'Find him a position in my garden.'

He watched as the man picked up his boots, still covered with the dust of the surrounding area. The single burst of gunfire from an AK-47 coming seconds later, explaining the reason. Wearily he slumped in his chair. He slept very little, content to spend the nights, which he hated, trying to stay one step ahead of his competitors - the military, and even his own employees - a huge task at the easiest of times. There was Alfred, of course, and accountants, plantation bosses, transport managers and shipping agents. Yet he had always maintained the old ways and that meant checking the checkers.

It was five thirty in the morning when the fax machine began to operate, a single sheet of paper, but it might as well have been a blow from the gold dagger. He read the contents, at the same time pounding the table in anger until his hands bled.

★ ★ ★

BOGOTÁ, COLOMBIA, 1994

The lights were burning late in the office of Henri Pastrana, head of the Investigative Police Department of Colombia, the PIP. It was not unusual, a matter of routine for most nights recently, this time however he was not alone. Sitting opposite were two of his most senior and trusted men, men who looked as if they had gone without sleep for a very long time. Which indeed they had. Guillermo Garbanza was the senior of the two men and therefore directly responsible for the smooth running of the department, which he did very effectively. But for the last two months in particular he had been experiencing major problems.

A short, stockily-built man, he looked as if he belonged on the other side of the law, but nothing could have been further from the truth. He had been a policeman for twenty-seven years, working his way through the rank structure in record time, involved in every type of crime and at every level. For the last ten years, however, he had concentrated on drug enforcement. It had always been his intention to specialize in that particular area, influenced mainly by the death of his father, killed for a sackful of coca leaves, the proceeds of which were to buy food for the family. He had never married, in his position it was a 24-hour job keeping himself safe, without the added burden of a wife and children. He had a friend of course. A closely guarded secret, and since he never attended social events there was never any need to be seen in public with her.

The meeting that night was routine, there wasn't enough spare time during the day, and so his boss had decided to hold them at bizarre times. He looked at his watch, just after midnight, and he knew they would not finish until dawn. He knew that Henri was under intense pressure from the Colombian Government, especially since the death of Renaldo Hernandez. The man, held in high regard by law enforcement agencies throughout the world and responsible for instigating the present campaign, had always known that he would continually be a target. He had been returning home from a visit to Amsterdam and had died in a hail of bullets on the tarmac of El Dorado airport. The men who had carried out the killing posing as catering assistants restocking the plane.

'Have we made any progress at all in tracing these hostages? Because the bottom line is, I'm getting grief from every corner of the world. How about you Guillermo?'

'I'm no further forward than I was a month ago, boss, all we know is that these people have been taken and why, but no confirmation of who is behind it. Although I think we can all guess.'

'I will not commit hundreds of men on supposition. I need a name.'

They were going over old ground as usual and his boss knew it. The probability was that it was one of the two big cartels - either Medellin or Cali - but there were also the less powerful independents to the north, and to a lesser degree the guerrilla groups of FARC and ELN.

'I know it all seems like bad news, but we have achieved a measure of success, including the capture of three large shipments destined for the USA and Europe,' volunteered his companion.

s boss was not impressed.

nd at what cost? Let me remind you that seven people are at this moment paying for that success and who knows there may be more. It would appear that every time we make a move on the likes of Betancur and Garrido, they know in advance of our coming.'

Garbanza was only too aware that there were men, even in his own department, who were in the pay of the two major cartels. It was something he had lived with for years, no longer trusting anyone but Henri. He placed the folder of documents he had brought on the table, a folder containing information on every category of illegal activity which had occurred that week, and their results. It would be another long night.

* * *

EL PASO, TEXAS.

The computer was a piece of equipment that did not respond to violence, he had discovered. In fact it had quite the opposite effect. It just switched off and no amount of encouragement from its abuser would make it do otherwise. Byron T Hollingsworth was not computer friendly. He was a pen and paper man who liked to see things written down. That way there was no possibility of the disaster that had just occurred. He had just spent the best part of two hours typing a report using the word processor on his desk, and now it had disappeared from the screen. No matter which key he pressed, the computer had decided to mess him about. It had been then that he had resorted to giving it a sharp knock, much to the amusement of the rest of the staff in his office at the DEA's El Paso Intelligence Center, to which he had been seconded.

Since retiring from active service in the field, he had spent the last three months in, what was to him, an unfriendly environment. Not that this had anything to do with his colleagues; he had endeared himself to them on his first day. His present boss had introduced him.

'Ladies and gentlemen this is Byron who is joining us from Washington and who I'm sure most of you have heard about.'

'Morning, folks. As you can see I'm big, black and also blessed, and I don't mind sharing the john with white folk.'

His assessment of himself was there for all to see, apart from the third element. But he had been blessed, with a loving wife and a nine-year-old daughter who he worshipped.

He had been allocated the section dealing with European affairs, a part of the world that he was not too familiar with, and was surprised at how well he had quickly settled in - apart from the computer, a technical innovation which hadn't been too plentiful on the streets of Harlem where he had started his career. At fourteen he had been on the other side of the fence, running with a neighbourhood gang, and dealing in anything that happened to be in demand at the time, including every form of illegal substance imaginable. The event which changed his perception of society occurred when he was seventeen, and resulted in the rape and death of his sister, by a rival gang, so high on drugs that two of them went even higher. The experiences during those early years had stood him in good stead, and when he eventually joined the Agency, he had the advantage of an insight into both camps.

'Byron, the boss wants to see you in his office, right now.'

Glad of the brief respite from watching a blank screen, he made his way to the far side of the room, knocked and went straight in to face a small, balding man wearing glasses, one lens looking like it had been cut from the bottom of a bottle.

'How is your workload, Byron?'

'I'm up to my neck,' he replied, honestly.

'Then you'll have to grow a bit taller,' and he threw a thin folder in his direction.

'There's something happening in Colombia. I'm not sure what, but I've been told to keep a particular eye on US citizens touring in the vicinity of Medellin and Cali, and as you know by now, me means you.'

Delegation, in Byron's eyes, was a charter for either the inept or the lazy. In the case of his immediate superior, both applied.

'It may have escaped your attention, but I'm on the European desk.'

The eye looking through the bottom of a bottle twitched.

'Not anymore.'

'Do I get any clues?'

'Of course Byron, Colombia is south of our present position, in South America.'

On his return, as if by magic, his computer had come back to life, his report intact, already falling onto the floor from the printer, and as he waited for it to complete its task, he glanced through the folder. It took no more than a minute, the details sketchy including a short appraisal of the political situation as it affected drug trafficking, a few figures as to estimated turnover, and a short list of six names. Two had been highlighted. Underneath in pen, a short note had been added indicating that the young couple's travel arrangements should have seen them back in New York two weeks earlier, but they were not. The reason for their absence of course could be obvious. It was not uncommon for tourists to be caught smuggling and thrown in to rot in a prison cell, in some remote part of the country. An alternative answer was that if they refused to smuggle in the first instance, then the maximum retribution was extracted. He thought the last page in the folder was blank, but it wasn't. It contained three lines and informed him of the death of Renaldo Hernandez, the Colombian Minister.

He spent the next few hours browsing through the Colombian newspapers, housed in a small library in the basement, and delivered on a regular basis. There was no better source of current information, providing you could read Spanish, and he found a good spread from the area in which he was interested. El Tiempo from Bogotá, and El Mundo, published in Medellin, were of particular relevance to his assignment. Both newspapers had Liberal affiliations and consequently they contained pages of political opinion, most of it directed in a derogatory fashion at the opposition parties. He did, however, find a small piece that interested him. It concerned the death of a Frenchman, killed, according to locals, following a gun battle outside the town of La Ceja, situated on the old Bogotá road. He tore the scrap of news from the page; his folder was already taking shape.

* * *

At almost the same time as Byron Hollingsworth was reading the papers, his immediate superior received a telephone call from the Administrator's personal secretary, a rare event, causing the eye to take on a whole new blinking rhythm.

'Yes, can I help?'

'I believe you have an operative there, name of Hollingsworth, and in which case, he is to report to this office the day after tomorrow.'

The message was short and to the point, the request of a man you would not like to cross swords with, especially when he had been personally appointed to his position by the President of the United States no less. Yes, Mike O'Grady was a powerful man indeed.

CHAPTER FOUR
Hartlepool, England

The last 25 miles of the A19 seemed to have taken an eternity, Simon thought, and not made any easier by the anorak sitting next to him. He had even borrowed a word from Wallace and Grommet for it, anorak-naphobia, a fear of boring people - to whom he gave short shrift. The man, in his early forties, had boarded the coach at Luton Airport and had immediately identified Simon as a receptacle for all the useless information that he possessed - the first of many gems coming as they approached a contraflow system.

'Do you know the definition of a cone? It's a geometric solid consisting of a plane base, bounded by a closed curve…'

To escape, he had even attempted to listen to his Walkman - but the man, undeterred, had on more than one occasion nudged him to point out something in one of the fields they happened to be passing. Insulting the man in a subtle sort of way hadn't worked either.

'What a Prolific Reader And Thinker you are,' he had told him. 'But I suppose you've been told that before, perhaps in abbreviated form?'

'Thank you,' he had replied, the acronym - PRAT - totally wasted on him. 'You going all the way to Hartlepool?'

Wondering where the next piece of useless information was coming from, he had nodded.

'That's where they hung the monkey for being a French spy, isn't it?'

He was surprised it had taken so long, the inevitable question asked all over the world when people discovered your home town. The legend, like most, had expanded with the telling. A monkey dressed as a French sailor had been washed ashore and then imprisoned, accused of spying. The fair-minded people had, however, allowed it a trial, where it condemned itself by refusing to speak. Amazingly enough, the unfortunate animal was consequently hanged from a gibbet erected just for the occasion, on the beach. It had in fact crossed his mind more than once, that it was only a matter of time before a sign was erected on the outskirts of town, welcoming tourists to 'monkey hanging country', and why not? He had noticed the trend was becoming quite popular, examples of which included; 'Cookson Country', 'the land of the Prince Bishops', and 'Captain Cook Country'. There could even be a place for 'the Home of Andy Capp.'

'So did they actually hang the monkey?'

He had not gone away.

'They did. So what's the reason for your visit North, researching the family tree?'

The poor man still hadn't cottoned on.

'No. As a matter of fact I'm making a surprise visit to my relations in Middlesbrough.'

He had never been so relieved in his life to see the lights of Teeside and, as they turned into the coach station, he relented slightly and wished the man a nice holiday.

Simon, at last able to relax for the final few miles, reclined his seat and reflected on the last five weeks - in particular his tour of Europe which he and his backpacking friend had enjoyed immensely. They had planned their tour to take in as many capital cities as possible but, at the end of the day, it would be the contents of their money belts that would be the deciding factor and in this respect they had been fortunate on more than one occasion. The first bit of luck happened on the cross-channel ferry to Calais, where having bought a drink they shared a table with a Northumberland-based lorry driver, taking tractor parts to Paris, and who offered them a lift as far as the French capital. The man was a typical Geordie, telling them about some friends he would stay with overnight and continually cracking one liners.

'The French are alreet if ye forget aboot the wine on the table instead of broon, and the fact that they eat things that hop up and doon.'

He was good company and Paris beckoned them in no time, wishing them good luck and adding a few words of wisdom before they parted company.

'Remember what ye mother telt ye, div'nt gan with no strange wimen, not that they aren't all strange, just mak certain all the reet bits are in the reet places.'

After spending the night in 'gay Paris' they had set off for Madrid by train the following lunchtime, deciding in advance to use the European rail system as much as possible. It was cheap and anyway they both qualified for a student railcard. Rome the 'Eternal City' was a two day stop which turned into four, due to the attentions of two pretty Italian girls and the realization that all they had come to see, couldn't be accomplished in the allotted timescale. The remainder of the trip took in Austria,

Germany and Belgium, and they arrived in Ostend with just about enough money to buy a fizzy drink.

He looked out of the coach window and found that they were already in the town. Ten minutes later, at the home of his parents, he was answering all their questions; well, most of them.

It was a week after his return that he seriously started searching for employment. He knew what he would like to do, but for the foreseeable future would have to make do with something mundane. Europe had awakened the travel bug in him and next time he was determined to try a bit further afield. Unfortunately that sort of undertaking would require the financial security of a permanent position. The opportunity presented itself via an advertisement in a national newspaper. A large supermarket chain at the forefront of the retail business required trainee managers, and although it wasn't what he wanted to do for the rest of his life, it was a means to an end.

In reply to his submitted CV and application form, he received an invitation to attend for interview at the organization's store based in York. Whilst his parents took the opportunity for a tour of the ancient walled city, he joined five other candidates in a small anteroom.

'How do you think he will do, George?' asked Joan.

'I'm as sure of him getting a job as I am of the Pope being a Catholic.'

'Does that mean you think he will?'

On the way back to the store he explained what he had meant, and he was right. They found Simon chatting with the other candidates, and he smiled broadly when he saw them.

'No need to ask how it went then, son.'

'I'll explain everything in the car on the way home,' he replied.

Joan sat quietly listening to her son - proud and happy that the interview had gone so well, until the South and London in particular was mentioned as a possible placement.

'Is there nowhere nearer home that you can train?' she asked.

'No. The only course centre is at Camberley, in Surrey. Anyway, they told me that the prospects for promotion would be much better in the South.'

She thought about the three years he had spent away at University, hoping that once he had attained his degree he would find something close to home. Wishful thinking she knew. He was his own man now. He was ambitious - always had been, forever talking about earning lots of money and what he was going to do with it, mostly to do with music.

The invitation to join the supermarket came as anticipated and three weeks later he reported to the training store in Camberley, ready and willing to learn the retail business. For the first week, accommodation was provided at a small hotel, on the understanding that once the seven days were up they must make their own arrangements. The hours were long and the course demanding but, even so, he managed to find a room which met his criteria. It was on a bus route, and it was cheap. The 'Crooked Gate' public house would not figure in any guide to 'England's Best Places to Stay'. It was a dark and poorly-kept hostelry, brightened only by the cosmopolitan clientele, who appeared friendly and were certainly noisy. This would be his home for the next six weeks whilst he settled into a new career, and then who could tell what would follow.

* * *

Maria knew her mother and father were having second thoughts about allowing her to travel unaccompanied to Europe, and she understood their concerns. The furthest she had ventured from home on her own was to the weekly market in Otavalo - a half-hour bus ride away, South of Ibarra. On the eve of her departure they sat around the kitchen table, joined by her grandmother, Hermania, who usually said very little - conveying everything by a smile or a look. Tonight however was the exception, and Maria was glad of her support.

'You must both remember the stock your daughter is from. She will do well, as our family has done for hundreds of years. Is it not so that one of most revered ancestors fought as a partisan with Martufar in 1809 at the taking of Quito, if only for a short time, and then again with Field Marshall Sucre to recapture it? In recent times your son took part in the border conflict with Peru and played a large part in bringing Dahik and twenty-three ministers to account for their misuse of public funds. I have no fears for Maria, because our family has survived since the days of Pizzaro and will continue to do so.'

She stood up from the table, her hands clutching the revered rosary that was never far away from her grasp.

'Many years ago chica, when your grandfather and I were together, we set out on a great adventure during which we made much sucre. This was good and bad. The good was that I would want for nothing; the bad was that it turned him into a greedy, selfish man. Shortly after your mamma was born, we parted and we have not seen each other since. But there are times when I still remember those days of excitement and adventure. Use the sucre I have given you to find that adventure.'

Maria felt more of an affinity with Hermania than she did with her own mother. Some of the happiest days of her life had been spent at her grandmother's house. She was still a fine looking woman, belying her sixty-two years of age.

'Where is grandfather now?'

The question she could see immediately was not well received by Hermania.

'That is none of your concern chica, and neither is it mine, but I am tired, remember well what I have said. Que le vaya bien!'

She kissed her gently on the forehead and retired to her room.

'Well Maria, tomorrow you will leave us and we have talked everything through, except for something that I thought of today. I would like you to travel in your 'Anako'.'

She looked at her mother quizzically. Her national dress was normally reserved for holidays and religious festivals, not for travelling.

'By wearing it you will stand out and therefore people may be wary of harming you. Do this for me.'

Her father nodded in agreement. Having thought about it herself she saw that it might have its advantages. She had packed her holdall and backpack earlier in the day, at the same time ensuring that her money and documents were secure in her money belt. That left just one more thing to do. Like every other night, the other members of the household were summoned and together they prayed, for the final time as a family.

★ ★ ★

The Terminal Terrestre was about two kilometres south of the town centre and the taxi that was to take them there duly arrived promptly at 6am. The journey took just over ten minutes and was undertaken without a word being spoken - the loud salsa music coming from the radio making conversation impossible. Although still quite early, the bus that was to take her to Quito was already three-quarters full with people who obviously worked in the capital, and as her father put her luggage in the keeping of the driver, there were only their good-byes to say. They hugged each other and then she boarded the bus, hearing her mother shout 'Buena Suerte' and wondering how much 'Good Luck' she would need.

They were moving before she had the chance to take her seat and so for a few seconds she stood, staring out of the rear window until her parents had disappeared from view. Most of the journey would be on the Pan American Highway with slight detours to Tabacundo and Cayambo - a journey she had undertaken many times with her two friends. Now, however, she was making it for perhaps the last time and her companion was as far removed from Patti and Anita as anyone could be. The old man who sat beside her wearing his soiled and worn Panama hat smelled strongly of rum and mumbled continuously - even when he appeared to sleep. After an hour with the heat and humidity not improving conditions any, she began to feel quite sick.

The final stop before the capital was Quinche and she took the opportunity to get some relatively fresh air and a drink. The break from the old man's increasing stench was enough to stem the urge to be sick, until they finally pulled into the north of the city and Quito Airport. The driver hurriedly handed her luggage down and then quickly sped off. She watched it go and suddenly felt very alone. It was her last link with something with which she was familiar. From now on everything would be strange and new. She would be alone to face the challenge of a new continent, a new culture, and for the first time she doubted herself.

As she walked to the aircraft, she took one last look back. When would she see her country again? But that was now in the past. She must look to the future, and with a renewed purpose in her step, she boarded the plane and took her seat.

The flight would eventually take her to Amsterdam where she would change and catch another plane to London Heathrow - hopefully arriving late evening. As she took her seat next to the window she was already taking in a new experience. She had never been on an aircraft before and was amazed at how large it was. The flow of passengers seeming endless; her companions for the journey, the last to board. The married couple were Spanish, from Madrid, and had been touring South America before visiting Europe on their way back to Spain. The woman immediately engaged her in conversation, complimenting her on the "Anako".

The take-off was the most exciting thing that had ever happened to her, and although tinged with sadness, the view from her window compensated for her melancholy thoughts. The sight of the Andes, far below, was something she would never forget, not taking her eyes from the window until the cloud enveloped them. Leaning back in her seat she tried hard to relax, choosing to listen to Eine Kleine Nachtmusik, her favourite Mozart composition and one of the many classical tapes she had received as leaving presents. Already her thoughts had turned to home, visualizing her mother and sister who would be busy washing, her brother, the artist, engrossed in creating another painting, and Hermania, reading as usual.

'Whereabouts in Ecuador are you from?'

She only just heard the question above the sound of the music.

'From Ibarra. It is in the north. I am going to London to be a sort of nanny,' she volunteered.

'It's a long way to go for work. Are you not frightened to be on your own?'

'Oh no! I'm sure that I will be met at the airport, and anyway I have a telephone number to ring when I arrive.'

The journey took less time than she had anticipated - mainly due to the conversation with the couple and the fact that everything that happened on the plane was new. She even helped the lady to buy some expensive perfume and was allowed to apply a few drops to her own neck.

Her first glimpse of Europe, because due to lots of grey clouds that was all it was, questioned her decision to wear the thin "Anako". Rain splashed the windows as the plane came in to land and it was not the sort of welcome to Europe that she had anticipated. As the aircraft slowly taxied to its position in front of the main Schiphol Airport terminal building a stewardess enquired as to her destination.

'Are you staying in Amsterdam?'

Maria understood the question without grasping all the words, explaining that she would be travelling on to London Heathrow, and secretly hoping that the stewardess would give her directions.

'I will show you where to wait until your flight is called. I think it leaves in about one hour.' She explained it very slowly and with the aid of her hands, gesturing to Maria to remain in her seat until all the other passengers had disembarked. Minutes later, she was walking across to the terminal building, accompanied by her guide, who explained to her on the way that her luggage would be transferred to the Heathrow flight, and that she should listen for a message, requesting passengers to make their way to gate number two. They shook hands, Maria thanking her for the help and watching as the smart, self-assured woman left her. She wondered if she would ever be so confident.

The building was crowded and this suddenly reminded her of Hermania's advice about thieves and pickpockets, her hand quickly feeling for the money belt strapped to her waist, sighing with relief as she discovered it was still in place. As she wandered around the huge building she took comfort from the sight of large numbers of young people like herself - bulging backpacks, tents precariously balanced on the top, all seemingly like her, in search of an adventure. Eventually, above the noise of what seemed like a thousand differing languages, she heard the call for her flight and quickly made her way through the correct gate and onto the London-bound aircraft. She began to feel more than a little excited as the plane neared its destination. It will be nice to see the English couple again, she thought. Her only contact with them for some time being by way of an answering machine; the telephone, outside of the larger cities in Ecuador, was not a household item.

She found the capital much the same as Amsterdam - cold and wet. Her first impression, one of miserable people, rushing about as if searching for a safe place to hide from an impending disaster. Locating her luggage had not been a problem and now, having cleared customs, she searched for signs that the couple were awaiting her arrival, or at least had made arrangements for her to be met. She was disappointed not to find either. Before leaving home, her grandmother had advised her to change some of the sucre into dollars, explaining that American currency was accepted almost everywhere, except as she now found, in British telephones. In order to get the right coins, she bought a drink, and then spent some time reading the instructions on the wall of one of the booths in order to make the call to her future employers. Eventually after much trial and error she heard a ringing tone.

'Hello.'

'Hello this is Maria Sandino, I am at Heathrow airport.' It was the culmination of months of practice

'I think you have dialled the wrong number dear.'

The telephone made a peculiar noise as the voice disappeared. She checked the number again, taking her time. The same voice answered her second call.

'This is Maria Sandino, from Ecuador,' she repeated, the lump in her throat getting progressively larger, or so it felt.

This time there were no words, just a click, and before she had replaced the receiver, she felt the tears.

CHAPTER FIVE
Medellin, Colombia

When the young Colombian servant entered the room he gasped in horror as he saw the splashes of blood that covered the table and the front of his employer's shirt. A pair of glazed eyes looked through him and the familiar bark sharply brought him to his senses, the order when it came, given with venom.

'Bring me some water and bandages!'

The servant hurried away. Returning almost immediately with the required medical supplies, he proceeded to treat Rodrigo's hands, gently drying and dressing them as best he could. As he cleaned away the remainder of the blood from the table and supplied a fresh shirt, he was given new instructions.

'Show Señor Jaramillo in the moment he arrives.'

'Si, señor.'

He slumped back in his wheelchair and stared at the painting on the opposite wall. It depicted Jesus as the 'Light of the World' and was inlaid with gold and silver. The placement was deliberate - catching the sun, and so epitomizing its theme. It had been a gift from Guido Suarez, the youngest son of the infamous Roberto, who had reigned supreme as the head of Bolivian Drug Interests until ending his days at the hands of Drug Enforcement agents. The valuable painting had cemented a lucrative deal between the two of them, Roberto supplying the raw coca, he turning it into the base product and refining it into pure cocaine and then supplying his many buyers in the US. The successful partnership had been terminated when the US Administration had stepped up its 'search and destroy' tactics, concentrating mainly on Bolivia's coca crop. The agents responsible for Roberto's death had been extremely lucky, finding him, virtually unprotected, visiting his family - something he did very rarely.

'You have had an accident Rodrigo?'

Alfred had entered the room unnoticed by him. Only a small thing but it annoyed him that he had been caught unawares.

'Of little concern, unlike the recent events which have brought you here. Explain to me.'

Although his friend and right-hand man he was not invited to sit. He stood uncomfortably. Taking an exaggerated deep breath he proceeded to inform Rodrigo as to the events of the previous twelve hours.

'Everything went as planned from here to Santa Marta,' he began with a confidence that he didn't really feel. 'The truck was parked at a new location in readiness for its cargo to be loaded onto our ship. Then, just as it was getting light, I noticed two military coaches and a small truck pull onto the park at some speed. The military and police immediately made their way to our container and ordered the driver to display its contents, which he did - knowing only too well that to pick out the contraband boxes of bananas from so many legitimate ones, was an impossible task. Then, as he was opening the rear doors, I noticed the small truck being positioned quite close to them, and it was at this point that I spotted the weighing machine.'

Suddenly the pain from his hands had gone. That part of the brain that controlled emotion taking over and sending waves of intense anger through his mind.

'So they had prior knowledge of the consignment.' It was a statement.

'It would appear that they did.'

He allowed Alfred to continue, but he had ceased to listen. The fact that the authorities had discovered this particular method of smuggling was alarming, and what concerned him even more, was that there was only one way they could have found out. They had used bananas as a way of smuggling the drug for two reasons. The first, because it was a produce exported by any number of South American countries, not all involved in his particular business - such as a country like Ecuador, where the fruit had originated. The second reason was slightly more devious and until now, successful - the secret being that the bananas remained virtually unaltered, at least to the naked eye. They remained as a bunch still connected to the main stalk, but at the other end a small hole was then made - large enough to allow a narrow tube to be inserted. The chemists at his many factories would then inject the fruit with a chemical substance that would not react with the cocaine, but would turn the contents of the banana into an almost watery mush which would be aspirated through the hole. The fruit could now be filled with the white powder. The hole was then sealed with a black wax, which produced the same effect as the original produce. Furthermore, the skin still retained its natural smell. There was only one way of detecting the substitute, and that was by weight. The fine powder weighed slightly less than the fleshy part of the banana.

He suddenly became aware that Alfred had stopped talking.

'You realize of course that this is the fourth consecutive consignment that we have lost in as many months, and not only are we losing dinero but, what is much more important, I am losing personal credibility - something which our American buyers will not tolerate.'

'Part of the problem is that the authorities are paying four times as much for information as we are for three months' work, Rodrigo.'

He knew that only too well, but peasants would always want more. No. Money was not the answer.

'Send the photographs of the dead Frenchman through the usual channel. Perhaps the concern of his Government for future tourists will provide us with the necessary breathing space to complete one of our transactions. Be sure, also, to inform our partners in Bolivia that they will be compensated for any loss.'

He watched Alfred leave before lighting a cigar. It was his only concession to smoking and, in all the years of trafficking, he had never sampled the goods.

A week passed, during which time the information concerning the Frenchman's death appeared in El Mundo, but without the photographic evidence. Not that it would have made any difference. Many people went missing, or were found dead in South America, on a regular basis. He had also ordered Alfred to oversee the death of one worker from each of the factories, as a warning against informing.

The latest of the captured consignments had cost him dearly. Five hundred kilos of cocaine would have brought him in excess of $300 million and, although the Bolivians would only be compensated for their coca leaf, he would still stand to lose $200 million. He knew exactly where he was - between a rock and a hard place, as the Americans were fond of saying. If he suspended operations he would lose money and likewise, if another cargo went missing - which in the present circumstances seemed likely - he would also lose out. The more he thought about it, the more convinced he became that he had no choice, the pressure from his buyers making the decision for him.

Twenty-four hours later he instructed Alfred to organize the next shipment. This time the valuable cargo would travel by air, concealed, ironically enough, in boxes identified as hazardous substances. In addition to the shipping and consignment papers being genuine and authenticated by a man who had received fair recompense for his trouble, the method had two further advantages. In order for any hazardous material to be investigated, a large number of people from different agencies had to be involved. The cost of mounting such an operation meant that the US Custom Service only carried out occasional searches. So far this method had always been successful. It was a tried and tested route - the plane leaving Colombia and flying north to the island of St. Lucia in the Caribbean, then after changing pilots, continuing on to Costa Rica, the final part of the journey undertaken by ship to San Diego on the West coast of America. The military base and a small fish-canning factory provided further security for the shipment. It was not unusual for cargoes of a hazardous nature to be seen heading for the base. Only on this occasion, the truck would be diverted to the factory where the white powder would be packed into tins and then distributed to various drops. He breathed a huge sigh of relief at the news from Alfred that the plane had taken off without any interference.

* * *

Four hours after contacting his boss, Alfred Jaramillo also received a telephone call. On the other end of the line an excited pilot explained to him - in between gasps for breath - the progress of the shipment. It was not good news. He had landed the plane, ready for the changeover as planned and watched as the relief pilot made his way across the runway accompanied by two men. What he hadn't noticed, until too late, was the fuel tanker, which had been positioned some one hundred metres away - blocking the runway. From all directions, armed men had appeared, and he had tried to steer the plane across an adjacent field, in order to save the shipment, only to crash the plane into the perimeter fence where it burst into flames. The man had obviously done his best, yet Alfred doubted whether Rodrigo would see it that way. He was proven right immediately the information was passed. His friend had erupted.

'This is America's doing, I know it. And now we will see whether the shipment was worth two lives. See to it that both American hostages are taken care of, and I want lots of photographs.'

He had rambled on, muttering about Pizzaro and doubt and death, until the tirade ended with the slamming down of the secure phone.

Alfred would see to it that the killings were carried out as ordered, but he was not happy and, although it would not be his finger on the trigger, he would be just as much to blame as the assassin. He had known Rodrigo for over forty years and never once had he wavered from doing his friend's bidding. In recent years, however, his enthusiasm for their precarious lifestyle had started to wane. A rich man in his own right, he felt more and more that the work was better suited for the likes of young Suarez and his generation, rather than two old men hanging on to yesterday. It had been so different in the early days - wheeling and dealing throughout the length and breadth of the country - illegal, yes, but never violent or destructive.

He reluctantly gave the order for the execution of the two Americans, knowing full well that the consequences would be rapid and far-reaching.

★ ★ ★

WASHINGTON, DC

To be called to see the Administrator of the DEA was a bit like a Catholic priest being called to Rome for an audience with the Pope. Whilst feeling pleased at being recognized in such illustrious circles, you were never sure it was for the right reasons until the actual event. Byron wondered about it until the plane left the ground. He had been told nothing by his immediate superior other than his presence was requested in Washington by Michael O'Grady. He was sure of one thing however - it was not to exchange small talk. Just eighteen months earlier, he had made a similar trip prior to attending a meeting in Curaçao, and so it was quite possible that this visit was in connection with that, although he hoped not. For over thirty years O'Grady had been making his mark in law enforcement - not only in America but also on the international stage. Initially as a deputy with the Erie County Sheriff's Department in the 60s, he had entered the New York State Police as a uniform trooper and later progressed to Narcotics and Major Crime Investigation. It wasn't long before he was promoted to sergeant, followed soon after by his appointment as Lieutenant in Charge of

Recruiting. It was at this point that their paths had first crossed.

Byron remembered it well. He had applied to join the Bureau of Narcotics and Dangerous Drugs, along with thirty other hopefuls - all white - and had waited in a small room, carefully going over the script. There was however one problem - O'Grady didn't have a copy.

'It would appear that you are in the minority out there, son, any particular thoughts on that fact?' had been for openers.

'If you're referring to my color, sir, yes I am. I understand, however, that according to the medical department, my brain is the same size and shape as the others.'

O'Grady had smiled, the only one of the panel to do so, but the remark obviously hadn't done him any harm, as he heard a week later that he had been accepted. His appointment, however, was short-lived as, soon after, the Bureau ceased to exist. During his time as President, Richard Nixon implemented Reorganization Plan Number 2, which consolidated all Federal Anti-Drug Forces under a single unified command within the Department of Justice. It was the creation of the Drug Enforcement Administration. O'Grady had very quickly become a leading light, and yet they still kept in touch - even if it was on a purely professional level - working together on a number of undercover operations, until politics intervened and his teacher and mentor became deskbound. Now the man he was going to meet controlled a workforce of over 7000 special agents and support staff, in addition to DEA offices in 50 states and the same number of countries - still finding time to serve on the IACP, the International Association of Chiefs of Police.

It was raining when the plane from El Paso touched down in Washington. He had forgotten how cold it was compared with the south and hadn't really dressed accordingly, so he was pleased and yet puzzled by the waiting automobile.

'Mr. Hollingsworth?'

The driver looked as surprised as he was. It wasn't normal practice for the top man to provide transport for one of the troops - unless of course he was about to send him on a suicide mission - the thought not one to dismiss lightly.

'So what's happening in the big city?' he enquired, once settled in the rear of the Buick.

'Nothing changes really. There's always someone trying to shoot it in your arm, put it in your mouth, or poke it up your nose, and if they can't manage that, there's always some bastard who wants to shove it up your ass.'

What a sad loss to the literary world. This man is wasted in his capacity as a driver, he thought. The man turned his head slightly, doing his impression of a chameleon - one eye on the road ahead whilst the other gave him the once over.

'You're the man they call the 'poet', aren't you?'

He nodded, unwilling to offer an explanation for a nickname he wasn't particularly fond of. Although, if he was honest, it had been of his own making. He had been given the name whilst training to be an agent at Quantico. The other members of the course had seized on the fact that there had been an English lord with the same name. The fact that it had been the aristocrat's surname seemed to have been lost on them, but his being a poet of some renown hadn't. Initially he had thought nothing of it, willing to go along with the joke - even quoting the man's verse and becoming quite an expert on his life - and then, in time, wishing he had never heard of Lord George Gordon Byron. But it was too late. He was stuck with it.

The rain had stopped by the time they reached his destination, a formidable looking building, not unlike the man he was going to meet, he thought. A lift took him to the top floor where he was confronted by a middle-aged lady who looked him up and down, asked his name, and then smiled.

'Please go straight in, Mr. Hollingsworth. You're expected.'

Mike O'Grady walked across the room with his hand extended; the handshake, when it came, strong and vigorous, the welcome genuine.

'Glad you made it Byron. Sit down, I've already ordered coffee and sandwiches to be sent in.'

They talked about things in general and, whilst he enjoyed the refreshments, O'Grady continually flicked through a thin file, making notes as he did so.

'How is your Spanish these days?' he enquired, suddenly.

'It's a while since I used it for any length of time, but I could sharpen up.'

The change in O'Grady's tone meant that they were now down to the serious business.

'Let me be straight with you, Byron, I don't usually brief operatives as you well know. Why keep a pack of wolves and howl yourself? - is normally the way I look at things. However there is a current situation in Latin

America that alters things slightly.' He paused and leaned forward.

'Unfortunately, in any large organization - such as ours for instance - more people being in the know, inevitably leads to more people knowing. In this particular case, it is necessary that only people who are actively engaged in deciding the outcome of the problem are party to any information at all - which is why I have dragged you away from El Paso.' He paused to order more coffee before continuing.

'The problem is in Colombia, and it's not just blow - although the situation isn't exactly unconnected with cocaine, as you will no doubt have guessed. Within the last couple of days two young American tourists have been reported executed, although it's not common knowledge as yet.'

'Were they carrying?'

'The Department's office in Bogotá has been monitoring the situation for some time now, and they are convinced that they were not.'

'Why can't they handle it? Let's face it they are on the spot.'

'And that's the biggest problem. Our agents in that part of the world are too well known. But there's also other factors involved in this. Forgetting about cocaine for a minute, Colombia's economic resurgence and political stability are in jeopardy. Let me take a few minutes to bring you up to the mark. Since 1989 the Colombian Government have done a U-turn regarding their attitude to coca mainly due to an upturn in the economy - coffee and oil having the biggest influence. Unfortunately, this 'crackdown', if you'll excuse the pun, has upset certain members of the drug fraternity, and they are seeing this renewed interest as an excuse to start taking hostages. At the moment, the Treasury Department is pouring money into the country, whilst various other agencies are providing people with the necessary expertise, to assist them with their oil production. The danger is, however, if this hostage taking becomes a habit, our people will be a bit reluctant about working out there.'

'Have we any idea who is behind these kidnappings?'

'According to our intelligence - which at the moment doesn't amount to a great deal there are three main players, but whether it's only one of them or all three we don't know.'

'So why me?' he asked.

'You're the best I have. I trust you, and besides, you know the country, the people and you speak their language.'

He knew O'Grady wasn't prone to flattery. The fact that he had been summoned from Texas was an indication of the importance of the mission he was asking him to undertake. The decision to go back into the field however, wasn't one to be taken without great consideration - especially because his last undercover operation in that part of the world had nearly been his last.

'I understand you know Guillermo Garbanza, Byron.'

It was a statement, and an understatement at that, he reflected. 'Gill', as he had nicknamed him, had been responsible for saving his skin during that last operation - a sting involving the number one fish at the time, Pablo Escobar. It had taken a year to set it up and one phone call for it all to fall apart, Garbanza and he were lucky to escape the ultimate wrath of the drug baron - the Colombian agent being the deciding factor.

'We have had our moments together, you might say.'

'I remember. Seňor Garbanza is now second-in-command of the PIP and feels that because of the latest killings, we might be interested in showing some hands-on involvement. He also asked after you.'

'He's a good man. Even when most of his colleagues were taking dinero, he was as straight as Pinocchio's pecker. So what's the state of play so far?'

O'Grady pushed his chair away from his desk and walked to the window.

'To be honest, it's all a bit hazy. Garbanza contacted me three days ago saying that he had been reliably informed of the landing of a cargo plane on the Caribbean island of St. Lucia - the following night - en route to Miami. The pilot, who would fly the final leg, was American and part of the cargo would include cocaine. We sent two agents from our Nassau office to intercept it, and got a result.'

'And who's the source?'

'That's where it turns from hazy to smogbound. According to Garbanza this is the third tip-off in as many months. All they get is a taped message.'

'How come we didn't let the shipment make the journey, and then do the business this end?'

It was a reasonable question.

'Your Colombian friend wants to keep the pressure on at his end - simply because whoever is behind these shipments could easily blame the buyer for things going wrong. The overriding factor, however, is that he knows that the Colombians are not the only ones taking the losses, and shortly the shit is going to hit the fan.'

'Sounds as if it already has. This hostage taking and execution of foreign hostages is a new tack as far as the cartels are concerned. Has Gill got anyone in the frame?'

He watched O'Grady return to his desk and the file.

'He's given me a short list of three - two Colombians, and a Bolivian, who would be a tough nut to crack, bearing in mind his background and connections. Roberto Gomez has a particular fancy for women who are related directly or otherwise to senior government officials, his current wife being the sister of Ricardo Punta, a minister in the Bolivian administration, who, if my memory serves me right, is no stranger to you.'

He nodded, the name brought back memories of a one-eyed, naked woman, and a light bulb.

'The two Colombians are General Luis Garcia Tejada, who although technically a Bolivian, after a failed coup and an unsuccessful attempt to abduct President Siles Zuazo, transferred his operation to Cali, where his cartel is nearly as powerful as that of the final suspect. He is Rodrigo Betancur. Now in his sixties, he has no offspring to hand over to, and no one has laid eyes on him for a number of years, mainly due to his reliance on a wheelchair.'

'What is Gill's gut feeling?'

'He has a tendency towards Betancur. But without any solid proof is reticent about mounting any operation involving large numbers of the military. And that's about as much as I can tell you.'

At this point Byron decided to bring the discussion to a more personal level.

'I said I'd give my wife a ring. No details of course, but she needs to know something.'

'Sure, I understand. Talk it over, but I'd appreciate a decision tomorrow. Time isn't our friend.'

'I'm reminded of a saying. Twice the thinking time, half the working time.'

'Lord Byron?' asked O'Grady.

As he walked to the door he looked back and smiled.

'Nope. Agent Hollingsworth.'

On the way back to his hotel, he gave some thought to the impending phone call to his wife Anne. She would not be happy, that he knew for sure, and he sympathized. His safe job in El Paso had steadied the boat through a stormy relationship - the cause attributed to his drinking and loss of confidence - due to his fieldwork. The desk also allowed him to spend more time with her and his daughter, Sara, now nine years old. He grabbed a sandwich and a coffee before making the call to Fort Worth, and was halfway through telling her about the situation when she stopped him.

'I know.'

'What do you mean, you know?'

'It's just been on NBC, about the tourists, in South America.'

He moved quickly to the television and switched to the News Channel, but he had missed the item.

'Naturally I'm not going to encourage you, but knowing you only too well, Byron, I bet you have made your mind up. Besides, these people, whoever they are, can't go around killing innocent Americans, especially youngsters.'

He was surprised, but at the same time greatly relieved. He had expected opposition. The conversation continued - mainly concerning domestic matters and Sara - until five minutes before the next news bulletin was due. He rang off. There were two photographs on the screen - a young man and woman, both in their early twenties. The broadcaster went on to explain that their bodies had been found by a peasant farmer returning from the market at Santa Fe De Antioquia, some 50 kilometres north-west of Medellin. He rang O'Grady immediately the bulletin had finished.

He was sitting reading the sports pages of the Washington Times and simultaneously sharing a conversation with O'Grady's secretary, when his new boss arrived.

'Where? How? And when?' he began, once they were alone.

'Slow down, Byron. It's not that simple. I'll give you the basic outline and then you can fill in the gaps using the folder I'll give you before you leave. Your cover will be posing as a mature ecological student, attached to Inderena. It's the Government body, based in Bogotá, responsible for National Parks. For the first few weeks you'll have no personal contact with Garbanza or our own office. If an emergency should arise you can use the Youth Hostel Association's office as a drop. The address is included in the folder. At first, your only contact will be a courier, name of Benito. He's a relative of Garbanza's, so he's sound. For the last three months he has been doubling as a Park Ranger and will be your guide as well as your link with Garbanza. You're to concentrate solely on Betancur. The other two are someone else's responsibility. Well, if there's no questions I'll wish you a safe return.'

They shook hands and half an hour later he was back in his hotel room - his six feet two frame at full stretch on the double bed -and absorbing the information contained in the folder. Along with most of the information given to him by O'Grady, there was an open return ticket from Washington to Bogotá, via Miami - the departure date in three days time - together with $500 and a quantity of pesos. There was also a photograph of Benito.

He would spend the next two days with Anne and Sara, who would help him buy clothing suitable for a mature student. Then it would be goodbye, again, and a return to something he had thought was in the past - tears.

CHAPTER SIX
London, England

She was oblivious to nearly everything as she sat in the airport building. Only the tears that were now streaming down her face made any sense. Thus far her life had been simple and uncomplicated. She had been surrounded by loyal and caring friends for so long, unfamiliar with periods of crisis. Unable to comprehend what had gone wrong, she continued to sit in a bewildered state until the flood of tears turned to a fine mist. Suddenly she became aware of the cameras, she had forgotten that she was still wearing the 'Anako'. She felt tired, alone, her knowledge of the language limited, and she had nowhere to go, all the things that her friends had warned her about on the way to San Lorenzo were happening. She pulled her belongings around her, finding some measure of comfort in the barrier they formed, and then dried her eyes.

'Hola. ¿Coma esta?'

Startled at hearing a greeting in her own language, she looked up. A tall man stood before her, a briefcase in his hand, his voice gentle. At first she did not answer. It was only when he sat down next to her that she replied to his question, informing him that she was not well at all. She looked at him closely, he was definitely from her part of the world, she decided, perhaps Peru.

'I know we have never met,' he began, 'so let me introduce myself.'

He went on to explain that he had been on the same flight as her from Amsterdam, returning from a business trip. Out of curiosity he had decided to see if she was being met - her being so young. He had subsequently witnessed her distress - and hence the introduction. The fact that someone had taken an interest did little to placate her. Bursting into tears once again, she nevertheless managed to tell him her story - in between large sobs.

'Have you got somewhere to stay?'

She felt his hand on her arm, an attempt at reassurance. She shook her head, everything and everyone appearing in blurred form - the effect of her sore eyes.

'I will suggest something to you. Not far from here is a cheap hotel where you can stay for tonight and which is on my way. If you like we can find a policeman, and I will tell him your story and what I intend. I can also show him my passport and any other particulars about me that he may wish to see.'

Her defences down, exhausted, she knew that she was about to break the first rule of travelling alone. Her grandmother had been most insistent that she should, under no circumstances, accept help from strangers. And yet she agreed.

'I will come with you.' It was almost a whisper, as much as she could manage.

He carried both her holdall and backpack to a waiting taxi, telling her a bit more about himself on the way. She was right. He was originally from Lima and had been married to an Englishwoman for the last fifteen years. The relationship had also produced two children, proudly showing her their photograph produced from his wallet. By the time they reached the hotel she was too tired even to listen, and it was left to him to explain everything to the woman who let them in.

'It will be fifteen dollars for one night, Maria.'

Her arms felt like bars of iron as she produced the money from her belt.

'Now I must go, I hope things go better for you.'

'Muchas gracias,' she said, quietly.

'De nada.' And he was gone.

Leaving her luggage in the hall she followed the lady up two flights of stairs to her room, where she collapsed fully-clothed onto the bed and fell asleep almost immediately.

It was still dark when she awoke, and for a moment had difficulty in remembering anything of the last 24 hours, then suddenly it all came back into focus. She looked at her watch, 6:30am. She had remembered the time difference at least. Although very little had happened to improve her circumstances, she felt slightly better for having the sleep. She even recalled the advice given by her mother about wearing the 'Anako'. It was just possible that the man who had helped her get to the hotel had been attracted by it. Once more she felt herself lapsing into sleep.

'Hello. HELLO.'

A loud knock on the door of her room and a woman's voice, shouting, causing her to sit up with a start. Outside she found the lady, who spoke quickly to her, the only word she recognized being breakfast.

'Si, I come.'

She hoped that she had understood the lady's instructions. Once dressed, she made her way down to the dining room, where the lady insisted, using a series of hand signals, that she eat all that was on her plate. Most of it she didn't like, but a good breakfast meant that she could miss lunch, so she did her best to leave a clean plate. Back in her room she showered, and felt better again. Her dilemma had not been solved, but she felt infinitely better than when she had first arrived. It was an hour later that she decided to experience the sights and sounds of the capital. And so, dressed in her warmest clothing, she ventured out.

* * *

Simon Halkin sat outside the General Manager's office, waiting to meet him for only the second time since he had joined the store. The man had introduced himself briefly at the start of the training course, but little had been seen of him since.

'Come in Simon. Take a seat, young man.'

He winced inwardly, hating being called 'young man'. To him it implied that he had not yet reached the mature stage of being just 'a man.'

They discussed his progress and promotion prospects, before he was finally informed of the location where his 'hands on' training would commence.

'I'm offering you a position as Fresh Food Manager at the Elephant and Castle, Simon.'

It was not what he wanted to hear, and the GM knew it.

'I know it's got a reputation - but it's run by a man who I trust, and you will be looked after. Anyway, you will be receiving a letter confirming the position, and let me take this opportunity to wish you the best of luck in the future.'

His feelings were mixed. It was a start on the management ladder, but the Elephant was a rough area of

London in which to work and besides, due to his financial position he would also have to live nearby. Still, looking on the bright side, he now had a week's holiday. And he would make the most of it, dividing the time equally between sleeping and listening to his music.

★ ★ ★

During the week's that followed her arrival in London, Maria found her way of life changing dramatically, day by day. She had already learned quite a few more words of English and had even found the Colombian Embassy. She had found it quite by accident, shortly after leaving the hotel, and they had been very sympathetic - putting her in touch with a club that catered exclusively for South Americans who, like herself, were new to the capital. During one of her visits, she had made friends with Conchita - a girl her own age and from Argentina. They enjoyed each other's company to such a degree that she was now sharing Conchita's flat in Southwark, south of the Thames. She had even found a job. It was only cleaning and serving at a small restaurant, but it paid for her share of the rent with a little to spare.

Shortly after settling into the flat she had written to her mother, and in her answering letter she was informed that the couple who had offered her the position as nanny, had been in touch. They apologized, but because of a change of location - associated with the husband's employment the position was no longer available. Maria felt no animosity towards them. She was aware of the poor postal system in her country and the delay was understandable.

On the monthly anniversary of her arrival in England she bought a white cotton blouse. Not significant in itself, it was, however, the first thing that she had bought - apart from necessities, and she was immensely proud of herself. It hung on the door of the wardrobe like a trophy, waiting to be paraded in public. Then one night, as they both sat reading, Conchita surprised her.

'Tomorrow night, Maria, we are going out. My treat.'

She had never ventured out at night, except for the occasional visit to the South American Club. But stories of their native countries dominated every conversation and they had soon tired of going.

'Where will we go?' she asked, excitedly.

'To a pub.'

She wasn't sure. But her friend assured her that they would only drink something non-alcoholic, and so it was settled. The following night another surprise awaited her.

'I think this skirt will go well with your new blouse, would you like to borrow it?'

She tried it on. Conchita was slightly larger than she was, but once her friend had pinned it at the waist it fitted her very well, parading around the room like a peacock and laughing loudly.

For no reason in particular they took the underground to the Elephant and Castle area, amusing themselves with the help of the large pink elephant at the shopping precinct before moving on in search of a suitable public house. Whether or not the 'Waning Moon' was suitable was questionable, she thought. But ignoring the whistles and rude words, they bought two soft drinks and found an empty table.

It was her first experience of an English pub and she was not impressed. It was dark, and apart from the jukebox at the far end of the bar, everything else was old and in need of paint. There were two things that interested her however. One was a notice stating that bar staff was required, and the other was a tall dark-haired man with piercing green eyes, sitting alone near the jukebox. She pointed the vacancy out to Conchita who listened to her intentions and then expressed her disapproval.

'I need the work, and it's not far from the flat. It will also be good for my English,' she insisted, encouraging her friend to talk to the man behind the bar on her behalf.

'Well if you are certain.'

Moments later Conchita returned with the man.

'Now then young lady, I hear you're interested in a job?'

'I don't know much English,' she said, hesitantly.

'Right. Don't worry about that, there's not many gets in here that do.' He paused. 'Have you done this type of work before?' The words slow and deliberate.

She shook her head.

'But I will learn.'

He turned to Conchita, and she understood only part of what he was telling her friend. 'He said you could start on Thursday for a trial period. It will be from 6pm until 11pm and he will pay you £40 for working four nights.'

Bubbling with excitement, she thanked the man. She would soon be able to buy her own skirt. Looking over her friend's shoulder she noticed that the man with the green eyes had gone. And yet something inside her was beginning to stir - a feeling that she would see him again. No, not a feeling. She would make a point of it.

* * *

His batteries recharged, Simon was now looking forward to the challenge of the Elephant and Castle store, eager to show his new boss that there was more to Northerners than pigeon racing. He had moved from one pub to another, the Waning Moon, being situated within walking distance of the store, and cheap. He had been there for three weeks, and he didn't usually visit the bar - but his rent was due and so he had decided to pay it, and at the same time take the opportunity to have a drink. It was full of local people, with a few Irish labourers thrown in for the 'craic', so it caused quite a stir when two extremely pretty young girls walked through the doors. The noise was deafening, and he wasn't surprised at the embarrassment shown by both girls, particularly by the younger of the two. Some time later he noticed Bob, the landlord, join them at their table - who on his return to the bar - revealed all.

'Well, that should keep you punters happy. That's my new barmaid over there Geordie.' Anyone north of Watford was a Geordie to Bob.

'Which one?' he asked, casually

'The smallest of the two. She's South American. Maria Sandino I think she said her name was. Worried about not being able to speak much English she is. And what with this place being full of Geordies and Micks she's not likely to learn any.'

He finished his drink and returned to his room. But he had already decided to frequent the bar more often.

* * *

She loved everything about her new job. Even when she knew that the local people where making fun of her, she laughed with them. And of course he would occasionally come down - sitting alone, but watching her. Then one night their eyes locked, and she returned his smile. Contact had been made, and she experienced a feeling towards a member of the opposite sex, which until then had been alien to her. During the days that followed their first meeting she treated herself to some lipstick. The purchase had not gone unnoticed by Conchita, who chided her about it.

'You are right, I am happiest when I am with him. He is strong and deep, and yet I know he cares. And he makes me laugh.'

Conchita wasn't a psychologist, but then she didn't have to be to understand what was happening to her friend.

As the weeks passed they became very close, both of them recognizing mutual interests. The cinema, music and of course travel, in addition to the value of money and the respect for each other's privacy, or 'space' as Simon called it. The inevitable happened spontaneously, rather than by design, one night after she had finished in the bar. The pub had been late in closing due to a family celebration, and taking up Simon's offer of a place to stay for the night, she had gone to his room where they sat talking and listening to music. She didn't know whether it was the effects of the wine, or the music. It didn't matter, it was her choice. They danced, forcing their bodies together, attempting to become one. Him with the awkward movements peculiar to European men, her exhibiting the natural sensual rhythm of the Latin American woman. The look she gave him said it all. The electricity suddenly arcing across the divide of two continents. She made the move. Letting him know that she was giving, making the decision for him, removing any thoughts that he may be harbouring about taking something he was not yet permitted to have. But he was.

She welcomed him, leaving nothing in reserve, her passion totally overwhelming them both. Her femininity releasing him from the confines of his natural restraint. Later, she lay nestled in his arms – content, the nightmare of her arrival in England forgotten, the sacrifices justified. She would have endured much more for him.

He stroked her long black hair, almost without knowing it he had committed himself to her well-being and personal happiness. For the first time in his life he felt totally responsible for someone, and he had no regrets.

★ ★ ★

The weeks turned to months, during which time he had taken Maria north to meet the other members of his family. George and Joan had taken to her immediately. Fascinated with stories of her life in Ecuador, and admiring her determination with which she had overcome the difficulties in reaching England at all. She was full of questions, showing the curiosity of a small child. What were dumplings? Pancakes? Laughing at toad-in-the-hole, and in return explaining that guinea pig and rice was a delicacy in Ecuador, failing to understand how they were treated as pets by the English.

They had shown her as much of the area as possible during her short stay. From the adjacent coast to the beautiful countryside thirty minutes away by car, Simon and Nick completing the tour by introducing her to the numerous wine bars and nightclubs. George knew she was impressed, and understood why. During his service in the Forces he had visited South America - although not her particular coastline. He had gone to the opposite side, the ship helping to subdue the mounting tension in

British Guyana in the sixties, and assisting the country to attain full independence. In Georgetown he had witnessed real poverty, culminating in near Stone Age conditions in Suriname. So he had an idea where she was coming from.

It was also during that weekend that he began to realize his son's depth of feeling for her. He was explaining to Simon something she had said, and attempted to mimic her poor command of English.

'I know exactly how she sounds, Dad.'

It was all that he said, but it was enough. It was a slap on the wrist, and he never did it again.

Although careful with money she had one particular failing, slot machines. He had commented on it to Simon after watching her spend some time putting twopences into something called a waterfall. Like a small child, she had been disappointed when nothing fell, ecstatic when a few coins cascaded into the tray.

'She's never had the opportunity before, like a lot of things,' was his son's guarded reply.

She spoke very little about her childhood to them, content to listen and laugh at Joan's attempts to embarrass the two boys, with stories relating to their younger days. But he knew from the look in her eyes that she had not had an easy time. On the one occasion that she did mention the early years of her life it was apparent that her grandmother had been a huge influence, rather than her mother or father, but she was reticent about saying too much. More evidence of how compatible her and Simon were - telling you only what they wanted you to know, no more.

The night before they returned to the capital she had made them all laugh, in response to Joan's question about the first time they had gone out together.

'He took me to a bar,' she began, haltingly. 'And because I had never been taken out by a European boy before, I asked my friend what I should drink. She told me to ask for a cocktail, called 'sex on the beach'. I think Simon thought I was very, er...'

Joan helped. 'A forward hussy?'

The following morning they were all early risers, the train for London leaving before seven, and again she had made them all laugh, saying goodbye.

'Ta-ra everybody,' she shouted from the taxi.

It sounded strange and comical coming from her, and he caught the look on his son's face. It was a look of pleasure, and he too was pleased.

* * *

Two weeks after their return to London, Maria received some bad news. Her mother was very ill and tearfully she informed Simon that she would be returning to Ecuador to visit her. He made the reservation, knowing that it would mean taking all her savings. But that wasn't important, it was the possibility of not seeing her again that made their last two days together so miserable. The day of her departure arrived only too quickly, and having taken the day off work, they had lunch together before making for the airport. They walked aimlessly around the building. Him talking incessantly, her for the most part crying, before making her way to the departure lounge. And at 9.15pm he watched Maria's flight leave England.

He missed her more than he thought was possible, Sunday taking an interminable time to arrive - the day they had agreed on for him to ring her. The line was bad. Echoes distorted her voice, his money greedily swallowed by the call box. But it was her. She explained that her mother was very ill and would need to go into hospital for treatment, which might be for some time. The prospects of a return to England before Christmas were not good. She confirmed the bad news the following Sunday. It would be the New Year before he would see her again, and it was then that he made his decision. It would mean taking all his holiday entitlement for the year, but if she couldn't come to England, then he would travel to Ecuador.

He spent the following weeks carefully laying his plans and saving every penny he could, counting the purchase of a new backpack as a necessity. In late November he had received all his inoculations and even bought the family their Christmas presents, his intention being to fly into Teesside on the return home in time for the festivities. On the first Sunday in December he rang Maria for the last time. She was excited, full of expectation at the prospect of seeing him again. She would meet him at Quito Airport and then they would travel together by bus to her family's home in Ibarra the following day.

The day of his departure from London dawned cold and grey. He knew that it was in complete contrast to the weather that would welcome him to South America, and having changed aircraft in Amsterdam he was soon on the United Airlines flight that would take him there. He had never been keen on flying, not that he had ever travelled for such a long period anyway. But it was fourteen hours away from seeing Maria again.

CHAPTER SEVEN

She had lost count of how many times she had visited the ladies' room in the Terminal building of Quito Airport. It wasn't surprising really, bearing in mind the number of drinks she had consumed, and the excitement she was feeling. She could feel her heart start to race as the aircraft came in to land, and then taxi into position ready for its passengers to disembark. Then she saw him. Unmistakable in his T-shirt and shorts - a real fashion genius - and she felt herself laughing, not at him, but because it was him. She stamped her foot impatiently, waiting for him to clear customs, and then she was throwing her arms around him, burying her head in his chest, sobbing.

'What sort of welcome is this?' he asked, smiling.

'I know, but it has been so long,' she sniffed.

A waiting taxi took them to a hotel. She had thought about taking him to the flat that her two friends still rented. But her plans didn't include an audience, and the frustration of not seeing him for so long exploded during their subsequent love making, leaving them both breathless.

'Is it always this hot and humid?' he asked.

'Sometimes it is hotter. El Niňo makes it so hot that many people and animals die. You will miss the cold of England, yes?'

'Not really,' he lied, knowing that if it did get any hotter he certainly would welcome some English weather.

'But tell me, what have you been doing.'

She told him about her mother who, although still not well, had been allowed to leave the hospital, and then about the other members of her family - all eager to meet him. Then it was his turn, until neither of them could talk nor listen anymore.

Lying by his side, she stroked his black, curly hair. How she had missed doing that. But then she had missed everything about him, and she would make up for those missing weeks in no uncertain terms - never leaving his side if she could help it.

She was gently blowing on his face when he awoke the following morning. Even at that early hour the heat was oppressive, making even waking an effort.

'Have you come all this way to sleep?' she joked. 'We have a bus to catch, before it gets too hot.'

They both showered, and he was reminded of how beautiful she was. Her long, dark hair falling to the middle of her perfectly contoured back - everything in proportion to her small figure. After a Continental breakfast in the hotel they caught a taxi to the Terminal Terrestre where, after a short delay, they boarded a bus heading out of the city and north to Ibarra.

'Did you ring your parents before you left?' she asked, once they were settled.

'Yes. From the airport. Joan was predictably a bit upset, but George was okay. He did, however, say that he'd read in one of the papers that a Frenchman had been taken hostage and then killed - but that it had happened in Colombia. He just said to take care.'

'What is 'predictably'?'

It was his greatest failing. She had done remarkably well mastering as much of the English language as she had. Occasionally, however, he was apt to use words that she hadn't heard before. He explained.

She was undecided whether to tell him what she knew, but then they had always been open and honest with each other.

'It has been in the news here quite a lot. It seems that it is the work of drug barons - who are being hunted by the military; only last week two American tourists were also murdered.'

The subject was then forgotten, and they talked of happier times, both in the past and to come.

The journey on the crowded bus was both hot and uncomfortable, and it was with some relief that two hours later he stepped onto the main highway that led directly to Maria's home. It was a short walk to what turned out to be a bungalow-type house, painted white, and with a small garden back and front. Most of her family and friends where gathered in two rooms - probably out of curiosity rather than any desire to welcome him, he guessed. But they were extremely friendly, although he understood little of what was being said, apart from the odd interpretation by Maria. She proudly introduced him to everyone, and he even managed an 'hola' and a smile to them all. Finally he met Hermania, Maria's grandmother, sensing immediately that there was a special bond between them. She belied her sixty-two years - looking fit, her handshake strong, and the only one to say 'welcome' in his native language.

He was shown to a small backroom by Maria where he left his backpack, returning to sample the huge array of food laid out in the front room, most of which was strange to him. During the next three hours - and with her help, he answered a variety of questions, mostly about his family and Hartlepool, until she sensed that he was exhausted. He was grateful for her intervention, and excusing himself he prepared for bed, still hearing her laughing and talking to her friends. She is happy, he thought. And because she was so close, so was he.

* * *

'Any word from Simon yet?' Joan asked her husband.

'No, nothing.'

He was not in the least surprised.

She took off her coat, disappointed that her eldest son hadn't thought fit to contact them again. It had been more than a week since his last phone call, informing them that he had arrived safely. He noticed her mood and tried the impossible - reassurance.

'There's no point in you worrying. You know what he's like, he'll ring us when he's ready or remembers. Walking about with a long face won't make him ring.'

He knew he was wasting his time. She was a born worrier, if she didn't have anything to worry about, she would worry about it. And yet sometimes he wondered whether their son did it deliberately, as some sort of education process.

'The thing is George, we don't really know all that much about Maria or her family, and still less about this country he's gone walkabout in. You read about all sorts of things happening to young people when they are abroad. Look at that man whose daughter went missing in Africa. Thousands of pounds he's spent trying to find out what happened to her, poor man. It must be terrible.'

He made pretence of reading the newspaper, but his thoughts were elsewhere. They had been married for nearly thirty years, and he still cared for her, but sometimes she could be impossible. During their time together they had raised two fine boys, the eldest twenty-three, and Nick, just eighteen, both him and Joan proud of their achievement.

He had recently retired from the Fire Service on ill-health grounds, although in reality he had lost his enthusiasm for a job he had once loved, no longer willing to watch its demise. He was now content to undertake simple, mundane tasks around the house, free from the pressures of having to make critical decisions, not only concerning the general public, but his own people. He had received a decent pension, which supplemented by Joan's wages from working part-time at a supermarket, allowed them to maintain a good standard of living.

She brought him a cup of coffee, still subjecting him to her worry of the week. She had a point, he had to concede that. They had only met Maria on two occasions and knew little about her or the family's background, and although she seemed to be nice enough their conversation had been limited. His major resentment of Joan was that she was under the impression that he didn't worry, when in fact he did. He just didn't see the point of advertising it. As the eldest of three children he had been raised to shoulder the responsibility for watching out for his brother and sister. It was a task he had probably undertaken too seriously - believing that in order to do the job in the right manner, a show of weakness wasn't a contributing factor. From an early age he had constructed an invisible shell around himself, giving the impression of a strong, confident and even an insensitive nature. It was false, but only he knew it. Somewhere inside the shell lay his true attributes. Loyalty, a determination to succeed, high standards and principles, and although sometimes not obvious, a devotion to his family that was second to none. He was also a romantic as opposed to his wife who was pragmatic, in every sense of the word. He knew that she lived for the two boys, involved fully at every stage of their development, whether it be in the classroom or on the soccer pitch. She was like a lioness guarding her cubs. Any approach she deemed threatening or even critical met with defensive fervour, and that included him - especially regarding Simon.

He continued reading the newspaper and at the same time rolled a cigarette when a small piece caught his eye, it concerned further killings in Colombia and read:

'It has been reported in the South American press today, that a further two bodies have been recovered on the outskirts of Medellin. They are believed to be both in their twenties and from North America, although their identities have not yet been released. Tourists planning to visit this part of the world are strongly advised to contact the Foreign Office before proceeding.'

'George, your coffee is getting cold.'

It wasn't only the coffee. The whole room had suddenly undergone a temperature change, but once again the shell was in place and he knew that Joan had noticed nothing.

During the days that followed he became an avid follower of any news items involving South America - switching television channels continually, fearing that he might miss even the smallest snippet. He remembered being questioned by a young firefighter who had recently become a father for the first time, asking him when he had stopped worrying about the boys.

'I never have. If you're a good parent it will probably happen when they find you a plot,' he had replied. 'Don't forget, there's a lot of you in them. As an example, both of my lads share my love of music, speaking of which I heard a song recently that summed it up for me:

'With my family all around me
I've all that I can hold,
I'm a beggar,
Sitting on a throne of gold.'

He relaxed for a moment and must have dozed off, the sound of the telephone startling him. Joan was there to answer it almost immediately, hoping that the voice at the other end was the one she wanted so much to hear. He turned down the sound on the television and heard her curt reply.

'No. We don't want any of your damn double glazed windows.'

* * *

'How long will you be away?'

'I've no idea,' he replied honestly. 'The South Americans have called for the cavalry and I've got the dubious honour of riding the big white horse, sweet thing.'

'Seems to me Byron that you're stepping into a pile of what the horse left behind.'

He laughed. Her quick wit had been one of the reasons he had found her so attractive in the first place, that and her insatiable lust for his body - a fact she would refute whenever he mentioned it. He watched from the window as Sara played in the garden with her friends, already showing the mischievous nature she had probably inherited from them both.

'Have you got everything?'

'A toothbrush in my top pocket and two packets of rubbers. That should be enough, babe.'

'Travel light Byron, forget about the toothbrush, with that many condoms you won't have time to use it anyway.'

It had been a time-honoured ritual with them both, an idiotic rhetoric, which they went through every time he went away. But it worked - easing the tension between them, and protecting their daughter from fear. Not that they kept her in the dark about his clandestine work, but she was at an impressionable age, and she had many years ahead of her to worry. Now, was not the time.

'How do you feel about going back into the field, and especially in South America?'

He knew his wife had put off asking the question until now.

'Like most situations, the Lord had words for it, babe.'

He was referring to the poet and not the Almighty, but she knew that.

'Now he adventured on a shore unknown,
Which all admire, but many dread to view:
His breast was armed 'gainst fate, his wants were few;
Peril he sought not, but ne'er shrank to meet.'

He put his arms around her trim waist, kissing the back of her neck.

'I'll be okay,' he whispered.

'Well, just think on. Forget the poetry and concentrate on the real world.'

She knew him too well. Sometimes he used the poetry as a shield against the effects of the real world - as she put it. It caught people off guard, expecting a conventional reply. Instead they got the abstract verse of a dead nobleman, and it amused him. They continued the ritual until Sara came in from the garden, then all three of them watched television until bedtime. When she awoke next morning he would be gone.

* * *

Hermania sat in the garden, watching Maria as she talked and laughed with her friend from England. She wondered if his childhood had been comparable with hers, but she doubted it. It had not been easy for any of the family, but the instability had left its effect on her granddaughter more than the others. Things had started so well for them. They had owned a house and land, making a good living, until the dispute, which had left them with nothing. An already wealthy landowner had become their neighbour and decided that the soil on their land was better than his, becoming increasingly violent when the family had refused to sell. They had resisted for a time, but then because the man had influential friends in Government, he was able to obtain documents stating that the land was his anyway. Up until that time there had been no legal requirement for owners of land to register their boundaries, and so the man had simply obtained the land by trickery and force. Maria's family had lived with her for the next few years, working on the farm, which was situated just outside of Banos. She smiled, recalling the times she had watched Maria struggling to keep up with the horse whose tail she was clutching, afraid of getting left behind. She had been four years of age when she had first started to work in the fields, even then showing the streak of independence which was now the envy of her brothers and sister.

She saw them walking towards her and pretended to read her book.

'I am taking Simon to the square, Abuela.'

She nodded an acknowledgement, and watched until they were out of sight, hoping that Maria had found a good friend. If not, he had found the worst of enemies - even though she was an old woman. Deep inside her she guarded a secret. An event that had happened many years before Maria's birth, the consequences of which enabled her to extract retribution, should anyone try ever again to harm the people she loved. She put down the book of poetry. It had been written by Octavio Paz, a Mexican, and the poem she had been reading was Piedra del sol, the story of the loneliness of individuals and their search for union with others. It could so well have been her story. She had the family around her, of course, but she had always felt that there had been something missing. It was possible that the events so long ago now had influenced her more than she realized.

CHAPTER EIGHT

They had planned initially to stay with Maria's parents for three days, but there had been a surprise awaiting him on his arrival which caused them to change their plans. Maria's mother had told her that there was no need to remain with them as she was well on the way to recovery and that, if she wished, there was now nothing to stop her returning to England with Simon. The good news had in fact created a problem. In order for her to return with him she would require a new visa. Due to the time she had spent away from Britain, and also a change of Government in Ecuador - with the subsequent alteration of policy regarding travel - the one she held at present was invalid. They set off early. Their goodbyes tinged with more than a little sadness, everyone realizing that if everything went to plan, she would not be with them for Christmas. Negro, her dog - who she had named after one of South America's major rivers - insisted on following her, and considerable time and effort was spent coaxing him back to the house.

They caught the first bus of the day to Quito, where she filled in numerous forms at the British Consulate, and was informed that a decision would await them on their return.

Before leaving England Simon had familiarized himself as to the country's general geography - finding himself absorbed in its long and mysterious history, in addition to an interesting blend of race and culture. His chief interests were in its rivers. The Amazon, Orinoco and Piranha providing not only a means of seeing the rainforests, but as a habitat for all sorts of unusual fish, some of which he knew, had yet to be named. The geographical marvels however were only part of the reason for wanting to see as much as possible. His other main interest was in the business opportunities available. Somewhere, he thought, there had to be a niche in the market that he could exploit. Maria had informed him that the Ecuadorean economy depended on three major exports, namely oil, bananas and shrimp, which to his way of thinking left big gaps in a number of areas.

Their main objective however was to follow the tourist trail and cover as much ground - and he hoped water - as possible, before Christmas. The country, he knew, was crossed by two parallel chains of the Andes Mountains, which divided it into three main geographical regions. These consisted of the Costa, or coastal plain, the Andean highlands and the Oriente, which was in effect the Amazon tropical rainforest. The latter region was located on the eastern side of Ecuador and it was this area that he was hoping to visit. He had left the planning of the trip to Maria, but she was aware of his wishes and he felt sure that a visit to the jungle would be included on the itinerary. His one reservation was about entering Colombia. Although not intending to cross the border, once in the jungle it would be difficult, even for a guide he imagined, to ascertain the whereabouts of any boundaries. He remembered his father's warning, about South America not being Europe, by any stretch of the imagination, and although he had been inoculated against most things, an antidote for dealing with the attentions of local bandits was not yet available.

The town of Banos had played an important part in Maria's life. It held a lot of memories for her, some she had tried hard to forget, but the majority of the time she had been happy living with Hermania, and it was to be their first port of call. The town bristled with jewellery shops, and he spent two hours following her as she darted in and out of them - reminding him of a rabbit and its burrow. The town's other claim to fame was its naturally occurring hot baths. Considering their location he thought this seemed somewhat ironic, and would have preferred the cold variety - once submersed in the water, however, he found it quite refreshing. Before leaving the town they bought each other a gift of jewellery - gold earrings for her, and a pendant for him - which she referred to as their 'Christmas presents'.

Because their visit into the jungle would necessitate an internal flight, Maria suggested that they return to Quito, where it was much easier to catch a plane to Iquitos, a popular starting point for such journeys. On their arrival back in the capital, Simon took the opportunity to ring England. It would be at least a week before he would be able to make an international call, and he was disappointed when there was no reply from his home.

The earliest available flight, they were informed, was the next day and so they spent their time sightseeing - that included a visit to the hotel where Maria had previously worked, the staff greeting her enthusiastically. She then took him on a tour of the capital of Pichincha Province, picturesquely situated on the slopes of the volcano of the same name and nestling in a fertile valley of the Andes Mountains. The city, Maria explained, was the oldest South American capital. He could see that it still retained a lot of its colonial aspect, notably the many Spanish baroque-style buildings. She was especially proud of its history, and considering that her ancestors had played an important part in creating it, she was a veritable encyclopedia of information.

That night they joined Patti and Anita, Maria's two friends, on a tour of the city nightlife, sampling the various music cultures - of which there were plenty - and also enjoying the local cuisine. Anita, in particular, enthusiastically asked questions about England, and listened intently as he told her stories about 'Hartlepol' as she called it. She laughed loudly as Maria translated the story of the monkey, and then the net that was spread across the road between the two Hartlepools - a futile attempt to contain a plague. It was after midnight when they all arrived back at the two friends' flat, the girls giggling incessantly in between whispered comments, which he neither understood, or for that matter wanted to.

They were awake early the next morning, eager to be on their way to north-eastern Peru and the starting point of their adventure, Iquitos. The Russian plane that they eventually found themselves boarding had seen better days. The seats were no better than hammocks, and the service non-existent, and so they were relieved when it touched down just outside the capital of Loreto Department. Maria had chosen the port because it was actually situated on the Amazon, and approximately 60 miles from the point at which the Maranon River unites with the Ucayali, so forming the mainstream of the famous waterway. She had never visited the city, but she told Simon stories that her grandmother had told her when she was small, of strange people who lived and worked in the surrounding area.

'There was a man who was one of the first white men ever to visit this part of our world,' she began. 'He would go into the jungle and persuade the poor Indians to trap the wild animals and then kill them. Then he would stuff them and sell them to the early tourists. He became so well known that he became very rich by sending them all over the world.'

They had been warned by a helpful Brazilian during the flight that they would be the targets of the many vendors who would be waiting to ambush them at the terminal building. They would promise 'jungle trips' at the cheapest possible price. The majority, however, were bogus, and he advised them to wait until they reached the city and find a reputable travel shop.

'Quite apart from some of them being thieves in their own right, there is also a minority who owe allegiance to the 'Shining Path'. He said it as if it was common knowledge, until Simon's quizzical look said otherwise.

'They are a violent terrorist movement dedicated to the overthrow of the Government, my English friend, with the intention of giving power to the peasants, but in reality the power would go to their backers, reportedly the Peruvian drug industry. Many people think that with the death of their leader the movement died also. A fact which is not altogether true. So be very careful who you decide to trust for your jungle adventure.'

Maria had no previous experience of hiring someone reputable to take them by boat into the jungle, and so the choice was always going to depend on a certain amount of luck. They eventually hired a man in his mid-twenties, named Enrico, who besides appearing to be quite sensible could also speak passable English. The boat was very narrow, and due to the amount of equipment that they were obliged to take, there was very little room to make themselves comfortable.

It was late afternoon when they finally got underway, feeling at first that the boat would capsize with any sudden movements. But after an hour of practice on the river their fears were allayed. Enrico turned out to be a good choice; enthusiastically pointing out places and objects that he thought would be of interest to them.

Memories of days spent camping came flooding back. The river, at that point, not unlike the one he and Nick had played on in their inflatable boat as young children. He disregarded the fact that there were not too many piranha fish in Yorkshire's River Ure.

It was getting dark when the canoe pulled alongside a small wooden jetty and Enrico informed them that they would spend the night in one of the basic wooden huts visible from the boat. Basic was an understatement. With walls of bamboo and a roof constructed of some kind of large leaf they looked positively uninhabitable, even for one night's stay. It got progressively worse as they entered their accommodation. Candles appeared to be the only means of illumination, and a small fire smouldering in the centre of the only room, filled it with a foul smelling, acrid smoke. The beds were also of bamboo, covered in some sort of fibre matting, and raised some two feet off the floor - presumably to discourage the attentions of any unwelcome nocturnal visitors.

Sitting close to the fire and manoeuvring various sized blackened pots sat a dark-skinned woman, who smiled as they entered, her remaining teeth similar in colour to her pots. Having deposited their backpacks on adjacent beds, Enrico invited them to join the woman by the fire where they were each given a bowl, the contents of which resembled a thin porridge. Maria gave him a reassuring smile, but he had already decided that the amount of time the substance was going to remain in his mouth was dependent on how long it took to reach his throat. He therefore had no idea of its taste. Having eaten, they walked down to the river's edge to wash, before stretching out on the bamboo beds in preparation for what Simon knew was going to be a long and uncomfortable night.

He wasn't disappointed and next morning Enrico explained to him the reason for the incessant, high whine, which had been responsible for his discomfort.

'It was the culex mosquito, or 'carapana' as the Indians call it. The whine used by the female is to attract the male - the sound produced by the wing beat of the insect.'

I'm glad something had a good night, he thought, his sense of humour gradually returning. Half an hour later he was tempted to kiss Enrico who, from a box in the canoe, had produced some eggs.

'I have discovered in the past, that Europeans do not take to the local diet, but as my little joke I let them try it. But then I surprise them.'

They heard him laughing whilst they had breakfast and he loaded the canoe, still maintaining a mischievous chuckle as they pulled away from the jetty.

The river twisted - becoming quite narrow in places - enabling them to get close-ups of the vast array of fauna and wildlife, and to be captivated by the beiju-beiju monkeys. Enrico explained that it meant 'kiss-kiss' - because of the sound they made with their lips. The morning passed quickly, and at noon they stopped in a small creek.

'We fish for our lunch today,' said their guide, producing two primitive fishing implements. 'The piranha are plentiful in this part of the river.'

They threw their lines into the water, watching Enrico thrash it with a stick.

'The fish come and see what is making the water so er, er…'

'Frenzied?'

'Yes. As you say, frenzied.'

His point was made some minutes later, when Maria squealed in delight - one of the dreaded fish taking her bait. Within half an hour six of them lay in the bottom of the canoe, having been clubbed to death by Enrico. Even dead, they sent a shiver down Simon's back. The fish were short and deep-bodied with a blunt face, the razor sharp teeth wedge-shaped, not unlike a shark's. Having made a fire on the creek bank, Enrico proceeded to cook them, each one speared with a wooden stake and still retaining their heads. As usual he was extremely informative.

'They are nervous and unpredictable, with no fear of man,' he began. 'The one's we have caught today are of the smaller species, the larger fish could bite through your leg. It is also advisable that women, for whom it is that time of the month, do not go into the river.'

Simon saw Maria look away, embarrassed.

The fish were not very appetizing, he decided, and was convinced that they would not go down well at his local fish and chip shop.

Mid-afternoon found them in a magical lagoon. It was filled with a multitude of diverse creatures, all seemingly co-habiting in perfect harmony. The canoe was escorted to the Cayman free bank by pink botos, commonly known in Europe as dolphins, beautiful creatures, and neither of them was surprised when Enrico informed them that they had the reputation among the local Indians for luring women into the river, and having intercourse with them.

'Will I be safe swimming with them, Enrico? asked Simon.

It was as if the dolphins recognized a kindred spirit in him. Having been reassured by their guide that 'gay' dolphins were an unknown entity in Amazonia, he slipped over the side of the canoe and was immediately surrounded. They glided effortlessly through the water, snorting at him when they got close, then allowing him to stroke their smooth, rubber-like skins. He waved at Maria to join him, then remembered what Enrico had said. Besides, he knew that she was a 'sinking ship' swimmer, not confident, but capable when the situation required it. Fifteen minutes later he was drying himself in the afternoon sun, recalling his younger brother's words. Nick had been on holiday to Mexico and during his stay had also swum with the beautiful creature, describing it as 'an experience not to be missed'. They didn't usually agree, but on this occasion he was right.

'Shall we have a look at the rest of the lagoon?' he asked, intending to go anyway.

Maria nodded, adding words of caution. 'But first we must tell Enrico what we are doing.'

They found him gathering wood for the fire on which they would cook their evening meal.

'I must first warn you, my young friends, that we are now in the southernmost tip of Colombia and, although fairly safe, be watchful. Do not speak to anyone you may meet, and if you see anything that you don't like, then return here.'

Clasping each other's hands they strolled into the dense undergrowth and heavy wooded area that was the

South American jungle. It was all he had hoped it would be. Macaws, parrots and toucans provided a cacophony of sound, their stunning colours heightened by the sunlight, percolating through the canopy like a million spears. Huge white butterflies followed them, fluttering around their heads, whilst the sight of the occasional tarantula spider reminded them of the need to be careful. He glanced at Maria. Was she thinking the same thoughts as him - that at that moment there was no one else in the world, and that this was the nearest thing to paradise. He could easily have remained there. Swimming with the dolphins, listening to the macaws, and being with her. He had forgotten about time.

'I think we should return, Simon.'

It was an easy place to daydream, and she kissed him, more to get his attention than anything else. As they approached the place where they had left Enrico they could see from a distance that he had already erected the tents. The smell of the evening meal - chicken and rice - drifted towards them. As they reached their camp for the night however, their guide was conspicuous by his absence. A sudden feeling of foreboding gripped Simon and he tightened his grip on Maria, whose small hand had already started to shake.

At first he thought it was a large species of monkey hanging from the tree. But as his eyes became accustomed to the gloom he realized that it was human, as were the four figures that stepped out of the undergrowth. Brandishing large machetes they screamed what he could only surmise were instructions to them both, whilst Maria, the increasing pitch of her voice an indication of her desperation, tried to inform them that they were 'tourista'. She suddenly sat down and crossed her legs, indicating for him to follow, the intruders standing over them pointing their machetes in the direction of Enrico's limp and lifeless body.

'They say that unless we do as they wish, we will be cut into small pieces and thrown to the piranha, or hung like poor Enrico.' He knew that she hadn't noticed the body until then, and it finally put an end to her composure, as she collapsed on the ground in a flood of tears. She was roughly brought back to a sitting position in order for them both to eat the meal that Enrico had been preparing for them. They reluctantly forced the food into their dry mouths, encouraged by the machete-wielding men. The reason became clear some minutes later, as he saw Maria again collapse on the ground and felt his own head spinning. Frantically he tried to focus on the pink dolphin as it leapt clear of the water in the lagoon. But he never saw it re-enter as he too was suddenly enveloped in a sea of darkness.

It was still dark when some level of consciousness returned, but it wasn't night - it was the hood that completely covered his head that was the cause of his loss of vision. He was vaguely aware of being carried. The splash of water, the sound of a vehicle's engine, the pain as he was thrown onto something hard and then bounced around like a ball, then nothing.

CHAPTER NINE
Investigative Police HQ, Bogotá

At roughly the same time that the 'poet' was taking his seat on board the Avianca-owned B747 bound for Bogotá, his good friend and saviour, Gill Garbanza, was entering the offices of the Colombian PIP, situated in the same city. His first stop was the coffee machine, his one and only capitulation to anything remotely associated with addiction, but he needed the boost first thing in the morning.

'Buenos dias, Bernice. ¿Como esta?'

His pretty young secretary smiled at him, returning his greeting. He knew that she would have already placed on his desk any reports, faxes or telephone messages that had arrived overnight, awaiting his or Henri's personal attention. Most of it would be routine, ranging from petty crime committed by kids as young as five or six, to a drug-related murder or murders for which he knew very little effort would be expended in finding the culprits. He knew, however, that his city wasn't any different to many of the big cities of the world, where crime was spiralling out of control. He quickly went through the sheaf of papers, pausing when he came to a single sheet on which Bernice had scrawled a message.

'The man called Emilio will ring you at 10am.'

He leaned back in his chair - a feeling of trepidation already beginning to surface. The man had rung on three previous occasions, always the bearer of bad news. He would be surprised if this latest message was any different. He immediately instructed the intelligence room to prepare themselves to tape the call, at the same time wishing he had the technology of the Americans. At 10am precisely his secretary put through the call to him.

'Sen̆or Garbanza?'

'Si.'

'Two more tourists have been taken. Simon Halkin, English, and his companion Maria Sandino from Ecuador.'

He knew it was a waste of time asking any questions - it was a taped message, but that's all they had established. Writing down the latest two names in his folder he noticed how embarrassingly long the list was becoming, or should it be lists, he thought, one for those who had been killed, and the other - the waiting list. Henri had already been at work well before his own arrival and so taking his folder with him, he went to give his boss the latest news.

'Have we made any progress at all?'

'I wish I could give you some good news for a change, unfortunately, as usual it's all gloom and doom. During the past month I've lost two operatives. The latest of them was supposed to infiltrate Betancur's estancia seeking work as a gardener, but nothing has been heard of him, so I am assuming the worst. Benito is at present working undercover with Inderena, but I've told him to be patient, and just to monitor Betancur's estate. I've also asked the Americans to send over an agent to work with him. Bearing in mind that two of their nationals have just been murdered it seemed the least I could do.'

'Just make sure that we don't lose him as well, it's bad enough our own people going missing.' There was a hint of cynicism in his voice, and it didn't go unnoticed.

'We go back a long way me and Hollingsworth, and he isn't the sort of man who just goes missing.'

He watched Henri's fingers tapping the desk, a nervous habit borne out of having to make too many difficult phone calls.

'We have got to start getting somewhere my friend, I know exactly what the Minister is going to say when I inform him of this latest situation, and I don't like being unemployed.'

* * *

FOREIGN AND COMMONWEALTH OFFICE, LONDON.

He watched the red light flickering for some time before he extinguished it by picking up the receiver.

'There's a call for you from our Embassy in Bogotá, Sir Charles.'

Charles Barnard waited for the call to be put through by his secretary, a perplexed frown beginning to wrinkle his forehead. As Head of the Consular Division such direct communication with an Embassy based in a foreign country was not only unusual, it was potentially dangerous, even if the line was secure.

'Sorry to contact you this way Charlie, but it's important that you hear the situation from me rather than a media source.'

He reached for the appropriate button on the ever-present record facility, knowing full well that the Deputy Head of Mission in Bogotá was not one to take chances and therefore the reason for the call was worthy of taping.

'The full details will be coming to you through the official channels, but in short the Colombians have informed us that within the last 48 hours one of our nationals has been taken hostage.'

'Have we a name?'

He heard the rustle of papers being shuffled before receiving the information.

'There's an added complication, Charlie. It would appear that there's an Ecuadorean girl with him, a Maria Sandino.'

The conversation finished and he played the recording of the brief message over a couple of times before contacting his secretary.

'I have two names Audrey. Simon Halkin who is one of ours, and a Maria Sandino from Ecuador, see what you can dig up on them both, and treat it as priority.'

He knew that she would have some answers for him within the hour. Halkin would not be a problem, but information on the girl, who technically speaking was not really the British Government's concern, would probably have to come from the Immigration Department's computer data bank. In the meantime he thought it prudent to inform Drugs and International Crime, as well as the FCO Information Department. It was in fact two hours later that Audrey supplied him with enough information on which to proceed. The details were scant, the single sheet of paper not containing anything that could be construed as out of the ordinary concerning either of them. The only item that caught his eye was the fact that the father had seen service with the Royal Navy. It would only be a problem however if he decided to take matters into his own hands. The last thing the FO needed was a 'loose cannon'. He smiled at the pun. His next call was to the Permanent Under-Secretary's office, to whom he gave all the details that he had to hand; the reply was as he expected.

'I'll leave it with you for the moment Charlie, but keep the office informed. By the way, don't leave it too late to inform the Member for Hartlepool, wherever that is. The family needs to be informed before the Christmas recess, but then I'll leave it up to you to sort out the details. Some present eh?'

The eyes and ears of the press had already made up his mind, knowing only too well that it was only a matter of time before they discovered the reasons behind the youngsters' disappearance, and so Christmas or not, the family would need to be told.

Donald Bevan was sitting in his usual position on the backbenches' of the House, when the Assistant Serjeant-at-Arms handed him the note. It was brief, requesting his attendance at Palace Street as soon as it was convenient. There couldn't have been a more convenient moment; the debate through which he was struggling to keep awake had dragged on interminably.

It was midday in the capital and so it was some time before he managed to hail a taxi, parliamentary privilege not yet extended to the taxi rank, unfortunately, he mused. The journey took thirty minutes. His cab continuously making detours to avoid the more congested parts of London, a city he disliked intensely. He couldn't imagine anyone wanting to live here out of choice. The only reason possible being the ability to make money or hide from some heinous crime, neither of which applied to him. A cliché or not, he had entered politics for what he thought were the right reasons. And that was to take an active part in the development of his native north-east and to do his best for the people who lived there. He had soon discovered however, that there was a large chasm between the ideology and the reality. His power as a backbencher was virtually non-existent. So far his only contribution to the proceedings of the House had been his maiden speech - customary, rather than controversial. He had been returned as the Member for Hartlepool on the last three occasions - principally because it was a safe Labour seat, the only deviation from that being in the sixties, when Kerans, the captain of the Amethyst, had been successful. It had been only a hiccup, however, and the Commander's exploits on the Yangtze River had been forgotten by the time he came to be re-elected. Consequently, as a 'foot soldier' it was with some apprehension that he entered the office of a leading member of the Diplomatic Service, the door behind him firmly closed by his secretary.

'Sit down Mr. Bevan, I make no apology for dragging you away from the House, but I'm afraid I have some bad news for one of your constituents.'

He listened to the news of the kidnappings with a mixture of sadness and hope. Contrary to public opinion, as a politician he still retained the ability to feel for the misfortunes of others, and yet, maybe here was an opportunity to finally make his mark.

'I understand you were intending to return north on Friday?'

He nodded, noticing for the first time the cold, grey eyes.

'I suggest that you leave first thing in the morning, for obvious reasons. I would rather the news was broken to the family by HM Government than by some less than creditable Fleet Street rag.'

Although the present situation had never occurred in his constituency before, he was vaguely aware of the procedure. There would be silence at first until all interested parties had been informed, and then a carefully worded release to the Press Association.

'Assure the family that everything is being done in order to secure the release of their son and his friend, and that they will be kept fully informed of our progress.'

How many times had Barnard said those very words, he wondered?

'One more thing before you go. Let me know what you think about the father, personality and intelligence, that sort of thing. You can leave the details with my secretary.'

He was dismissed. In politics you read between the lines and he knew that the interview had come to an end.

There was no answer from his home, so he left a message on the answerphone informing his wife that he would be arriving earlier than she had anticipated. He then booked a seat on the 6.55am train from King's Cross to Darlington leaving the following day.

He woke early, eager to leave behind the hustle and bustle of the capital in exchange for the more sedentary pace of Hartlepool, and although not looking forward to the task that lay ahead, he breathed easier as the InterCity rolled smoothly northwards.

It was an hour into the journey that he decided to make a few notes, and also examine fully the information, which Barnard had supplied. George, the father, had served for some years in the RN eventually leaving with the rank of Leading Hand, and while not exactly Rear Admiral of the Red it did show some ambition. The same could be said of his career in the Fire Service, noting that for the majority of his adult life the man had been in a disciplined environment. He had travelled extensively, independent of his time in the Forces, a photocopy of his passport showing visas from a wide range of countries. Joan, his wife, was described as a shop assistant, but very little else seemed to be known about her. The same also being applied to the youngest son, Nicholas, who had followed his father into the Fire Service. Of the missing son there were a few lines indicating that he was a university graduate, and that he had been visiting his friend in Ecuador when things had gone drastically wrong. He assumed that the girl's Foreign Ministry would be investigating her disappearance, but also suspected that the FO would have instigated inquiries of its own. Pausing for a moment he reflected on his own position, appreciating the fact that he was no more than a middleman between the parents and the FO. His involvement was small and restricted, confined to giving assurances and reporting back to Barnard, and yet he knew that it was important to do both well. It went without saying that it would be a stressful time for all concerned, including him. But he must be careful not to let his compassion lead to promises that he was in no position to guarantee - openness and honesty not being an integral part of a politician's character.

The incident that changed his intended way of dealing with the matter occurred at Doncaster. The woman - in her mid-fifties he guessed - took her seat opposite him, placing her newspaper and paperback book on the table. She smiled, picking up the book and at the same time revealing the title. It was called 'The Missing Children,' and the coincidence caused him to take a sharp intake of breath.

'Looks like an interesting read, if you don't mind me saying.'

It was said as casually as he could manage. The woman lowered her glasses, turning to the back cover that contained a synopsis of the contents.

'Harrowing rather than interesting I would say, but at the same time thought provoking.'

He doubted the wisdom of asking more, but almost lemming-like couldn't resist.

'It concerns the fate of a number of Argentine children and their mothers' attempt to compel the Government to provide details as to their whereabouts. They suspect that they are languishing in the country's prisons - held on spurious offences; many of them maybe not that lucky. So, every Thursday, they parade in the main square of the capital, the Playa del Sol, carrying placards containing photographs and details of their missing offspring, hoping that the Administration will enlighten them, which never happens.'

She laid the book on the table, looking out of the window, as if reflecting on the pain that the women were forced to endure.

'So none of the children are ever returned?'

'Rarely. The women go to their representatives of course, but they are men with no real influence, puppets, so their efforts are fruitless.'

It was getting too near to home, and he was beginning to experience real feelings of inadequacy as he silently joined her in gazing out of the window.

'Politicians,' she sighed suddenly, ' we never learn do we? They are elected by the people and then do little to repay that trust. I suppose it's a bit like paying someone to rob you. Still we don't have the problems of these poor women, thank goodness. Can you imagine ever losing one of your children - no matter what the circumstances?'

He couldn't. But what he would try to do was to be as honest as he possibly could with two people he was on his way to meet.

* * *

BOGOTÁ, COLOMBIA

Byron Hollingsworth felt the heat immediately the aircraft doors were opened, the walk down the stairs already causing his breathing to be laboured. It was as if the sun was concentrating every one of its 4000 megawatts of solar energy on his particular piece of El Dorado, Bogotá's main airport. By the time he reached the terminal building he was convinced that he had lost weight, the sweat from his neck already running in rivulets down his back.

'You look warm, Mr. Hollingsworth.'

He recognized Benito immediately. The short cropped hair, the boxer's flattened nose and the build of a weightlifter had been clearly defined in the photograph that O'Grady had included in the folder.

'Hot and sweaty would be a better description.'

He offered his hand, and wished he hadn't, as his fingers were suddenly crushed. Walking at a hurried pace through the building he knew instinctively that they would get on, the man's unending chatter interrupted by bursts of laughter, putting him immediately at ease. As they left the airport at a speed equalling that of the aircraft that had brought him to the city, his guide explained that he had worked for Gill for the past ten years, sharing more than a few scrapes in the process.

'But this is different, señor, it is a nasty business.'

'Still nothing to go on then?'

'Guillermo has a gut feeling that it is Betancur, and usually he is very good, but there is no evidence with which he can move against him.'

The friendly Colombian had, Byron decided, been a Formula One racing driver in a previous life, as they ignored every speed limit on the way to the Old City. Twenty minutes after leaving the airport they pulled onto a restaurant forecourt - Benito explaining that they would eat before he delivered him to his hotel. He had chosen well, the Italian cuisine, supplemented by a bottle of the same country's wine, enjoyed by them both.

'I hear that you too have had your moments with Guillermo, yes?'

'I owe him my life, Benito, but he will have told you the story.'

'He does not tell stories, my friend, he is a very private man.'

'Then I will tell you. Many years ago, when we were both young field agents, we joined forces to operate a sting operation against Pablo Escobar. It had been a good plan, a lot of work, thousands of dollars invested as bribes, sweeteners, and it had enabled Gill and myself to infiltrate Escobar's cartel. He was a special target, a rising star, because not only did he turn the coca into its base form, he was also capable of refining it and producing the finished product. After months of dangerous manoeuvring, we eventually persuaded the cartel that we had a market place in the States - amongst the organized crime syndicates. There was a condition however. Escobar himself must fly to Mexico to cement the deal, owing to the vast amounts of money involved. We arrived at his 'fortress' just to the south of a place called Melgar by private plane, ready to take him to the 'meet'. Unfortunately it was we who were met. No sooner had the plane taxied to a halt than armed men swarmed all over it and we were forced at gunpoint to lie on the crude runway. After attempts to question us, using rifle butts as their interview technique, Gill who had remained with them and was regarded as one of their own, was ordered to take us into the wooded area and dispose of us. Instead of carrying out his orders he shot the two accompanying men and we managed to escape.'

'Did you ever find out why it had gone wrong.'

'Some months later, after an intensive inquiry into the whole affair, it was discovered that the contents of a Mexican border official's bank account, had quadrupled overnight. When questioned he admitted to supplying information to the local major cartel, concerning the increase in the movements of large numbers of FBI and DEA agents into Mexico. This information was then conveyed to Escobar who naturally smelled a rat.'

For the next half an hour they discussed the worsening situation concerning the hostages and killings, until Benito decided that it was time to book into the hotel. He knew exactly what to expect the moment he saw the exterior. A real estate man would have called it 'a residence with character', which was their jargon for 'falling apart', as indeed it was. Benito laughed.

'I was told not to get you anything too comfortable.'

'Do you always obey orders to the letter,' he replied, grabbing his bag.

'I will pick you up here at six in the morning, seňor.' And with that he sped off.

The room he was allocated confirmed his worst nightmare. It reeked of sweat and damp, and a trickle of what he assumed was urine came from an open toilet, home to a family of cockroaches. He didn't even put his bag down, deciding that he would look for something slightly better - like a cardboard box, he thought. It was beginning to get dark as, quite by accident, he discovered Gill Garbanza's place of work, causing him to stop and wish that he could walk in and greet his old friend. He walked on, knowing that to do so would certainly put at risk the lives of the hostages and the operation as a whole.

'Perdon, seňor.'

He knew immediately what was happening, not realizing where his legs had taken him until it was too late. The two men hustled him into an alley, not big men, but made bigger by the knives they were brandishing in his direction. He didn't have to be asked and reached for his wallet, throwing it down at their feet, whilst they pointed at his hands, indicating that they also required his rings and watch. To resist meant at least certain mutilation, at most - death. He never got the opportunity to remove any of the jewellery, as two dark shadows appeared from nowhere, expertly disarming his adversaries and forcing them to lie face down in the filth of the alley. It was all over in a minute, and as the would-be thieves were led away he caught the whispered words of one of his saviours.

'Seňor Garbanza sends his regards Mr. Hollingsworth, but please return to your hotel.'

The realization that 'Gill' had once more saved his life caused him to pause for a moment before picking up his wallet. The men had gone, but he knew that there would be replacements.

CHAPTER TEN
Colombia

Simon was the first to come round, groggy, a severe headache and an intense desire to be sick greeting his return to consciousness. He could vaguely make out the outline of Maria lying a short distance away, her long black hair covering her face, motionless. Crawling over to her, he put his cheek to her mouth - relieved to feel her warm breath. He remained by her side, stroking her forehead. Unable to think, his memory returning only in fragmented form, he had no idea how long he lay there, until the black cloak enveloped him once more.

'¿Como se llama?'

He held his chest - the sharp pain caused by the rifle in the hands of the man who was now bending over him.

'Simon Halkin.'

The effort was causing more pain.

'¿De donde es?'

A second voice.

'Inglaterra.'

'¿Que hace?'

His knowledge of the Spanish language was now exhausted.

'No entiendo,' he replied, as the butt of the rifle was aimed in his direction once more.

Maria saved him from suffering further pain, coming round she answered for him, before replying to their questions about herself. The two men grunted, satisfied that they had achieved what they had been ordered to find out, and then climbing a short wooden staircase, disappeared through double doors. Outside he heard the turning of a key in a padlock, then silence, apart from his and Maria's breathing. She moved closer to him, and finding his hand held it tightly; he could feel her shaking - or was it him?

As his eyes became accustomed to the dark he noticed that they were in some sort of cellar, the floor was concrete and cold, the walls constructed of uneven stone shapes. Shelving lined two of the walls, of a type once home to hundreds of wine bottles left to mature. Now the only evidence of the cellar's former use were the broken remains of one or two carafes and a quantity of paper and straw - in which the bottles were presumably packed.

'Why are we here, and how long Simon?' Maria asked, through chattering teeth.

His answers would be only a guess, so he changed the subject. By now they were both shaking uncontrollably, partly due to the cold, but mainly due to shock, he thought, a symptom every bit as deadly as their captors. They had been clad only in T-shirt and shorts at the time of their capture, clothing which now was quite inappropriate for enduring the cold Colombian night. They hugged each other tightly - each trying to impart some of their own body heat, until suddenly the sight of the straw gave him new hope.

'Gather all the straw and paper and pile it in the corner against the wall,' he urged Maria.

Minutes later they were totally immersed in the filthy refuse, the smell overpowering, but both feeling slightly warmer, and eventually falling asleep in each other's arms.

It was the sun percolating through the cracks in the rough wooden doors that roused him from a fitful sleep. That, and the sound of Maria crying. She didn't look well at all, and he was beginning to wonder how he could gain the attention of the guards when he heard the padlock being removed. At first he couldn't make out who it was - the figure appearing in outline due to the brightness of the sun - and it wasn't until he had descended to the bottom of the steps that Simon got a clear view. He wasn't a guard that was for sure - his clothing and bearing indicating that he was more likely to be their employer, confirmation coming almost immediately.

'How are you Simon Halkin?'

He spoke very good English and joined them in the corner of the room, yet appeared to ignore Maria completely.

'No doubt you are very hungry?'

The container, which the man placed on the floor, contained four large empanados and coffee, which they both wolfed down, ignorant of his presence until the food had disappeared.

'You are also cold, yes?'

The question answered with a question.

'Why are we here?'

'I think the phrase is 'victims of circumstance'. You were indeed in the wrong place at the wrong time.'

They watched him leave, their questions still unanswered.

'Do you know how long we have been here Simon?'

He didn't, and it really didn't matter. What did was to make the best of their predicament, something that was going to take a lot of doing. He still couldn't remember all the details of their journey after being taken, but parts of it were now beginning to surface. He could recall being taken out of the boat and dumped into some kind of truck, then occasional stops for toilet and food, some of the journey undertaken on rough tracks, then the bumping stopped - as if on a highway. At some point they were transferred to another vehicle, and he remembered hearing men shouting, arguing, but nothing made sense. Somewhere along the way they had been robbed of everything, including the few Christmas presents which he was keeping for their return to England.

'We must walk, Maria.'

He was starting to feel the effects of cramp, and their condition was such that they didn't need any further complications. She followed his example, clinging to his arm as they circled the room. They had completed three laps of the room when he heard the padlock being removed, and seconds later two dirty sleeping bags together with a couple of rough ponchos were thrown down the stairs.

'I need the toilet, Simon.'

She put on one of the ponchos. He walked up the stairs and banged on the door, whilst she shouted at the guards, hearing them laugh at her discomfort. Eventually one of them opened the door and approached her, covering her eyes with his bandana and leading her up the stairs. With their backs turned Simon followed them and managed to get onto the bottom step, from where he was able to get a quick glimpse of the terrain. The door was slammed shut. It was enough time however, for him to realize that they where no longer in the jungle. The sight of cattle in an open field with a backdrop of heavily wooded hills a far cry from the rainforest where they had been taken, and the unfortunate Enrico left to rot.

It was as he was donning the poncho that he heard her first cries for help, shouts at first, turning to screams moments later. Racing to the top of the stairs he peered through a large crack in the wooden door, a feeling of anger mixed with despair as he saw Maria struggling with the guard, her poncho and T-shirt lying on the ground some distance away. The huge guard completely covered her small figure, whilst his companion stood watching and laughing, until a shout followed by a gunshot brought Maria's ordeal to an end. He saw her scramble away, grabbing her shirt and the poncho, covering herself, head bowed. At first he didn't see the source of her assistance, it wasn't until the man who had brought them the empanados helped her to stand that he was aware of the identity of her benefactor. He escorted her back to the cellar where the three of them stood silently until a burst of gunfire prompted him to explain.

'The man will not bother your friend again, I will not tolerate such actions, I apologize.'

'And do you also apologize for us being here in the first place?' Simon's anger was causing him to appear more courageous than he actually felt.

The man said nothing, but his eyes spoke for him, glaring, and then he turned abruptly and headed for the stairs, stopping short before facing his prisoners.

'I will say this to you Simon Halkin, if that is your real name. You have witnessed how women in this country are regarded. They are kept rather than accepted as equals, of little or no importance. You however, an Englishman, may be of some value, it remains to be seen.'

'What do you mean, if that is my name. You have our documents?'

'No I do not. They are being withheld by the people who brought you here, until proper payment is made. Only then will I have proof of who you say you are, not that it really matters.'

He said it with finality. His parting words had sent a shiver through Simon's whole body, and suddenly he felt very, very frightened.

⋆ ⋆ ⋆

HARTLEPOOL

It was late evening when they returned from a spell of early Christmas shopping - George heading straight for the kitchen in search of a hot drink, whilst Joan checked the answerphone. He watched her through the open door of the hallway, writing down names and numbers of people who she would call back once the television 'soaps' had finished. She was especially enjoying the seasonal shopping spree this year, due mainly to the fact that Simon had informed them, on his arrival in Ecuador, that Maria would be accompanying him when he arrived back home on Christmas Eve.

'It makes a change to be able to buy for a girl, instead of three men,' was her reply, when he had commented on her enthusiasm. He had also noticed that what had started out as a few 'bits and pieces' had now turned into a sackful.

'Any of those calls for me?' he enquired.

'Someone called Derek Bevan rang. Must be for you, I don't know anyone of that name.'

The hot drink was forgotten instantly. No drink in the world would have been able to disperse the coldness that he felt at that precise moment. With shaking hands he returned the politician's call.

'This is George Halkin, Mr. Bevan. I understand you've been trying to contact me?'

'Would it be possible for you and your wife to come and see me at my home?' The voice sounded almost apologetic.

'Can you tell me what it is about?'

'I'd rather not over the phone. If I give you my address can you come tonight?'

He agreed. Politics was something of a grey area to him. But when the MP for your town said he would like to see you, everything became black and white.

'Was it important, George?'

'You had better come through,' he said, already in the process of putting on his coat.

George said nothing during the short drive to the MP's house. It was in complete contrast to his wife's incessant chatter - which he knew was borne out of nerves and a feeling of foreboding. They were met at the front door of the large rambling house by Mrs. Bevan, who showed them into a small study occupied by her husband, who quickly provided two chairs.

'I'll come straight to the point Mr. and Mrs. Halkin. Two days ago the Foreign and Commonwealth Office received a communiqué from our Embassy in Colombia, stating that your son and his friend had been taken hostage by, at the time, an organization or persons unknown.'

The long-overdue tears were now streaming down Joan's face. George placed his arm around her, and at the same time tried to retain some semblance of composure himself.

'I think we both know Mr. Bevan that this unidentified organization is in fact a major drug cartel. So if you don't mind, stop treating me like a fucking mushroom and tell me what you really know.'

He noticed Bevan take a sharp intake of breath, no doubt alarmed at the ferocity of the outburst, he thought.

'I can only tell you what I know, which isn't a lot. The problem has now escalated from an internal conflict, to one of international proportions, fuelled by the taking of so many different nationalities.'

He was interrupted by a knock on the door and the entrance of his wife bearing tea and biscuits.

'Would Mrs. Halkin like to come into the living room? It's much warmer,' she offered.

At first Joan refused, but then decided that it was better to leave her husband to ask the important questions, without the distraction of her bursting into tears every few minutes. George waited until the door closed.

'Before we go any further Mr. Bevan, let me tell you a little about myself. Very briefly, I'm no one's fool, I like people to be up front and I'm not prone to taking in water at the first signs of anything unpleasant. The very nature of my work during most of my adult life has prepared me, quite adequately, to handle problems. So if you think that there are aspects of this business that I may not be able to come to terms with, think again. Now I know that you haven't got all the answers, and probably never will, but I'll ask anyway. I have a fair idea from the press coverage why, but have you any idea who has got my son, and where?'

He saw Bevan reach for a notepad.

'For me to be as honest and open as I possibly can with you I need some assurances. During the next few days the local, and even the national press, are going to be knocking on your door. At this very moment the FCO are releasing these details to the Press Association. On no account must you quote me to these people. Will you guarantee that?'

'You have my word.'

'The Colombian Authorities are fairly sure that the man behind these kidnappings and er…'

'Killings, Mr. Bevan, or if you prefer, executions. Either way it amounts to the same thing.'

'Yes, killings. Anyway they think it is a man called Rodrigo Betancur - head of the largest drug cartel in Colombia, and possibly the whole of South America. One of the biggest problems however, is that they don't know the exact location of the hostages, and to move on him without that confirmation, would mean their certain death, a fate already experienced by a number of unfortunate tourists. Two hours ago I received a fax from London informing me that a truce had been offered. It also stated that the Colombian Administration were prepared to open negotiations with whoever was responsible, providing that the executions stopped.'

'So the bottom line is that my son's life is in the hands of various diplomats and the inevitable prospect of long drawn out negotiations with no certainty as to the outcome, and that is dependent on this murdering drug baron accepting the truce anyway.'

'You're answering your own questions, Mr. Halkin.'

He was right. Bevan had nothing more to say, or tell him. Collecting Joan, they were shown to the door by the MP. His parting words predictable.

'It goes without saying that I'll keep you fully informed of any developments, and if you ever need to ring me, please don't hesitate.'

Joan had stopped crying, but her red and sore eyes bore testimony to what she had endured for the last few hours. He also knew that there were lots more tears to be shed in the privacy of their home, and not all by her.

* * *

MEDELLIN

Rodrigo placed the newspaper El Espectador on his desk. The headlines stated that the Government of Colombia was prepared to talk to the perpetrators of the recent kidnappings. Alongside it lay an envelope, containing details of the latest hostages, and delivered by Alfred.

'Sit down,' he said, heavily.

Alfred Jaramillo had never seen his friend in such a depressed mood, he looked tired, worn out.

'Tell me your thoughts on this.' He pointed to the headline, his finger trembling.

'I will tell you what I know, and then what I think. There has been the expected increase in diplomatic activity since the death of the Americans, and I also expect a further increase with the taking of the Englishman. That is not however, our only problem. Our coca suppliers in Bolivia, as well as our two main competitors, are feeling the effects of increased military activity, so in reality we are about to be squeezed from both ends.'

'They wouldn't dare,' shouted Rodrigo, 'I'd crush them.'

'Maybe that's what the Government is hoping for. A war between us would be doing their work for them, because I doubt whether the main reason for this offer is the safe return of the prisoners.'

'Are we no nearer discovering the identity of this traitor in our ranks?' Rodrigo growled, changing the subject for a moment.

'No compadre. I have stopped all shipments for the time being, so maybe it is a good time to talk.'

'But not directly, do it through Cali.'

During all his years in the drug business Alfred had maintained one basic rule above all else, never tell anyone everything, and that included his friend for over forty years. The envelope containing the details of Simon Halkin and Maria Sandino was far from complete, a crucial piece of information withheld, information which one day could save his life.

* * *

CALI, COLOMBIA

The most spectacular views of the city of Cali, apart from its 'Las Calenas' or beautiful women, were to be observed from the magnificent church of Iglesia de San Antonio, which was where Ernesto Videla found himself. He was not, however, interested in either the ladies or the scenery at that moment. The meeting with the man from Medellin was totally occupying his thoughts - the product of a coded telephone call. It had been short and to the point. 'Manana Calle 5' was the only instruction given, but the man would know its significance. The coded system had kept him anonymous - and so out of prison for over thirty years, literally living by his code. Everyone he dealt with had their own, exclusive to them, and apart from an initial enquiry he would never conduct business any other way. The man representing the Medellin drug cartel had been allocated a system based on a street map of Cali; it was simple and yet effective. Each Calle or

Avenue was given a number, next to which a rendezvous point had been allocated, chosen by him. The contact simply gave a number, and on this occasion that number corresponded with the church on the hill.

His portfolio of contacts and clients had, over the years, grown immeasurably, his expertise at providing anything, no matter how large or small, a legend in the dark circles in which he moved. Neither religious nor political, his master was dinero, of which he now had plenty, and yet because of his clandestine business he had never been at liberty to enjoy it fully. Sitting at the rear of the church, he watched the man approach the small side chapel opposite, placing a plain brown envelope next to the ornate font and not leaving his pew until ten minutes after the man had left. Quickly collecting the envelope, he made his exit out through the vestry, noting that it was addressed to the Head of the PIP in Bogotá.

* * *

FCO, LONDON

Charles Barnard was about to get into his coat prior to leaving for his flat, when the phone rang. It was Derek Bevan.

'How did your meeting go?'

'As I expected from the mother, lots of tears, but the father kept it together very well.'

'What is your first impression of him?'

'I'm convinced that he won't be fobbed off with bureaucratic jargon and empty promises, and he strikes me as being fairly resourceful when he needs to be.'

'Could this be one of those occasions?'

'Maybe. But it's difficult to see what he could do on his own.'

Charles Barnard wished the backbench Member of Parliament for Hartlepool the compliments of the season. Bevan would never rise above mediocrity, he thought. The one thing you never did in politics was to underestimate people.

CHAPTER ELEVEN
Bogotá, Colombia

The 'poet' knew instinctively that he would not be spending Christmas with Anne and Sara - he was becoming too involved and he detested unfinished business. Since his arrival in the capital very little had happened and he was getting increasingly frustrated. He knew, however, that eventually the shit would hit the fan and he wanted to be there when it did. Although no Americans were officially listed as missing any more, he was more determined than ever to help apprehend those that had murdered them, and he couldn't do it from Fort Worth.

The day after his confrontation with the would-be thieves, Benito had taken him for a sightseeing tour of the city, pointing out, rather belatedly, areas where it was unsafe to venture. He had also mentioned to his guide that he was unhappy about the accommodation that had been provided, agreeing to move into the small office that had been provided by the Director of Inderena.

It was during the second week of his stay that Benito decided to take him further afield.

'We are going to take a trip to the outskirts of Medellin,' he announced, shaking him from a deep sleep one morning.

'How long will we be away?'

'Who knows, compadre? Two nights, maybe longer.'

'Any particular reason for this trip?'

'Guillermo wants you to see the area in which Betancur's estancia is situated.'

The drive through the city was as he expected - at breakneck speed, his driver showing no regard for other road users or pedestrians alike. His curiosity eventually got the better of him.

'When did you learn to drive Benito?'

'Long time ago, before I work for Guillermo. I am bodyguard for General Rene Barrientos, 'La Caudillo,' er, how you say, strongman of Bolivia, yes, that is it. I learn when I am with him, and because I am so good he made me his personal driver.'

This Barrientos must have been a little too fond of his own 'wacky baccy', he thought. Once on the new Bogotá to Medellin road he began to relax a little, taking in snatches of peasant life as they passed through small villages.

'What do you think of this hostage business, Benito?'

'We have a bloody history in our country, Sen̆or Hollingsworth. From the Incas and Conquistadors of many hundreds of years ago, to the FARC, ELN and EPL of today, life has always been cheap and we have accepted it. I think maybe that it is only because these missing people are foreigners that there is so much trouble, and if they have been given too much burundanga then we are too late to save them anyway.'

'What is this burundanga - a poison?'

'It is a drug made from the Borrachero tree. It has no taste or smell and can be put in anything - cigarettes, candy, beer or food, too much burundanga and you die. There have been many visitors here who have mistakenly taken maybe a drink or a cigarette from a stranger as a show of hospitality - only to find themselves under the influence of the burundanga and most of their possessions taken. You have a saying Seňor, beware Greeks bearing gifts, yes? That is good advice here in Colombia.'

He must have fallen asleep because it was afternoon when he felt the Landrover sharply come to a halt - throwing him forward slightly. They had stopped at a roadside café, and whilst he yawned and stretched, Benito provided some food and coffee.

'Tell me about this man Betancur.'

In between mouthfuls of chicken and rice he listened to Benito giving him a potted history of the cocaine smuggler, interrupting him when an unfamiliar name was mentioned.

'Who is this Alfred Jaramillo?'

'He is the long time friend of Rodrigo, they go back to the early days, and there was also a woman, but I don't know what happened to her.'

They had been on the road for nearly twelve hours when finally he caught sight of the city, set in a narrow valley and surrounded by forbidding mountains - barriers in nearly all directions. Entering the city from the north-west, Benito drove straight to a hotel named the 'Arod', situated about one and a half kilometres from the centre.

'I have been here with Guillermo,' he explained, 'it is safe and if he needs to contact us he will know where.'

* * *

PIP HEADQUARTERS, BOGOTÁ

The contents of the envelope lay on Henri's desk, a single sheet of paper and four photographs.

'Do we know when or by who it was delivered?'

Guillermo Garbanza shook his head.

'We will check the security camera of course, but the chances of us positively identifying anyone, probably disguised, from a photograph taken at night is remote.'

Together they spent some time scrutinizing the wording of the single document that lay before them. It contained four conditions;

1. The Drug Enforcement Agencies of both the USA and Colombia are to cease immediately, all interference in the business interests of LMA Shipping and Exports. This will continue for an indefinite period, during which time one or more of the hostages may be released.

2. The PIP is to publish, via a national newspaper, the name of any individual providing them with information involving the business interests of the above company.

3. The release of any impounded merchandise belonging to the above company.

4. We have enclosed photographs of the individuals who are at present held by us and are alive. For them to remain so depends on the above conditions being met.

Both men said it simultaneously.

'It's Betancur!'

'And what's more he knows about Emilio,' added Garbanza.

'Well he knows he has an informer, he obviously doesn't know who.' answered his boss.

They had known for a long time that the LMA Shipping and Export Company had on various occasions been used as a front for drug smuggling, and they had also known that it had been part-owned by no less a man than Rodrigo Betancur. He was obviously unaware that they held this information. And so he had made his first mistake, and although they were no nearer discovering the location of the hostages, they were both convinced in whose company they were being kept. Henri requested Bernice to contact the Minister whilst Gill listened to his boss's instructions.

'Where is our American friend at the moment?'

'Benito has taken him to Medellin for a few days, mainly to get the feel of the place.'

'Good. Tell him to stay there until he hears differently.'

On the way back to his office Guillermo reflected on the information contained in the envelope. Progress? Yes, but nothing really to get excited about. He knew for a fact that the Colombian Administration would never agree to the terms, and so they had approximately one month to locate the hostages and that included the rapidly approaching two week holiday period. It was the only time when the cartels showed any sign of benevolence, allowing the majority of their workers to return home for the various festivals. He wondered if Emilio would be one of them. Although the man's information had so far been mainly retrospective, he was the only link, tentative as it may be, with their adversary, and therefore it was time to give some serious thought to the possible identity of the man.

Reaching for the pen and notepad on his desk he began by putting his random thoughts on paper - a practice that had always enabled him to see things more clearly. Short, taped calls, asking for nothing in return, information accurate; it was as if the man was trying to destroy everything from the inside, but then why? He hadn't noticed Henri enter his office, suddenly startled by his boss's voice.

'You will not be surprised to hear that the Minister has told me to sit on the photographs and document, Guillermo.'

'Are you sure he said 'sit'?'

It was an unusual outburst of cynicism not unnoticed by Henri.

'I wasn't given a lot of choice, my friend.'

'Then we must wait for Emilio to make his, and hope he chooses us.'

* * *

If Byron had not been wearing the seatbelt he felt sure that he would now be sprawled on the bonnet of the Landrover.

'This is as far as we can go and still remain unnoticed,' said Benito.

They had taken the road to Honda initially, but after thirty kilometers turned off onto a dirt track and were now perched on a rock outcrop, prevented from continuing by a wooden gate. Crudely nailed to the gate was a notice indicating that any trespassers would be very fortunate to read the notice again.

'From here as far as the eye can see belongs to Betancur,' declared the Colombian.

The 'poet' gazed down at the spectacular landscape laid before him, such a crime that a man so steeped in evil should posses anything so beautiful.

'He who ascends to mountain tops, shall find
The loftiest peaks most wrapped in clouds and snow;
He who surpasses or subdues mankind,
Must look down on the hate of those below.'

He said it almost to himself, but his companion had overheard his utterances.

'What is that you speak of?'

'It is poetry, my friend. Written by my namesake many years ago, a strange member of the English aristocracy.'

'It is good, maybe you can teach me.'

He thought that educating the ex-bodyguard of a Bolivian drug smuggler as to the finer points of Lord Byron's verse would be akin to teaching a heavyweight boxer how to engrave pinheads.

'The hacienda must be well hidden, I don't see any sign of it.' The change of subject was deliberate.

'True. The only way of seeing it safely is from the air, and on the ground there is only one road in, always well guarded.'

The mobile telephone in the Landrover interrupted their conversation. It was answered by Benito, who sat in the passenger seat saying very little.

'It was Guillermo, we have to talk,' he stated, but there was no warmth in his voice.

They sat together in the vehicle discussing the details of the call, at the end of which, each of them waited for the other to speak. He took the initiative.

'Did he say when he wanted a reply?'

'He does not need one. The one who remains behind is to call him once the meeting has taken place.'

It was ten minutes before he spoke again.

'You will make the call, and I will tell you why it must be me that meets this man. I have experience of this type of work, and although it was a bad time for me I feel that I have something to prove to myself. Besides, Gill will expect it to be me. Also, should I need to get out in a hurry, I will need someone who knows the country, and that is as important as anything I may have to do.'

Benito offered no argument. Not because he was relieved that the American had volunteered, although that was true, but he knew that this man had come to Colombia knowing that at some point, the decision he had just made was inevitable. Silently they stood together on the rocky outcrop, each with his own thoughts, until this time it was Benito who spoke first.

'Let me buy you a beer in Medellin, compadre.'

* * *

The mysterious informer, known only as Emilio, made his choice a few days before Christmas. Garbanza took the phone call personally, and he knew immediately that this time the message was not taped.

'Señor Garbanza. This is Emilio.'

'Si, this is Garbanza.'

'In two days time, at noon, in the village of Carmen de Viboral, a truck will wait in the square for thirty minutes. The man in charge has orders to recruit temporary workers to look after stock over the festive period. He will also have orders to look for a man with a white Panama hat.'

The line went dead before he could say 'gracias', so he said it to himself, over and over again. For the first time in months he felt exhilarated. It was as if his body had discovered a new source of energy, and his walk to Henri's office had a spring to it that caused Bernice to smile. He felt sure that during the next few days, as the result of one phone call, he was about to achieve a major step forward towards a confrontation with Rodrigo Betancur. Henri's first question was predictable.

'Who will you send in?' Frowning when he heard the answer.

'I'm not sending anyone. It is their choice, and yet I know who it will be. Byron Hollingsworth hasn't come all this way to stand on the sidelines.'

He watched and waited for Henri's reaction, knowing that he was playing the devil's advocate with his own thoughts.

'When will you inform O'Grady?'

'At this time of the year he is probably on what they call a 'happy holiday', so there is no immediate need to let him know what is happening.'

'And the American's family?'

'I'm sure Byron will have considered them before he decides what course to take.'

The question and answer exercise went on for some time before Henri made his decision.

'Do it.'

The euphoria that he had experienced earlier had evaporated by the time he came to call Benito, fully recognizing the risks that he was about to ask his friends to undertake. And yet he had no choice.

* * *

How long they had been imprisoned in the cold, filthy and stench-filled room Simon had no way of knowing. The only thing of which he was certain was their deteriorating state of health. Neither of them had been allowed to wash and, denied the use of a brush or comb, their hair felt like coconut matting. The English-speaking man had not returned, and the guards seemed to show more interest in the local drink, 'chicha', than them, which he was not too unhappy about. Maria however was causing him some concern, sleeping and being constantly sick for much of the day, and he suspected that her experience with the guard had caused her to go into shock for a time. He noticed too, that he was beginning to develop spots and sores all over his body, the physical evidence of some unknown visitor, feeding on him during the hours of darkness - a frequent occurrence. He shook Maria gently.

'Maria you must try to walk.'

She turned on her side, curling her slender body as small as she could make it, and mumbling incoherently in Spanish. Although light in weight, he soon felt the effort of manoeuvring her around their prison, and after only a few minutes they both collapsed into the pile of straw and newspaper. She was now clutching her stomach and moaning loudly, her skin hot to the touch, the poncho wet with perspiration. Staggering to the stairs he managed to climb to the top and banged on the doors at the same time shouting for help.

'¡Un médico, por favor! Please, please help us.'

Careering down the rough wooden stairs was the last thing he remembered.

How long he had remained unconscious again he did not know. What he did realize however, was that they were in a different place. Not able to raise his head fully, he could see enough of the room to know that their cellar had been exchanged for a cabin, and that it contained four bunk-type beds, two of which he and Maria were now occupying. He was also aware that his clothes had been removed - covered now by only a thin colourful blanket, whilst in one corner a large black woman sat reading.

'Por favor,' he croaked, and saw her look in his direction.

'Espero,' was all she said, and then hurriedly left the cabin.

The next face he saw belonged to the English-speaking man who had ordered the execution of the guard, and who was now peering down at him and feeling his pulse.

'How are you feeling?'

'Better. But how is Maria?'

'She is better also.'

He closed his eyes, relaxing a little in the knowledge that although they were still the prisoners of this man, he had obviously played his part in their recovery.

'What is wrong with us?'

'The doctor said you are suffering from bacillary dysentery, and so has left you some tablets to take. I will see that you get them at the appropriate time, together with food and fresh water.'

'Thank you.' He offered his hand, but it was ignored.

'Do not take my concern for you and your friend as a sign of weakness, Simon Halkin. You are still confined here and will remain so until we decide otherwise.'

As Simon watched him leave he thought of two things. The first was that the man believed who he said he was, so he presumably now had their documents. The other was that he had been reminded in no uncertain terms that the man was still a menacing and cold cocaine smuggler.

Irrespective of whatever else he was the man kept to his word, the large black woman ensuring that they took their tablets with every meal during the next few days. They were fed the same food as their jailers - plato montanero. Maria explained that it was a variation of ground beef or salt pork but always with rice and green banana. The improvement in diet and the prescribed drugs had seen a substantial improvement in her health. She had even taken to helping the black woman clean the cabin, although not a word passed between them. The guards also said very little, content to talk amongst themselves, drink and sleep, although there was always one who remained fully alert.

It was late one night as they lay in their respective bunks that she broached the subject of home, never mentioned by either of them until then.

'What do you think our parents will be thinking, Simon?'

'I think they will be as unhappy as we are, maybe more so,' he replied, knowing only too well that George and Joan would be at their wit's end with worry.

'And we will not have Christmas, with a tree and lights, baubles, a fairy or litter.'

'Glitter,' he corrected her, knowing that such a slip under normal circumstances would have had them both laughing.

He knew that she had never tired of hearing about the arrangements that his parents would be making for their arrival. The stocking which his mother would hang on the mantelpiece, now decorative, but a reminder of when he and Nick were both small. The huge dinner which she would be expected to eat and the crackers which they would pull. Dropping silently to the floor from his bunk he knelt at her side, holding her head gently in his hands.

'Why do you look at me so, Simon?'

'Because I care for you,' he replied, stroking her hair.

'Will we soon be safe?'

'I can't answer that, but we must try very hard not to give into these people, and as long as we stay together we will be okay.'

'I will think of the Christmas tree.'

Returning to his bunk he lay awake for some time. So like her, he thought, no one knows where we are, the prisoners of dangerous and evil men, and yet she thinks of a Christmas tree. He knew at that moment however, that it was the naïvety of her that was turning his caring into something more.

⋆ ⋆ ⋆

One of the problems associated with drinking strange beer was that not only were you unaware of the quality of the product, but of the quantity you were capable of consuming. At ten o'clock next morning, had Byron been thinking clearly, he would have borne testimony to that very fact. They had toured, he estimated, every bar within a two kilometre radius of the hotel, until they found a man who had carelessly left his white Panama hat on the seat beside him on visiting the toilet, only to find it missing when he returned.

'How are you feeling, compadre?' asked Benito mischievously.

'Do I know you?' he replied, not lifting his head from the pillow. Every movement of his mouth was an effort, just managing to force his lips apart to drink the dark-green liquid which his companion had given him.

'Why did we have to steal the hat? Why couldn't we have bought one?'

'Where? This is not Washington, most places are closed for the holidays.'

He felt his eyes closing, unable to ask any more questions.

Two hours later he awoke from a deep sleep, feeling more refreshed than he had in his whole life, and feeling hungry.

'What was in that drink?' he asked, realizing the marketing potential of an instant cure for hangovers.

'It is better that you don't know, my friend. One thing I will tell you, try taking it back to America and you will find yourself in a lot of trouble.'

Over a meal of chicken and rice in the hotel restaurant they talked of the forthcoming operation, Benito reminding him of a few survival fundamentals.

'The moment I leave you in Carmen de Viboral you are completely on your own. Trust no one, these people have eyes and ears everywhere. Never ask questions and remember that the man who hires you may not be involved with the informant. Guillermo does not know why this Emilio wants us on the inside, therefore you will have to think on your feet and handle any problems in your own way. Finally, if for any reason you think that your cover has been compromised, or that your life is in danger, head for the village of El Retiro. Unfortunately I can't tell you how to get there, because I don't know where you will be taken, but I will wait for you there for as long as it takes.'

'What if I have information for Gill?'

'Then the informant will contact him. That is not your concern, is that clear?'

He nodded. But he wasn't happy about working so completely in the dark, and so they scrutinized a map of the area for the remainder of the afternoon, until he felt a little more familiar with the location of the rendezvous point.

When they had finished it was early evening, and he knew that he couldn't put off doing any longer what he should have done earlier - and that was to ring his wife and tell her that he wouldn't be home for Christmas.

⋆ ⋆ ⋆

Rodrigo hated holidays and festivals, not least because it was about families uniting, the renewing of longstanding friendships, neither of which he had put much faith in, apart from Alfred. He knew that he could have had the pick of the world's most beautiful women, but that would have meant sharing his wealth, and so the selfish part of him had made his life one of loneliness and mistrust. He watched his friend remove his boots, as he had a thousand times before, and then walk over to the table on which he placed a report of the month's business.

'Have the peasants started leaving yet?'

'Si, the rest will leave tomorrow, Rodrigo.'

'And their replacements?'

'I am sending one of my most trusted men to Carmen de Viboral to recruit men who will be suitable.'

'You trust too easily Alfred. You must be careful, at this time of year we are always at our most vulnerable to the infiltration of our enemies. If it will prove a point, shoot one of the remaining hostages, but keep it quiet.'

He listened, but knew that he had no intention of shooting anyone just to make a point to a few peasants.

'How are they?'

'They are hostages, and as such will learn to survive until we decide otherwise. If they die - then it will save us a bullet.'

He knew it was what Rodrigo wanted to hear.

'Good. That is all for now.'

Alfred put on his newly-polished boots and left.

CHAPTER TWELVE
Hartlepool

It was normally a warm house - one of those dwellings built during the early part of the century by men who had yet to hear of breeze blocks. And yet, returning from the meeting with Derek Bevan, George found it devoid of any warmth.

Suddenly he felt exhausted, worn out by the news of his son's disappearance. But it was more than that - he felt angry. It was anger aimed at himself, and he knew that it was misplaced, but that was the way he felt and until he saw Simon again it would remain with him. Questions filled his head. Why hadn't he been more inquisitive as to where his son was going? Insisted on an itinerary. What was he intending to visit and for how long? And yet he knew that he had faced every parent's dilemma, how much to ask and say, content to let Simon make his own way across the world. Part of the anger reflected his inability to help find a solution to the problem - the hoped for successful outcome in the hands of complete strangers, which was completely alien to him. All his adult life he had been concerned with the solving of other people's problems. As a young man serving his country and its inhabitants all over the world, and latterly doing a similar thing for his county. Now, when the problem was on his own doorstep, he was helpless to do anything but listen to the likes of Bevan telling him that 'everything was being done', which they both knew was meant to pacify, rather than inject confidence.

He saw Joan light another cigarette, her hands shaking uncontrollably, her eyes glazed and seeing nothing but her offspring's pain.

'Why don't you go to bed?'

'I wouldn't be able to sleep anyway. What are we going to do, George?' her voice trembling and hoarse.

He leaned forward, holding his head in his hands, fighting back the tears that he knew were there, but now was not the time.

'I don't know. All we can do for the moment is wait and see if the diplomats can come up with something.'

'Will you tell Nick when he comes home?'

He nodded, as he watched her wearily climb the stairs.

The night seemed to last an eternity, a mixture of hand-rolled cigarettes and coffee his only companions, until at some point, just as it was getting light, he must have dropped off to sleep.

It was the key turning in the lock that woke him, for a moment a feeling of panic, as he realized who it was and what he must tell him.

'Couldn't sleep, Dad?'

'No. Make me a coffee will you, son?'

By the time Nick walked back into the room he had prepared himself for the ordeal ahead.

'Sit down, Nick.'

As he told him of the previous night's events, he noticed for the first time things about him that before that morning had seemed insignificant. The colour of his eyes and hair, the way he fidgeted with his tie, the small scar over his eye that he had forgotten about - sustained during his days as an amateur boxer.

'Did they say when we could expect any news?'

'No, but I wouldn't be surprised if it was later, rather than sooner.'

For some time after Nick had gone to bed - tired after a busy night of fire calls, he sat thinking, becoming more morose by the minute, until a Christmas card on the mantelpiece caught his eye. It was from the local Council and had been specifically sent to Simon - as it was every year, in recognition of his sporting achievements and the credit it brought to the town. Since eleven years of age he had been active in a number of sports, representing the town and county at rugby until leaving for University. He had even been awarded a 'Rising Star' award - an honour presented by the Council to young men and women who showed more than average potential in their chosen sport. The card contained a verse, which until now had seemed trite and not really in the spirit of Christmas, but suddenly it was relevant. As he read the verse, he felt the emotions of the last twenty-four hours surge through his body, the tears dropping onto the open card.

'I'll lend you for a little while a child of mine', he said.
For you to love the time he lives and mourn for when he's dead.
It may be six or seven years, or twenty-two or three,
But will you till I call him back, take care of him for me?
He'll bring his charms to gladden you, and should his stay be brief,
You'll have his lovely memories as solace for your grief.
'I cannot promise he will stay, since all from earth return,
But there are lessons taught down there I want this child to learn.
I've looked the wide world over in my search for teacher true, and
From the throngs that crowd life's lanes, I have selected you.
Now will you give him all your love, nor think the labour vain,
Nor hate me when I come to call, to take him back again?
I fancied that I heard them say, 'Dear Lord, thy will be done!

For the joy thy child shall bring, the risk of grief we'll run.
We'll shelter him with tenderness, we'll love him while we may,
And for the happiness we've known, forever grateful stay.
But should the angels call for him much sooner than we've planned,
We'll brave the bitter grief that comes....and try to understand.'

The verse was attributed to no one in particular, but obviously written by a grieving parent at the death of a child, and although the unthinkable had not yet happened, he wondered whether in the scheme of things, the Guardian of Destiny was about to call.

⋆ ⋆ ⋆

FORT WORTH

Anne was holding Sara, so that she could place the newly-made fairy on top of the Christmas tree, when the telephone rang.

'Hi babe, it's me Byron, everything okay?'

At first the echo made it difficult for her to hear clearly.

'It's a terrible line, but yes everything is fine. When will you be home?'

She knew instinctively that the delay wasn't caused by the quality of the line.

'Byron, you are coming home for Christmas, aren't you?'

'I'm afraid not Anne, something has come up here that I just can't leave.'

'This is the work of that bastard O'Grady, isn't it?' She could feel herself losing control.

'At the moment I doubt whether he knows what's happening, so don't go and give him a hard time. There's nothing he can do anyway.'

'So when can Sara expect her father home?' She knew that she was being unfair, but it was her concern for him that was making her say things that she didn't really mean.

'I don't rightly know, I suppose the answer is, as long as it takes.'

They talked about family and Christmas, until there was nothing else left to say.

'Be careful Byron, and we'll be thinking of you.'

She sat with Sara on her knee, stroking her hair, thinking about the man she cared for, so far away. Everything had been fine since his move to El Paso. There had been no more worries about the dangers he faced in the field, the bad experience years before overcome. And it had been bad. Lots of sleepless nights, mood swings - all the symptoms of post-traumatic stress turning her man into a complete stranger. It had taken years for him to completely recover from his ordeal - as it would anyone coming that close to a violent death. And then O'Grady had sent him to Curaçao. Had it been to test him, to see if he was able to go back into the field? Not that it mattered, in the end Byron himself had decided that he had something to prove. But at what cost?

'When is daddy coming home?' The question asked between large yawns.

'He has some business to finish, and then when he does come we will have another Christmas.'

As she carried Sara up to her room she thought of her husband's unnecessary chivalry. He had never fully confided in her, preferring to hide behind a man who had been dead for over a century and a half - using him as a cloak. During the desperate days of his depression he had even written about it, including it in a poem which he had given her some time after his recovery. She found it in the box containing photographs and old birthday cards, then sat silently, reading his words.

This family has been my salvation,
Saved me from turmoil and grief,
To you who helped me achieve it,
My gratitude, for your belief.
Discarded my cloak of indifference,
Broken the shell that I made,
Revealing at last true emotions,
Gone the role that I played.
Released from my bondage of pretence,
I now can enjoy every breath,
Give my soul to you, who matter,
Until comes the time of my death.
My destiny not yet made clear, I
Pray that in years yet to be, I
Continue, like I have endeavoured,
To love you, mine own family.
Ab uno disce omnes, absolvi meam animam.
Byron T Hollingsworth.

She remembered asking him what was the significance of the Latin quotation.

'It reflects what I feel, Anne, 'from one learn all, I have relieved my mind,' he had replied.

But he hadn't - not completely. She folded the single sheet of paper and placed it back in the box. Maybe what he was doing in Colombia was the answer he was looking for.

* * *

BOGOTÁ

Henri walked to the filing cabinet and removed the bottle of port. He wasn't a prolific drinker - the bottle kept primarily for special occasions, or for the visit of a fellow police chief. Half filling the two glasses he handed one to Guillermo.

'What will you do over the holiday period, compadre?'

'I will probably spend most of it here. My friend has returned to her family for Christmas and so I need something to occupy my time.'

'You know you are welcome to spend a few days at my home.' But he knew that the offer, like so many before, would be refused.

'Thank you, Henri, but I have this man in my sights after all these years, and I am afraid of losing him.'

'I have never asked you this before, Guillermo, but why this obsession with Betancur? You have known many evil men in the past and yet his freedom gives you so much pain.' He waited, watching his friend finish the port in his glass.

'I was eight years old when my father first took me with him. I would sit on the sacks of coca as he pushed the cart, and he would laugh at me as I sang a silly song, something about 'coco makes you loco', I think that's what it was. We had a small piece of land - given to us by the Government, not much, but enough on which to grow some vegetables and a small crop of the coca leaf. Once a month, my father would sell his three sacks of leaf to a local dealer, who paid him only enough on which to survive. It was during one of these trips that we were ambushed by what we thought at first were local thugs, my father, a stubborn man, refusing to hand over the leaf.

They were all well armed, and yet he still refused, until one of the men shot him. I quite naturally was in hysterics, and yet still managed to hear the killer's parting words, 'Rodrigo Betancur thanks you for your donation'. From that day to this the man has haunted me, and although he did not do the shooting, it was done in his name and therefore in my eyes he is responsible.'

Henri poured him another glass of port.

'What of the rest of your family?'

'My mother died shortly after the death of my father. The remaining brothers and sister staying with the land, except for my youngest brother who moved to El Retiro and owns a bar there. Not a bad place for Benito to spend his time.'

They sat quietly enjoying the port until the bottle was empty, leaving the building together. Henri felt full of festive cheer, looking forward to the holiday, quite the opposite to his companion's disposition - which he knew had more to do with revenge than Christmas.

⋆ ⋆ ⋆

IBARRA

The period of prayer was longer that night, the message from the Embassy in Quito compelling them to spend more time than usual in front of the statue of the Madonna. The telegram had been short - informing them only that Maria and her English friend where missing somewhere in Colombia. She had hoped that the killing of a river guide on the Peruvian-Colombian border had in no way affected the plans of her granddaughter, but following the arrival of the telegram, Hermania had suspected the worst. Her fears were confirmed the following day, as the local newspaper declared that the two friends had been taken hostage - adding to the growing list of missing tourists. She sat, like she had for many nights, letting the rosary slide through her wrinkled hands and wishing she was thirty years younger, when she would have been more than capable of going in search of the youngsters. She looked across the room at Maria's father, not a bad man, but weak and devoid of any imagination or ambition, prepared to sit and wait for his daughter's return. Maybe she was being unfair, what could he do anyway? The same applied to the boy's father, a man she had never met or seen who at this moment was thousands of miles away, with no hope of even attempting to find his son. She could not visualize what the boy's family were feeling at that moment, and so she said five Hail Marys dedicated to them. Her faith was all that she now felt counted in life, never once doubting that there was a God, not even at that moment. It was too easy to blame Him for all the world's evil doings when in fact most were the actions of non-believers. And anyway, sometimes God needed a helping hand from mere mortals to punish the wicked.

⋆ ⋆ ⋆

CARMEN de VIBORAL

Byron was sure about two things. Firstly, that the market place was about the size of a basketball court and secondly, that everyone from within a hundred kilometres of the small town had chosen that day to visit it. Benito had dropped him off on the outskirts of town and he had walked down the steep hill - taking in the picturesque houses and tidy gardens. He had decided to reach the town three hours ahead of the pick up time, hoping to sharpen his Spanish by engaging the locals in conversation, which he did immediately.

'¿Permiso Señor, estoy buscando un hotel cerano?'

The man had pointed to a hotel on the opposite side of the square.

'Gracias.'

Ordering a beer he chose a table giving him a complete view of the square, whilst at the same time enjoying the warm sunshine, although regretting the fact that he could not be with Anne and Sara in the comparatively cold climate of Texas.

The informant however was no fool. His choice of the holiday period quite deliberate in getting someone into the organization, and the minimum number of people knowing about it, including those on Garbanza's staff.

He spotted the green station wagon making its way down the hill. And then after making a tour of the square, it stopped some distance away, facing the way it had come, it's engine still running. Waiting until the last possible minute, he ambled over and confronted the driver, a large, rough-looking individual wearing a Castro-type hat, the large lump at his waistline indicating that he was armed.

'Estoy buscando trabaja,' he said quietly, deliberately not looking directly at the man.

'¿De donde es?' The man spraying him with saliva as he spat out the words.

'El Retiro, señor,' giving him the name of the village with which Benito was so familiar, and therefore he had been well briefed.

'Que hace.'

Byron raised his arms and hunched his shoulders, a gesture meaning nothing in particular, to which the man grunted and indicated that he should board the station wagon.

In all, there were eight men crammed into the back of the vehicle as they left the square, men who had no idea of their destination, or maybe even their future. He looked around at his companions from beneath lowered eyes. They were a mixed bunch - ranging from the half-clean to the peasant sitting next to him, who emitted a stench that was already making him feel nauseous.

Approximately a kilometre out of town the wagon came to a halt and filthy, black bags were placed over their heads - completely shutting out both the sunshine and the view, the latter being the obvious intention. The journey continued in complete silence. The only noise coming from the wagon tyres as they made their way along a series of rutted tracks, of which there were plenty in that part of the country. Trying to plot their progress was impossible. They could be going around in circles, he thought, so any attempt at measuring time was pointless.

How long they had sat in the darkness before their transport stopped would have been complete guesswork, but suddenly the wagon came to a gradual halt, and shortly after the hood was removed. At first everything was bright yellow, but as his eyes became accustomed to the light he could make out two men some distance away having discussions with the driver. Eventually they all approached the rear of the vehicle - the best dressed of the three casting his eyes over his new workers.

On removal of the hood he had immediately donned the dirty white Panama hat, the sign of recognition requested by the informant. He waited, wondering what would have happened if there had been two of them, noting however, that his companions wore either straw hats or bandanas. The well-dressed man pointed at him and his stinking companion, who he had nicknamed 'Mell'. They were immediately bundled unceremoniously to the ground from where they watched the station wagon disappear.

Regaining his feet he was aware that there was now only one man with them, dressed in green camouflage and carrying a small machine gun he shepherded them down a steep track at the end of which lay a small clearing.

The sun was still high in the sky, so he estimated that it hadn't taken them that long to get here, his watch having been removed at the same time as his wedding ring and in the safe keeping of Benito.

There were three cabins in the clearing spaced approximately ten metres apart, and it was to the middle one of them that he and Mell were directed, pushed through an open door that was instantly closed. The inside of the cabin bore more than a passing resemblance to a refuse dump, the permanent inhabitants obviously possessing the domestic habits of a wild animal, although he doubted whether Mell would notice.

Sitting on the edge of a broken bunk bed, not daring to expose any more of his body to the filthy mattress than was necessary, he took stock of what was to be his living quarters for the unforeseeable future, and it didn't take long. The cabin consisted of six beds, the same number of rickety chairs and a table, whilst in one corner a sink filled with cracked or broken crockery appeared to be only just secured to the wall. The stench from both his companion and his accommodation was already overpowering and eventually forced him outside where he sat leaning against the side of his cabin, making mental notes of the location.

The clearing was situated at the bottom of a track, and as he had noticed previously, contained three cabins, one of which was positioned further away from the others, and outside of which sat three armed guards. Through the trees he could see that the upper part of the track terminated at a large house, only part of which was visible. It was however an important part, because directly in front of it was a pillar supporting an iron gate. During his basic training to be an agent the instructors and trainees had talked at length about the importance of accurate and detailed reconnaissance, great emphasis being placed on landmarks. Terrain, treelines, and even the position of the sun were all important. But it was objects like the one at which he was now looking that could pinpoint locations, and that object was a winged horse sitting on top of the column. A shout from one of the guards opposite, followed by an instruction to return inside brought his 'recce' to a halt. But he had seen enough, and he suspected that the cabin, which was being so well guarded, contained what he had been sent to find.

CHAPTER THIRTEEN

It was Nick's turn to be on rota that Christmas and he had been looking forward to it - particularly as his brother and Maria were spending it with them. He had never been one for spending a lot of time or money on presents, but this year had made an exception - painstakingly trying to find something special for the South American girl. It would have been her first taste of an English Christmas, but now, neither of them would experience it, which was the reason he had joined his parents in the living room. They sat staring at the television that had been continually tuned to one or other of the news channels since news of Simon's disappearance had reached them. Joan had lavishly decorated the room; no expense had been spared in her search for novelties and tree accessories. Even his father - who normally exhibited apathy to the whole process - had provided them with a real tree this year upon learning that Maria had never seen one.

His mother looked frail and tired, slumped on the sofa still wearing the dressing gown that had been her constant companion for the last 48 hours, and his father looked no better, solemnly breaking the silence.

'We now know that Simon won't be coming home as we expected, in fact we don't have any idea of when we will see him again. Under the circumstances it seems unthinkable that any of us could enjoy Christmas without him. So the question is, what do we do?'

He waited for Joan to wipe away more tears, and for his son to collect his thoughts.

'We should wait for him, maybe it won't be too long.'

It was Nick who put into words, what until then had only been in their thoughts, but it was his wife who went further.

'We should wait for both of them!' She paused, taking a deep breath. 'This will be the first Christmas that we have not been all together.'

She stood, and then walked over to the tree and switched off the lights.

'The day my son comes home will be the day that they are switched back on.'

George watched her leave the room. As with so many other women - he was *her* son, never ours, as if he had played no part in Simon's conception.

'What about you son, will you open your presents?'

'They will keep,' he replied, knowing that his mother wouldn't be sat watching him open them, something which gave her a great deal of pleasure. It was embarrassing sometimes the way she still put out the sacks that she had kept since their childhood, but they had never complained - understanding her reasons for doing it.

The ringing of the doorbell prevented any further conversation between them. It was Anthea, Nick's girlfriend. George waited for her to poke her blonde head around the living room door and ask how he was, like she normally did, but she didn't, and he knew then that it had begun. It would be like this until the problem was resolved, he thought, like people diagnosed as having cancer, friends and even family felt uncomfortable, not quite sure of what to say. He heard them whispering in the hallway and then minutes later Anthea made an appearance.

'How are you, Mr. Halkin?'

He felt sorry for her, she was only a young girl and still growing in confidence, but yet to attain the maturity of adulthood.

'I'm okay,' he lied.

She did her best to find something constructive to say, but after five minutes he suggested that her and Nick take a walk downtown.

Left on his own he reflected on earlier years, recalling the time when the two boys had been particularly fractious.

'I've cancelled Christmas this year,' he had joked. 'Santa wrote me a letter and said that because you both have been misbehaving he wasn't calling at this house.'

Joan hadn't been amused, and told him.

'That's a terrible thing to say George, think of all the people in the world without children, and who would change places with us tomorrow.'

Could it be that the remark had come back to haunt him? Chastisements by some malevolent force for his attempt at sick humour.

It was a joke no longer. The three of them had decided that Christmas in the Halkin household had been put on hold.

* * *

'What is it Simon?' She had seen him hurriedly make his way to the only window in the cabin.

'One of the guards is shouting at a peasant worker and ordering him to go inside.'

'I saw some of them leaving,' her voice only just above that of a whisper. 'They will be going home for the holiday.'

He could see the way she was feeling and so he put on a brave show for her.

'So will we Maria, very soon.'

'And we will have no Christmas.'

He thought frantically of a way to prevent her dark mood turning to despair.

'Sit down and I will tell you why we will not miss anything.'

They sat facing each other at the table as he tried to remember the sermon he had been compelled to sit through at Sunday school.

'When I was small, a man told me a story and now I will tell it to you. As you know, two thousand years ago Jesus was born in a stable in Bethlehem and to celebrate his birth, three kings brought him precious gifts, the most precious in all of the world. They travelled very far to bring him these gifts, in fact so far that they did not reach the stable until a long time after he was born. Upon entering the stable they said to Mary, 'We are sorry that we have missed the birth of your son, but we have brought him these gifts,' and they laid them next to the crib. She replied that because they had undertaken a difficult journey and yet still come, they should rejoice all the more. 'My son has no need of your gifts, it is you who are precious to him.'

He paused, surprised and pleased that he had remembered the story after so long.

'So you see Maria, Christmas can be any time that we want to make it, and we will have it, I promise.'

She had always been content with the simple things in life. But simple she was not, and she understood exactly what he had tried to do for her. Lapsing into deep thought she recalled her excitement on being told by her mother that she could return to England. The pleasure of buying presents for Simon's family on their return to Quito. A bottle of Tequila for Nick, liqueurs for George and earrings for Joan, but now in the hands of thieves and murderers.

Where the idea came from was a mystery, but suddenly he became aware of an urge to decorate the cabin. Encouraging a perplexed Maria to collect as many old newspapers and magazines as she could find, he set about collecting the many discarded bottle tops, of which there were plenty due to their guards insatiable appetite for the 'chicha'. He then showed her how to tear and fold the paper in order to form patterns, and then once completed they hung them around the cabin, much to the amusement of the black woman and even the guards.

'Now I will make you something special, close your eyes and don't open them until I tell you,' he said, smiling.

Again using the newspapers and magazines he made her a Christmas tree, on which he hung the bottle tops, suspended by threads taken from his poncho, and placing it on the table told her she could now look. He could see her eyes filling with tears, the first time for days, as she touched the twinkling bottle tops.

'It is very nice,' she sniffled, reaching for his hand, 'thank you.'

'Buenos, seňor.'

It was the first time the large woman had said anything remotely aimed at him since their arrival, so he took her acknowledgement of his expertise as a double compliment. Sitting down at the table she proceeded to hold a conversation with Maria, maybe she too was feeling lonely at such a time of year, he thought.

'She tells me that her husband and two sons were killed during the violent '80s, but Alfred gave her a position here, looking after the peasants and guards. I feel a little sorry for her, this is all she has, Simon.'

He agreed. It wasn't much of a life as he watched her disappear behind the curtain, which was her space, to prepare the evening meal.

'What are you thinking?'

The question startled him, and he was undecided whether to tell her not.

'You can be honest with me, you know.'

'Of home, what we would have been doing, what everyone else is doing.'

Her smile caught him by surprise, a rare occurrence since their imprisonment.

'You English, you show your unhappiness so silently, instead of talking about it, yes?'

The sudden appearance of the English-speaking man prevented him from answering her, and then causing them to give each other questioning looks as he placed a bottle of wine and three glasses on the Spartan table.

'I will not add to your personal discomfort by wishing you good health, but accept this drink in the manner in which it is given. Unfortunately for us all, business is exactly that.'

They both accepted the drink - but without thanks, savouring the taste of something that wasn't brackish.

'What day is it?' Maria spoke for both of them.

'It is Christmas Day,' he replied.

'Can you tell us how long we will be here?'

'That, Simon Halkin, is one question I cannot answer. I have no idea of what the future holds for you, but I will say this to you, there is a passage in the Bible from

Matthew which states, 'a man's enemies will be the members of his own household'. I do not expect you to understand at the moment, but remember what I have said.'

He left them, no wiser, but for some reason with a little hope.

* * *

Byron knew exactly what day it was, it was the day his wife and daughter would be sat around the Christmas tree opening their gifts, whilst his would remain untouched until his return. He had been awake early after a torturous night, his companion's incessant snoring and the smell in the cabin allowing only short periods of sleep. It had also been early when one of the guards had burst into the hovel, issuing them with various tasks; him assigned to feeding the stock twice a day which consisted of pigs, chickens and a few cattle. His duties also included collecting the newly-laid eggs that he was to hand to a guard, who in turn took them to the cabin at which they spent so much time.

It was a blessed relief to be out in the open again, and for a second time he took the opportunity to become aware of his surroundings. The clearing was halfway up a valley, with heavily wooded hills on three sides and a track winding its way through the open end, reminding him of the early westerns he liked to watch, when the cowboys would herd the stolen horses into a dead-end canyon. Below the clearing was the stockyard, a cluster of roughly assembled shacks containing the livestock, whilst again, on every side of the valley some sort of crop flourished as far as the treeline.

He discovered very quickly that feeding corn to the chickens required the concentration span of a ventriloquist's dummy, and so his thoughts turned to his present situation and specifically what he was now supposed to do. He assumed that the man who had met them and subsequently pointed to him, was in some way involved with the informer, if not the man himself, but no contact had yet been made so it was purely supposition. Still, he had been there less than 48 hours and the informer was unlikely to shake his hand and spill the beans as soon as he had arrived.

The guarded cabin posed another question. Although there had not been any physical evidence as such, he felt that all the indications were that some of the inhabitants hadn't pre-booked with their local travel agent. Deciding that at present he could do nothing about those two problems he concentrated on something he needed desperately to know about, and that was the direction of El Retiro. He remembered the advice from Benito about not asking questions or being too inquisitive, so asking 'Mell' was out of the question. The more he thought about it, the fewer the options became until he resigned himself to the fact that there was only one. To take the chance of heading over one of the hills could easily end in disaster, and so he decided that when push came to shove he would follow the track through the neck of the valley.

The incident happened quite by accident as he and 'Mell' were returning to the cabin at the end of the day. A young man, hands thrust deep into his pockets, was making his way to the sentry-box sized toilet accompanied by a guard. Byron immediately laid his hand on the shoulder of his companion urging him to slow down and take in the fresh air. He waited for the boy to leave the toilet, and noticing that the guard lagged well behind, quickly walked in front of him and collapsed on the ground holding his chest. The boy was at his side very quickly.

'What is your name? Tell me, hurry.'

He saw the astonished look on the boy's face as he answered.

'Simon Halkin, I am English.'

And then the guard and 'Mell' joined them.

Still holding his chest he was roughly helped to his feet, and told to go to the cabin, any enquiries about the state of his health being totally absent. But even if his complaint had been genuine, the short exchange with the boy would have made him feel a hell of a lot better.

Sitting silently on his bunk bed he made a mental note of all the information he had so far gathered, even congratulating himself on his progress in such a short time. The fact that he had identified the house as having two winged horses at the front gate would have been enough to contact Gill, but now having obtained positive proof that the hostages where being kept there made contact with Benito imperative.

The information however posed questions that put his next move in doubt. He had partially infiltrated the cartel due to the efforts of the informer who was in possession of the same information as himself, so why hadn't he passed it on? No, he decided, there was more to this than met the eye. The phrase 'bigger picture' was one that came to mind, he thought, and at the moment he hadn't even seen the 'trailer'. For the first time since he had left Washington he began to wonder whether O'Grady had been straight with him. He was even beginning to doubt the reasons he had been given for his attendance at the meeting in Curaçao. Had that been part of the plan also? As he lay on his bunk listening to the snores of his fellow worker, his final thought before falling asleep was that his reason for being where he was had become too fucking obscure.

⋆ ⋆ ⋆

WASHINGTON DC

The 'happy', in 'happy holiday' had in Mike O'Grady's case disappeared some years before. It wasn't that he was unhappy, he would just have preferred to have spent that particular Christmas at his desk, although he knew perfectly well that further progress wasn't possible. The bottle of Southern Comfort had been full when he had taken it out of the cabinet earlier that evening, now it was barely half, and his wife had noticed.

'Something on your mind Mike?'

'Mm, just work.'

'It's not like you, bringing the Agency home with you.'

She was right as usual. He had never had a problem with switching off once out of the office, maybe he was rediscovering the emotion of compassion, or was it just that he had committed a man he liked and respected to an uncertain future. He had preferred the uncomplicated Narcotics Bureau, not happy at being an offshoot of the centralized Justice Department. The Administration had fallen for the fallacy that bigger meant better. It didn't, it led to an overlapping of interests and the very situation that now weighed heavily on his mind. Since the dissolution of the Bureau and the inauguration of the DEA his organization had become increasingly involved with covert operations instigated mainly by the FBI, and occasionally with the CIA. He had never felt happy collaborating with either, and it was the latter of the two that was now the main cause of his discontent.

'Does it concern Byron?'

She had met him on only three occasions, but his open and friendly manner had been to her liking, and she also knew that her husband felt the same.

'He's involved, yes.'

She left it there, knowing better than to push him on the subject and continued reading.

The 'poet' had been involved since he had agreed to attend the meeting in Curaçao one year before, a meeting instigated by the CIA with well-intentioned motives but a highly dangerous format. They had received information, as only they could, that a certain Bolivian politician, namely Ricardo Punta, was planning to take over a major Colombian cartel. To implicate him however, purely on hearsay, was impossible. But what gave the story its credibility was that for some time he had been unhappy with his own organization's ability to produce the finished cocaine and then distribute it. Punta was no fool, aware that the huge profits came from the drug's export and not as he was doing, simply supplying the coca leaf.

As Director of the DEA - and since it was a drug-related matter, he had been instructed to send an agent to the meeting to achieve, if possible, three things. That agent had been Byron and he been instructed in the first instance to gauge the possible commitment of the South Americans to a plan involving the abolition of coca production. Secondly, to confirm Punta's objection to the whole idea, but finally and most important of all, to convince him that the Colombian and American Administrations in partnership, were going ahead regardless, thereby forcing him to make his move quickly.

The meeting produced the desired effect. Within the space of six months, the Bolivian's representative met with Alfred Jaramillo on three occasions, the CIA obtaining photographic evidence of one of the meetings. The photograph was invaluable for two reasons, it not only identified the targeted cartel as under the control of Rodrigo Betancur, but it also gave the CIA a lever with which to blackmail Jaramillo. For six months, using a third party, the right-hand man of the most powerful drug baron in Latin America was now under the control of the CIA, and like most of their operations, no-one knew, not even the Colombian law enforcement agency.

The taking and subsequent killing of hostages was something that they could have done without, not out of any sympathy for the dead tourists or their families, but because it complicated matters. If it ever came to light that the CIA were responsible for allowing the deaths of Americans, irrespective of their motives, heads would roll, literally. Jaramillo however, in order not to arouse the suspicions of his boss, had to comply with his demands, and following the deaths of the two American tourists it had been decided to send a man to Colombia in order to facilitate the escape of any more threatened hostages any way that he could.

He paused to replenish his glass, this time noticing his wife's disapproving glance but ignoring it and returning to his thoughts. It had been his idea to allow Jaramillo to furnish Garbanza with certain information on shipments, knowing full well that at some stage they would have to get fully involved, and therefore a few sweeteners would go a long way to placate him and Henri once the truth came out. How far away they were from that happening he didn't know, but the moment that Punta came to see his intended acquisition was the time that the largest supplier of coca leaf and the most prodigious purveyor of misery and death would be in the same place. That would then be the time to act.

'I think it's time you went to bed, you look tired.'

She leaned over and kissed him on the forehead.

'Can the deaths of a few ever be justification for the saving of millions?'

He saw her quizzical look.

'You sound like Byron, but in answer to your question, no. But then again - thousands of years ago there was a man crucified with that idea in mind. So who am I to say that He was wrong.'

Again he knew she was right, and that's why he felt and looked tired.

CHAPTER FOURTEEN

The Halkin family greeted the New Year with muted optimism. Relieved that Christmas was behind them they awaited any news of Simon and Maria, from whatever quarter. If it hadn't been for the festive decorations it would have been hard to imagine that it had been that time of year at all, such was the despondency that pervaded every corner of the house. Apart from brief visits, the remainder of the family and close friends had respected their wishes for privacy, and George had reminded them that they had their own lives to live, not to get too embroiled in someone else's misery.

From Bevan, or the FO, he had heard nothing, although he hadn't been surprised at that - gaining some crumbs of comfort from the fact that no news was slightly better than bad news, a train of thought not shared however by Joan. Sleep was becoming her only barrier against her emotions, and even when she ventured downstairs her personality had changed to one of morose indifference, barely looking at him or Nick.

She had reluctantly returned to her part-time job at the general dealers for the short spell between Christmas and New Year's Eve. Her reason being that at least for a few hours she would be free from the constant reminders of him, although he was never out of her thoughts.

If he was honest with himself it was also starting to get to him, the photograph of Simon in his cap and gown which hung on the wall of the living room, the small mementoes he had bought them during his travels, the fairy made at nursery, which Joan still insisted went on the tree. It was doing them more harm than good, and yet neither had the courage to remove them.

The return to the shop had sadly been counter-productive, the constant well-intentioned enquiries about her son only adding to her misery, and after two days she had left.

It was also about this time that strange things began to happen. The Christmas cactus, which they had nurtured since their sons were small and which had flowered without exception for twenty years, failed to produce a single petal, as if it too recognized the absence of any reason to celebrate. Then there was the visit by the pigeons, which was most odd. Living so close to the coast they were familiar with the sight of seagulls swirling above the house or scavenging in the garden, but to see hundreds of pigeons completely covering the lawn was unnerving. They remained from early morning until noon on Christmas Day and then, as one, flew off, never returning.

He took his wife a cup of tea, but she was sleeping again and so he drank it, sitting on the side of the bed and trying to read her thoughts. She had always been there for Simon and Nick, whether it had been on the football field or schoolwork, never overbearing, but involved. Now he could feel her frustration at not being able to help her eldest and it was obvious to everyone but her, that his disappearance was having a serious effect on both her physical and mental health.

Nick took most things in his stride, attributing his philosophy to the fact that if something was going to happen then it would, and no amount of worrying was likely to change it. So it came as a shock when he discovered that he was concerned for both his parents.

The change in them both had been dramatic - his mother wallowing in misery, and George angry and frustrated at the lack of progress - so he was expecting the worst when the local newspaper, *The Recorder*, sent a reporter to the house. His father's mistrust of the media went back years, to an episode involving a family friend who due to an accident had lost most of his hair and was therefore in the habit of wearing a toupee. Whilst sitting outside a local bar the hairpiece had blown away and was then used as a ball by a group of youths. The unfortunate scene had been observed by a columnist for *The Recorder*, who finding the whole affair to his amusement, had included it in his weekly column. The friend had been upset, his father furious, and had immediately written, not to the Editor, but to the Chief Executive of the newspaper group, enquiring as to his awareness of the quality of journalism practised by his employees. Within three days the friend had received a letter of apology and the column was never included in the paper again. Typically, his father had refused credit and put it down as a lesson for him and Simon.

'Never be satisfied with people who think they can help you, go straight to the people who can,' was his comment.

A further indication of his dislike for the Press occurred during a discussion they had been having concerning road traffic accidents and procedures in general, the conversation conducted logically and calmly, until he had asked George about handling the Press. It was at this point that the eyes narrowed and his tone changed.

'What do you know about an animal called the strandwolf?'

'Not a lot,' he had replied.

'Then I'll enlighten you. It's a species of hyena possessing great jaw power, a scavenger waiting to prey on the misfortune of other animals, even its own kind. It feeds on carrion, tearing the animal apart without any compassion or feeling, oblivious to its suffering. Over the years you'll see them at road traffic accidents and fires, hovering on the edge of the incident, identifying the weak and vulnerable, ready to pounce. They call themselves reporters, but in reality they bear more than a passing resemblance to the wolf who posed as a grandmother in a famous fairy story.'

Nick had been surprised that the young reporter had escaped with his life, but he was astounded at the fact that he had managed to interview George, questioning him about it once the young man had left.

'Had a change of heart Dad?'

'I may be feeling a lot of things at the moment, but weak and vulnerable aren't two of them.'

'What did you tell him?'

'What he wanted to hear, that Simon and Maria were undercover and had been detained by the Colombian Authorities whilst they helped them with a trafficking problem.'

He didn't believe what he was hearing and rounded angrily on his father.

'But that's a pack of lies, and you know it.'

'I'm aware of that, son, but the pest was satisfied. I may have to wait a little longer.'

Bewildered, he had gone to bed; a strange man his father. But as he lay on his bed he thought that maybe it was going to take a strange man to get his brother back safely.

George wasn't in the least bit surprised that his son had been angry. It would appear to the youngster that his father had deliberately gone out of his way to cast a slur on his brother, but then he had become accustomed to being misunderstood. The desire to form close personal friendships had always evaded him, preferring to make do with acquaintances who he could take or leave depending on his mood at the time. What Anthea thought of him he could only guess, not that it mattered, but his request to her and Nick on Christmas Eve must have had her fearing the worst. It had been a cold, clear night and he had asked them both to accompany him into the garden. His real emotions encased in the hard shell that he had spent a lifetime building around himself, he had stood in the middle of the lawn gazing up at the moon.

'Irrespective of where you are in the world, everybody has one thing in common, they share the same moon. As a young boy in the Navy, I would stand on the deck of the ship and imagine that at that very moment my mother and father were also looking at it. I realized of course that because of the time difference that wasn't possible, but somehow it brought them nearer knowing that we could both observe the same object. There will be a night when Simon and Maria will also look at the moon and in that way we will have shared something with them.'

Whether or not they did it to humour him wasn't important, but the two of them stood alongside him, faces turned to the sky, each with their own thoughts. It probably didn't mean a lot to them, but to him it had been a special moment and since that night he had done the same thing on more than one occasion.

Enquiries from the national newspapers began the day after the story of the two missing backpackers appeared in

The Recorder, and with one exception, his reply was no comment. He deliberately chose the tabloid press because of its circulation; the Sub Editor both delighted at the exclusive and amused at his explanation.

'So there is no truth in this report whatsoever, Mr. Halkin?'

'It's true that we have not heard from either of them for some time, but as to the remainder of the story I can only assume that the young man who came to interview me has an exceptionally active imagination, or that his shorthand isn't all he thinks it is.'

'What did you actually tell him?'

'That I suspected that they were under the covers, as young people do, somewhere in Colombia and that they may have been retained to examine Simon's idea for setting up a tourists' motoring organization, which I think he was calling Traffic-King.

He was aware of a short chuckle, before the man thanked him and rang off. In due course a small piece appeared in *The Recorder*, apologizing for any embarrassment caused by the article. He wasn't sure whether they meant to him or themselves.

During the first few days of a bitterly cold and snowy January, Joan's physical condition began to deteriorate to an alarming level. The family's GP had prescribed anti-depressants and sleeping tablets for her, but he knew, as well as Nick and her husband however, that he was treating the symptoms and not getting through to the cause.

It was following one of the doctor's visits that Nick approached his father with the idea. On the face of it, it had meant to be somewhat of a device to keep up their spirits, until, that is, they had spent some time discussing the matter, and suddenly the whole thing became feasible.

'Why don't you try to contact someone in the FO and go and see them personally Dad? You're always telling us to go straight to the top, and although Bevan may be doing what he can, he's hardly in a position to achieve anything constructive.'

He had dismissed the idea out of hand, explaining that dealing with politicians was infinitely more difficult than reaching the head of a newspaper group. His son however had not been disuaded.

'Well let's at least look at the options.'

'Which are?'

'The first one that springs to mind is leaving everything in the hands of the diplomats which, to my way of thinking, would involve monthly reassurances such as 'every avenue is being explored' and 'you will be kept fully informed of any developments'.'

At least the lad had been listening when he had told them of his latest conversation with Bevan, and he was right. These so-called developments could take months, even years, and he was positive that Simon didn't have either. Besides, how could you deal diplomatically with people who had already murdered. There was also the question of motivation. The Government was not personally involved and therefore was highly unlikely to pull out all the stops in an effort to bring the matter to a speedy conclusion.

It was at this point that he thought of the Middlesbrough man, Keith Mangan. A backpacker like Simon, he had been captured by a group called Al Faran, and nothing had been heard of the lad for nearly two years. They too had started to kill their hostages - starting with a young Norwegian. The names of previous hostages came to mind quickly, McCarthy, Waites, to name but two. And how much could you rely on diplomacy? It probably had more to do with political blackmail or bribery. He wondered how their families had dealt with the uncertainty, years of it.

'Go on, son, what else is on your mind?'

'I know this will probably sound easier said than done, but why can't we look for him ourselves - hire a guide or someone who knows the country?'

It was indeed easier said than done. Quite apart from the fact that the country was in excess of one million square kilometres in area, he had no starting point to speak of. Europe had been different, Simon leaving a daily itinerary of his travel plans, but this time there had been no information, due to Maria planning the trip. He also felt sure that the FO would already be monitoring his movements just in case he was contemplating doing what his son was proposing, and wouldn't be at all surprised if details of his passport hadn't been sent to the various control centres at the major airports.

Nick's final contribution was to suggest a reward, either for information or their actual release, although this seemed unlikely considering the large amounts of money already in the cartels' accounts.

The more he thought about the situation the more unreal it appeared, as if he was listening to someone recounting the details of a film. A so-called lapsed Roman Catholic, he still believed that there was someone or something that controlled the scheme of things, and in times of stress he still did a thing that could be construed as praying. He preferred to think of it as calling on departed members of the family for assistance, or to watch over them. He knew it was unfair to use them in such a way, but that was family; they where there when you needed them, unconditionally.

The phone prevented them from discussing it any further. It was Bevan, and he was passing on something that he didn't want to hear.

'I've just received word Mr. Halkin that a Japanese tourist has been found shot. You will probably read about it tomorrow but I thought I would give you the news personally. I'm afraid there's still no word on your son or his friend.'

It was January 3, and at that moment he decided to take his youngest son's advice. On January 4 he would do something positive.

* * *

The peasants had started to return to the estancia following the holiday, treating the new face with suspicion, probably wondering why he had been retained whilst the remainder of the temporary workers had been released. 'Mell' had been one of them, but his new companions did little to improve the standard of hygiene in the cabin, and by the turn of the year he was becoming progressively disenchanted with his position in the clearing. Somewhere along the way he had picked up a few obscure Latin phrases, tucked away in his subconscious, one now released itself, 'ultra vires,' translated into colloquial English it meant 'fucking useless', a feeling that was totally alien to him.

It hadn't helped his feeling of frustration to receive a cleverly concealed cry for help from the hostages' cabin, the young man showing a mature level of initiative, he had thought at the time. The large black woman - who saw to all their needs, if you were that way inclined - had brought him his evening meal, placing the tin plate on the table and then leaving without a word. He had looked at it in the forlorn hope that it would turn into something more palatable, turkey with all the trimmings it was not, and yet eat he must. Scraping some of the meagre salad onto his only eating implement, a spoon, he found a number of newspaper cuttings, single words, and removing the remainder of the salad laid the words on the table. At first it meant nothing, but after a few minutes of juggling them about he found himself reading a message.

'Socorro dos travellir Señor Señorita Inglaterra Ecuador'.

They were asking for his help, and because of some obscure plot - that he had yet to be made a part of - he was unable to comply with their wishes. Screwing the paper into a ball he threw it at the cabin wall, venomous, like a snake spitting out its poison, conscious of the fact that he was losing control. That night he made the decision that if nothing happened within the next 48 hours he would head for El Retiro.

It happened quicker than that. The following day he was escorted by one of the guards through the gates with the winged horses and up to the house, where he was left to wait in a large gazebo type building, an integral part of what could only be described as a mansion. Minutes later he was approached by a small, wiry man dressed in a chef's uniform, and told to follow him to the kitchen.

'Señor Jaramillo is in need of another waiter for tonight, he has guests, very important business men, and so he has selected you to carry out this duty,' he proclaimed, although giving the impression that he was not happy with his master's choice.

Having been shown to a bathroom, twice the size of an apartment, he showered, then dressed in dark trousers and white shirt which had been laid out for his use, and made his way back to the kitchen. The chef was busy preparing the evening meal and without a pause gave him more instructions.

'Seňor Jaramillo wants to see you concerning tonight.'

He was given directions and soon found himself in a large study, the man he had been sent to find sitting in a large leather chair. He had to admit that Jaramillo did not look like your archetypal drug smuggler, in fact the face and eyes had an almost benevolent glow about them. As he stood looking down on the man, he was reminded of Haidee's irate father in Don Juan:

'... the mildest manner'd man
That ever scuttled ship or cut a throat,
With such true breeding of a gentleman,
You never could divine his real thought.'

The final line of the poem however was a warning - appearances were not only deceptive but also misleading, sometimes to the point of compromising one's own position, which wasn't healthy in his particular chosen occupation.

'You are an associate of Guillermo Garbanza?' The question asked in a voice barely above a whisper.

'I am a peasant who wishes to work on your estancia, seňor.'

'You are anything but, Mr. Hollingsworth. Please sit down.'

He did as he was asked, still uncertain about the moment of admission.

'You are here at my request, and you are an American Drug Enforcement agent. Now I would appreciate a little more openness. How much do you know of your country's intentions in this matter?'

'I doubt whether my country, as you put it, are even aware of my existence at this present time. I am here talking to you on the instructions of Señor Garbanza, and not the DEA, as you are obviously well aware, although the reason is still unclear.'

The man was genuinely surprised.

'Furthermore, I have no idea what I'm supposed to do now that I am here, perhaps you can throw some overdue light on the subject?'

Jaramillo said nothing for a few minutes, content to gaze at a photograph on his desk, it was of a pretty, young woman, obviously taken some years before.

'In a very short time three men will arrive here, important men, and should the meeting go as planned, and you do as I ask, you can walk out of here unhindered taking with you the people I have detained. I presume you have a contact somewhere nearby?'

'There is a man in El Retiro waiting for me. How far is that?'

'By truck it is not too far and to the east of here, over that hill.'

He pointed through the open window.

'What is it that you want me to do tonight?'

'Very simple, you must take a photograph of myself and my visitors but we must all be included in the same photograph, that is important, yes?'

He waited for Byron to nod in agreement before continuing.

'There is a place behind one of the panels in my dining room from where you can observe the whole room, the camera will also be there, but I will show you all of this shortly.'

'What exactly is going on here, seňor? First I'm asked to live like a pig for God knows how long without any explanation, and now I'm being asked to take photographs, again without a reason. I think it's time someone put me in the picture.'

He saw Jaramillo shaking his head before he had finished speaking.

'There is too much at stake here, even Garbanza and his boss are not aware of the implications. There are only three people outside of this house, of whom I am aware, who know everything, the Head of your CIA, your own Director, and a go-between whose identity is not known to me.'

Profanities in abundance filled his head, each one directed towards O'Grady - a man who he thought he knew.

'And now I will show you the dining room, Mr. Hollingsworth.'

The clock on the wall of the kitchen showed eight thirty as he heard the automobile pull into the long drive, followed by the crunch of gravel as the three men approached the house. He heard the guttural exchanges of formalities and then the door to the dining room closing. At nine, he walked through the same door holding a tray containing four bowls of soup, but they never made it to the recipients, one of whom he instantly recognized as a man he had sat opposite in Curaçao, Ricardo Punta. The piping hot soup burnt his hand as it cascaded to the floor, but it was nothing compared to the searing pain as a bullet tore into his shoulder, tearing away the flesh and smashing bone as he made for the open doors to the garden. Blindly, his chest bursting as he fought for every breath, he ran like a crazed animal, whilst all around him men screamed, and floodlights made the night into day. How long it took him to get to the treeline he did not know, the pain in his shoulder erasing any attempt at thought, but make it he did, fear his inspiration, fear that failure meant certain death. As he sat with his back supported by a tree he tried desperately to control his heart rate, sky high and increasing the flow of blood, now running off the end of his fingers, the occasional piece of flesh dropping onto the grass beside him. Tearing roughly at the remaining sleeve on his shirt he fought to stay in control until he had made an attempt at a tourniquet, the twisting of the small branch quickly decreasing his level of consciousness, until it disappeared totally.

CHAPTER FIFTEEN

Having attained the number one position in the Drug Enforcement Agency the hard way - namely through its ranks - O'Grady was only too aware that shit always came down. It was a dubious privilege of rank that when things went well you got the pat on the back, but when they didn't it was a different kind of 'pat' that landed. And so it was that Friday morning. The details of Byron's encounter with Punta had come via Cali, passed on - like so much more information during the preceding months - by a man known only as the 'fixer'. It had been the CIA who had approached him, confident that in his area of expertise there was nobody better. And so it had proved. The man was a born hustler, sometimes playing two hands at a time, as he had for the last six months. In addition to blackmailing and controlling Jaramillo for the US, he had also been feeding Colombia details of the hostage situation, and at the same time becoming an extremely rich man.

It was two o'clock in the morning and he was still at his desk, the weight of what had occurred during the previous two days causing him to hunch his shoulders as he reflected on how one piece of unforeseen bad luck had wrecked a major coup. There was no doubt in his mind at all that Punta would now be frightened off, wary of entering Colombia for some time, so the plan to bring down him and Betancur was now in shreds. Guillermo Garbanza's anger had steadily increased during the phone call that had been necessary, informing him of recent events.

'The bottom line is then, O'Grady, that the hostages were always going to be secondary. I just hope that you can come to terms with the fact that you allowed innocent people to be executed so that you could indulge in a game of cat and mouse. When will you Americans learn that you have no God-given right to save the world on your own. The truth is that you're not very good at it, but then Hollingsworth found that out the hard way.'

The news about Byron had been like a stab to the heart. The fact that he hadn't known Garbanza was sending him undercover not one bit of consolation, but then he couldn't have warned him anyway. Anne had been told, but there were few details he could give her, other than her husband was wandering around a Colombian forest, lost, and with probably a fatal gunshot wound to deal with. So he had decided to tell her a half-truth - that there had been an incident, but everything was in hand and he would shortly be coming home. He prayed that he was right.

The official termination of the project had come, not unexpectedly, in a sealed envelope from the State Department and now lay on his desk, a brief document that he had read a hundred times. It instructed him to curtail all links with Alfred Jaramillo and the man in Cali. The explanation was typical of the hypocrisy practised by most Administrations, stating that as there were no longer any Americans at risk, there was no longer any requirement for US involvement. The fact that he had an agent down and fighting for his life, if he had been lucky, irrelevant, and the bad news continued to arrive one hour later.

The computer in his office operated continually, the Internet his eyes to the world and his only contact with the anonymous go-between. The message from the 'fixer' was, as usual, in code and it was the final nail in the coffin. It stated that, 'the chameleon has reverted back to his original colour'. It was apt, the lizard changed its colour when it was frightened or in response to environmental changes. The message referred to Alfred Jaramillo's reluctance to cooperate any longer, irrespective of the threat of blackmail, not that it mattered anymore.

As the night came to an end so did his conflict. He had wrestled with his conscience for hours. On the one hand he had been told officially that the operation had been aborted, and yet self-respect told him that to abandon a valued agent and the remaining hostages was fundamentally a criminal act. Knowing full well that his proposed actions could cost him his career, he nevertheless made two telephone calls. The first was to Bogotá, and the other was to the FO, specifically to the Head of the Drugs and International Crime section in London.

⋆ ⋆ ⋆

The quick reference section of the central library was full of material and books on missing persons, unfortunately they referred to those missing in the UK, and not abroad. He had searched the shelves three times before he discovered something that might be of some use. It was Dodds Civil Service Directory, a reference book containing the names and addresses of nearly everyone employed in a prominent position at UK Government level. Taking it to one of the many cubicles, his intention was to identify the most senior Consular official dealing with South American affairs and contact him personally, even if it meant camping at the man's front door. He found what he was looking for fairly quickly, writing down Charles Barnard's official address and even the telephone number of the FO. It was at this point that the pen slipped from his fingers and landed on the open book. Looking down he noticed that the tip of the ballpoint was pointing to a department designated the Drug and International Crime Section, and directly below and nominated as its head was the name Robert Morrow.

Leaning back in the chair he was transported back over thirty years, to his time in the Royal Navy and a certain Royal Marine Captain of the same name. Maybe it was a coincidence, but then on the other hand, what if it was the same man? He wrote down the address and replaced the book.

It was a fifteen-minute walk back to the house and for every step of the way he considered what his next move would be now that he had something to work with. Bevan, he knew was merely a go-between, a mouthpiece for someone higher, and therefore to tell him anything or ask for his help would probably mean any chance of reaching Morrow would be made very difficult, if not impossible. No. It would have to be the direct approach. But how? A man in Morrow's position would only see him by appointment, of that he was certain, and that would be only the first hurdle to negotiate. By the time he arrived back home he had decided what to say to the ubiquitous secretary he was bound to encounter on ringing the acquired telephone number. Sitting by the phone he carefully wrote the script, then having read through it three or four times made the call to the FO. He was surprised at how easy it was, expecting all sorts of awkward questions before he was allowed access.

'Which department do you require?' The monotone voice, obviously the private exchange operator. He told her quickly.

'One moment,' followed by the inevitable strains of some obscure piece of classical music.

'Drugs and International Crime Section, Mr. Morrow's secretary. Please state your name and agency.'

He had anticipated the request for the latter for no other reason than it sounded more professional than just a name.

'Halkin, George, Assistant Coordinator, Children's Health Organization Worldwide. We organize and distribute large quantities of food and medical supplies to the majority of the Third World countries.'

'And your business with this department, Mr. Halkin?'

He took a deep breath, the words, when they came, spoken confidently, without hesitation.

'I have evidence that there are people within this organization who are using its humanitarian purpose as a cover for distributing what you would term contraband goods.

'Have you contacted your local Police Authority on this matter? That is usually the first step, and then they usually pass it on to us.'

Again he had anticipated well.

'I had fully intended to speak to them, but circumstances as recent as yesterday have forced me into this position. I have positive proof that two container vehicles leaving this country on Friday will contain more than just food and medicine. There is also one other piece of information which I would appreciate you passing on to Mr. Morrow, it concerns an operation on which we worked jointly some years ago, 'Hurricane Guardship'.

He could hear the faint tapping of keys, visualizing the contents of the conversation now portrayed on a computer screen.

'Can I take your number, Mr. Halkin? I will get back to you when I have spoken to Mr. Morrow.'

For three hours he lay next to Joan, her motionless form the evidence of an increasing amount of anti-depressant pills and various forms of sedative, and yet when the phone rang her eyes opened slightly.

'Mr. Halkin?'

He confirmed her assumption.

'I have made an appointment for you to see the Head at 4.30pm tomorrow, would that be suitable?'

He contained his relief long enough to agree.

'And by the way, there was no need to try to be so clever.'

He apologized and took down the details - but there was no guilt being felt by him as he lay by Joan's side.

'Who was that?' she murmured.

'Just some man I have to see, nothing important,' he lied.

He was doing it again; not solely to guard her from the possibility of disappointment, it had more to do with his fear of failure. It had always been inside him, the urge to do things his way, rarely confiding in even the closest family member until a problem was either resolved or impossible to complete. A 'bottle person' his brother had labelled him, implying that there was always a cork firmly in place until the contents of the bottle were released, only sometimes the cork popped itself, the resulting mess catastrophic. Even Nick would only be told so much, his son's priority would be looking after Joan, a task as important as his own during the coming days and with that in mind he began to pack a small bag.

* * *

Robert Morrow's day had started quietly enough, but within a period of four hours he had received two phone calls that changed all that. At first they had seemed unconnected, until the name Halkin had been mentioned, making the highly improbable link between Washington DC and a town in the north-east of England called Hartlepool. The transatlantic conversation with his opposite number had been surprising enough, O'Grady requesting the assurance of a secure line several times before divulging the reason for the call, the occasional question rapidly becoming a list.

'I take it this information is unofficial and known only to a handful of people then?'

'Damn right, Bob, and fewer than that. In fact the only Colombian who knew anything was Renaldo Hernandez, a politician, assassinated some months ago.'

'And this drug trafficker, Jaramillo, has now thrown his toys out of the crib, but may still have Halkin and the girl?'

'Only the contact in Cali can confirm that.'

The contact O'Grady was referring to was known to him, not by name, but he guessed that every Law Enforcement Agency in the civilized world had at some time used his services, and he was no exception.

'I have to ask the question Mike, why the sudden cooperation? These aren't your people that are missing.'

Although separated by thousands of miles he sensed the man's pain as he answered.

'One of my most trusted agents is unaccounted for, a man named Hollingsworth. Nothing has been heard from him for some considerable time, he's wounded and I imagine lost, and now that we have done a Pontius Pilate my only hope of seeing him back here is you and the Colombians.'

'How much do they know in Bogotá?'

'I had to come clean when Punta saw our man, so they probably are slightly ahead of you, I don't know for sure.'

He paused, not quite sure of how much more he needed or wanted to know, and yet there had to be another query.

'How much of this fiasco of yours is known in official HM Government circles?'

'Nothing at all as far as I am aware. Only a handful of people in the whole world knew the full details, none of whom were on your side of the water.'

He had heard enough and probably too much at that, but he thanked O'Grady anyway, but it was more out of sympathy for the man than for the information he had passed on.

The first thing he noticed about the transcript of his secretary's telephone conversation with Halkin was the acronym contained within the organization the man purported to represent. At another time, in another place, CHOW had been used by matelots as a term for their expectations on returning home from sea, a cryptic message to loved ones printed on the back of an envelope containing a final letter home. It translated to 'Coming Home, Open Wide' a reference to man's more basic instincts rather than any desire to feed the world, even though it was often referred to as 'chow time.' During his time at sea, he had never tired of admiring the ingenuity of the 'lower deck' to invent words or corrupt the most simple of games, Ludo being one that sprang immediately to mind, or 'uckers' as the sailors had renamed it. It was basically the same game with a few refinements, although to an outsider or 'civvy' the invitation in the wardroom to 'partake in a game of Ludo', sounded a million miles away from the cry of 'any of you fuckers for uckers' frequently heard below decks.

Glancing down at the sheet of paper it was apparent that he was known to Halkin, although how he had traced him after so long was a mystery. The name would have meant nothing to him if it had not been for O'Grady's call, and yet they must have served on the Whirlwind together at some point, a distant association the man was now using as a means of gaining an interview. As Head of Section his initial reaction was not to get involved and leave it to the diplomats, they would undoubtedly be in at least weekly contact with their counterparts in Colombia. As yet it was not his department's concern, probably never would be, and any interference could lead him on a path now trodden by O'Grady. The facts that altered his way of thinking was that he too had children and could therefore sympathize with Halkin, but his overriding reason for making the decision to see him was born of loyalty. The man had served his country, and for that at least he deserved a hearing.

* * *

Henri and Gill Garbanza were in total agreement following the telephone call from America, in that, what they had regarded as a goodwill gesture in allowing a DEA agent to participate in the downfall of Rodrigo Betancur, had in fact put their whole plan in jeopardy. They both realized that what had seemed like a bright light at the end of the tunnel before the holiday had suddenly turned into the possibility of someone sealing it completely, at both ends.

'Where do we go from here, my friend?'

The question was a request for options, not answers, and Garbanza was at a loss on both counts.

'I contacted Benito the moment I heard about Hollingsworth from that devious bastard O'Grady, but so far he has been unable to discover his whereabouts. One thing is clear however, we and the Americans have been using the same intermediary, although if it's any comfort at all, we have not been paying him.'

'Maybe we should have made him an offer.'

Their eyes met at the same instant.

'And maybe it's not too late to do just that. Did O'Grady give you the means of getting in touch with this contact of theirs?'

Garbanza shook his head.

'But he wants his agent back, badly.'

'Contact him tonight, tell him that with the help of this go-between there is a good chance that he will see Hollingsworth again.'

There was a hint of enthusiasm returning to Henri, Garbanza noticed.

'There is one thing in this business that bothers me boss. Now that we know what has been going on, why have we been informed about the hostages at every opportunity? This informer has asked for nothing in return for his information.'

'Maybe it's not the time, compadre. It may well be that he has something in mind at a later date.'

'Like what?'

'Once we have contacted him, he may tell us. Now ring O'Grady.'

He did, and one hour later he returned, but with more than he had bargained for.

'It would appear that our American counterpart feels the need to bare his soul.'

'They say that about confession,' Henri replied, sardonically.

'Not only did he give me the e-mail address of his contact, but he was also generous with two further pieces of information, including a few pieces of the jigsaw. According to him, the CIA entered into an agreement with our Administration prior to the Curaçao convention, the main point being, that should they bring about the downfall of both Betancur and Punta, the acquired land would be assigned to an appointee of their choice. This appointee, on acquiring this land, would promise to oversee the growing of a more conventional form of crop than coca, and under no circumstances condone the manufacture of illegal substances. Apparently, Jaramillo has been growing disenchanted with his lot for some time, and had therefore decided to sell-out to Punta, the crunch coming when they would meet with Betancur - now a very sick man - and force him into permanent retirement. The Americans somehow found out about the plot and took photographs of meetings between Punta and Jaramillo, threatening to take the evidence to his friend, who would certainly have had him executed. So they proceeded through an intermediary to blackmail him into doing their bidding, promising him that if everything went to plan he would be allowed into the States and given a new start.'

Henri was finding it very hard to believe that all this had been going on without his knowledge, and said so.

'Unfortunately Renaldo Hernandez took the information to the grave before he could inform us. His successor however has been using the hostages as a delaying tactic - preventing us from moving in too quickly.'

'How do you mean?'

'You know as well as I do compadre, the problems associated with an armed assault in a hostage situation, and although our Administration has allowed the media to tell the world about the tourists, time and again they have reiterated that the answer is by diplomacy and not force.'

'By diplomacy they presumably meant when the CIA gave them the go ahead, and eventually ourselves.'

He answered his own question.

'Did O'Grady give any reason why Jaramillo allowed an agent to infiltrate the cartel?'

'No. He was unaware that Hollingsworth had gone under.'

Henri's nervous habit of tapping the desk returned with a vengeance, and Gill could almost hear his mind at work.

'Where does this leave us, boss?'

'Before I answer that let's hear what our friend in Cali has to say. Maybe he has the solution.'

* * *

Fear wasn't an emotion that Alfred Jaramillo experienced very often, that was usually left to others, and he was usually the cause of it. But, as he awaited the return of his visitors he could feel sweat accumulating in the folds of his wrinkled skin, and it wasn't due to the warm night air. He had tried to be clever, realizing too late that to bring the American onto the estancia could cost him his life, when it should have had the opposite effect, protection. Yet he could never have known of their previous meeting. It had been the man in Cali's idea, persuading him that to trust the Americans to keep their side of the bargain and exempt him from prosecution or extradition, in addition to providing a new life in the States, was naïve in the extreme. Trusting people was also a new experience for him and so he had allowed the go-between to talk him into allowing the agent to provide a tenuous means of insurance, should the meeting with Punta turn into something else. He thought of the irony of it. The photograph had been his own idea, evidence which would prove that the Bolivian had made the acquaintance of a known drug trafficker, a fact which his country's Administration would find hard to explain, especially when there was no record of him having entered Colombia. Hollingsworth he had hoped to use in a similar way, his chef taking a similar photograph earlier as they sat in the study. Of course it could be explained away, but America had a long and disastrous history of failed CIA operations and Watergate-type embarrassments. Would they risk another? He doubted it. Anyway it was now academic, he had shot himself in the foot. He just hoped that the American agent had been luckier.

The man who now entered the room was not Punta but one of his henchmen, returning to deliver a final message.

'Señor Punta wishes you luck in your explanation to Rodrigo concerning the employment of an American agent, Señor Jaramillo.'

He waited until the screech of the vehicle tyres on the gravel died away, then poured himself a large glass of port. The henchman had been right with his sarcastic remark, Rodrigo would see right through him, and even if his excuse, as yet unthought of, was accepted, there would still be Pizzaro's curse, doubt; enough of it for his long-time friend to order his execution. Crossing the large room he unlocked and then opened one of the drawers in his bureau, removing an envelope and then checking that its contents were still intact. The envelope contained a single item of information, and yet he had known since the Englishman and his friend had been taken, that one day it could save his life.

CHAPTER SIXTEEN

At first, Simon thought that a rescue attempt was in progress, the sound of gunfire and shouting getting louder until suddenly it subsided with the opening of the cabin door and the brusque entry of one of the guards.

'¡Vayase ahora!'

'We have to go outside,' whispered Maria, leading him by the hand. They followed the large black woman into the cool fresh night air, an unexpected reprieve from the oppressive atmosphere of the cabin.

'What is going on, Maria?'

The guards, who had now been joined by a stranger, were becoming increasingly agitated.

'I think they are looking for someone, maybe one of the peasants has tried to get away.'

His hopes dashed that help had not arrived, he took consolation from the fact that it was probably the American who was the cause of the guards' frantic endeavours. He placed his arm around Maria's shoulder as they were hastily ushered back to the hovel, taking the opportunity that the last few minutes had provided to reassure her.

'I think it is the American who spoke to me that they are looking for, and maybe he has gone for help now that he knows where we are.'

The events of the night had helped restore much of the faith that he had lost during the days following his attempt to contact the American. What he had expected to happen on the strength of a few smuggled pieces of paper he wasn't sure, maybe he had hoped for too much. The one thing that he had never lost faith in however, was his parents', and particularly his father's, tenacity in taking whatever measures they could to return him and Maria to their respective homes and families.

George's philosophy of life had been formed during his time in the Navy, guided by a set of rules he called his 'tenets', a mixture of beliefs, dogma and principles from which he never wavered. It was more than likely that already he was treading on toes or upsetting petty officials in an attempt to get some answers or assistance. Following in his father's footsteps was quite impossible, he knew that, and really had never attempted to do so, but he had adopted some of his principles, although one or two he had learned the hard way.

One such incident had happened shortly after Christmas, when he and Nick had been very young. He had been entrusted with his younger brother's safekeeping, although Joan had been in another part of the house. Nick was of an age where he was into everything, including the computer on which he, Simon, was trying to play a game, and was being continually interrupted by Nick's insistence on joining in. Tiring of his brother's attentions he had given him a plastic torch to occupy his mind, only to discover moments later that he had removed the batteries and placed one in his mouth. Joan had managed to remove the offending obstruction but had informed George on his arrival home of the close encounter.

'As the eldest of the two you had responsibility for your brother's safety,' he had begun, 'and because of your selfishness you allowed Nick to play with something that he didn't understand. It was not good sense, so learn from it.'

He had, and still was.

The day following the shooting they were visited by the man from the house, Simon noting a distinct change in his tone, and surprised by the unexpected invitation to follow him back up the hill. Like two orphaned waifs, the filth and smell now an integral part of their bodies, they stood in the huge hall awaiting their fate.

'It is some time since you showered, yes?' He didn't wait for an answer, 'My bathrooms are at your disposal, and if you leave your clothes with the servant they will be more presentable when you return to your cabin.'

Simon was wary, but Maria didn't hesitate and followed the female servant until she disappeared from view.

'There is nothing sinister attached to my offer, Simon Halkin, but you may please yourself.'

And ten minutes later he was glad that he had. The beard which had matured since his capture gave him a Latin American look, he thought, as he gazed into a mirror for the first time in months, his black, sleek hair adding to the appearance.

Together again, in what he assumed was the man's study, he could only stand and stare at his companion. The transformation in Maria was quite breathtaking. Her long, black flowing hair had replaced the infested matted mess of the last few weeks, whilst her face shone out once more like the moon on a pitch-black night. They sat, each in a dressing gown, feeling as though they had been reborn, Simon thinking of a scene from a Victorian parlour, one of the servants acting as chaperone. The study was quite large and contained all the amenities of a well-run business, prominent amongst which he noted a state-of-the-art computer, together with a fax machine and small photocopier. From his position he could also see the contents of the man's large desk, a collection of books and a variety of stationery products. Nothing very unusual, apart from the ornate photograph frame which portrayed a striking young woman, not unlike Maria.

* * *

The East Coast Express left Darlington on time leaving Nick Halkin on the platform. George stood by the door, reluctant to take his seat until his son had disappeared from view, a son in whom he had placed a great deal of responsibility. He had taken Nick up on his offer of a lift, discussing on the way his fears for Joan, and leaving instructions that any further deterioration in her health and he was to call the doctor immediately.

It was not until the train left Doncaster that he decided to review his strategy of dealing with Morrow, appreciating that once in the man's company he would get but one opportunity to solicit his help. Having used the ploy of 'old ships', - a matelot's term for men who had served together on the same vessel - to gain access to him, a different approach would be needed when they came face to face. He had never begged for anything in his life and was loath to start now, but if that's what it was going to take then he would do it, pride was not an issue. A more palatable scenario was that the man had not lost his appetite for risk-taking and, without putting his entire neck on the block, would at least stretch a point or two, knowing as he did that protracted negotiations were not in his son's best interest.

The train pulled into King's Cross on time, giving him plenty of time to have something to eat before making his way to Matthew Parker Street. Leaving the station, he recalled the last time Joan and him had visited the capital, stumbling, quite by accident, into a friendly Greek café, and after five minutes walk he discovered that it was still open for business. Ordering a mug of tea and an all-day breakfast he found an empty table near the window, noticing immediately that many of the patrons had the tell-tale cabby's badge pinned to their jackets.

Engaging one in conversation at the next table, he asked, 'Could you take me to Matthew Parker Street when I've finished my meal?'

'Certainly guv. You from the North?'

'Hartlepool.'

He saw the instant recognition and waited for the inevitable reply, surprised at the retort.

'British West Hartlepool.'

It had been a few years since he had heard the phrase. A standing joke in the three armed services, there were two prerequisites for visiting West Hartlepool - as it was named prior to the '70s. One was an up-to-date passport allowing you entry to what the locals termed 'God's allotment', the other, to be clean-shaven - for obvious reasons.

'You ex-forces?' The question unnecessary - an impulse.

'The 'pusser', nine years man and boy, every finger a marlin spike as we used to say.'

George allowed himself the luxury of a smile, memories of happier times revived by a complete stranger. The journey took no time at all, the friendly cabby dropping him at his destination well ahead of the appointed time of his meeting with Morrow. The secretary invited him to wait in an adjoining ante-room where he thumbed through a selection of magazines, mostly with a tendency to the more political side of life. At 4.35pm he was beckoned into the office of Robert Morrow by a tall, youthful-looking man, who the years had obviously treated kindly.

'Mr. Halkin? I'm Bob Morrow, please take a seat and tell me what I can do for you. By the way I understand that we are 'old ships'.'

'Many years ago,' he replied. 'I remember you as the officer commanding the detachment of Marines on HMS Whirlwind, my first ship. If you recall we were deployed for nine months on the West Indies station.'

'Exciting times.'

'They were indeed, especially the one's that I was part of. You probably don't remember but I accompanied you and your lads on numerous occasions in your search for caches of weapons and explosives on the cays.'

'That's where you are wrong George. My memory is as good as ever and you were the electrician that made up the landing party, to check our wiring to the detonators. And you know why I remember?'

'Probably because you practised on one of the Navigating Officer's landmarks.'

'Something he never forgave me for doing.'

The recalling of the event caused them both to laugh, and George felt that his credibility had been established.

'I'll try not to take up too much of your time and it's been a real tonic for me going over old times, but I think that you're aware of my reason for coming to see you.'

Morrow nodded.

'I made some enquiries prior to you arriving and to be perfectly honest this department has its hands well and truly tied. I'm afraid this isn't the Navy of thirty years ago George, when we could exercise a certain amount of flexibility. The rules in this business - unless you're out in the field - leave no room for latitude at all, and a further obstacle is that a missing Foreign National is the responsibility of their own country, not ours.'

He had expected this initial setback, and although the signs didn't look good he hadn't made the journey south to give up without a fight.

'Let me revert back to our days in the Navy once again. Without exception, anyone who found themselves before the Captain on some charge or other requested you as their defending officer. There was a good reason for that, and it was that you invariably got them off the hook, more than once you got them out of deep shit. Well I'm in the crap again Mr. Morrow, and I need a defending officer, if only to point me in the right direction.'

'And believe me, it gives me no satisfaction at all to sit here and refuse you my help, but this is a Foreign Office matter, not technically international crime.'

'Someone has kidnapped my son, with the intention of killing him, damn it! What would you call it, technically?'

He hadn't meant to lose his temper, that wasn't the way to secure the man's help, but they were entering the realms of beaurocratic bullshit and he wasn't having any of it. There was an uncomfortable silence, possibly shorter than it seemed to him, and he took the opportunity to remove his baccy tin from his jacket pocket and place it on the desk.

'Do you mind?'

Morrow shook his head.

'That's something else I remember about you, the tin.'

Having rolled himself a cigarette, George slid the battered tobacco container across to the man who had recently been on the receiving end of his outburst.

'Like riding a bike, you never forget how to roll one.'

They sat enjoying the smoke in silence, before Morrow replaced the lid on the tin, but not before his visitor had noticed a small card being secreted under the tobacco.

'I still can't be of any assistance George, and all I can say is that I hope your son is returned safely and good luck.'

He didn't know what the card contained, but as he left the building in search of a public house in which to discover its contents, he felt sure that Morrow had made some attempt to guide him.

From his third storey window Morrow watched as George Halkin left the building, before crossing to his desk and picking up the phone.

'What have you got on for the next couple of weeks?'

'Nothing.'

'A man called Halkin will be in touch. It isn't official but see what you can do for him. One more thing, I don't want to know.'

He replaced the receiver and finished smoking the hand-rolled cigarette. The meeting hadn't turned out the way he had intended, but in the end his decision had been influenced by a picture; the picture of two men in an inflatable boat off the coast of Cuba. One had been the father, the other his son, and he didn't want the same to happen to Halkin.

It had always been one of life's mysteries to George, how the quality of beer could vary so much on such a small island. He looked at the headless pint of what the barman had loosely termed 'best bitter' and decided that rather than drink it, he would just use it as an excuse for being there. The card that Morrow had surreptitiously placed in his tin bore a simple message, 'Pandora's Removals', followed by a telephone number. Leaving the already stagnant pint, he made for the payphone at the end of the bar and rang the number - a pleasant female voice confirming the name of the firm.

'My name is Halkin and I was advised to ring this number by a colleague of mine regarding a removal.'

'One moment Mr. Halkin.'

He was aware of a faint conversation in the background before the female voice returned.

'If you care to call at our office, Mr. Kelly, our contract manager will deal with your inquiry. By the way we close at six o'clock, so if your removal is of an urgent nature I can give you instructions for how to get here.'

He replied that it was, and subsequently wrote the instructions in the back of his diary. The address was just off Sloane Square, and fifteen minutes later the cab dropped him at the entrance to a small cul-de-sac, at the end of which a barely legible sign advertised the removal firm. The well worn flight of wooden steps led him into a comfortable, rather than stylish outer office, where a smart young lady sat behind a desk reading what appeared to be an upmarket magazine.

'George Halkin, I rang earlier.'

'Ah, yes. Mr. Kelly left some information in an envelope for you. If you wish to discuss your removal further then everything you need to know is there.'

He took the envelope and thanked her, subduing his urge to tear it open until he was seated in an adjacent café. It contained three items of information, and concluded with an instruction to destroy the envelope the moment he understood its contents. Looking at an enclosed map and an address of where he was to proceed, he discovered that it was quite close and easy to follow. The instructions thereafter however, caused him, for the first time, to question the wisdom of what he was attempting to achieve. It was becoming all too cloak-and-dagger for his liking, something he was not familiar with, and he felt uneasy. It didn't last long, the appearance of a young couple in the café reminding him of his self-imposed commitment to helping Simon and Maria in any way possible, and moments later he had flushed the burning remains of the envelope and its contents down the café's toilet.

⋆ ⋆ ⋆

The face was brown and wrinkled; like a piece of old brown parchment that had been screwed up and then an attempt made to smooth it out. Long, straggly hair fell onto bare shoulders, whilst bared, uneven teeth protruded from beneath an equally straggly beard. The hand that was gently rubbing his shoulder was suddenly withdrawn, its new task to offer a cup of foul-smelling liquid to his lips. He drank it, reluctantly. The sound of the waterfall, building to a crescendo filled his ears. Then he was floating on a thermal current high above it, looking down on trees that were not green but all the colours of the rainbow. Suspended by some invisible cord, he felt totally relaxed, as if mind and body had been removed. Was this death? A witness to your own departure? If it was, then he had carried his admiration for Byron too far, succumbing like him to finality on foreign soil. The scene below was becoming confused, the river meandering through the rainforest, providing food and water for the inhabitants of the primitive dwellings, and yet there in the midst of this throwback of a village was a Landrover. He was floating again, but this time downwards; there was no feeling of landing, just an awakening.

'Byron, Byron wake up, it is me Benito.'

At first the face was just a blur. Then slowly it started to take on an identity. It was true - it was the Colombian.

'My head's pounding, where am I?'

'Still in the land of our fathers, thanks to your Indian friends. If they hadn't found you when they did you would now be muerto, my friend.'

'For one horrible moment I thought I was dead. What the hell have they been feeding me? Or shouldn't I ask?'

'Very wise, Byron, they have their own ways of dealing with sickness these people.'

His eyes fully focused he was beginning to feel slightly better, even managing to raise himself to a sitting position, pleasantly surprised at the lack of pain from his shoulder as he did so.

'I know the whereabouts of the English boy and his friend, or I did. How long have I been here?'

'Garbanza was informed of your shooting five days ago, by O'Grady of all people.'

He then proceeded to tell the 'poet' the events of the last week, including how he had traced him through a priest visiting El Retiro.

'He's got a lot to answer for that bastard. Have you managed to inform my wife that I'm okay since you found me?'

'All taken care of. Now I must get you out of here.'

He was starting to feel dizzy again and offered no objections as he watched Benito expertly place his arm into a sling, the inhabitants of the village taking a keen interest in the operation. Shaking as many hands as he could, they made their way to the waiting Landrover, the only evidence of a return to civilization he had seen in nearly a week, if in fact that's what he was returning to.

★ ★ ★

The reimbursement for services rendered had been satisfactory, there was nothing to complain about in that department, but to dispense with his expertise in such a way had left him feeling more than a little offended. Ernesto Videla wasn't accustomed to being treated in such an offhand way, even by a superpower, and the curtailment of his agreement with the Americans had been occupying his thoughts since the day he had received the curt e-mail message. The American dollars had only been the tip of the iceberg, the real benefits coming from the land he had been promised once the operation had been successful, an operation now dead in the water. Not that it was any of his doing, as usual the Americans had tried to go it alone and come unstuck, secrecy and deceit together with the ability to manipulate not their forte, although they were obviously of the opposite opinion.

The climb up the hill to the church was becoming more difficult, like most of the tasks that he had carried out during the last thirty years, and he was reminded once again of the land he had been promised that could have changed his life. He took his seat in the usual pew awaiting the man from Medellin to arrive at the 'drop,' the request coming the previous night. Their arrival was almost simultaneous, the contact leaving the envelope in the side chapel and leaving without even a look around. The fact that the man had something for him had come as a surprise until he realized that he would have been unaware that the Americans had pulled out. Opening the envelope in the vestry he found that it contained photocopies of three documents: the page from a passport, a copy of a birth certificate, and finally a cutting from a newspaper article. He was not normally an excitable man, but as he walked down the hill there was added impetus to his step; Alfred Jaramillo's cook had done well.

CHAPTER SEVENTEEN

Alfred had refrained from visiting Rodrigo for as long as he dare, reports of his friend's erratic behaviour only making the eventual meeting a highly charged affair, with the outcome uncertain. He had decided on an early morning arrival for no other reason than it was better to get the matter settled whilst his wits were at their sharpest, the advantage of being a morning person. Rodrigo wasn't, he was a nighthawk, a lover of darkness and shadowy places. The helicopter touched down and he made his way to the house, his hands shaking as he removed his boots before entering the large room.

'How have you been Alfred?' An affable enquiry that would have fooled many.

'There have been better periods in my life.'

'Unquestionably.'

'You also do not look your usual self.'

It was true. The man looked grey and drawn, his posture in the wheelchair awkward as if nursing injured limbs.

'Matters which have come to my attention have done nothing to improve my condition, I assure you.'

'An error of judgement Rodrigo, no harm to you was intended.'

'But an American agent in our midst. You say that is harmless?'

'He was clever, I had no idea.'

He could see from Rodrigo's face that this was not working.

'An American agent and a Bolivian Minister. Strange bedfellows, would you not agree?'

'We both know what Punta is really involved in, Rodrigo, and his visit to me was a step away from him coming to you with an offer.'

'The man can offer me nothing which I have not already got at my disposal, what reason could he have for visiting me?'

'Neither of us is getting any younger my friend. This business with the Colombian Authorities has taken its toll, and when we die who is there to take over from us?'

'So you intended to sell out? And to a Bolivian at that.'

'Not without your consent and cooperation.'

He hoped that Rodrigo would not see through the lie.

'We have known each other for most of our lives, Alfred Jaramillo, and for the first time I doubt your word, not disbelieve it, but doubt it.'

'Then I am deeply sorry that I have caused you such pain, and for nothing, because Punta is no longer interested.'

'Maybe the agent unwittingly did us a favour.'

He saw Rodrigo change his position in the chair, a slight wince showing on his face.

'I am tired of this charade with the Authorities. How many of the hostages have we remaining?' he asked, painfully.

The change of subject caught him off balance.

'The Englishman and the girl from Ecuador.'

'Then have them killed. Put an end to this pretence that at some point it will be resolved. It will not, we know it and the Administration know it.'

Now was the time, not only to attempt to save his own life, because he knew Rodrigo's only answer to doubt was death, but maybe he could prevent at least the girl from becoming another victim. Nervously he removed the contents of the envelope and laid them before his boss.

'More surprises, Alfred?'

'I suspect that it has more to do with fate than the element of surprise.'

He watched as Rodrigo put on his spectacles and scanned the sheets of paper in front of him.

'So they are the documents and a newspaper clipping concerning the girl hostage. What of it?'

'They are proof that the girl is in fact your granddaughter.'

The only noise in the room at that moment was the sound of the papers being hurriedly shuffled.

'I am in no mood for trickery, I must warn you.'

'It is no trick, look at the newspaper cutting of the grandmother, she is old like us, but it is Hermania.'

His nose nearly touching the cutting Rodrigo scrutinized the photograph, still not convinced when he next spoke.

'There is a likeness, yes, but what further proof have you that this girl is indeed related to me by blood?'

'My suspicions were aroused when I managed to recover her passport, her place of birth being Ibarra the town to which I knew Hermania had moved from Banos. I then managed to obtain a copy of the mother's birth certificate, which listed her own mother as one Hermania Gavira. It is irrefutable proof that Maria Sandino is your granddaughter.'

'And this makes a difference to what I have told you must be done?'

He was not surprised at the answer; he had known him too long.

'You would murder your own blood, Rodrigo?'

'I must give some thought to this matter, but as to the Englishman nothing has changed.'

He reluctantly agreed and turned to go.

'You are a fortunate man Alfred. Before you walked through those doors you were a dead man yourself. Look to the girl until you hear from me. As you probably suspected, she is all that is keeping you alive.'

* * *

It was 5.30pm and dark as George approached the designated hotel where he was to meet the man who could hopefully help him return his son. The doubts about his course of action still lingered, and although Morrow had appeared to be a decent enough bloke, there was no guarantee that whoever he was about to meet would have the same principles. He turned into Knightsbridge, heading for Kensington Road and the Albert Hall, following his instructions to the letter, and three cigarettes later he found himself outside the unusually named Two Thirty Hotel, a four-storey Victorian building on Queensgate. The entrance was guarded by an elderly gentleman, who he recognized as ex-forces by his bearing and firm voice, enquiring as to George's business, then showing him to the lift. Making sure that he took it by himself he pressed the three button, exiting the compartment at the indicated floor and quickly made his way down the stairs to the second, where he located room number 16 and without knocking walked in. The room in which he now found himself was tastefully decorated, without being too 'over the top', a typical example of somewhere he might take Joan for the weekend.

'Mr Halkin?' The question boomed across the room from a man taking up much of the sofa on which he was languishing.

'Yes. Mr. Kelly?'

'That'll do cobber.' The accent still very much in evidence.

They shook hands, the Australian's hand totally enclosing his own. A big man in every sense of the word.

'Can I get you a tinny or anything?'

'A lager will be fine,' he replied, the sight of the stagnant pint still firmly in his mind. He thanked him, noticing that he had taken a notepad from his briefcase on the way back from the small refrigerator.

'Now then, let's get down to the nitty, George isn't it? Right then what's the problem?'

It took about fifteen minutes to explain to the easy-going Australian what had happened during the last six weeks, Kelly constantly making notes and drinking lager, and he was on his fourth 'tinny' when he spoke again.

'I'm gonna be on the up and up with you here George. The fact that Colombia is involved makes the outcome difficult to predict, and should I take on the job it also makes it very expensive. The upside - and to be honest with you I'm struggling to find one - is that not only am I the best at what I do, but to my knowledge I'm the only one in this country who does it. Which brings us to the financial side of things, so before we go any further what's your status?'

'The money isn't a problem. I've recently retired with a lump sum which is immediately available, with the capacity to double it if required.'

'As you say then, no problem.' He made a note on his pad. 'Have you access to a computer and the Internet?'

'Not personally, but my brother has.'

Again he made a note.

The questions continued, some straightforward others more obscure, but obviously important to Kelly.

'Right, let me break a few things down for you George, then when you've heard what I've got to say you can make a final decision as to whether you want me to go ahead or not. At the end of the day it's entirely up to you, and by the way don't think you've wasted my time if you decide otherwise.'

He listened intently as the mercenary - although he would never refer to him as such, explained his conditions.

'There will be an initial payment of £50,000 paid into a Jersey bank, the details such as name, sort code and account number etc. I will give you before you leave. If you're not familiar with this method of money transfer, your own bank will explain it to you and do the necessary. This initial payment will be used to pay my three associates a retainer, reimburse what we call a 'fixer' and pay for transport, weapons and other bits and pieces which may crop up from time to time. Now like I said, that's the initial cost. If I bring your son and his 'Sheila' back safe and sound it will mean you coming up with a further £50,000; if I don't then it will still cost you £20,000, because to be honest with you George this isn't my hobby. It sounds a lot of money, probably a lifetime's saving for you, but there's more than your son's existence at stake here.'

'If you had asked for twice as much I would have found it, Mr. Kelly.'

'I don't doubt it for one minute cobber. Now comes the difficult part to take onboard. If you agree to my conditions it must be done on trust. There can be no contract or written agreement between us, because if things do turn to rat shit any attempt at redress by you would compromise other parties. Is that clear?'

'I understand what you're saying.'

'Good. One final condition. When you head back north you will not hear from me again. You will not try to contact me or anyone else that you have met since you have been down here, in fact George I am persona non grata as far as you are concerned. But what's more to the point your son's safety depends on you keeping to the conditions I have laid out.'

'How long before you can move?'

'Depends on my contact in South America. If he's on the ball I can be in place within four days.'

'And the chances of success?'

Kelly reached for another 'tinny' before he replied.

'All I can guarantee is that you will have the best men that money can buy earning their corn for you. I can't say any more than that.'

He wouldn't have disagreed - impressed by the way the man had conducted himself, confident, almost to the point of being arrogant. He stood, ready to leave.

'The money will be on its way to you first thing tomorrow, Mr. Kelly, and bring them home will you?'

They shook hands.

'By the way, why Pandora Removals?'

'According to the mythical story when she opened the box all the bad things in the world came out of it, only Hope remained. That's exactly what I deal with George, bad things and hope.' He smiled, giving the impression that he actually enjoyed it.

'I am 'deus ex machina' George, take care cobber.'

As he left the hotel in search of a cab he made a note of the Latin phrase in his diary; he would look it up when he arrived home.

* * *

Henri Pastrana wasn't sure whether the contact in Cali would acknowledge his message, particularly as he was using the American's codeword, but after speaking with his Minister he was more than hopeful. His superior had informed him that the British Foreign Office could in no way condone an attempt to free the hostages using force, and that if they disregarded the wishes of HM Government then be it on their own heads. The message was clear enough, explaining to the go-between that the pull-out by the Americans need not necessarily mean that the original agreement could not be resurrected. The deal however was conditional on him continuing to supply information on the remaining hostages and also any other items of interest, which he was obviously in a position to acquire. The one bit of good news that week had come from Benito, Guillermo particularly relieved that the American had recovered so well from his ordeal.

'No reply yet boss?'

Henri shook his head, indicating to Garbanza that he should take a seat.

'It would appear that the man in Cali is no longer interested, now that the dollars have ceased to flow. The question is, do we really need him now? Hollingsworth has informed us of where the hostages are being held. Surely it's time to move, before they kill off the remainder, or even take more tourists. How long do we wait Henri?'

He had no idea, and told his deputy as much.

'Unfortunately the British are a particularly patient race, they are not hot-blooded Latins, and they will urge our Government to continue to negotiate until the last possible moment.'

'Correct me if I am wrong boss, but there are no negotiations taking place.'

'That's not what the British Foreign Office have been led to believe. And there are other considerations to be taken into account, my friend. You were part of the bloodshed that occurred in the late 70s and early 80s and I am sure that you would not want to see a return to that era.'

'That is for certain. They were dark days indeed.'

'For that reason alone our Government is loath to give permission for an all-out military attack on the likes of Betancur. It could have the effect of uniting every drug trafficker, bandit and guerrilla movement, not only in Colombia, but in all Latin America. What I am about to tell you now makes me certain that our friend in Cali will be in touch.'

Up until that point Guillermo had only been half listening. He now took a keen interest in what his boss was about to divulge.

'The reason I think the man from Cali will contact us, is not because of what grows on top of the land belonging to Betancur and Jaramillo but what is being produced underneath it. Oil, Guillermo, billions of barrels of it, and the go-between has known of its existence for some time.'

'But how? Our own Government would have known, surely.'

'One representative in it did. A man who we all thought was beyond reproach. Renaldo Hernandez instigated this whole mess with a view to becoming one of the richest men in Latin America, and whoever executed him on the runway at El Diablo did us a favour.'

'When did you find this out?'

'As you know, I went to see the Minister yesterday, at his request, and he informed me that quite by accident they had discovered certain documents relating to Renaldo's term in office. These papers had been kept in his personal safe and only recently come to light, but on closer inspection where found to have originated prior to the Curaçao meeting. Being in his position he was aware of America's interest in once again gaining a foothold in Bolivia - for whatever reason, the main stumbling block being Punta, whose hatred of anything American went back years. The Americans informed Hernandez of the 90% probability of oil and so a deal was struck, America being permitted to take out the three drug traffickers in return for the land, which they would develop with their man in control.'

'But how was Hernandez going to profit?'

'Because my friend, he insisted that the Americans turn the land over to the man in Cali, who in fact was in partnership with him. If it had gone to plan everyone would have benefited. With Punta discredited the way would have been clear for the Americans to improve their position in Bolivia. Hernandez and the Cali connection would then share in the spoils brought about by the oil revenue.'

'So where did it go wrong for Renaldo?'

'Pure supposition, but there is more than a possibility that with the plan in place, Hernandez was surplus to requirements.'

'The man in Cali.'

'He would be my choice also.'

'And obviously still interested in a deal that would see him taking over Betancur's estancia?'

'That is why I feel almost certain that he will make contact.'

The following afternoon Henri Pastrano was proved right. An added bonus being that the envelope left at the PIP headquarters' reception desk by the shadowy figure contained information that would open up a whole new course of strategy.

* * *

It was early morning when he arrived back in Hartlepool, having made the last train north from the capital, the frost thick on the ground causing him to hold the wall of the house as he fumbled for the lock. The gloom and cold from outside seemed to have followed him in, and even before he took of his coat he put the kettle on. He was sitting by the fire having decided not to disturb Joan when he heard the lounge door open, Nick closing it quietly behind him.

'How did it go Dad?'

'Better than I expected, son. The man that I went to see was the one I hoped he would be and he was able to put me in touch with someone else. He seemed to know what he was about and is probably our best chance of success.'

He then went on to tell him the rest of the story.

'What are you doing up at this time of the morning anyway?'

'I've been keeping an eye on mam every couple of hours, but she just lays there, saying nothing.'

'I know, it's hard on us all but it's particularly difficult for her. You get to bed now and I'll see to her.'

He finished his cup of tea and crept into the bedroom, gently lying on the bed beside her. He wished that she would wake and start asking him questions. It was something that he had found irksome in the past, because he had never been deliberately secretive; it was just that sometimes things were better left unsaid. He had lost count of the number of times the two boys had entrusted him with some piece of information, only to request that he was not to tell 'me mother, you know she'll only worry'. But then there was the 'Catch 22' situation which applied to their present predicament. If she did recover and start asking what was happening, should he tell her and build up her hopes, or tell her nothing and risk a reoccurrence of what was happening at the moment. He decided to cross the bridge when it came and to his surprise found himself falling asleep.

A similar thing had happened to him on three occasions that he could remember, all unexplained, the first being the call from his mother shortly before her death. He had been awake minutes before the phone rang, her voice weak and feeble pleading for his help, a plea which he answered immediately and provided her with assistance, although her life came to an end shortly afterwards. The second had been the burglary - some sixth sense alerting him to an intruder who he had disturbed in one of the boys' bedrooms, not apprehending him but his presence enough to chase him off. Finally there had been the old woman on the street corner who he had pulled back from the kerbside moments before a lorry - of which they had both been unaware - took the turning too sharply and mounted the pavement at the very spot on which she had been standing. Maybe some people did possess a 'third eye' or then again, did it belong to someone else. It had happened again, the feeling that something was wrong. Fumbling for the bedside lamp he switched it on, illuminating Joan's face, her lips and lobes of her ears already turning blue, the unmistakable symptoms of cyanosis. Nick - in response to his father's shouts - rang for the ambulance, adding that it was required for a heart attack victim and hoping that when it arrived it would be manned by paramedics. Together now in the bedroom they put their years of training into practice, a husband and son combining their efforts to keep a wife and mother alive.

CHAPTER EIGHTEEN

John 'Ned' Kelly had been born and raised in Sydney until the age of fifteen when - following the death of his mother in a road accident - both he and his father had made the journey to England. During the first two years in his new country he had worked with his father, a plumber by trade, but soon found the work repetitive and boring, so it was only a matter of time before he decided to do something with a bit more excitement attached. That something was joining the Army. He was born to it, and by the time he was twenty years of age had attained the rank of full corporal. A sergeant at twenty-three he then decided to apply for the SAS Regiment, and although it meant a reduction in both rank and pay he felt the urge of another challenge more than compensated for the loss. The selection process posed few problems for him and he was readily accepted into their ranks, winning the coveted beige beret and 'Who Dares Wins' badge at his first attempt.

There then followed an intensive year of training carried out in various countries and extremes of conditions, before he was eventually seconded to the Counter Revolutionary Warfare (CRW) wing and posted to Northern Ireland where he completed three tours. The outbreak of the conflict in the Falkland Islands saw him as part of 'D' Squadron 22 SAS walk into Grytviken without a shot being fired and during the latter days of his career he was in much demand all over the World as an instructor in CRW.

He had first met Morrow in the Falkland's town, the 'bootneck' officer, as they were known, scrounging a cuppa off him and his mates. They had all been part of the same attack force - Morrow the officer commanding a detachment of Marines from HMS Antrim, and during a conversation over the 'brew,' he had mentioned that this was his last 'op', having been offered some sort of position in a Government Department. Five years after Grytviken, and following his release from the Army, he had bumped into Morrow purely by accident at the Red Lion public house in Westminster. It wasn't a watering hole he frequented - a favourite haunt of political types and their commentators and so not really his scene but he had been in that part of the city anyway.

Since leaving the Army he had been employed on numerous building sites as a general labourer, like so many ex-forces personnel before him, his expertise in hostage release and parachute jumping not in great demand. His employers at that time had been cowboys, paying little more than beer money, and so the offer of a job from Morrow had been gratefully accepted, especially as it utilized his soldiering skills and paid well. His new boss explained that because he invariably had to operate within the confines of Government red tape and strict guidelines, it was sometimes impossible to act quickly enough. He was therefore looking for an alternative method of preventing known criminals using the laborious system as an escape route. The arrangement was highly unofficial, but so far it had been very successful mainly due to the comprehensive register of worldwide contacts which Morrow had compiled over the years, and which was now in his hands. It had come as no surprise to him that there were men who made their living from supplying any mortal thing on earth, from information to arms, and not above carrying out the most heinous of contracts.

The same night that Halkin had been to see him he consulted the folder, where, under Latin America, he found the code word and the method of contacting the man in Cali. Using his laptop computer he then set about putting his requirements into the designated coding system together with a request for the possible location of the hostages. Having completed these preliminaries he was now in a position to make contact with the 'fixer' at the e-mail address contained in the folder.

It was now quite late, but before he vacated the hotel room and returned to his office he decided to accomplish one more task, and that was to pick the team that would eventually enter South America.

* * *

It was twelve hours after Joan's admission to the General Hospital that George was allowed to see her, his wife lying motionless in the midst of an array of humming machines and numerous lengths of tubing.

'She's comfortable and stable,' replied the sister in charge of the intensive care ward in answer to his enquiry, but he sensed without any conviction.

He stayed for an hour, holding her hand and talking quietly, words of encouragement, his mouth inches from her ear. Nick relieved him, allowing him to visit the bank and organize the transfer of the money required by Kelly, the bank manager explaining how it would occur in language that he understood.

'It's quite straightforward really, Mr. Halkin. Your instructions will be passed by our computer system to our

Head Office who in turn send the amount stipulated through the Clearing House Automated Payment Service to the beneficiary's bank Head Office. You're in plenty of time to make what we term the 'gateway' which closes at 3.30pm, so the beneficiary will have the amount in his account today. Unfortunately the bad news is that we have to charge for this service.'

He signed the relevant paperwork and returned to the hospital - allowing Nick to return home and change into his uniform ready for the night shift. The hand on his shoulder woke him from a restless sleep. It was 8 o'clock and the doctor responsible for the ward was making a final check of the patients before he too retired for the night.

'I think you would be better in your own bed, Mr. Halkin. There is nothing you can do here.'

He is too young to be looking after my wife, he thought.

'Will she get better?'

'We will talk tomorrow when the picture is a little clearer.'

The sister smiled at him, condescending, yet he knew that she was doing it for the right reasons.

His grip on the steering wheel of his car tightened with every metre of the journey home, imagining that it was at the throat of the man responsible for his son's incarceration - the bastard who was systematically destroying his family. And who was next, him?

⋆ ⋆ ⋆

'Read it to me again, Guillermo, slowly.

Both men had scanned the contents of the envelope with incredulity written all over their faces.

'I have enclosed the following newspaper cutting and the additional explanation as a sign of good faith. The woman in the photograph is Hermania Gavira, the grandmother of the captured Ecuadorean girl and the ex-lover of Rodrigo Betancur. Until recently, Betancur was unaware of any family, but would have cared little if he had known. He is now in poor health and maybe more responsive to suggestions that they meet. I fear that Alfred Jaramillo's day's are numbered, and feel that in return for assisting in his demise, apart from any other way in which I can be of help, acquisition of his estancia would be an acceptable remuneration.'

'Not only devious but articulate with it,' Henri muttered.

'But not something we have the authority to agree to.'

'Who said we haven't? From the very start we have been lied to, kept in the dark by the Americans, betrayed by one of our own politicians, and generally treated like lepers. Well it's about time we started to play them at their own game. Let me ask you a question, Guillermo, have you made a will, or written a letter of intent?'

'Well yes. But why is that relevant?'

'Because I am going to agree to the man's wishes and hope that Jaramillo has also made provision for someone, that would then make the deal with Cali not worth the paper it's written on.'

Garbanza wasn't sure, the tone of his voice making it clear to his boss.

'It's a hell of a gamble, what if you're wrong? How do we explain this to the Minister?'

'If I am wrong I wouldn't have to, and as my successor I would make it clear that you were unaware of my decision. Now before you talk me out of it ask Bernice to give you the most recent letter from the Ministry, then tell her to take an extended coffee break, but to leave her computer switched on.'

Minute's later Garbanza watched as his boss covered the letter with a blank sheet of paper, everything that is but the heading. He then made two photocopies.

'How is your typing my friend?'

He sat down in the secretary's chair without answering Henri. It would have taken Bernice probably ten minutes to compose the two letters, but as a two-fingered and five words a minute typist it took him nearly an hour, and yet Henri was pleased with the result.

'Now we fax them to the drop address that he's stipulated.'

'Why don't we monitor the location, pick him up when he arrives?'

'Because Guillermo, if he's as clever as I think he is, it will not be him that does the collecting. Besides he is just a means to an end, his turn will come.'

They sent the letters, one promising the man in Cali ownership of Jaramillo's estancia, but only on condition that Rodrigo would permit Hermania and her family to visit him. The second letter gave Government assurances that Alfred would be granted an amnesty and passage to a country of his choice. It also included written permission to transfer any funds that he had accumulated, should the visit be accomplished.

When Bernice arrived back at her desk there was no evidence of what had occurred during her coffee break. There was however a note, requesting her to make two reservations on a flight to Quito, Ecuador.

* * *

'How is the shoulder, Byron?'

They were sitting having a meal in a bar in El Retiro, washed down with a glass of the local beer.

'Much better, the pain has gone, it just aches slightly.'

'We will stay here tonight and return to Bogotá in the morning. No doubt Guillermo will be glad to see you back.'

'I'm not going to Bogotá. I'm going to find that house again and get them kids out of there.'

The fork containing the remainder of his meal never reached Benito's mouth.

'That is not such a good idea, even for a fit man.'

'And I suppose this was.' He touched the sling that still supported his arm, not really necessary, but he was wary of removing it.

'There may be plans in progress that we know nothing about, and any interference could jeopardize their success.'

'Know nothing about, just about hits the nail on the head Benito, which is why I'm fed up with being treated like a fucking mushroom.'

'I do not understand.'

'Kept in the dark and fed shit from time to time.'

He knew the analogy would be wasted on him, it was more a need to vent some anger. But he was determined not to become another Terry Waite, who had been given similar treatment during the Iran-Contra affair involving the Lebanese hostages. Waite finding himself a victim instead of what he had intended, a saviour.

'No, my friend, if I'm going to self-destruct then I'll press the button, not some faceless, manipulative son of a bitch.'

They finished their meal in silence, not sure about where the conversation was taking them.

'The next move is yours, Benito, because as far as I'm concerned you're still my control.'

He knew he was putting the man on the spot.

'I always thought poets were shy and sensitive, compadre, not hard and ruthless.'

He smiled.

'Like my namesake - they can be both. His poetry came from his imagination and observation, but his fervour for indulging in revolutionary politics came from the heart.'

'If I agree, what are your intentions?'

'There is a stockyard close to the clearing, but some distance from the house, it would be possible to hide there until the opportunity presented itself. But first I must locate the house with the winged horses.'

'That should not be a problem. I suspect that there are people here in El Retiro who may know of such a place. I make one condition, Byron, and that is that I come with you. You may have the brains - which will certainly be required to carry this thing through - but I have the muscle and cunning which may be useful should your plan fail you.'

'The Dead have been awakened - shall I sleep?
The World's at war with tyrants - shall I crouch?
The harvest's ripe - and shall I pause to reap?
I slumber not - the thorn is in my Couch.'

Benito didn't understand a word of it, but there was something about the way the American said it that impressed him. It had nothing to do with understanding, it was the undeniable passion of the man, a commitment to people he didn't know, and in a land that wasn't his.

'You are indeed a strange, strange man Byron.'

★ ★ ★

For the very first time in his life, Rodrigo was under the influence of the drug that had made him an extremely rich man. He had been driven to it by a mixture of pain, loneliness and uncertainty. Compelled to leave the real world if only for a short respite, and hoping to find the answers to questions he couldn't resolve by the process of rational thought.

Alfred's revelations about Hermania and her granddaughter had come as a shock, causing him uncharacteristic feelings of wanting to belong. He knew that death was not far away. Every day the searing pain caused by the bullet becoming more intense, his attitude to those around him less tolerant. The smallest of indiscretions irritated him to the point that he was now ordering beatings for his servants, a dropped glass, or late meal, punishable irrespective of the reason.

Over a period exceeding forty years any semblance of basic humanity had been torn from him, replaced by a total disregard for compassion, and yet this new development had triggered in him a long lost desire to see Hermania again. They had been close - once, Alfred, her and him like one. He shivered uncontrollably, the hallucinatory world of cocaine taking him down an unknown path, removing his defences and exposing dormant weaknesses. The Englishman mattered little - the order for his execution already given, even if he was a friend of his granddaughter. The girl was a different matter - the daughter of his daughter, the same blood running through her veins.

Loath to admit it in his presence, Alfred had been right. They were not getting any younger and sooner or later their Empire would crumble, they in turn left to rot, although convinced that death would precede that event. The cracks - in what he thought was an impenetrable organization - were now turning into huge chasms, the informer who had virtually brought his business to a standstill, still not identified. Then there was the recent affair with Punta and the American agent, more evidence that the enemy was closing in.

He could feel the effect of the drug beginning to diminish, returning him to the pain and the doubt. It was conceivable that Jaramillo had a point, maybe it was time to relinquish his hold, try to see out his remaining days without having to continually look over his shoulder, or wear the pistols. The wearing of arms - something he had only recently adopted was a throwback to the early days. Until now his men on the outside had shouldered the responsibility for his continuing survival, now he even doubted their loyalty. The cocaine had helped, not only to alleviate the pain but also in deciding the path he would take. Jaramillo and the girl would join him, but only after certain aspects of his affairs had been put in order.

* * *

They had returned to the squalor of the cabin, both of them feeling much better, if somewhat perplexed, by the unexpected show of concern by the man from the house. From the calendar on the desk in the study Simon calculated that they had been in the man's hands for nearly six weeks, and he was still no nearer discovering the reason. There were strange anomalies, the fact that they were being kept against their will contrasting with isolated displays of civilized behaviour by the man, and then there was the photograph.

'Did you see her, Maria?'

'She was very pretty. Perhaps it was his wife.'

'She looked like you.'

She smiled, a rare occurrence since their capture.

'She looked like a lot of South American women, it is the black hair and the dark eyes.'

He wasn't convinced and spent the next ten minutes watching her as she gazed out of the window. Suddenly she turned and caught him.

'Why do you stare at me so, Simon?'

'You remind me of what a real feminine woman should be like, that is all.'

'You have women in England also, remember?'

'I sometimes wonder. Every time I return home I see more of them with tattoos, hear them swearing, watch them drinking pints, even fighting in public. They dress like men, some play rugby and soccer, there are a few who have even taken to boxing, and somewhere along the way they have lost their femininity. There is perhaps a lot of truth in what my father says, that in the space of twenty years the opposite sex has risen from inferiority to equality and some think they have reached a position of complete superiority.'

She listened as if understanding all that he was saying, but just hearing his voice was enough. Joining him on the side of the bunk she laid her head on his lap.

'No matter what happens I promise not to be a boxer.'

They both laughed, causing the large black woman to emerge from behind her curtain, but only for a moment, returning to her solitary world.

He looked down at Maria. He knew that she would always make him laugh, not unlike his mother, sometimes not meaning to but just by the way it came out. On one occasion they had all gone away to a popular holiday camp where he and Nick, due to the excitement, had misbehaved, causing Joan to inform them that 'the next time we bring you on holiday, you're not coming.'

His father had been unable to refrain from laughing which resulted in making the matter worse.

Maria brought him back to the present.

'If the man has allowed us to shower do you think that we may soon be going home?'

She had put into words the possibility that he had not even dared to think too much about, it had however crossed his mind.

'Let us wait and see Maria, but what will be, will be.'

* * *

He couldn't decide whether it was due to his popularity or notoriety, although he suspected strongly that it was the latter, but within the last twenty-four hours his services had been requested on two occasions, from such diverse locations as Bogotá and London. The problem was that they were obviously inter-linked, although whether their originators knew of the other's intentions was another matter, and therefore the requests required some thought.

To supply the weapons and transport required by London would take twenty-four hours, and probably less, the large arsenal that he had built up over the years readily available in a warehouse just south of the city. He had started small, but the Contra-Sandinista war in Nicaragua during the 80s saw his stock increase with an almost equal amount of Russian and American weapons being traded by the unpaid peasant soldiers for food with which to feed their families. The major turning point for him as a 'fixer' however, came with the election of Violet Chammoro - the widow of Pedro. When she took office in 1990 the Contras disarmed, leaving him to purchase enough American weapons to equip an army, and all for virtually nothing. The weaponry, both large and small, was loaded onto a ship and transported down the Pacific Coast eventually reaching Colombia after a few officials had been paid considerable amounts of dollars to turn a blind eye.

London had also requested a helicopter, and although he had the capacity to stock those as well, it was just as easy to import one from Brazil as and when required. His major concern was the request by the English for the location of the hostages. There was only one possible answer to why they wanted the information, and that was that they intended to take out their own National, or maybe even the girl as well, and that was not the way he saw things happening. The agreement with Pastrana was dependent on the girl being in the care of Betancur, and that could hardly be achieved if she was on an aircraft bound for who knew where.

Approximately one hour of careful thought later he had the answer. He would satisfy London's requirements immediately - except for the location of the hostages, which would be supplied at the last minute - that would then give Jaramillo time to take the girl into safe keeping. He would also offer Pastrana a piece of advice, and that would be to call London and find out what was going down.

CHAPTER NINETEEN

The phone calls to the men he had chosen to accompany him to Colombia had been made the previous night, all accepting, as he knew they would, his invitation to join him at the hotel located on the outskirts of the capital. They would remain there until all the arrangements for the 'op' had been completed, only then would he and his three companions make any attempt at an 'extrication'. The men he was going to meet belonged to an elite club, hand-picked by him and who he knew either personally or by reputation, each from a different social background and highly individual, but they all had one thing in common. They were men capable of killing a fellow human being and walking away unscathed, always in mind, and to date, in body too. It wasn't however as easy as the movies made it out to be. In the real world it took a special type of man to stand eyeball to eyeball and pull the trigger. Factors such as self-discipline, attitude and the detached mind to carry it out and then live with it afterwards were all important, and to that end they all believed that if you couldn't handle the grief, then you didn't handle the gun.

As the cab manoeuvred its way out of London he thumbed through the file reminding himself of the specialist qualities each man possessed.

Mick Chandler had a similar background to his own. Now thirty-seven years of age he was ex-SAS, the 'bandit country' of South Armagh his second home during his time in the Province. In his day he had been a bit of a 'loose cannon', a law unto himself, openly disregarding the Rules of Engagement or 'yellow card' as it was known, which they all had to abide by. During his second tour he had shot and killed a sixteen-year-old civilian. It was the turning point in his life, realizing that he had been lucky to escape a custodial sentence he became a reformed character overnight.

Turning the page he smiled at the second name in the folder, Jerry O'Connor. 'Whinger' O'Connor was, and always had been, a misanthropist. Not only did he mistrust everyone, he simply hated mankind in general. His only friend and confidant was his dog Cerberus - who he had named after the many-headed dog which had guarded the gates of Hades. The German Shepherd had been aptly named. According to myth it had been one of the Labours of Hercules to bring the dog down to Earth - his hardest task - something which the Royal Marines' hierarchy had failed to achieve with O'Connor. As a member of the Special Boat Service however, he had played a significant part in taking out a large section of the communication link between Saddam's bunker in Baghdad and the rest of Iraq.

His final choice had been Alec Burns - an amiable Scotsman from Dundee and in his late twenties. He was an enigma. Intelligent and yet wayward, his background was one of money, mainly due to his father's ownership of a whisky distillery and his mother being second cousin to a Duke. Unfortunately the lad had never fitted in, and subsequently had never returned to the family home since being discharged from the Army. Before the break-up however, his father had paid for him to obtain a pilot's licence - the intention being that he would pilot the family helicopter on business trips. Alec had obviously taken to it, and his nerve and expertise had more than once saved them from coming unstuck.

He closed the folder satisfied with his choice, although realistically he could have chosen any one of a dozen men on his books. Since he had formed the organization - code named Orpheus - he had used them all at different times and on a variety of 'ops', predominantly abroad, but occasionally on home ground. During the five years that Orpheus had been running he had discovered that most Administrations required something similar - removing or destroying anything unsavoury that was interfering with the well-oiled machine of Government; he was in effect a 'cleaner'.

The taxi pulled onto the forecourt of the hotel, and minutes later he had located the three men, already well into a session judging by the amount of empty glasses on the table. Chandler spotted him first.

'Good to see you again Ned, what's yours?'

'Get me a lager Mick.'

He shook hands with each of them, adding that he was glad they had been able to respond, and then with a lager in front of him, briefly outlined the reason for their attendance. He planned to go over the 'op' in detail when he had received confirmation from Cali, which he hoped to receive within the next twenty-four hours, but until then it was time to catch up and reminisce. It was Mick Chandler again who spoke first, a master storyteller.

'Remember that Rupert we had at Hereford, Ned. He was in the habit of giving us lectures on leadership, a right tosser. Anyway this particular day he was rabbiting on about leading from the front like he had done and all that shit, when a voice from the back yelled, 'The only trouble was you were fucking retreating at the time'.'

It opened the box, each contributing, including him.

'I once took a squad of recruits up onto the Brecon Beacons and saw that one of them was struggling. So to try to give him a bit of encouragement I told him that, where there was a will there was a way. Why do you think General Hannibal took those elephants across the Alps, I asked him.

"Was he looking for a circus, Sergeant Kelly?' he asked.'

The raucous laughter continued, as did the lager.

It was good to be back amongst men with so much in common with himself, and the tales of previous exploits - some of them recalled with pleasure, others conveyed with anguish. It was early morning when they began drifting off to their respective rooms, leaving him to wait by his laptop computer in readiness for the anticipated message from Cali.

It arrived four hours after his companions had retired to their rooms, the 'fixer' confirming that he would deliver the necessary transport and weapons to an unused airstrip near Sevilla, a small town outside Cali. They would be picked up by taxi and taken to the drop, and only then would they receive all the necessary information and most important of all, the coordinates pinpointing the clearing. The delivery date, he noted, was in two days' time.

* * *

The intensive care unit at the General hospital was situated on the top floor for two reasons. The noise synonymous with hospitals was kept to an absolute minimum, in addition to which the building had been designed with a special lift stopping at no intervening floors but travelling straight down to the ground floor, which was where the mortuary was located.

The night sister had rung him half an hour earlier asking him to attend, and as he and Nick walked down the deserted corridor she met them at the door of Joan's private room.

'Any word of your son yet George?'

'No nothing, but why the call? Has something happened?'

She told them both to wait in an adjoining room and shortly afterwards they were being told to sit down by a tall, grey-haired man in an expensive suit.

'My name is Fairbrother, Mr. Halkin, and I'm the senior consultant here in a branch of medicine which deals mainly with determining the functioning, or in your wife's case non-functioning, of the brain, but that's it in its simplest terms. Don't get the wrong impression, I'm not talking down to you, but it is important that you understand exactly what I'm going to tell you.'

'I appreciate what you're saying and please keep it as simple as you like.'

He glanced across at Nick, saw the tears starting to form in his son's eyes.

'To risk stating the obvious, your wife's state of health is deteriorating rapidly, with little or no sign of any physical abnormality to account for it. In cooperation with some of my colleagues, we have come to the conclusion that your wife's condition is due to what we term a physiological-psychological problem. Now I did say at the outset that I wouldn't confuse you with medical jargon, so this is what it means. Our bodily functions, the physiological element, are greatly influenced by what occurs in the brain, the psychological side of things, and should anything upset the balance - say by some terrible experience, or a disability, then one can affect the other.'

George nodded, he had more or less known what Jean's problem was, here was the confirmation.

Fairbrother continued. 'In her present state all her thoughts are negative and we are fairly certain that is why her body has ceased to function. What we have to try to do is to discover a medium capable of supplying her with something positive to concentrate on.'

George had a good idea of what was coming next.

'We are now firmly of the belief that the event which is causing your wife to behave as she is at present is the absence of your son, Simon. He is the medium, the trigger if you like, and I'm afraid for your wife to survive she needs him badly.'

He didn't really want to know the answer to his next question, but it had to be asked.

'Is there any way of estimating how long in her present state she will last, before switching off altogether?'

He had watched his father go through the same process, before admitting defeat.

'Virtually impossible to ascertain,' he lowered his voice slightly, 'but time is not on our side. I'm sorry George but there's very little we can do for her apart from carry out certain functions for her until she decides otherwise.'

He thanked the consultant for being so candid, both him and Nick remaining in the room for some considerable time after he had left, silent, each with his own thoughts.

'Do you want to go in and see her, George?'

She lay as usual without moving, even more instruments monitoring her, more tubes feeding her, each machine sustaining life. He sat on one side of the bed whilst Nick occupied the opposite side, holding her hands, talking to her. If only she could look into his heart and see the pain he was feeling, but she was not that perceptive. He had done his best, still was - in his way, not always guaranteed to be right, and yet done for the right reasons; but then again life didn't have the rewind facility of a video recorder. You couldn't wipe the tape clean and start again when you felt like it, if only relationships were that easy.

His father had been right, the cutting of the first-born's umbilical cord was just a physical act, replaced by an invisible thread that was stronger and more durable than anything so far invented, and it was irreplaceable. The bedside cabinet was filled with get well messages and cards, all sent by family and friends, their intentions well meant, but serving little or no purpose. The one message that would bring her back conspicuous by its absence. They both kissed her on the forehead before leaving, Nick lingering. He had changed. Gone was the heart-on-the-sleeve, open-book attitude, he was in the initial stages of constructing his own shell.

* * *

The two seats, which Bernice had reserved on the flight to Quito, were now occupied by Henri Pastrana and Guillermo Garbanza, both men deep in thought as the plane levelled out. It wasn't until some time into the flight that Henri made any attempt at conversation.

'What did you tell Bernice?'

'That the moment she received any word from Cali she had to contact us at the number I had given her.'

'How sure are you that the grandmother will cooperate?'

'I wish I were as sure about a lot of things. If I was in her shoes, considering the way she was treated, and then someone came along with the means to get even, I would jump at the chance. And anyway, your career depends to a large extent on me being right, and when have I let you down?'

Henri didn't need to answer, his companion already agreeing to put his own life on the line if Hermania agreed to their plan.

They where met at Quito Airport and driven straight to their hotel, the driver reminding them that he was at their disposal for as long as required, his delight obvious when Henri told him that he need not return until the next day, giving the man the night off. The young lady at the reception desk allocated them their rooms and they were about to walk away.

'There is a message for you, Señor Pastrana.'

She passed him a note.

'I have to ring Bernice, immediately.'

'I'll wait for you here,' replied Guillermo, finding a comfortable armchair in the lobby and awaiting the return of his boss.

There was a perplexed look on Henri's face as he walked across the lobby.

'The man from Cali has been in touch, but it is not the message that we expected, in fact I am not sure what it means. Does the name Robert Morrow mean anything to you?'

'Morrow, Morrow, of course he is the Head of International Crime in London, but why?'

'Because Cali advises us to ring him as soon as possible.'

'Did Bernice give you the number?'

Henri nodded, he was thinking of the time difference.

'By the time we settle in and have a meal he should be available.'

Two hours later he was proved right, the call being put through by Morrow's secretary, and after introducing himself, he asked some critical questions.

'Have you anything going on in my part of the world at the moment, Mr. Morrow?'

'How do you mean, going on?'

'Any activity?'

'I haven't, no.'

Henri detected the emphasis on the 'I'.

'Are you aware of any?' The pause answering his question before the word came.

'Possibly.'

He was thinking on his feet, the way the man was answering an indication of an unsecured line, or simply mistrust; he compromised, hoping Morrow would get the message.

'There is something that you should know, sir. A marriage has been arranged and the girl is promised, but the boy is free to choose, good day.'

Guillermo waited for Henri to compose his thoughts.

'I suspect that London have made their own plans for releasing the hostages,' he divulged eventually.

'I thought as much from your reference to the fact that they could try for the boy but the girl was off limits.'

'Let us hope that Señor Morrow is as quick-witted as you, my friend.'

It was late afternoon the following day when Bernice contacted them again, relaying the news from Cali. Rodrigo had instructed Alfred to bring the girl to his hacienda and to arrange for her mother and father, with

Hermania, to visit him also, he would guarantee their safety. How the go-between came by his information Garbanza could only guess. A man on the inside? Not that he gave it too much thought; he had other things on his mind, like a meeting with Hermania Gavira.

They were on the road early the following morning, not certain how long it would take to reach Ibarra, and whilst the driver was content to listen to the local radio station, he and Henri acted like tourists and talked about anything that came to mind. The proposition which they would put to Hermania had been agreed upon the previous night and so there was no need to discuss it further, not that they would have done considering the proximity of the driver. It took them less time than they had anticipated, a further surprise being the size of the town, much larger than either of them had envisaged.

'How about breakfast, Henri?'

It seemed early to suddenly appear at someone's door. The driver was helpful and drove them to a restaurant that he sometimes used, where they stayed until Henri agreed that it was time to make their move. They found the family home of Maria Sandino without too much trouble, a large dog in the garden the first to greet them, followed closely by a woman who Guillermo took to be the girl's mother.

'Buenos dias. ¿Donde puedo encontrar Hermania Gavira?'

The woman answered uncertainly.

'Un momento.' Disappearing into the house, to return a few minutes later in the company of an older woman.

'Can I help you?' The voice was firm and strong, confident, unlike the younger woman.

They introduced themselves, providing adequate identification before she led them inside and invited them to take a seat.

'You have news of Maria, yes?'

'We have, but it is not good,' replied Guillermo.

'Not good, or bad? There is a difference, Señor Garbanza.'

'Before I begin will you answer me two questions, do you know a man called Betancur or another named Jaramillo?'

'I have heard of them naturally, they are the devils who have my granddaughter.'

'That is not what I asked.'

For the first time her reply was not immediately forthcoming.

'They had different names many years ago.'

Henri leaned forward in anticipation of his deputy pressing home their advantage - having made the admission.

'I have received word that Maria is to be moved to the hacienda of Betancur.'

'Then you must prevent that from happening. Policemen, soldiers perhaps, he would be no loss and the world a better place in which to live - especially for my granddaughter.' She said it calmly, without raising her voice, almost an intonation perpetuating indifference.

Garbanza explained the possible repercussions of such an action, to which she replied that although understanding the problem she didn't have to agree with his motives for not wanting to use force.

'There is a more subtle way, Hermania, if you will agree.'

'He will see me?'

The woman still retains her intuition, he thought.

'Maria's mother and father also. I understand he has never seen his daughter?'

'My daughter, not his.' It was a sharp rebuke. 'He must be dying, why else would he allow this to happen?'

'That is not important, but the opportunity to free Maria is, and to do it I need your help.'

'With respect, señor, why else would you have come personally? I cannot however speak for my daughter or her husband.'

'They would not be required. Because Rodrigo or Jaramillo have never seen either of them, I would act as the father and a female agent represent your daughter. It would give me access to him, something I have spent my life trying to achieve.'

'Then maybe we can both put a ghost to rest, señor.' It was what he had been hoping to hear. 'When will it happen?'

'Soon, which is why I must ask you to return with us to Bogotá. We must be in a position to move quickly.'

'I will collect a few things after I have spoken to my family. Please, make yourselves comfortable.'

In the privacy of her room she packed a small suitcase with clothes, then, satisfied that she had enough, reached under her bed and removed a small wooden box. The final two objects that she placed in her suitcase were from the box; a small velvet drawstring bag and a leather case, the contents of which she had never handled in over forty years. Now she was ready.

They both watched from the automobile as she said her farewells, Garbanza impressed by the walk – purposeful, as if she was impatient to meet their quarry.

* * *

Initially, Bob Morrow was totally confused by the cryptic message from Pastrana, not only by its content, but by the very nature of the call itself. He knew he was safe in assuming that the man didn't possess a crystal ball and so the alternative was that he was employing the same man as Kelly. His days as the Intelligence Officer on the Whirlwind came to his rescue regarding the message, his conclusion being, try for Halkin but leave the girl. He leaned back in his chair. Not accustomed to being told by a foreign agency what he could or couldn't do his gut feeling told him that there was something bigger happening on the other side of the world, and that feeling alone prompted him to contact Kelly.

'I'm afraid Mr. Kelly has gone away for a few days,' was the reply to his call to Pandora Removals.

'Not yet he hasn't, dear. Now you contact him immediately this conversation is finished and you tell him to ring this number. He will know who it is, do you understand?' He replaced the receiver before she had time to answer.

The authoritative manner in which he spoke had, on more than one occasion, been more influential than any threat in convincing people that they should adhere to his request, and when the phone rang five minutes later it proved his theory correct once again.

'Its Kelly, Mr. Morrow.'

'There's a complication at the other end. The inventory does not include the Ecuadorean piece.'

'Okay.'

Kelly would not be happy with the change of plan. As an ex-professional soldier and non-commissioned officer he would already have finalized the rescue attempt down to the smallest detail, and he didn't like doing it to him.

He and his men however where travelling into someone else's territory and the last thing that anyone wanted, was to screw up maybe years of dangerous undercover work. Still, he was curious and wondered whether the Americans were in on the act, or had got wind of anything going on. If anyone would know, it would be Mike O'Grady, so he rang him.

* * *

Alfred Jaramillo had read the facsimile from Rodrigo with the same sort of feeling that a prisoner on death row would read an adverse reply from the Governor. Without him having to do anything, Rodrigo had agreed to take the girl and allow the closest people he had to family to visit him, everything Cali had asked for. It should have pleased him, the fact that no effort was required on his part, instead it had the opposite effect. The fax had an air of finality about it - as if his friend of forty years was gathering together the fragmented parts of his life, in the shape of people. To what end he did not know - maybe just to see them, to say farewell, or maybe to dispense with them completely, the latter being the reason for his uneasiness. It would be three days before he would find out the answer, enough time to make certain arrangements so that, in the event that he did not return, his affairs were to a certain degree settled. It was time to think about the future of the English boy.

CHAPTER TWENTY

The four men sat in the departure lounge of London's Heathrow Airport. Wearing smart suits and carrying only hand luggage they could easily have been mistaken for businessmen, which in a way they were. They sat in pairs, Kelly accompanying Alec Burns, whilst Chandler and O'Connor awaited the call for their flight some distance away.

He had planning down to a fine art - even the last minute phone call from Morrow failing to disrupt his plan significantly - always leaving himself options. Preparation to him was everything. The difference between a highly successful mission and a pig's ear of one, regardless of the quality of the troops. If the plan was crap they might as well run headlong into batteries of Russian cannon. And it didn't start with the action. It all began now which was the reason he and Burns were taking a different route to the other two, and would leave first. It was the conventional way and they would arrive first, flying them to Amsterdam to change aircraft, before proceeding on to Bogotá, with a fuel stop in the Dominican Republic in between. Chandler and 'Whinger' would follow two hours later on the Miami flight, thus entering South America from a different direction. They would then all meet up in Colombia's third largest City, Cali. He heard their flight being called and they both made their way through the passport control and departure gate onto the plane for the relatively short flight to Schipol.

Their stay in Amsterdam had been short. And now, settled on the Pan American jet, he reminded himself of the arrangements with the 'fixer' and the general logistics of the intended 'snatch'. That's what it would be. In, snatch the bod, and out. For this very reason he had made it clear to Cali that there was to be no hanging about. Once in position they would expect to get on with the job immediately, any delay putting everyone at risk. He recalled O'Connor enquiring about the man's reliability at the briefing prior to them leaving.

'I've never used him before, but he reckons he's got the goods and until we get there we won't know any different.'

'What goods has he got? Not half a dozen obscure Albanian shotguns I hope.'

'Judging from the catalogue in the folder it's mainly Soviet and Yank stuff, none of ours. But it will be familiar.'

'What will we be carrying Ned?' It was Whinger again, the other half of the actual snatch team and who would also double as the 'bang man', positioning any necessary explosive devices.

'I've asked for either the AK-47 or M16 assault rifle, plus a couple of 9mm Brownings, which the catalogue states he has.'

'How about back-up? I take it that's my job'

'Spot on Mick. Usual routine, sort out a lying-up position and cover the area, all being well you should have an M60, although whether the asbestos gloves will come with it I'm not sure.'

They had all smiled at the reference to the hot barrel, a feature of an earlier model of the machine gun. He had then turned to Alec.

'The chopper I can't guarantee, that he imports in, as and when, you'll just have to figure it out when it arrives, Alec.'

'Nay problem.' It was what he usually said.

'There's one or two other bits I've asked for. Thermal Imagers or passive night goggles, flash-bangs et cetera, but like I said, we won't know exactly what we're working with until we get there.'

He had paused to see if there were any more questions, not in the least surprised by their absence.

'One more thing. Last night I told you there was a Sheila involved, well she's now off the list, but if she's with the boy give her the 'sleepy time' anyway.' He looked at O'Connor.

'All right Whinger?'

He nodded his head in agreement, but his eyes said something different.

'What are we using, thiopentone?'

'Yep. It's as good as anything, and it stops them wriggling about.'

He felt Alec nudge him, one of the cabin crew handed him a drink.

'All sorted Ned?'

'I hope so, the lad's life depends on us getting it right.'

'You okay about this?'

'Yea, sure.'

But he wasn't sure. Like O'Connor he didn't like last minute alterations. He was not as sure now as he had been when he had told Halkin that he was 'Deus ex Machina' - the one who puts matters right at a critical moment, and they didn't come much more critical than when one of your kids went missing. The drink in his hand and the word 'missing' reminded him of an incident in the sergeant's mess at Aldershot some years earlier. He was in the company of four mates, one who didn't look particularly happy with life. At one point the bloke went for a 'leak' and he took the opportunity to enquire about his long face.

'He's just lost his wife,' was the reply. 'We told him to have a look in the lounge, but it didn't work, they were obviously pretty close.'

It was black humour. Not irreverent, nor did it trivialize the event - it was a way of handling it, common to the forces and emergency services alike as a safety valve. To outsiders it appeared cruel and insensitive, to those who on a day-to-day basis dealt with death and destruction, it kept the men in white coats at bay. But you could never adopt it with children, no matter how old they were.

'What's happening to the boy when we get him out?' Alec as positive as ever.

'We'll drop him in Quito before we leave, he can make his way to the Embassy and they can get him home. I doubt these people have left him with his original clothes never mind his passport. Anyway, as you know, it's never been our policy to take them the whole trip.'

He settled back in his seat, there was nothing more to be done until they arrived at Sevilla and then there would be more than enough.

* * *

It was the first time that she had ever been in an expensive automobile, overawed by the smoothness of the ride. Granted the roads are much better than they were forty years ago, she thought, little more than cart tracks then, and more roadblocks and checkpoints.

Garbanza had wanted to return to Quito and fly to Bogotá from there, but the opportunity to visit the places of her youth was too good to miss and she had persuaded him to leave from Ipiales, just across the Colombia-Ecuador border. As the vehicle sped northwards the place names, so long forgotten, rekindled memories of the last time she had been in this part of Latin America. They where approaching the border, the sign for Tulcan, the gateway to Colombia, and a favourite crossing point for them during their smuggling days. The darkness of night providing some protection as they raced across the border in the dilapidated truck, her driving, whilst her two companions fired their pistols above the heads of the Guardia. Drugs, weapons, it mattered little, any sort of contraband was their way of surviving. The only way. And then, exhilarated by the rush of adrenaline - she and her man would make love under the stars and later, naked, would play like children in the Rio Napo. Her granddaughter knew nothing of this, why should she? Her mother was not even aware.

Pastrana had said almost nothing since they had left Ibarra, content to gaze out of the window as they passed through places that she had not seen for half a lifetime, Mocoa, San Agustan where they had nearly come to grief at the hands of a vigilant soldier.

She wondered how they had uncovered her relationship with the man she was going to meet, a secret she had kept well hidden, or so she thought. He had disappeared before Maria's mother had been born, stealing away without a word, leaving her money to salve his conscience, money she didn't need.

'The country has changed since you were last in these parts, yes?'

Beside her Garbanza was trying to make conversation.

'We very rarely had time to appreciate it, señor, besides it was usually dark.'

He smiled. He would have liked to have known her when she was a young woman.

'How do you feel about seeing him again?'

'There will be no tears or laughter, señor.'

She had loved both men dearly, but time had drained her of any feeling for either of them. The photograph of them in her bedroom was not a reminder of happier times - but a vehicle for her hate. She had never married - content to assist in the upbringing of her daughter's children. A man would be surplus to her requirements, her independence established whilst still a young woman. She reflected on how greed - an integral part of human nature could destroy relationships similar to hers. The misguided concept that the dollar could produce happiness or the peso purchase everlasting friendship. In her case the two men's crusade in search of more sucre had purged her heart of any semblance of love.

They reached Ipiales at noon where another first-time experience awaited her. Journies undertaken by air had always been something that other people did, never her, yet here she was, and she had to admit to enjoying it, which was quite the opposite to Bogotá. The ride to the hotel where she would be staying was through the centre of the city - a large sprawling mixture of dirty buildings and uninviting calles, a million miles away from Banos and Ibarra, relieved when she finally entered her allocated room.

'There will be a señorita in the next room should you require anything, and she will also inform you when we will be travelling to Medellin. I will return however before that to go over the arrangements with you before we leave.'

She thanked Garbanza and waited for the two men to leave before sinking into a comfortable chair. Her final thoughts before falling asleep concerned her own arrangements.

* * *

Byron had entered the estancia from a different direction from which he had so hurriedly left it during his previous visit. It had been a good choice by Benito, who knelt by his side, hidden by the thick foliage of the trees yet within a short distance of the hacienda. He had done well, the Colombian, scouring the haunts of El Retiro and the surrounding area until he had discovered someone who knew the location of the house with the winged 'caballos'. It had been a forty–five minute drive and they had left the Landrover in the care of the Indians who had saved his life, taking with them only the mobile phone and the PPK pistol from the glove compartment. In the light of day Byron could see no possible way of approaching either the house or the clearing without being discovered, and so another location would have to be found, which meant circumnavigating the estancia. He left his companion, keeping to the treeline.

Benito watched him disappear into the trees then settled down, his binoculars close by with which to monitor the American's progress. He had told him about the phone call to Garbanza, not willing to shoulder all the responsibilities of their intended involvement and fully expecting his boss to disapprove. He hadn't, but he had issued a word of warning. They were under no circumstances to compromise the safety of the hostages -

but to keep a close eye on the movements of the girl and Jaramillo, any movement of either in the direction of a helicopter, reported to him immediately. Byron returned an hour later, sweating and gasping for breath.

'These hills take it out of you, my friend.'

'Did you see anything that may be helpful?'

'Not really. Things seem pretty much the same as when I left, although there's a better location further round which gives us a good view of the clearing whilst still being able to observe the house.'

'What of the guards? How many?'

'As I recall there's four at the house, and then the three in the clearing.'

'Not good odds, Byron.'

'No, I agree. But then again this is not Custer's last stand.' He mumbled the last few words, more to convince himself than Benito.

'It's time to move anyway, before it gets dark.'

The Colombian carried the small backpack containing spare clothes, a little food and a pair of binoculars whilst he led the way. They arrived at the spot he had chosen thirty minutes later, and donning the extra clothing settled into the undergrowth and waited for night to fall.

* * *

Even dressed in the shorts and shirt, which they had changed into during the fuel stop, he felt the heat and humidity draining away his strength. The flight from Amsterdam had been tiring enough but by the time they touched down in Cali he felt absolutely knackered. It was Alec who noticed the card with Kelly's name on it held by a man at the end of the small terminal building.

'Taxi for Mr. Kelly?'

'Si señor,' replied Alec, his Spanish now exhausted.

'Por favor.'

He gestured for them to follow him to his vehicle, its appearance resembling something found on a stock car racing circuit, and sounding the same.

'No expense spared, eh Ned?'

There was no answer.

The taxi took them north out of city and onto the main highway, and it was almost an hour later that they saw the sign for Sevilla. They could see the town in the distance but turned off onto a rough track well before reaching it until suddenly coming to a halt outside a small tin hut. Apart from a windsock and a primitive fuel pump there was nothing else in sight but a vast expanse of red-coloured dust. Removing their hand luggage from the vehicle they both stood by the door of the hut whilst the taxi driver, using his hands to good effect, conveyed to them that he was now returning to the airport for their friends.

'Bit short on home comforts aren't we Ned?'

'I hope we're not going to be here long enough to need any.'

He looked around him, their location bore all the hallmarks of a cartel drop, either taking the drugs out or importing them from elsewhere in the country.

They changed out of their casual clothes into the contents of the hand luggage - a pair of dark-blue overalls and lace-up boots, only the ski masks remaining in the bag until they were required. The hut was devoid of anything in the way of furniture and so, surrounded by the ubiquitous red dust, they sat on the hard concrete floor and waited.

He heard Whinger's voice above the sound of the taxi.

'Who are we working with on this fucking job, Lawrence of Arabia?'

'Welcome to hotel shithole,' replied Alec, as the newcomers walked through the door.

'You've been in worse places,' added Kelly.

'True, the absence of any sort of life reminds me of Montrose on a Tuesday night.'

They all laughed except Alec.

It was an uncomfortable three hours later that they heard the approaching helicopter, all four men sitting outside the hut, watching as it circled and then covered them in dust as it landed. As the rotor blades came to a standstill, the pilot jumped to the ground, he was young and good looking, expensive sunglasses perched on his head.

'Looks like a right flash bastard,' commented Alec, putting into words what they were all thinking.

'Buenos dias, señors.'

'G'day, any problems?' asked Kelly.

'Nope, she flies rather well, don't let her age fool you.'

His English was good, very good.

'Your man's done well, Ned. I never thought we'd get a 'Huey', said Alec.

'The Iriquois will take you anywhere, and safely. I have flown her from Brazil without any trouble,' interjected the pilot. 'I will also accompany you on a test flight should you require it.'

Alec nodded in agreement.

'I was told to give you this,' said the Brazilian, handing over a large envelope.

'Right start unloading the toys and bring them inside before they get clogged up with this dust.'

He took the envelope and made his way back to the hut. Alec had not been wrong; the man in Cali had done well, he thought, as he sorted through photographs of the target area in addition to sheets of necessary and useful information. He cleared a layer of dust from the floor and laid everything out, finishing at the same time that the weapons had been unloaded from the chopper.

'Everything okay?' he asked Chandler.

'Just about spot on. There's a couple of things we'll have to look at, but me and the boys are happy with what we've got.'

'How's the Brazilian getting out of here?' he asked.

'There's a car coming for him shortly.'

He walked over to his bag and removed an envelope, handing it to Chandler.

'Give him that, then when he's gone come inside and we'll go over a few things.'

Halfway through making his notes he heard the Brazilian's transport arrive, and shortly after he was joined in the hut by the other three.

'Happy with the chopper, Alec?'

'Nay problem.'

'Good. Here's the coordinates and a map of the area we will be heading for. I need a flight time and a landing and holding location.'

Whilst the pilot retired to a neutral corner, he detailed the plan to his 'snatch team'.

'I plan to go for the extrication two hours before dawn tomorrow, which gives us about eight hours to check all the 'toys' including the radios, and make sure we all know the score. From these photographs it looks as if our best way of approaching the clearing is through the crop field, giving us cover until the last fifty metres. Mick, you will set up directly opposite the house at the treeline, you should be able to cover everything from there. Now, according to our friend in Cali, two guards remain on duty outside the hostages' cabin whilst a third one kips, which means me taking out those two before you come back and join me having dealt with Rip Van Winkle.' He looked at Whinger who nodded, understanding fully.

'How about the house? There's bound to be activity from there once the ruck starts.' It was Mick.

'Fair point, and for that reason Whinger will rig the track prior to the main assault, but you'll have to press the tit, he's going to be occupied.'

They discussed everything at length once rejoined by Alec, it was a job with a standard operating procedure which they all knew; in, snatch the bod and out, using the minimum of gear to effect the maximum result.

'Finally we head for a place called Mitad del Mundo which is about 22km north of Quito where we ditch the chopper, not literally I hasten to add, Alec.'

There was a quiet chuckle before he continued.

'There will be transport waiting to take us to the airport, and on the way we'll drop the lad off.'

They spent the remaining time cleaning and checking every item of equipment, sliding condoms over the barrels of the weapons, wrapping everything else in a transparent film until ready for use, which he calculated would be in about six hours time.

* * *

It was Benito who spotted the movement in the clearing.

'Byron wake up.'

They had been taking it in turns to get some sleep.

'The guards are moving about.'

He took the proffered pair of binoculars.

He could see them clearly, all three were moving towards the hostages' cabin, and then a fourth man came into view, it was Alfred Jaramillo, all four men disappearing into the cabin. The air faintly carried her cries of protest towards him as she was escorted outside by one of the guards, followed by the drug trafficker, all three making their way up the track to the house.

'What is going on, Byron?'

He took some time in answering, his thought processes working overtime.

'It looks as if the girl is on the move.'

'I must try and contact Garbanza.'

'Not yet, there will be time for that.'

'Shit, Byron, this is not the time or the place for you to play at being a one-man army.'

He wasn't listening.

'That stretch of grassland next to the house we noticed earlier, I reckon that's where the helicopter will land, and if I can get to that then…'

He never finished, on his feet and picking up the backpack.

'Come on, compadre, when I'm on that chopper you can call your boss.'

Retracing their steps they were half way to the house when they heard the sound of the helicopter's rotor blades. His arm was now starting to hurt with the exertions of the last few hours, the thought of reaching the house on time acting as a painkiller. They eventually made it, both of them covered in sweat and numerous scratches, the effects of the undergrowth.

'What now, Byron?'

He was too engrossed in examining the helicopter to answer. It stood about twenty metres from their position, totally shut down, silent. Moving to his left he could see that the pilot was still sitting in his seat, casually reading a magazine with the aid of a flashlight. He returned to Benito.

'Give me the pistol, and do not ask any questions, there isn't time. I am going to try to get onto the helicopter and you will remain here and watch what happens to the boy.'

'For God's sake, Byron, what if you are recognized again?'

'By whom? Jaramillo already knows who I am and Betancur has never seen me. No. If that helicopter is going to where I think it is, then I'm going as well.'

They were his final words to his companion, who from the safety of the trees watched a dark shadow run across the open ground.

CHAPTER TWENTY-ONE

Simon could feel the coagulated blood mixing with the heavy growth of hair that had accumulated on his face. His head felt as if part of the cabin roof had landed on it - the intense pain retarding his thoughts for some time. He was also aware of loose teeth, painfully moving as he tested them with his tongue. Slowly, his memory returned, equally painful. The absence of Maria confirmed that the recent events were not some figment of his imagination, but the reason for his woeful appearance. It had all happened so quickly. The three men had burst into the room - two of them grabbing her and then lifting her small body clear of the floor. She had struggled throughout. A useless attempt to evade their strong grip and then calling to him. He had run headlong into the third of the guards, a huge fist sending him sprawling to the floor, his chest cavity purged of air. The man from the house had watched, unsmiling, explaining that she would come to no harm. He had attacked the guard again. This time the heavy butt of a rifle smashing into his face, removing all conscious thought, replacing it with her increasingly faint cries for help. Then nothing.

Staggering like a drunken man to the window, he searched through the approaching darkness for any sign of her. The clearing was empty, except for the two guards who had taken Maria. He turned to find the large black woman approaching him with a dirty, wet rag in her hand. Gently, she did what she could to clean his face, until the rag was no longer dark grey in colour, but bright red. He sat, for how long he did not know. His own words had returned to haunt him, 'we will be all right as long as we are together'. The words had been to reassure her, but he now knew that they had been a crutch for him also. He had used them as a means of sustaining his self-control and strength. Now they had been brutally separated - her fate unknown to him.

It was the sound of the helicopter that prevented him from drowning in a sea of self-pity. The area surrounding the cabin was suddenly bathed in light. Making his way to the rear of the cabin he was able to watch it land through a crack in the wooden wall, the pilot gently putting it down on a patch of flattened grassland. He turned away as all but one of the lights were extinguished, realizing its function. It was about to take Maria away from him, maybe forever. It was then, even though the late evening air was warm, that he shivered. What was to become of him? An English backpacker, a nobody in this vast expanse of a country, corrupted by the likes of the man from the house. It was another indication of the way that the absence of Maria was affecting him. Not once since they had been taken had he thought of what could happen to him? His concern had been for her.

The bright lights returned. Through the crack he could vaguely see two shadows moving down the track towards the helicopter. He could not see her clearly, but he knew it was her. The walk, her head unbowed.

'Maria, it's me, Simon,' his mouth pressed agonizingly hard against the rough wooden wall as he shouted her name repeatedly.

There were no words in return. Then the two shadows suddenly transformed into real people. It was her. She was accompanied by the English-speaking man, who held her arm, whilst he could see some sort of gag covering her mouth.

He was still calling to her as he heard the door to the cabin burst open and heard the guttural curses of the guard. Then once more the pain returned, this time to the back of his head, forcing him spirally downwards into a pit of despair.

* * *

In his youth he had been an accomplished athlete - a 10.5 second man over one hundred metres - but the intervening years had left their mark, and normally it would have taken him more like ten minutes to cover the same distance. But not today. He realized only too well that once he left the cover of the undergrowth he would get one opportunity to board the helicopter. Keeping as low as possible without hindering his progress too much, he approached the machine from the rear, relieved at reaching it without discovery. He could see the pilot quite clearly now. The man was still reading his magazine, totally engrossed in coloured pictures of women with unbelievably large breasts. By the side of the seat rested a small machine gun, but the pilot never reached it. As Byron revealed himself the magazine fell to the floor, the man riveted in his seat at the sight of the pistol now pointing in his direction. Byron joined him in the cockpit, crouching down behind the man before a word was spoken.

'If you make a sound Seňor I will kill you and fly this helicopter out of here myself. Do you understand?' he bluffed.

The man nodded, staring straight ahead.

'Why are you here?'

'I am to fly Seňor Jaramillo to the hacienda of Rodrigo Betancur.'

'When?'

'I was not told that. Just to wait here until he comes.'

'Then we will both wait, quietly, yes?'

It was dark with the flashlight now extinguished, but he managed to locate the pilot's firearm. He thought of Benito in the undergrowth, defenceless, and decided that he would drop the machine gun off before they left.

His arm had started to ache again, his cramped position doing nothing to ease the discomfort. He must have remained in the same position for some time before, unexpectedly, the whole area was illuminated. The pilot shifted nervously in his seat, until the metal object inserted just above his thigh settled him. Peering over the man's left shoulder, Byron could now see two figures walking his way. The taller of the two he recognized immediately, the girl he assumed was the Englishman's friend. They were now within shouting distance of the helicopter and Jaramillo's voice broke the silence.

'You can start the helicopter, Phillipe, we are ready.'

The pilot half-turned in his seat.

'Seňor?'

'Do as he says, but nothing else.' His hand tightened on the pistol grip.

The girl saw him first. A sad little face, he thought, but pretty. She entered the compact helicopter some way ahead of Jaramillo, crouching down beside him. The Colombian entered from the opposite side to that of the pilot, easing himself into the remaining seat.

'Buenas noches, seňor.'

He saw Jaramillo turn sharply in his seat - the man's eyes focusing on the pistol pointing in his direction.

'There is no need for any of this, Mr. Hollingsworth, as the girl will tell you.'

He was confused.

'You are obviously unaware of what is happening, or is about to happen once we reach the hacienda of Rodrigo?'

The girl's expression had not changed, but she nodded in confirmation.

'Then you had better explain.'

Although he missed the odd word - due to the incessant noise from the rotor blades, he heard enough to put together the proposed plan. He would have to take a lot of what he was being told on trust. The girl spoke for the first time immediately Jaramillo had finished.

'And Simon, what of him?'

Byron answered her, his hand on her shoulder.

'He is being taken care of. Don't worry.'

He then instructed the pilot to hover just above ground level close to where Benito was hidden. The Colombian agent would be glad of the weapon, he knew, as it disappeared into the undergrowth. It took only a minute for the helicopter to gain height.

'You are coming with us all the way?'

'All the way, seňor. Like Daniel into the den.'

* * *

She was deteriorating rapidly. George had no medical experience whatsoever; it was just so obvious to everyone that Joan's condition was critical. The visits to her bedside by the nursing staff to check on the monitoring equipment had become significantly more frequent during his visits. A smile was the only response to his questions. He was alone with her now, the subdued lighting in the private ward only adding to his gloom.

Random thoughts flickered through his head. Good times, when laughter had come easily. Her and the two boys had provided most of the humour in his life. His contribution had been mostly at the cost of too much drink, the only thing that had allowed his hard shell to be penetrated. It hadn't all been his fault. A disciplined upbringing, leading to a life of disciplined employment, first in the forces and later in the Fire Service, leaving him with little room for flexibility. Then as the boys grew into men, a new phase. More secretive, occasionally manipulative. His protectiveness of her being misunderstood, and because she was the way she was he had carried the burden for them both.

The arrival of Fairbrother prevented him from sinking any further.

'How is she doing?'

The answer was written all over the consultant's face. He pulled a chair next to his and sat down.

'The hardest part of being a member of my profession, George, is admitting defeat. The longer we practise, the more convinced we become that working small miracles is part and parcel of the job. Sometimes we can work the miracle, but to do that we need the cooperation of the patient. Joan, I'm afraid, has locked everyone out. At this moment she is in a deep coma, and there is no way, with the best will in the world, that anyone can reach her. With the exception, maybe, of your son, Simon. The decision is now hers and hers alone. I don't know whether you are a religious man George, not that it's a prerequisite for prayers to be answered, but that's what it has come down to. Her only chance of coming out of this unscathed is contact with your son, and even then it may be too late.'

George reached into the pocket of his jacket and removed a small wooden box. Fairbrother looked on quizzically.

'It belonged to my great-grandmother, it's a snuffbox. Inside are two strands of hair. A black one that came from my father, the other silver, my mother's. In times of trouble I call on them. Who knows? Perhaps they can influence the scheme of things, persuade the Guardian of Destiny to intervene.'

He knew that Fairbrother wouldn't understand any of what he was saying, his way of preserving life much more of a practical nature.

'I hope you won't take this the wrong way, but you see sometimes I have more faith in the power of those in another place, than even the most skilful of mortals.'

'I've never underestimated the power to which you refer, George, believe me.'

He accepted the consultant's prognosis and filed it. The grieving would come in the privacy of his own home, not in full view of Fairbrother and the sister. His was not the Wailing Wall way. A public exhibition of grief, no matter how genuine, not his way of handling it. He kissed Joan on the forehead. When he returned home he would once more hold the box until his call for help had been accepted, or rejected.

* * *

Hermania Gariva walked slowly towards the door of her hotel room, and admitted the woman who Garbanza had left behind. She looked about the same age as her own daughter, in fact she was probably the substitute, she thought.

'I have heard from Señor Pastrana, he will send an automobile later this morning.'

The woman sat down on the edge of the large bed.

'You have news of Maria?'

'Only that she has been taken to the hacienda of Betancur.'

She felt her pulses race, it was an unconscious reaction to what she was feeling - hate.

'She will be okay, Garbanza will see to it.'

The woman was telling her something she already knew. Maria was a survivor. Since her difficult childhood she had been beset by problems. The disappointment of finding herself alone in a strange country without a friend until the English boy Simon. The illness of her mother. And now her present predicament. But she was like the reinforced house in Ibarra. The outer concrete would crack and crumble due to the passage of time, but the inner steel tendons would never break.

Another knock on the door interrupted her thoughts. Garbanza was let in by the woman, immediately settling himself into a comfortable chair.

'I have come a little earlier than planned to discuss certain arrangements with you, señora.'

She said nothing, now was not the time.

'When we arrive at the hacienda we will without doubt be searched for a weapon. I assume you are not carrying one, but I have to ask?'

'I am an old woman, señor.' She looked him in the eye.

'Not so old, I think.' He smiled. The man was not stupid.

'Once we have gained entry to the hacienda that is your part in this finished. You must not interfere. Your granddaughter's life may depend on it. The military will be waiting some distance from the hacienda ready to move in the moment that I signal. That signal will be from a pistol carried by Alfred Jaramillo, who will not be subject to the same level of scrutiny as ourselves.'

She thought of the irony of it all. The man was now helping the Authorities after being a thorn in their side for so long.

'You will not arrest this man, Alfred?'

'He has been of assistance to us, Hermania.'

Again she held her tongue.

'And so, if everything goes to plan, you will be reunited with Maria within the next twenty-four hours.'

She wasn't listening. They left the hotel in Garbanza's automobile, driven by a large man in a fedora hat. The vehicle was filled with the smell from a large cigar fixed firmly in his mouth. She sat in the rear next to her substitute daughter, the velvet drawstring bag in a pocket, the leather case causing her some minor discomfort. She was thinking of arrangements, but not Garbanza's.

* * *

COLOMBIA. Wednesday, 0300 hrs.

The only light in the vicinity of the tin hut was coming from a small spotlight mounted on the front of the 'Huey'. Its steady beam falling on the four ex-soldiers, seated, backs against the wall of their temporary accommodation. Kelly was just coming to the end of their final briefing, the third since they had arrived. He didn't care if they were unhappy about the repetitiveness of it. The six Ps were his personal code - pre-planning prevented piss-poor performance.

'Right fellers, it's now coming up to 0300, so set your watches. We leave at exactly 0400, which if Alec is right about the flight time should see us in position an hour later. We use channel six on the Motorolas unless it's to contact Alec in which case it's four. You'll listen out on both.'

The Scottish pilot nodded.

'One last thing. Priority, as always, goes to getting the bod out. If the 'op' turns to rat shit and we have to leave anybody behind, head for the designated emergency rendezvous point. We'll come back for you when the lad's been dropped off.'

He expected and got no questions about what he had just told them. They had all been trained in escape and evasion techniques during their time in the forces. The ERV chosen by Alec because of its access suitability. He looked at his companions, not unlike professional sportsman in an obscure kind of way. The money for the job was not the overriding factor, it was the winning. The satisfaction of doing something well and being the best at what you did, and they were. All dressed identically, they clutched their weapons, and at precisely 0400 boarded the chopper. He was the last, a final check that nothing had been left behind in the hut. Then he too joined them in the 'Huey'. No joking, no whinging, it was shit-hitting-the-fan time, at least it was for the Colombian guards sitting outside a wooden cabin, and anyone else who got in the way.

* * *

Ernesto 'the fixer' Videla sat on his patio, a large Cuban cigar in one hand whilst the other held a glass of an excellent French wine. It was the nearest he ever got to a celebration, and at this moment he had something to celebrate. In a few hours time his life of living in the shadows would end. No longer would he have to remain an anonymous 'pulpo', an octopus reaching out with its tentacles in different directions at the same time. When the Brazilian returned with the helicopter he would inspect his newly acquired property, the estancia of Alfred Jaramillo. As owner of one of the richest areas of land in Colombia he would no longer have to rely on his subversive activities. It was a dream come true. Overnight he would become a legitimate businessman, his misdemeanours a thing of the past. And there had been many.

He was a man without a conscience, a luxury he couldn't afford when dealing with drug traffickers, arms smugglers and even assassins. He had used such a man at El Dorado airport. He had been compelled to reveal his true identity to Renaldo Hernandez, the Government Minister and his partner in the American agreement. It had been a decision instantly regretted, but one he had corrected within a short time.

The American pull-out had been a setback, of that there was no question, but not for the first time in his life he had been fortunate. The discovery of the identity of the Ecuadorean hostage had put his ball back in play, and he felt in a much stronger position than ever before. The request from London had been an added bonus, although it seemed at first that it could have caused complications. It could not have turned out better. Not only would the mercenaries remove the last remaining hostage, but there was a possibility that any guards still loyal to Jaramillo would also be taken care of, permanently.

He savoured the last of the wine, pleased at what he had accomplished. There was now only loose ends to tie up. Entering his study he walked across to the computer and for the first time in his life 'logged off' and then switched it off completely. The records he had kept of the thousands of transactions, he would come back for. Dealings with high profile businessmen, Government Agencies and international organizations that had paid for his services over the years. Secrets that people would kill for. He opened the safe that had been specially constructed for him in the concrete floor and removed his pistol. It would seal the fate of his 'inside man', Jaramillo's cook. The man knew too much of this latest affair. The Glock model 17 would also provide him with protection, in case Jaramillo should decide to return to his hacienda.

He returned to the patio and continued to draw on the cigar. Tomorrow was the start of a new life, he thought, and a new name, maybe Emilio.

CHAPTER TWENTY-TWO
Colombia. Wednesday, 04:45 hrs.

The early morning mist was starting to cover the forest canopy, making visibility in the helicopter virtually non-existent, and the darkness didn't help. Sitting in the rear of the 'Huey', Kelly was becoming concerned.

'Is this lot gonna cause us problems, Alec?' he shouted above the noise of the engine and rotor blades.

'I won't know until we reach the target area and have to go down.' He remembered the remarks made by his instructor. 'Anyone can fly an aircraft, it's the taking off and landing that makes you a pilot.'

He peered down at the mist. It was collecting in small valleys and then rising. According to the information supplied by the 'fixer' their target was on high ground. He just hoped the man had got it right.

'How long before we know for certain?'

Alec glanced at his map of the area.

'We should be able to see something in about fifteen minutes.'

The landmarks he was hoping to see were two hills, one slightly higher than the other with a flat spot in between, ideal. It would mean a bit of a 'tab' for the boys but there was plenty of cover should they need it.

It was ten minutes later that he spotted them, looming like two women's breasts out of a soft grey blouse. He smiled at the analogy. Glancing again at the map to check his position he proceeded to head the helicopter on a reciprocal course.

'Everything okay, Alec?'

'Nay problem, but I don't want to fly over the clearing and risk giving the game away. I'm going to make another run and this time it'll be for real. You ready?'

Kelly looked at each man in turn, receiving the thumbs up from both O'Connor and Chandler.

'Roger that.'

'About two minutes, Ned.'

Kelly tightened his grip on the '47' as the chopper began its descent.

'Going down boys. Fifty feet, twenty, ten, five, standby. Out, out, out.'

They hardly felt the 'Huey' land, the engine killed before the last of the team was out. Alec watched them disappear into a patch of mist, five metres apart and moving quickly. Ned made the cover slightly ahead of his two companions.

'Delta one, this is Alpha one.'

He heard them in turn report back to the chopper that they too had reached the trees. Alec was acknowledging each one in turn. Suddenly they were together and moving off up the hill. It was hard going, the dampness from the mist making it slippery underfoot. They were breathing hard when Kelly indicated that they had reached the top. If he had remembered the photograph accurately the trees should continue for another hundred metres, before terminating at the edge of the crop field. They took a short 'breather' before slipping and sliding through the forest, just managing to stop themselves at the treeline.

'We'll do a quick recce before moving any further.' Kelly spoke quietly; he didn't even want the wildlife waking just yet. The PNGs gave him excellent vision and it wasn't long before he detailed his plan.

'There looks to be a spot one hundred metres to our left for setting up the M60, you should have an uninterrupted field of vision from there. You can also see anyone coming down the track towards the clearing.'

Chandler nodded and moved off.

'Any sign of the guards, Ned?'

'Not from here. We should see them when we move further round.'

Whinger followed some two metres behind as Kelly led the way to their new position. They didn't have to travel far before all three cabins were visible.

'This will do fine. We'll go from here.'

With the aid of the night goggles Kelly picked out the two guards seated outside one particular cabin, making a mental note that one was missing. He knew O'Connor would also have noticed.

'Bravo one, at the treeline.'

The subdued tones of Chandler confirming his arrival added to the eeriness of the early morning atmosphere.

'How long to set the charges at the track?'

O'Connor looked over at the half-exposed house.

'Fifteen minutes at most,' he replied, already on his way.

From the cover of the trees Kelly monitored his progress, as well as keeping an eye on the clearing for any sudden activity. He couldn't be certain but it looked as if the two guards were armed with AK-47s. Not that it mattered. The element of surprise would nullify even the best weapon. He lost O'Connor for a moment as the 'bang man' crossed to the opposite side of the track. Moments later the radio crackled.

'Charlie one, on my way back.'

'Alpha one, roger.'

The words were hardly out of his mouth when the third guard emerged from one of the cabins. The man's need to relieve himself had solved one of Kelly's problems. He hadn't been certain of his location - now he was.

O'Connor joined him, breathing heavily from his exertions.

'Get your breath back, we'll go in five minutes.'

He informed the other two members of the team, then checked his weapon. The luminous hand on his watch seemed to take an age to reach the appointed time.

'Alpha one, moving off.'

They crawled, keeping as low as a snake's belly, into the crop field, the produce, whatever it was, making it an uncomfortable ten minutes. The PNGs were now surplus to requirements, the whole clearing now visible with the naked eye. Outside the main target cabin, twenty metres in front of them, Kelly could see both guards, their weapons cradled on their knees, unconcerned. He looked at O'Connor and raised three fingers, three minutes and then they would take life. He took long, deep breaths, focused, looking directly at the men he was going to kill.

'Charlie, Delta, going in.'

They were both on their feet and running, before either of the guards reacted. A short distance to his right he caught Whinger throwing the 'flash bang' and then he was on one knee, taking out the nearest guard from ten metres. The second guard's weapon never reached his shoulder, a bullet to the chest curtailing the attempt at retaliation. He was at the cabin - the door nearly kicked off its flimsy hinges.

'Lay on the floor, on the floor.'

He saw the terrified look on the boy's face as he yelled his instructions. Saw a large black woman also obey his commands. Outside there was the sound of a single shot, shortly followed by the arrival of his companion. He watched as O'Connor administered the 'sleepytime' to both the prone figures, and then the boy was over his shoulders.

They had reached the edge of the crop field when the first of the explosive devices lit up the sky, rapidly followed by the second. Halfway across the field they heard the M60, two short bursts then silence. They rested briefly at the treeline, using the respite to transfer the boy to a fresh pair of shoulders and contact Alec. The climb back up the hill was painfully slow, Chandler joining them halfway to the top, and finally all three dragging the 'bod' the last few metres. Kelly heard the chopper before he saw it, all in, when it eventually came into view. The boy went in first and then the team scrambled onboard, collapsing due to a mixture of fatigue and the adrenaline rush of the past thirty minutes. Kelly watched the ground disappear beneath him as the 'Huey' gained height, whilst Alec set a course for Mitad del Mundo.

* * *

COLOMBIA. Wednesday, 08:00hrs.

The 'poet' had to admit that the hacienda belonging to Rodrigo Betancur was something else. They had arrived the night before, but even in the darkness the pink and white buildings had looked impressive. The head of the cartel had not been well enough to receive them on their arrival, and so they had been shown to a guest room to await his summons. He had been shaken roughly by a huge white man whose accent indicated that he had South African origins. Sitting on the edge of the bed his thoughts focused on the forthcoming confrontation, steeling himself for the ordeal ahead. It wasn't everyday that you found yourself in the same room with the worlds' most prodigious drug pedlar. The realization that he was about to place himself in a position of extreme vulnerability was causing beads of sweat to form on his forehead. He would be relying on one trafficker to keep his identity secret from another. Not ideal. Jaramillo had already shown his true colours, changing his allegiance when things had turned sticky, and then altering his plans again to suit. The man was also armed. He had admitted as much during the helicopter ride, explaining it away as insurance against Betancur's 'doubt paranoia', whatever that meant. Presumably he was confident that as a regular visitor, he would not be searched, something that would undoubtedly happen to himself and the girl.

He left the room and walked out into the courtyard, portraying a confidence that he was certainly not feeling. Maria smiled at him. But it was a weak smile, indicating that she too was feeling anything but satisfied with the impending meeting. She looked remarkably well considering what she had been compelled to endure during the previous weeks. Only small in stature, yet obviously her small frame contained a huge heart, with a willpower to match. She would hold up. The $64,000 question was, would he and Jaramillo? As the three of them strolled towards the entrance to the hacienda, he took his position behind the other two, in keeping with an employee's place. Sharp, razor-like stones attempted to cut his sandals to shreds and he was relieved to reach the steps without injury. Reaching the top, any further progress was prevented by an armed guard.

'Perdon, señorita.' He indicated that she should raise her arms, then deftly, but discreetly searched her.

Jaramillo watched, exempt from the process. Then it was his turn, rough hands being less discreet, but finding nothing - his pistol left on the helicopter wrapped in his discarded sling. The doors opened revealing a huge room, breathtakingly decorated. Expensive and rare items hung from the walls, whilst the fittings and furniture indicated incalculable wealth. He took it all in quickly, concentrating finally on the man sitting in a wheelchair behind a huge desk. He was a pathetic sight, not most people's archetype of a man holding his position, in fact quite the opposite. He sat at an awkward angle, face without expression, the eyes hooded like a particular species of hawk. But it was something quite remarkable that held Byron's attention. Almost supernatural. Resting on the desk was a gold dagger, whilst protruding just above Betancur's waistcoat he saw the handle of a pistol.

'That dagger, on whose hilt a gem
Were worthy of a diadem,
No longer glittered at his waist,
Where pistols unadorned were braced.'

In another life Rodrigo could have been Lord Byron's Selim, the Death Maker. The coincidence was unnerving.

They stood in his presence, no invitation forthcoming for them to sit.

'I see you have brought the girl, Alfred, but who is this stranger?' The reference to him made with a faltering, yet menacing voice.

'He is my personal servant, Rodrigo, and therefore yours.'

He felt the hooded eyes burning into his own.

'And you say this is my granddaughter?'

'It is so.'

A thin almost skeletal hand waved in Maria's direction. Uncertainly she approached the desk.

'Hermania Gariva is your grandmother?'

'Si, seňor.'

Byron was impressed by the firmness of her answer.

'We shall see very shortly, come and stand by me.'

She did so without hesitation.

'And what of you Judas?'

Byron's heart missed a beat.

'I do not understand, Rodrigo. Why do you refer to me in such a way?'

'The reasons are many, but at this moment it is your footwear that betrays you.'

The 'poet' stood transfixed as he saw Jaramillo look down at his boots. He would never forget the look on his face as the bullet from Betancur's pistol smashed into his chest. He made an attempt to prevent the drug trafficker from falling heavily to the floor.

'Leave him, let him fall into Hell.'

Surely it was the Death Maker reincarnate, Byron thought. Was he to be next?

The guard who had frisked them earlier burst into the room, his weapon making a sweep of the room before coming to rest. It was pointing straight at his head.

'There is no need, what had to be done has been accomplished. Go.' As if the effort had been too much, Betancur slumped back in his chair.

Byron said nothing, almost statuesque, breathing heavily.

'There is a study through that door, take the girl and wait until I send for you.'

The spindle-like hand pointed the way, and in unison they obeyed. Closing the door, Byron put his finger to his lips.

'I will explain who I am presently, Maria. Now sit down and wait for your grandmother to arrive.'

* * *

COLOMBIA. Wednesday, 10:00hrs

It was a journey that she had never envisaged herself undertaking. A return to the past for her, as opposed to ensuring the future for Maria. As the automobile continued towards the outskirts of Medellin she noticed that they were not alone. Some type of aircraft was accompanying them, whilst two military vehicles followed at a discreet distance. One thing occupied her thoughts. Maria had been special to her since birth. She still retained the innocence of those first few weeks of life, untarnished by the attractions of a commercially-biased world. The English boy was lucky, and yet maybe not. Two people separated by thousands of miles, from different cultures. Oblivious to each other's existence until a chance meeting. Maybe it had nothing to do with being 'afortunado'. She glanced across at the man sitting next to her; he too appeared to be deep in thought.

Guillermo Garbanza was, so far, pleased with the way things were going. The call from Bernice relaying the news from Benito about the boy's rescue was one problem solved. His only hope now was that Hollingsworth and the girl had come to no harm. He had instructed the excited Benito to remain at the estancia in case Jaramillo returned. Now the only hurdle was the successful entry to the hacienda. He estimated that another ten minutes would see them approaching their destination, the accompanying entourage of policemen and soldiers stopping some two hundred metres short, hidden until required. Henri Pastrana was with them, which made him feel a little more comfortable with the situation.

The glint from the helicopter, high overhead for so long, had disappeared. They were close. The driver slowed and then brought the vehicle to a halt metres from a wooden gate. He hesitated before stepping out, carefully opening it, ever vigilant. Then they were on their way again, a rough track bringing them within sight of the hacienda at the bottom of the hill. A compound area surrounded it, and Garbanza noticed two helicopters, stationary within its boundary wire. They came off the track and on to a tarmac road that led directly to the main gate of the compound, stopping just short. The large gates swung open and four heavily-armed men immediately surrounded the vehicle. Garbanza lowered the window, an AK-47 appearing inches from his face.

'Señora Gariva is here at the request of Señor Betancur.'

The man peered into the automobile whilst another ordered them to vacate it.

'The vehicle will remain here with its driver, you will be escorted the rest of the way.'

The man spoke in Spanish, but it was obvious that it was not his native tongue. Probably Rhodesian, he thought. He had heard that many of the 1st SAS Regiment had been recruited by the cartels when it had been disbanded in the 1980s. They were hardened soldiers, involved in many operations on the Zambia/Mozambique border and inflicting heavy losses on the ZIPRA and ZANLA forces. Robert Mugabe's successful election had provided the likes of Betancur with a formidable army. It had also been a major factor in deciding on a more subtle approach, rather than a one involving force. They had arrived at another set of gates. A small door was opened for them, allowing entry into a large courtyard.

'Wait.' The order barked.

They were searched, him more thoroughly than either of the two women, before being allowed to climb the steps to the hacienda. The sweat on his face was starting to mingle with a four-day growth of hair, causing him to scratch. It wasn't really an attempt at a disguise, more in keeping with the part he was playing, like the simple brown suit he was wearing.

The doors opened. It wasn't Betancur that he saw immediately, but Alfred Jaramillo, slumped against a wall, his chin resting on a blood soaked shirt. The room, bathed in sunshine, had nevertheless become cold.

'So you have come?'

It was not the sight that Garbanza had expected. He knew the man was ill, but he looked critical.

'At your request, not mine.' Hermania's voice as chilling as the room.

'You look well, señora.'

'You have forgotten my name, Rodrigo?'

She saw him squirm, aware that he was not familiar with being spoken to in such a way, especially in front of others.

'I have forgotten nothing.'

She looked across at the figure lying awkwardly against the wall.

'You have forgotten friendship, it would appear.'

'His choice, not mine.'

She saw him looking at the female agent.

'She is our daughter?'

'No, Rodrigo, she is my daughter. And his.' Her finger steadily pointing at Jaramillo.

He squirmed again, this time more pronounced.

'Then the girl, she is nothing to me?'

'But she is everything to me. Where is she?'

He said nothing, but lifted himself slightly in his chair.

'Are you not forgetting, señora, where you are?'

It was a threat that she was ready to counter.

'I am in the presence of a sick and evil man. Someone who I once loved and shared my bed with. A man who could have possessed my very soul and I would have given it to you gladly.'

She paused, composing herself, aware that emotion was causing a rise in the pitch of her voice.

'Instead you chose to follow Satan's path. Cherishing the sign of the dollar in preference to the sign of the Holy Cross. And for what? So you can die a lonely, embittered old man. It is not the bullet that still tortures your body, Rodrigo. It is a lack of humanity that is eating away your spirit that brings you close to death.'

Not only could he not answer her, he could no longer look her in the eye. She knew then that she had broken him. But it was not enough.

'I will ask you once more - where is Maria?'

His voice was weak, only just audible.

'The door to your right.'

Garbanza nodded to the female agent, who hurriedly made her way to the indicated door. Seconds later they appeared - Hollingsworth first, then the girl. She walked to Hermania and put her arms around the woman's waist.

Garbanza didn't see it happen. She must have used the girl to hide the removal of the weapon. But he saw the effects of the two bullets that exploded into Betancur's head. He saw the man and his wheelchair disappear beneath the desk, followed by the clatter of the pistol as it fell from Hermania Gariva's hand to the floor.

Hollingsworth was the first to react. Garbanza watched as the American DEA agent sprinted across the room to Jaramillo's body, removing an automatic weapon from beneath his jacket. At almost the same instant, one of the guards burst into the room managing to fire once before he was cut down by the 'poet'. Further firing was coming from outside, Henri Pastrana and the military, he thought, and he was right, his boss nearly falling over the dead guard as he ran into the room.

'Everyone okay, apart from the obvious.'

Garbanza nodded, preoccupied with watching Hermania walk towards the painting of the 'light of the world'. She turned it to face the wall.

'There is no more light in their world, only darkness.'

Kneeling she held the head of Alfred Jaramillo, then kissed his cheek. Maria stood close to her - she had never left her side.

'This is your grandfather, Maria. Not a bad man like Rodrigo, just misguided.'

'I know,' said the girl, recalling the wine, the shower and the words he had spoken, 'thine enemies shall come from within thine own household'. He had tried his best to look after her.

Henri Pastrana waited until she had arranged her dress, pulling the two halves together just below the waist, discarding the leather holster.

'You must come with us Hermania, I am sorry.'

She had expected it. Who would know how many deaths he had been responsible for over the years? But she bore the responsibility for his, a calculated, premeditated act of murder. She would be punished for it, but she would never regret it. It had purged her heart of forty years of hate.

'Give me a few moments with Maria.'

He agreed, feeling guilty about what he was compelled to do.

Maria watched as her grandmother took the small, velvet, drawstring bag from around her neck, removing a blue coloured box. Inside the box lay a ring which Hermania placed in her hand.

'Before I leave you, niño, there is something I must explain to you. Many hundreds of years ago, our ancestors came to this continent with Francisco Pizzaro. He was a man much like Rodrigo, and interested only in the treasures of the Inca people. During his conflict with them, he tricked the great Inca Emperor, Atauhallpa, into giving up everything of value he and his people possessed. It included his own ring, the 'Ring of Vulcan'. Pizzaro gave it to our family in payment for their loyalty, and it has been passed on as generations come and go. It is very valuable, not only because it is made from gold and emeralds, but for a more important reason. It was said by the 'ancients' that the gold and precious stones came from the very centre of the earth, from the volcano at Cotopaxi, the 'Shining Peak'. They say Vulcan, the God of Fire, forged it and that for true lovers it possesses mystical powers. Take your English friend to the slopes of Cotopaxi, for only there is the power to forge your spirits, and place the ring on each other's finger in turn. I know my child that you care for him, but you must not tell him of your intentions. If he is the one he will be guided by the son of Jupiter and Juno, and you will know he is the one.'

She took the ring.

'He is safe?'

She saw the smile appear on her grandmother's face.

'Seňor Garbanza has said so.'

Her emotions were mixed. She would find the man she cared for, but lose the woman she loved. As they walked down the steps her tears were confusing. Was it with happiness or sadness? One thing she knew for certain was that she would take the 'Ring of Vulcan' and Simon Halkin to Cotopaxi.

CHAPTER TWENTY-THREE
Mitad Del Mundo, Wednesday

Kelly looked at the figure lying on the floor of the 'Huey'. What a fucking state, he thought, the long hair and unshaven face making him look twenty years older than he was supposed to be. There was blood all over him, indicating that at some stage he had attempted to do their job for them. Still, they had done the business and he was more than pleased with the way the 'op' had gone. It had been 'clean'. No casualties had been incurred and they were now on their way home, the team already changing into civilian clothes. He noticed the boy stirring.

'Maria, MARIA,' he yelled, grabbing Chandler.

'Calm down, cobber, you're with the friendlies.'

'Who are you?'

'We are, my son, the Angels of Mercy, or should that be, Avenging Angels.' The reply from O'Connor bringing laughter from them all.

'Where is Maria?'

'Your Sheila's okay, believe me.'

Simon still felt groggy, the effect of whatever had been pumped into him whilst in the cabin, he thought.

'But who are you really?'

'That's not important, but what I'm about to tell you is. You up to it,' asked Kelly.

He nodded.

'We intend to deliver you to the Consulate in Quito, not literally, but somewhere close. Once there you will be, what we call, 'debriefed'. They will want to know what has been happening to you since you were taken. They will also want to know how you got away. You must not, under any circumstances, reveal any British involvement in your release. Your father will explain its importance when you arrive home.'

So George did have something to do with this. How did he know people like these? A very strange man his father, he would never know everything about him. But then who would?

'Are you listening, cobber?'

'Sorry, and by the way, thank you.'

'Nay problem,' he heard the pilot shout.

'But they will want to know how I got free.'

'Tell them the hostage fairy rescued you, tell them anything you fucking like, but not the truth. To do that puts you and your family in a lot of trouble, believe me.'

He did. The last thing he would want to do was upset these men.

They were now over a populated area, small, whitewashed houses appearing, a more than welcome change from three dilapidated cabins, his view for so long.

'When we get down there will be two cars waiting, you will get into the front one, okay?'

The Australian was giving him more instructions.

'When will I see Maria?'

'That I can't say, but you will see her. Now don't forget what I've told you. And by the way, phone home as soon as possible, they've been a bit worried about you.'

He smiled. He did as he was told, and from the rear of the car watched them crowd into the vehicle behind. He waved, and they saluted back, and then both vehicles took the highway to Quito.

* * *

THE ESTANCIA OF ALFRED JARAMILLO.

Benito was of the opinion that very little in life could surprise him. His days on both sides of the fence had catered for most eventualities. But he was mistaken. The firearm narrowly missing his head had been more of a shock than a surprise, as he had settled down for the night, his leather poncho keeping out the cold night air. He had been employed on many stakeouts. A thankless task, observe and report. He had observed Hollingsworth together with the girl and Jaramillo taking off in the helicopter and presumed that he was responsible for the firearm issue; unconventional, but he had been grateful. This was not the sort of place to be without a visible means of support. Tiredness had enveloped him like the early morning mist that would come, and he had slept fitfully.

It had been the breaking of a branch that had disturbed his sleep. He knew instantly that he had been joined in the undergrowth, but could see nothing. Not daring to move anything but his head, he had sat for some time peering into the gloom that was the mist. And then a further movement in the crop field, followed by a bright flash. Two dark figures were now running, and then the unmistakable sound of gunfire. Activity from the house and then two consecutive explosions, throwing bodies into the air. And then the most frightening sound, machine-gun fire from no more than five metres away. He froze. The running figures again, heading for the trees, a movement to his left, then silence.

It was later that morning, the mist replaced by a blistering sun, before he ventured into the open. There was no movement to be seen anywhere, a graveyard.

He stood, tightly clutching the machine gun. No shouts, no gunfire. Cautiously he walked towards the cabins, discovering the bodies of the three guards, their bodies twisted in unnatural positions. The hostage cabin was empty, except for a large black woman who lay motionless on the floor. He satisfied himself that she had a pulse before moving in the direction of the house. The track looked as if it had been attacked by landmines, huge craters containing more guards. The columns, which had once supported effigies of Pegasus, lay in pieces. The immortal winged horse that had sprung from the blood of the slain Medusa, then carried Bellerophon on his great deeds, fragmented. The house had escaped unscathed, which was more than could be said for the remaining occupants. He found them in the kitchen, still in shock, the cook was the only coherent one among the three of them.

'What has happened, seňor?'

'Nothing for you to concern yourself with, the men who caused the damage outside have gone. They will not return. Now we will all go into the large room and wait.'

'You are also a friend of the man from Cali?'

The question caught him completely off balance.

'You mean the one who calls himself Emilio?'

'That is him. I also work for this man and he will be here soon.'

The realization of who he was talking to came later rather than sooner. So this was the man who had been getting the information out.

'Yes, I too am waiting for him to arrive.'

They sat for some time, the conversation engineered to extract more detail about the 'fixer'. It was only when he was satisfied that the cook had no more to tell, that he decided to lock him and his fellow workers away in a small study, the man protesting vehemently. Alone in the large room he made himself comfortable, then contacted Bogotá.

★ ★ ★

Byron spoke to the man sitting next to him in the helicopter.

'Where are we going, Gill?

Garbanza smiled. He hadn't been called that in a long time.

'Benito has been in contact with Henri. We are going to the estancia to await the arrival of our friend from Cali.'

He felt his arm. It had started to throb uncontrollably.

'How is it?'

'I'll survive, which is more than can be said for those we have just left.'

They discussed it, along with what had been happening prior to the fateful event. As things became clearer, he got angrier. O'Grady and the Administration had all but hung him out to dry. He had rung Anne and Sara from the hacienda, a tearful exchange, until he assured them both that he would be home soon.

The carnage that had once been the orderly estancia belonging to Jaramillo came as a shock to him. As the pilot put them down on the spot from which he had left the previous night, a smiling Benito met them.

'No sign of our visitor yet?' asked Garbanza, waving to the helicopter pilot to take off.

The Colombian shook his head. They walked to the house, Benito full of questions and then telling them about the early morning raid. As they sat talking, Byron could feel himself drifting into sleep. The events of the last twenty-four hours, in addition to his painful shoulder, beginning to surface as fatigue.

'There's plenty of beds in this place, Byron.'

'I'll be okay.'

'You won't, so when he arrives stay out of the way.' Garbanza was firm.

He walked around the room, and then to the door of the house for a breath of air, prevented from doing so by the sound of the helicopter. Rushing back into the room he announced the arrival of the man they had come to arrest.

'I meant what I said - stay out of this, Byron, if it comes to a shooting match you have done your share for today.'

Garbanza was right. The killing of the guard, although necessary, had left him feeling reticent about handling another firearm. Benito positioned himself behind one of the doors, awaiting the man from Cali's entrance.

He was not what Guillermo Garbanza had expected. An exceptionally tall man, he stooped to clear the top of the doorway as he entered the room. His suit had been tailored by a craftsman, of that there was no doubt. Just enough cuff showing, revealing an expensive gold watch. A perfectly groomed beard partly hid a long, thin face, but it was the eyes that were the dominant feature, darting, searching. He placed his briefcase on the floor before speaking.

'Can I ask what you gentlemen are doing in my house?'

'Your house, seňor? We understood it was the residence of Alfred Jaramillo.' Garbanza answered.

'Then you were misled, it now belongs to me, as does the estancia.'

'And you are?'

Ernesto Videla shifted his feet.

'Of no concern to you or your friend behind the door.'

Benito emerged, but retained his position behind the 'fixer'.

'You are wrong, señor, it is my concern, because I am here to arrest you.'

'I have papers that make your task difficult to say the least. But as a matter of interest on what charge?'

Garbanza took a step forward and pointed to the briefcase.

'Maybe the evidence is in here. I'd like you to open it.'

Benito was now directly behind the man, snatching the pistol from the case as he revealed its contents.

'You are expecting trouble?' Garbanza met the man's piercing eyes.

'One never knows, señor, but maybe this will satisfy your curiosity?'

He recognized the photocopied fakes that he and Henri had produced.

'Hold them up to the light and describe the watermark.'

He watched the man's darting eyes franticly searching for something that wasn't there. It was only original Government documents that contained the distinctive watermark - a crest, not present in the photocopying paper. And Henri Pastrana had known all along, letting him in on the secret only that very morning.

'I think that maybe you have some explaining to do, as to why you are in possession of fake Government documents, señor. Anyway that will do for now.'

The man had lost his self-assurance. Within a few minutes he had been reduced significantly in size. Garbanza seized the opportunity.

'And your name again, señor?'

'I am Ernesto. You may know me better as Emilio.'

'No. I know you as a man who would use the circumstances of the less fortunate to his advantage. You are no better, I suspect even worse, than the traffickers on whom you have been informing. You are also a vain man, which makes me think that you have retained the evidence of your many dealings, a fact, which if I am proved correct, will see you in prison for the rest of your life.'

Benito had applied the handcuffs during his boss's assessment of Videla's character flaws and future prospects, then released the remainder of the hacienda's staff from the study.

There was no sign of the helicopter that had brought Videla to them as they left the house. Already, the military were starting to arrive, as good a reason as any for the pilot to desert his passenger. As they took to the sky, Byron took in the scene, much as Lord George Gordon may have done at Waterloo.

'As the ground was before, thus let it be;
How that red rain hath made the harvest grow!
And is this all the world has gained by thee,
Thou first and last of fields! King-making victory?'

Benito smiled, not at Byron, but at the mystified look on Garbanza's face.

'It is poetry, Guillermo, by an English Lord, called...'

* * *

QUITO, ECUADOR. Thursday morning.

They had travelled through the night, Pastrana insisting that both the female agent and the man in the fedora hat should accompany her. Maria had never been in an automobile that could reach speeds of 120km per hour, and she had found herself at the airport before really settling. There had been no flights to Quito immediately available, and so they had been forced to wait until nearly midnight. She had watched the lights of Bogotá disappear, far below, relieved to be on her way out of Colombia. Yet she knew that she would return. If Hermania were to be imprisoned then she would be compelled to visit her.

She had fallen asleep on the aircraft, a deep sleep, waking only when the woman agent shook her roughly, informing her that they where approaching Quito.

Before she had left the hacienda, Henri Pastrana had told her that Simon would be at the British Consulate. And at that moment that's where the automobile which had been waiting at the airport was taking her. She could feel herself trembling at the thought of seeing him again. Leaving him in the clearing in such a badly beaten condition had left her feeling empty. But no longer. The news from Pastrana that he was well had filled her with something that she could not explain, instead, she would show him. The vehicle pulled into a small courtyard and stopped. She was unable to move as she saw Simon open the door, the tears already stinging her eyes. He sat beside her, and she touched his swollen face, gently.

'Where have you been, Maria?'

They laughed, realizing the pointlessness of the question.

He helped her from the automobile, holding her free hand. The other clutched a velvet drawstring bag tightly. But that would come later.

⋆ ⋆ ⋆

HARTLEPOOL, ENGLAND. Thursday morning.

It was after midnight when Nick and Anthea returned to his house. They had been to the cinema and then afterwards gone for a meal.

'Are you coming in for a coffee?'

'I won't bother if George is still up,' she replied.

It wasn't that she didn't want to see him, it had more to do with intruding on his privacy. When he wasn't visiting Joan at the hospital he was searching the newspapers for even the smallest item on anything remotely to do with South America. It had been over a year ago since she had met Nick, frequently visiting his house. In all that time she had never been completely comfortable in George's company. She would never understand his sense of humour for one thing. Then there was his individualistic way of talking. She recalled watching a television talk show in the living room whilst waiting for Nick one teatime.

'Do you watch this?' she had asked him. He had looked over the top of his spectacles at her.

'There are quite a number of occasions, Anthea, when I talk to the dead in preference to the living. Unfortunately, due to programmes like this, its becoming harder to distinguish between the two.'

She hadn't known how to take his remark. But that was true of a lot of things he said. At the present moment he was asleep in the chair, so they sat in the kitchen drinking coffee.

The telephone ringing in the hallway gave them both a shock. Nick, fearing the worst, answered it.

'George?'

'No. It's his son, Nick.'

'Right. I don't think we've met, but my name is Bevan. I'm your local Member of Parliament, is your father available?'

George had also heard the phone. The nights spent on a Fire Station had groomed him into being a light sleeper.

'Hello.'

'Excellent news, George. Within the last hour we have received word that Simon has turned up at our Embassy in Quito. The other piece of news is that he will ring you at approximately one-thirty, which by my reckoning is in about thirty minutes time. Are you still there?'

He was taking it in.

'Yes, yes I'm still here. It was just a shock.'

'I understand.'

'How was he released?'

'Not quite sure at present until he's been debriefed, but it seems there was a raid on the clearing. Probably a rival faction, anyway in the chaos he managed to get away.'

Rival faction my arse, he thought. Kelly had come through. He had kept his promise.

'And Maria. What of her?'

'Again, we don't know the full details, but we understand that she is with him. Anyway, I won't hog the line, but I'll speak to you later.'

He thanked the MP. His hands were still shaking as he replaced the receiver.

'Well. What's the news, dad.'

Putting his arm around Nick and Anthea he steered them back into the living room telling them about the phone call.

'And now we have things to do. You know that karaoke machine that I'm always complaining about? Will it tape like a normal hi-fi system?'

He could see from Nick's expression that it was the last thing he expected to hear in the present circumstances.

'Well, yes.'

'Then bring it down and position it next to the phone. If it's Simon's voice that your mam wants to hear, then hear it she will.'

CHAPTER TWENTY-FOUR
British Embassy, Quito.

Simon had been insistent. He would not answer any questions about his captivity and subsequent release until after he had talked to his parents. The Head of Mission had reluctantly agreed to his demands. The call had been arranged and two hours after his and Maria's arrival he spoke to his father for the first time in nearly two months.

'How are you son?'

'I'm okay.' Relieved that he couldn't see his battered face.

'And Maria?'

'Fine. She's here with me. How's mam?'

He listened to his father's explanation of events. The euphoria of his release receding as the facts became clear.

'I want you to do something that may yet bring her round.'

'Anything you ask.'

'Just repeat everything after me.'

It took fifteen minutes to complete and then his father resumed his questioning.

'When can we expect to see you?'

'I'm not quite sure, but it will be as soon as I can. In any case I'll ring at least once a day to keep in touch.'

'Okay, son. Take care, and give our love to Maria.'

He explained everything to her. She in turn translated the news to her recently arrived parents. The Embassy official stood patiently in the background waiting to take a statement from them both.

Three hours after their arrival, Simon decided to get it over with. He had invented a plausible explanation for his release and the sooner he satisfied the official the sooner they could make plans to leave.

'So you have no idea who these men were, or where they came from?'

'No idea,' he lied, the use of his name and the clear instruction to 'get down' during the rescue deliberately omitted from his statement.

'And presumably you have no recollection of how you reached the Embassy?'

'About as much as our initial capture and journey to the clearing. I vaguely remember being in some sort of vehicle. But with the beating I took everything that's happened to me isn't very clear at all. Like I said,virtually identical to when I was first taken to the estancia.'

The man pressed him. He was not convinced, but then he couldn't disprove the version of events. The interview finally came to an end and he signed the statement as a true and accurate record. If it were later found that it was not, then he would answer for it at home. It took some time to complete the necessary paperwork. Eventually however they were allowed to leave the Embassy and together with Maria's parents, they left for Ibarra.

They had been provided with a car to take them and it was during the journey that Cotopaxi was first mentioned. Ordinarily he would have had no hesitation in accepting Maria's offer to accompany her. Anywhere. But the news of his mother's illness complicated matters. He did however have a little leeway. Their passports had been found on the dead body of Alfred Jaramillo. But they would have to be processed and visas issued before either of them could leave the country, so in the opinion of the official it would be two days before they could expect to get clearance. Negro, Maria's dog, and Patti her friend met them at the house and it was difficult to tell who was more glad to see her. He left them talking, excusing himself as being on his way to bed, but not to sleep. He should have been tired, probably was, but the conversation with Maria in the car would not allow his mind to rest. She had revealed very little, saying only that she wished him to visit the volcano before returning to England. It was important to her, he knew that. But so was his mother's survival. Two women. One who had cared for him since childhood, the other willing to take over, maybe for the rest of his life. He had told the official at the Embassy that it was urgent he returned home quickly and, once the paperwork had been sorted out, to book him on the first available flight. But he would travel to Cotopaxi with Maria, he had decided.

⋆ ⋆ ⋆

BOGOTÁ

Henri Pastrana's office had never seen so many happy faces. He had instructed Benito to go out and buy three bottles of champagne, and then he and Bernice were to join Garbanza, Byron and him for a small celebration.

'The Minister is pleased, Henri?'

'Very. He sends his congratulations.'

Guillermo Garbanza didn't need them. The satisfaction of seeing the men responsible for his father's death suffer the same fate was enough. He walked over to Byron.

'How is the shoulder?'

'It's fine. I'll get it checked out when I get back to the States.'

'I thought we had lost you, my friend.'

'I keep thinking about something I said to my wife before I left. I told her that you had sent for the cavalry, and there was I being saved by the Indians.'

The room resounded with laughter.

'What will happen to Hermania?'

It was Bernice who introduced a more sombre note to the proceedings. Henri explained.

'She will have to appear before the magistrate - probably tomorrow. If only the woman had kept to our agreement.'

'It sounds as if she had a lot to avenge. A woman not only scorned but also deserted, and then her granddaughter threatened with death. I may have been tempted myself. But surely, the fact that she helped bring the two men down will go in her favour.'

Although Henri sympathized, he also knew that his secretary was seeing things from a woman's point of view. The fact of the matter was that Hermania had committed a premeditated execution, borne out by the carrying of the firearm with which she had carried out the deed. But the real tragedy was that she would probably have to stand in front of the same magistrate as Ernesto Videla. A small consolation was that once they investigated his affairs at length he would inevitably make more appearances than she would.

'What were the documents about, apart from the passports, that you found on Jaramillo, boss?'

'They relate to Maria's mother. Alfred must have feared the worst when he took the girl to see Betancur. So he made provision for his daughter. Because of his death she now inherits his land, and a large amount of sucre. The remainder of his ill-gotten gains will probably take us years to trace.'

'Does she know?'

Garbanza was genuinely pleased that the family had gained something from the mess.

'Not yet. I'll let the dust settle for a day or two. Then when I've checked the paperwork out with the lawyers, I'll go and see her.'

The champagne bottles were empty. The celebration finished. As Garbanza left the building to accompany Byron to the airport he thought that tomorrow would be just another day. Dealing with petty criminals, prostitutes, dealers and pushers corrupting the streets of Bogotá. And yet maybe, just maybe, there would be another cartel.

⋆ ⋆ ⋆

The taped conversation with Simon had gone exactly as George had planned. Him responsible for the dialogue, Nick taking care of the technical part of the proceedings. It had never been his forte - recalling the time when he had waited for one of the boys to return home from school in order to operate the video. It hadn't taken long, his son referring to the term 'high speed dubbing,' whatever that meant. Anyway it worked. The message from Simon had been repeatedly taped and then successfully tried on the Walkman that they would take to the hospital.

'Do you think it will work?' asked Anthea, starting to feel that she had been forgotten about, but understanding why.

'I hope so pet, because we've run out of options.'

He knew that the alternative was to stand idly by and watch his wife's life slowly ebb away. The three of them made their way across town, reaching the hospital in record time, but were then halted in their tracks by the duty sister.

'I'll have to consult with Mr. Fairbrother.'

She was new to George and he took an instant dislike to her official attitude.

'How long will that take?' He was biting his tongue.

'I'll see if he's on his pager. If not then you'll have to wait until he is.'

But he wouldn't. He had made his mind up. The sister was hardly out of sight when he gave Nick the nod.

'Go and put those headphones on your mother's head - and be careful not to move anything. I'll sort this control freak out.'

He knew he was being unfair. The woman was only doing her job, but sometimes red tape was there to be cut. And he couldn't think of a better time to reach for the scissors. It had always been his way, 'Do what you think is right at the time,' he had told the boys on more than one occasion. If it turns out to be the wrong decision, you can put the comic down your trousers later. This time he had no reason to protect his backside - the sister returning with the news that Fairbrother had sanctioned the use of the tape, and then suddenly realizing, due to Nick's absence, that they had jumped the gun.

'The reason we have these procedures, Mr. Halkin is for the patient's safety. Didn't it occur to you that this tape recorder that you have brought into the ward could affect the monitoring equipment at your wife's bedside?'

She was right.

'I'm sorry sister. But when your ship is sinking and someone throws you a lifebelt, you don't check to see if it is Department of Trade and Industry approved before you put it over your head.'

He left her thinking about it. Nick was sitting at Joan's side as he entered the side ward, the Walkman and headphones already in place. They had done all they could. It was now all down to a piece of plastic, inside which was a message. It would be repeated over and over again.

'Mam. This is your son Simon. I am safe and on my way home with Maria. Very soon we will see you again, but only if you get well. You must start thinking about us all being together, so that we can have Christmas. Whatever you do, you must never give up. I will see you soon. I love you very much. Mam. This is...'

He wiped the sweat from her forehead, noticing the true colour of her hair. The rinse she used had faded, in its place the grey of worry and stress. Taking the wooden snuffbox from his jacket pocket he placed it in her hand. He had called upon it to help deliver his son from the hands of evil men. Now he was asking that his wife be returned to her family. He leaned back in the chair, oblivious to the strange looks from his two young companions.

'Thank you for Simon. But please help me once again.'

Those of whom he was asking for help were not of this world. But then there was no one who was that could grant his wish.

* * *

THE SLOPES OF COTOPAXI

Simon was awake early. It had been a night spent thinking, punctuated by short periods of sleep. He had changed during his period in captivity. It seemed to him that, in a perverse sort of way, he was better for the experience. Things that he had thought important had been placed in their correct order of priority. His captors had been a prime example. Two of the richest men in the world and yet unable to take full advantage of their wealth. In effect, they had been no better off for forty years, than he and Maria had been for a few weeks. He also sensed that his feelings had changed - not only with regard to her, but things in general. George had once remarked that he was like the Titanic - deep and reluctant to let parts of it appear on the surface. It was probably true to say that confinement had concentrated his mind, made him think more about certain aspects of his character.

What Maria had in mind for him that day she had kept a closely guarded secret.

'We are going to the Parque Nacional de Cotopaxi,' was all that she would tell him.

Guillermo Garbanza had left the vehicle that had transported them from the Embassy at their disposal for the remainder of their stay in Ibarra. So following breakfast they both settled into the rear of the car, taking the Highway south. After a few miles they stopped to allow him to ring home. Nick answered, informing him that there had been no change in their mother's condition. Returning to the car he relayed the news to Maria who knew exactly how he was feeling, having been down the same path, months earlier.

'By the way, what is in the suitcase that you have put in the boot?'

Her answer made him laugh - mimicking George.

'I cannot tell you - I am the ocean deep.'

They took the scenic route. Simon finally able to see some of her native country, arriving in the National Park late afternoon. His first impression of the 'Shining Peak' was everything he thought it would be. Towering nearly six thousand metres, the snow-capped peak disappeared into the clouds.

'How near can we get?' he asked the driver.

'I will take you to the bottom slopes, there is a small refuge where climbers meet before setting out on the upper slopes. It is not used at this time of the year.'

He was true to his word - stopping the car a short walk from the wooden hut.

'I have brought a picnic. I will get it from the suitcase,' said Maria, leaving the car first.

The three of them sat on the lush grass that surrounded the volcano, whilst the driver proved to be an expert on everything to do with Cotopaxi.

'It is the highest continuously active volcano in the world,' he began. 'Its shape is perfect, except for one little cone - the 'Cabeza del Inca'. He pointed out the Head of the Inca. They talked until the light showed signs of fading.

Then the driver gathered together the remnants of what had been an enjoyable meal. He placed the basket in the car and returned with the suitcase.

'I will return in one hour.' And then he left.

'What is going on Maria?' Simon thought it was time for an explanation.

'Just a few more minutes and then you will know.'

He watched her as she walked to the refuge clutching her suitcase and then disappearing inside the hut. He stood, gazing up at the mighty volcano. The fires burning deep inside the crater now reflected in the darkening sky. Flames, dancing like demons, enhanced by the whiteness of the snow. Then she was before him. Dressed in her very best dress of white and gold. He had never seen anyone so beautiful. She took his hand. Producing the ring she placed it on his finger. Perhaps it was the picnic wine, but he was aware of a trembling beneath his feet as if the earth was trying to open. The taste of obsidian that spewed from the volcano filled his senses. He was warm, no hot. Was it the heat from the forge of Vulcan? The voices of long dead Inca Emperors cried out to him, 'SHE IS THE ONE!'

Maria retold the story confided to her by Hermania.

'And so I will place this ring on a man's finger only once. You must do what you feel.'

He knew exactly what she was asking. Removing the heavy gold ring, he took her small hand in his. Slipping it over her finger - its huge size came nowhere near her skin. But it was not an adornment, it was a symbol of something very special. He looked once again at Cotopaxi. It was a forging of spirits, and he welcomed it. Thousands of miles away in a small room she had given him her body. Now, on the open spaces of Ecuador, he had pledged her his life. No words were needed.

As the car returned they walked to meet it. Two people from opposite ends of the world. Him - a product of capitalism. Her - a simple peasant girl. He knew his father would have supplied the reason. 'Brought together by those who knew the scheme of things.'

* * *

Gill had shaken his hand and wished him a safe journey, before speeding off in the Landrover. So he had bought a drink from the Terminal bar and awaited his flight to be called.

'Heading home?'

He looked at the man perched on the stool next to him. Smart, and judging from his slight accent, from Texas.

'Yep. And you?'

'Yea, after another wasted journey.'

'You in business?'

'Yea. The oil business. My company received information from a Government source, if you know what I mean,' the man winked, 'that an official in the Bolivian Ministry was interested in selling off some land. When we looked, we thought it might be promising, being in the oil belt an all. Anyway it didn't turn out as he and us had planned. Then we got the call again. This time it was from a guy in Colombia, who I was supposed to meet yesterday. But he appears to have gone and got himself arrested.'

Byron turned away and smiled.

'Our search for gold,
A greed, unchecked.
But find it not.
Our plan is wrecked.'

'You a philosopher or something?' the man asked.

'No. I'm a poet.'

Of his future plans, there was no doubt.

CHAPTER TWENTY-FIVE

On their return to Ibarra Simon and Maria found that there had been no word from the Embassy concerning a departure date. Maria's parents had travelled to Colombia to be at Hermania's side and that apart from her younger sister and Negro, the house was theirs.

'Are you still happy about coming to England?'

They were in the garden enjoying a cold drink.

'There is little I can do for my grandmother - except pray, and that I can do anywhere,' she replied.

They were now into the second day of their freedom and Simon's eagerness to return home was starting to turn to frustration at the delay. If it took this long to sort out a passport how long would it have taken the diplomats to free them?

During the telephone conversation with his father, George had mentioned that he had received a letter from the supermarket. It assured him of his continuing employment with them. He knew that it wasn't what he wanted and that he was capable of more than being responsible for ordering the required number of tins of beans.

Although his face still felt sore to the touch, the healing process had already begun. He had, however, been advised by the Embassy official to attend the local hospital in order to receive treatment to the many sores that still covered his body. On their way to keep the appointment, Maria was unusually quiet and withdrawn.

'Having second thoughts about coming to England, Maria?'

She held his hand tighter than was intended.

'No. It's not that. I keep thinking of the two cruel men who betrayed my grandmother, and if I will ever see her again.'

'They were not always cruel. Unfortunately when they found wealth they lost everything else - realizing it too late.'

'Will you change when you are rich and famous?'

He lifted her clear of the ground, swinging her around like his father had done to him as a child.

'Yes. I will beat you every night with a big stick,' he replied, laughing.

But she knew he wouldn't. The memories of how he had taken a beating in order to protect her from the guards, too vivid. How he had tried to make her a Christmas, too near her heart. She clung to him tightly, as she always would.

There was good news at the hospital. Due to his inoculations in England he had not been seriously infected. The doctor assured him that the cream and tablets with which he had been supplied, would soon clear up the sores. If only things were as simple in another hospital, located on the other side of the world, he thought. George and him had things in common, of course, but it was his mother he was really close to.

He had joined Maria and her sister in front of the Madonna the previous night. They used prayer as a pledge of their faith, but he knew that he was using it as a last resort. But then so did most people. They returned to the house where a message from the local post office instructed them to ring the Embassy in Quito. Hearts pounding they ran all the way. It was the news that they had been waiting for. The passports and visas had been validated and they were now free to leave. Two seats had also been reserved on a flight to Europe for the day after tomorrow. He rang home, the good news flawed by getting no answer.

That night they dined out. Over a simple meal he talked of his hopes and dreams whilst she listened. Then it was her turn. She talked about seeing a real Christmas tree, and 'litter'. This time they laughed until the tears fell into their meal.

⋆ ⋆ ⋆

HARTLEPOOL

George heard it on Sky News. It took fifteen seconds to partially dispel the uncertainty and misery of the last two months.

'In a statement issued to the Press Association early today, the Foreign and Commonwealth Office stated that two young backpackers - their movements unaccounted for since mid December last year have turned up safe and well at the British Embassy in Quito, Ecuador. There are no other details at present.'

'Nor will there be.' He wasn't in the habit of talking to the television - he just said what he was thinking. It had been thirty-six hours since Simon's initial phone call, with no improvement in Joan's condition. Three sets of new batteries for the Walkman and constant attention from him and Nick had still not resulted in any progress. Other members of the family had also been constant visitors to her bedside but like him they were not serving any purpose. He looked at the clock - ten minutes past seven, time to make tracks for the hospital and relieve Nick. The events of the last two months had seen a considerable change in his youngest son. More considerate, much more responsible, and their relationship had become much stronger. He arrived at the ward in time to catch him inserting another set of batteries.

'Any change son?'

'None at all, although I thought I saw her lips move once, but it must have been a trick of the light.'

'Well, you push off now. I'll see you in the morning.'

It was two hours later that it happened, and it wasn't a trick of the light. Just a slight movement, but he caught it. He rushed to her bedside and placed his ear over her mouth.

'Mam, Dad.' It was faint, but there was no doubt that it was her voice. Reaching for the alarm button, he pressed it repeatedly, and at the same time removed the headphones and Walkman.

'What is it George?' The sister was beside him almost instantly.

'Put your ear to her mouth and listen.'

He sat and watched, expecting an immediate response from the senior nurse.

'I'm sorry, but I can't hear anything.' She looked at the monitoring equipment. 'But there is an increase in activity. I'll be back shortly.'

As she hurried from the room he once again listened. The two words repeated, this time a little louder. She fell silent as Fairbrother entered the room.

'I'd like you to wait outside George.' The consultant already was noting the equipment readings.

He did as he was asked, watching the increased activity in the corridor. Machines were being moved in and out of the ward at regular intervals. And then the sister smiled at him.

'What's happened?' A tremor in his voice.

'Mr. Fairbrother will be having a word with you shortly,' she replied.

But the smile had given him renewed hope, and moments later he was allowed back in to see his wife. Physically she hadn't changed - still lying motionless, but then her primary condition had been caused by a psychological problem so maybe it was one step at a time. Fairbrother confirmed his train of thought.

'As you can see George we've been able to dispense with some of the paraphernalia that has been surrounding your wife's bed, and although we can't afford to be complacent or totally happy with the situation, it would appear that Joan is back with us. By the way - she said Simon's name, that's probably what you heard.'

The room was quiet, the hustle and bustle had finished and he sat alone at her bedside. He would ring Nick shortly, but first he removed the small box from her hand and placed it back in his pocket. He knew exactly what she had said.

* * *

LONDON

Sir Charles Barnard was becoming impatient to the point where it was turning to annoyance. The news that the hostages had somehow been released had of course been a relief - but it was the absence of any details that was the cause of his frustration. The Permanent Under-Secretary would shortly want a report on the matter and information from both Colombia and his own department was at a premium. Robert Morrow was a possible solution to his problem, but the man was annoyingly late. He had never entirely trusted the former

Royal Marine who he suspected - contrary to Foreign Office policy - did things his way rather than along more conventional lines. Since the damming report produced by the Commons Foreign Affairs Committee, which had unreservedly labelled the Department a 'shambles' and accused the Permanent Under Secretary of 'failing in his duty' to brief MPs over the gun-running operation by London-based Sandline, everyone had come under the magnifying glass. But Sandline had only been the final nail. Over a number of years - particularly involving the safe release and return of hostages - the Department's record had been nothing to be proud of, many examples still remaining unresolved, those cases that occasionally came to light resurrected by loyal family members. The flickering red light on his phone broke his train of thought.

'Mr. Morrow has arrived, Sir Charles.'

'Send him in, please.'

He remained in his seat until the Head of the Crime Section settled himself into the chair opposite, only then did he stand and greet him.

'Sorry for keeping you waiting, Sir Charles - but there was an urgent matter I had to sort out, and speed was of the essence.'

'That's something we both have in common at the moment, Bob.'

Morrow was immediately on the defensive. On the few occasions that they had met in the past or talked over the phone Barnard had been much more formal during their exchanges. On the face of it they were equals, both being head of their respective departments. He knew however, that Barnard felt that there was a certain kudos attached to his position - no doubt linked to the fact that he dealt mainly with diplomats, as opposed to the low-life of the world's criminal fraternity. Then there was his knighthood - in his own mind a further reason to take the high ground, which he did frequently.

'I take it you think I may be able to help you in some way, Sir Charles?'

He was aware of the newspaper crossing the desk and on closer inspection noticed that a particular article had been circled.

'Good news obviously. And yet a bit of a mystery, the circumstances appertaining to their release. Don't you think?'

His training as an Intelligence Officer triggered the warning light.

'I'm sure it's a mystery that both families can come to terms with.'

'Quite so. If only that were true of the Foreign Secretary.'

'What of your staff in Quito? They have, I assume, debriefed the lad at least.'

'Naturally. But his recollections of the final few hours of his captivity were limited - due to some sort of drug.'

Morrow was beginning to feel more comfortable.

'And Bogotá, the PIP seem to have played a major part in the girl's release?'

'They, naturally enough, are claiming that the success of the whole operation was due to them. They are also reticent about releasing any details, unfortunately.'

Morrow was inclined to disagree - but in any case he had covered his tracks.

The reason for his late arrival had been due to two phone calls - one of which had been to Guillermo

Garbanza. He had thanked the Colombian for his cooperation and then enquired as to his amnesia.

'It's improving, Mr. Morrow, it now only affects my ability to remember phone calls, especially of a cryptic nature.'

He knew however that he was not out of the woods yet.

'Does the name John Kelly mean anything to you?' The question shot across the table, like a bullet.

'An Australian. Yes, I met Kelly in the Falklands. But where's the relevance? I haven't met with Kelly for a number of years.'

He deliberately omitted the word 'contacted.'

'It may quite simply be a coincidence, but nevertheless we are interested in his movements - particularly over the last few weeks. Let me explain. There have been a number of cases in the past involving anxious relatives - frustrated at the apparent lack of progress made by the FO in tracing their missing offspring - decided to take matters into their own hands. As a father myself I have a certain amount of sympathy. However, my official position requires that the complete opposite apply. In order that these people don't, inadvertently, should we say upset the applecart, and indeed for their own safety, we impose certain safeguards. As an example we enlist the help of the Immigration Department, who keep a wary eye open for anyone trying to leave the country who we would rather remain here.'

'And the boy's father came into that category the moment his son was taken?' The procedure wasn't exactly news to Morrow.

'Precisely. Kelly however did board a flight for South America together with a companion within a couple of weeks of some hostages being executed.'

'Why the interest in him?' He shifted his position in the chair slightly.

'Because the Immigration Department through their Investigative Branch have suspected him of being what they term a 'jockey'.

Morrow knew exactly what the term meant - it referred to men who illegally escorted women from a foreign country into Britain - for a price.

'It would appear that Mr. Kelly is capable of undertaking anything for money, and maybe Halkin's money,' Barnard resumed, averting his eyes just long enough to allow Morrow to take a long hard swallow - he hadn't known.

'So it would appear that your association with this man would not have been in the interests of the British Government. Do you not agree.'

'As I have already stated, Sir Charles, the man was simply in the same war.'

'I'm relieved to hear it, but sorry that you can't shed any light on this latest situation.'

But I could, and so could Kelly he reminded himself as he left Barnard's office, which was why the second phone call had been to the mercenary - ordering him not to return to the UK until contacted. Due to the news of his alternative employment however, the man was now a liability. But then he had dealt with them before.

* * *

'Good evening ladies and gentlemen, this is the captain speaking. I hope you have enjoyed your flight. We are now making our final approach to Teeside International where the temperature on the ground is a cool three degrees Celsius…'

Maria tightened her seat belt even more and then placed her head against Simon's shoulder. He glanced across at her and smiled, then felt the wheels of the aircraft touch tarmac. The other passengers were hurriedly removing their belongings from the overhead lockers, but the two friends remained seated. He was enjoying the moment. He was back in England. They were the last to vacate the cabin, apart from the crew, who wished them well as they finally left. And then, as if by magic they found themselves in the arrival hall, staring at a man waving his arms in the air. He's changed, thought Simon. The hair now completely grey, the eyes hooded and he's lost weight. Then the smell of tobacco as arms enveloped him, his collar becoming wet, tears.

'Welcome home, son.'

He could feel his father shaking.

'You can't imagine how good it feels, dad. How's mam?'

It was Maria's turn for a hug.

'On the mend. So hurry up and sort these news people out, then we can go and see her.'

Simon hadn't noticed until then the vast array of photographers gathered just outside the Terminal main doors. George watched them walk hand-in-hand to meet the media, confident that his son would handle them with discretion.

'Can you give us any details about the time you spent in Colombia?'

Cameras flashed causing them to shield their eyes.

'Until I have been interviewed by the Foreign Office again, I can only tell you that since mid-December last year myself and Maria have been in the hands of a Colombian drug cartel.'

'How were you treated?'

'When you consider the fate of the other hostages - we have no complaints.'

George rolled a cigarette, and then two more before Simon brought the questioning to a halt. He brought the car to the entrance and amid further camera flashes the three of them headed for Hartlepool. During the thirty minutes that it took to reach the hospital no mention was made of their captivity, the conversation was about Joan.

'She even smiled when I told her that she would see you both today - the first time for months.'

'Just how serious was her condition - before I phoned?'

'She was having her final meal on death row.'

The warmth of the hospital was a welcome relief from the cold air outside, Nick and Anthea already sitting outside Joan's room and rising as one to greet the new arrivals. Few words were spoken, there was no need - the light in Nick's eyes, the intensity of the handshake and lingering hug for Maria pronounced their feelings for each other.

'I think there is someone in here that would like to see you both.' It was the sister - holding the door open. George waited until the four of them had disappeared into Joan's room before heading for the smoking area. It was deserted and so he picked the most comfortable chair. It would be a long night, but a night unlike any other.

'Tired, George?'

The sister had taken the opportunity for a sly smoke.

'I hadn't realised how much until now.'

'Saving life can be a taxing business and especially the way you did it.'

'I learned a lesson from a man - a lot of years ago. He too lost his son for a while. Unfortunately when they did meet again it was only for a short time before they died. He paid the ultimate price to see his son again. It only cost me money. How's my wife anyway?'

'As you would expect - improving by the minute. Give her a week of Simon and you can expect her home.'

'Is that a threat?'

She smiled at him, but it was a knowing smile.

'You don't fool me George, but I bet there's a few that you have. I have one at home just like you.'

'What do you mean - like me?'

She sat opposite him, her head resting on an upturned hand.

'Someone who believes that his position in the family pecking order is no longer as Cock of the North.'

He said nothing, neither agreeing nor denying.

'Men of your age find it hard to accept a change of role, can't come to terms with the fact that we, as women, are so much more independent than you would like us to be. Think back for a moment to when the two young men in Joan's room were boys in need of a father's firm hand, something on which your wife relied. Remember also that it was on you that she depended for the family's financial stability. I can give you a thousand examples of how indispensable you probably were. But changing circumstances inevitably lead to a shift in relationships, and whether you like it or not George - women are better at it than men. I'm not saying that you've enjoyed the last few weeks but what it has done is put you back in control, something that you have missed.'

'Isn't that a man's role?'

'You have no more right to wear that mantle than I have, and I certainly don't see myself as a 'control freak'. The walls are thin in here George.'

'Sorry about that.'

'Don't be. You're not the first man to think that a women's position in this world should be no higher than the horizontal.'

He laughed, nearly choking on the newly-rolled cigarette.

'I have to admit that there's more than a bit of truth in what you say. There have been occasions since I retired, when I felt as though I had been made redundant in more ways than one.'

She nodded.

'Go and join your family George, it's where you belong and always will.'

And so he did.

EPILOGUE

The warning siren indicating that the lock gates were about to operate made him sit up with a start. The masts of the yacht glided slowly along the wall of the quay until the whole vessel suddenly slipped into view. The big red ball that was the setting sun bounced off each window as it passed him. It had been a long time since he had seen such an end to a day - more used to guarding against the ravages of a north-easterly wind than enjoying a Caribbean sunset. George leaned forward, his chin resting on cupped, rough hands; it had been a long year. The problems caused by Simon and Maria's capture and the subsequent effect on Joan, he knew, had taken its toll. He had enjoyed the belated Christmas celebration, following Joan's instructions to the letter, as she churned them out from her armchair. As predicted by Fairbrother, Simon's reappearance had been better than a trip to Lourdes, and he had allowed her to leave the hospital ten days after the return of their son. A real tree had been purchased - much to the amusement of the local forestry workers - and duly decorated with glitter and lights, the latter leaving his wife somewhat bemused.

'I thought you said there would be a light for each one that would be here George. I make that six of us and yet there are ten lights.'

He had wanted to remind her of an earlier conversation shortly after she was able to talk, but decided against it. It would be hard for her to understand that there would be unseen guests.

'Can you remember anything while you were in the coma?' he had asked her.

'Nothing. Except for a feeling that I had.'

'What sort of feeling?'

'I don't know really. I suppose it was like falling and then being suddenly lifted, but there was no sign of anyone. I remember when I was a little girl walking hand-in-hand between my mam and dad, and then being swung in the air. But before my feet touched the ground they would stop me. Yes, it was as if it was happening again. But like I say it was just a feeling.'

The unseen guests maybe. But he knew exactly what she had experienced. There had been times in his life when a particular sound or smell had, for just a second, invoked a feeling, a reminder of the past.

It had been a bitter-sweet Christmas celebration for Maria - the fate of her grandmother causing continuing mood swings. She had rung her friend Patti, still in Quito, who informed her that although the authorities in Bogotá had allowed her to return to Ibarra, she must still stand trial for the killing of Rodrigo at a time yet to be decided. But then there were times when real pleasure showed on her face - especially when she showed off the ring. He had never been a devotee of jewellery, but he had to admit that it was something special as well as extremely valuable, prompting him to advise her on its safekeeping.

'Wouldn't that be better off in a bank?'

Maria had looked at him suspiciously.

'In my country people do not trust them - they take your sucre and then they close, leaving you with nothing. No, it is for me and Simon to share and enjoy. I will keep it safe.'

The warmth of the sun was slowly turning to the coolness of the moon, and he pulled his jacket tighter around him. A seagull swooped down then disappeared over the roof of the Old West Quay, heading out over the North Sea. He recalled telling Nick how they were the souls of past Sub Officers, returning to shit on firemen - as they had done in life. They both appreciated the joke. If only they had shared more.

* * *

The pub was busy and it had taken her an age to get served with the pint for George and her own soft drink. She could see him as she passed the bandstand, sitting at an awkward angle. But it was his tin, lying discarded on the ground, the strands of tobacco blowing towards her, that set the alarm bells ringing. The glasses fell from her hands, the liquid splashing her legs as she ran towards him. But she knew it was too late. She beckoned to a passing dog-walker to call for an ambulance, then sat beside her husband. His hand was cold, lifeless, but she rubbed it anyway recalling the difficulties of the past twelve months that they had both endured. But she also knew that the coming weeks would be the hardest yet - or would have been. Now the shell was empty, he had no more to give. With him it had been all or nothing, there had been no in-between. Maybe his Guardian of Destiny - his God - had finally decided that enough was enough, his testing time completed. He had talked so often about when his time came and his hopes to be included amongst those who control the scheme of things. She hoped so. He would be good at it. She picked up the tin that had been his constant companion since they had first met. It was devoid of any of its original colour, battered and now empty - the coincidence was not lost on her.

'Death. Has this immortal soul
Passed its latest test?
No longer needed in this shell;
Another task? Perhaps, but first to rest.

Michael Hagon 2005

THE SEQUEL
THE WAGGARITE CONSPIRACY

The three men who occupied the table by the open fire waited until the stranger at an adjacent table left before one of them spoke.

'Did the solicitor say how long it would be before anything happened?'

Jack Patterdale picked up his glass of whisky with a slightly shaking hand, waiting for the answer before putting it to his lips.

'He said he couldn't be sure, and that we would be informed by letter of any developments. I think he was trying to tell me not to ring anymore; snotty kid.'

Dan Kendal put down his newspaper and removed his glasses. Short and stocky, he was the complete opposite to his two companions, who were more inclined to think before they spoke.

The third member of the company noisily emptied the sticky mess that was the contents of his pipe into the tin ashtray. It was a ritual he had carried out for years and the three friends waited until it had been refilled and then lit before resuming the conversation.

Ben Studley took a few long draws, then filled the air with its pungent aroma.

'How long has it been now? he asked.

'How long has what been?'

'Since George was buried.'

'Five weeks yesterday,' answered Patterdale. He had counted the days much like a child would at the approach of Christmas.

'I met his wife in town the other day, she seems to be getting over it well enough.'

Dan Kendal made a noise with his nose, not quite a snort.

'Well they do, women. I remember reading the results of a survey carried out by some group or other, involved with the over-fifties. They found that women lived longer after the death of their husbands than the other way about. Yep, they've got the capacity to get over most things - unless it's the one-eyed trouser snake and then it's a different matter.'

Jack and Ben looked at each other, both shaking their heads at the same time.

'And I suppose you're the expert on marital matters. How long were you and your lass together? If I remember rightly it wasn't long enough to fill a pisspot.

Patterdale found himself the recipient of a scowl for his outburst.

A barmaid removed the now full ashtray, her disapproval evident as she slammed a clean one on the table. Dan watched her as she walked away, the trim waist and long legs a reminder of happier times. He was now fifty-six and his life had been dogged by a succession of failed relationships, starting with Edna. They had married when they were both eighteen, meeting at a local dance hall and quickly establishing that a mutual appreciation of brown ale and Elvis was the basis for a lifetime of commitment. Caroline - the only child from what could only be described as a loveless marriage - had been born a year later. It had been too soon and it didn't take them both very long to realize it. Within two years Edna had remarried and he had raised Caroline as best he could. Along the way he had wandered in and out of different women's lives - never happy with any of them, brief periods of contentment, followed by deep resentment. The barmaid had reminded him of Caroline, his eyes suddenly becoming moist, his throat dry.

'Another pint Dan?'

'Is a pig's arse pork?' A deliberate attempt to shake off his feeling of self-pity.

'I'll take that as a yes.'

Jack Patterdale lifted his large frame out of the chair and headed for the bar. His size had been a distinct advantage during his previous career as a policeman - a Chief Superintendent in fact. He had joined the force at the age of twenty-three, taking the advice of the local 'beat bobby' and enjoying the challenges of law and order until arthritis in his hands had forced him into retirement. Now in his seventies, he was the eldest of the trio of friends; old enough to remember the difficult early days of growing up in an area like Longhill. It would have been easy to take another path. The majority of families were hard-working and honest, living on what they could borrow, some on what they could find, but it had been just as easy to pursue a life of crime. Betty, his wife, had died five years before, having given birth to two daughters. Then, much to his delight, a son, who had entered his life like a blast of oxygen entering a room on fire, giving him renewed strength and a relationship that few fathers would experience. He had grown into a fine strapping lad and at nineteen, and without any persuasion, had also decided to make the force a career.

'You want serving big feller, or are you just here for the free black pudding?'

'Two pints of smooth and a Grouse.'

He looked at the plate containing the black chunks, a particular favourite with a lot of the pub's patrons. It looked like burnt charcoal and he shuddered at the thought of the colour of some of its recipients' stomachs. He returned to the table and carefully placed one of the pints in front of Ben Studley.

'Cheers Jack.'

Studley passed a huge hand through a shock of snow-white hair that fell onto his shoulders. In his prime he had been a man to be reckoned with, and even now could handle men half his age with ease. An amateur boxer of some repute in his youth, at sixty he still looked fit. He had worked at the local steelworks until a combination of red dust and the heat had forced him to look elsewhere, and quite by accident had become involved in local politics. He had a natural aptitude for the job, able to talk to anyone, irrespective of their position, and soon gained a reputation for honesty, integrity, and getting things done. Married for nearly forty years, his wife Elsa had, after a difficult birth, produced a daughter, Patricia. They had decided that one child was enough, and twenty years after her birth Patricia married. Her choice of husband alienated her from him and Elsa. The man turned out to be a complete waster and the only worthwhile thing Ben gave him credit for was producing his granddaughter, Anna. He worshipped the ground she walked on, watching her grow from child to teenager, until shortly before her fifteenth birthday his world nearly collapsed. She had been returning from a night out with her parents, when the car was involved in a serious accident.

All three had been rushed to the town's General Hospital. For his daughter and her husband it had been too late, they had died in the ambulance, but Anna had survived. After a long and painful recovery period she had gone to live with him and his wife, eventually going on to study Economics at Durham University. Following a year 'out' she had then both surprised and delighted him by announcing that she was seriously considering a career in local politics.

'If you don't hurry up and drink that pint it'll be as flat as Nellie's chest.'

Dan's crude comment referred to a well-known local lady, reputed to favour men with her company for as little as a half of beer and a full-strength cigarette.

'Funny how nobody seemed to know her surname. Still, I don't suppose anyone would have admitted to it anyway.'

Jack and Ben had always suspected that Dan knew more about Nellie than he was letting on.

The pub was beginning to fill with early-evening drinkers. It was popular with a wide cross-section of the community - due mainly to the cheapness of the beer. Young working girls in tight skirts mingled with men old enough to be their fathers, whilst business men, posing with their mobile phones, rubbed shoulders with all-day drinkers, with hardly enough money to afford two tins and a piece of string.

'You lads all right?'

It was the offer of a drink, shouted across the room by an old woman clutching a 1940s-style handbag.

'We're all right pet,' Ben answered for the three of them.

'Well, any time you're ready give us a shout.'

It had been happening for the last month. It was as if they were returning heroes, feted by all and sundry, the backslapping never-ending, smiles of appreciation wherever they were recognized.

'So we wait for Haddaway and Shite to request our attendance now, do we?'

'Don't keep calling them that or you'll start believing it. Bright and Breckon have been okay to us so far.'

Ben was starting to lose patience with Dan, a four-pint maximum drinker and he was now over his limit. But Miles Breckon - the senior partner - had looked after their interests ever since the present nightmare had begun. The law and solicitors were all new to him and since the night they had all been taken into custody, he had been a frightened man. Yet fair or not, Breckon and his colleagues had never given them any impression other than that they had a job to do; sympathy with their predicament maybe, but professional, certainly. Right from the outset and without exception they had put their hands up to the charges - much to the disapproval of their legal representatives. Miles Breckon was blunt.

'You are being too honest for your own good gentlemen, why are you disregarding our advice?'

'Because we did it and there's no point in saying otherwise.'

Ben had put it in a nutshell.

'That's not your decision to make - it's not that simple. The fact that your friend is no longer with us may have a bearing on how we proceed.'

'If your planning on interviewing George Halkin there may be a few people interested in sitting in,' Dan had replied.

Miles had been quick to answer.

'Which brings me to the point I'm trying to make. Until you tell me the part he played in this alleged conspiracy I'm hardly likely to get the full picture. Believe me gentlemen, his participation could well be the deciding factor regarding your future freedom, or the lack of it. For Christ's sake Jack you of all people must know what I'm talking about?'

Jack Patterdale did. He hadn't completed thirty years in the force without learning something about the process of law. Breckon was referring to principal and secondary parties, insinuating, in a roundabout way, that if George had been the instigator of the principal offence, there may be a way out for them. He was also aware of other relevant factors - repentance, provocation, oblique intent, all potential ways of reducing their liability whilst totally shifting the blame onto their dead friend. But it wouldn't happen. Prior to their attendance at the police station, each of them had agreed to accept equal blame and they were men of their word. No amount of persuasion or coercion would alter that. He felt sorry for Breckon, a man trying to do his best without too much cooperation from them, but that was what they had agreed. The streets of Longhill - Beacon, Florence, Hill and Portland - no longer existed, but the loyalty that they had bred would never disappear.

Patterdale looked down at the newspaper lying on the table. The headline dramatic, yet true –

THE WAGGARITE CONSPIRACY: CHARGES

He finished his drink; yes, that's what it had been and that's who they were.